T0051106

PRAISE FOR KYLIE BRANT

"Kylie Brant is destined to become a star!"
—Cindy Gerard, *New York Times* and *USA Today* bestselling author

"A complex, page-turning mystery plus a heartfelt romance blend into a fast-paced story that kept me reading until the wee hours."
—Allison Brennan, *New York Times* bestselling author of *Make Them Pay on Deadly Dreams*

"Dark and compelling suspense."
—Anne Frasier, author of *The Body Reader*

"*Pretty Girls Dancing* is a complex and character-driven mystery that will keep you turning pages until late at night."
—Kendra Elliot, Daphne du Maurier Award–winning author of *A Merciful Truth*

"*Pretty Girls Dancing* is Kylie Brant at her chilling best as she delivers a compelling thriller with a shocking twist."
—Loreth Anne White, author of *A Dark Lure*

COLD DARK PLACES

ALSO BY KYLIE BRANT

The Circle of Evil Trilogy

Chasing Evil
Touching Evil
Facing Evil

Other Works

Pretty Girls Dancing
Deep as the Dead
What the Dead Know
Secrets of the Dead
11
Waking Nightmare
Waking Evil
Waking the Dead
Deadly Intent
Deadly Dreams
Deadly Sins
Terms of Attraction
Terms of Engagement
Terms of Surrender
The Last Warrior
The Business of Strangers
Close to the Edge
In Sight of the Enemy
Dangerous Deception
Truth or Lies

COLD DARK PLACES

A CADY MADDIX MYSTERY

KYLIE BRANT

THOMAS & MERCER

This is a work of fiction. Names, characters, organizations, places, events, and incidents are either products of the author's imagination or are used fictitiously. Any resemblance to actual persons, living or dead, or actual events is purely coincidental.

Text copyright © 2018 by Kim Bahnsen
All rights reserved.

No part of this book may be reproduced, or stored in a retrieval system, or transmitted in any form or by any means, electronic, mechanical, photocopying, recording, or otherwise, without express written permission of the publisher.

Published by Thomas & Mercer, Seattle

www.apub.com

Amazon, the Amazon logo, and Thomas & Mercer are trademarks of Amazon.com, Inc., or its affiliates.

ISBN-13: 9781542040198 (hardcover)
ISBN-10: 1542040191 (hardcover)
ISBN-13: 9781503951761 (paperback)
ISBN-10: 1503951766 (paperback)

Cover design by Rex Bonomelli

Printed in the United States of America

First edition

For Brecken Hayes, whose sweet smiles lift my heart.

Eryn: Then

Eryn was very quiet. Mama hated to be woke up at night. She was always at her crossest then, her voice sharp, with edges that scraped and burned. And sometimes even when it was morning Mama couldn't wake up. She was so sleepy Eryn couldn't shake her hard enough or say her name loud enough to make her open her eyes. Mary Jane always shooed her away then and said Mama needed her sleep. Then she shut the door, and Eryn couldn't talk to Mama until after lunch.

But lunch was a long time away now. The sky through Mama's windows was still dark, except for a fat moon and sprinkles of stars. Clutching her sketchpad, Eryn crawled on her hands and knees to the side of the bed, quiet as a mouse. Mama said a big nine-year-old girl didn't need to be climbing into bed with her. But Eryn could sit here, close. Mama didn't have to know. The bedcovers were bunched and hanging from the mattress because she always kicked them off. In the mornings, Eryn liked to come and hide in the mound where they curtained to the side. Mama didn't mind her there then, as long as she didn't get disturbed until a "decent hour."

Eryn hadn't been able to fall asleep tonight. There was a racket in her head, the noises ping-ponging until she had to move, had to shake them loose. When she'd first slipped from bed, she'd whirled and spun and skipped around her room until the twitchiness in her arms and legs had gone away. Then she could concentrate. She'd already finished two drawings tonight. But this one would be better. It'd be the greatest thing she'd ever done. Mama framed Eryn's best works and hung them on the wall. But only if they were *perfect.*

Eryn burrowed into the draping sheet and comforter. Soft pleats of fabric tented around her, but she could still peek out. She laid her sketchpad on the rug in the slant of moonlight. When a wet gurgle disturbed her, she tucked her head down to focus. Then there was only the cool sheet brushing her bare shoulder and the ticking of the clock as she wielded the pencil in her hand on paper. Shapes took form beneath it, transferring from her mind to the sketchpad with barely a hint of thought between the action and the result. The hours always danced by when she sketched. At night Eryn drew what she pleased, but she'd learned not to draw the dark images that sometimes filled her head. Those sketches made grown-ups whisper in hushed voices. Mama would get little lines between her eyes and look at Eryn in a way that made her ashamed and afraid. So now Eryn drew castles and dragons and beautiful princesses trapped in a tower. Adults didn't get upset over pictures of castles.

Eryn didn't go to school anymore because Mama said they didn't spend enough time on the arts. But Eryn knew it had more to do with the phone calls from school and the long meetings with her teachers and principal. Uncle Bill said Mama always left those meetings in "high dudgeon." After first grade, Eryn was homeschooled, which meant she was often alone doing lessons on the computer. Mama taught art class, though. Eryn liked those times most of all, when she had Mama to herself, even when she insisted Eryn stretch her artistic wings and learn more difficult drawing and painting techniques.

The wind moaned quietly outside the windows, and a floorboard creaked from the weight of the ghosts living here. Eryn had once asked Mama if Pullman Estate was haunted. She'd given an ugly laugh and said only by misfortune and broken dreams. Eryn wasn't sure what the words had meant but decided maybe it wasn't just people who could be ghosts.

She set her pencil down and tilted the pad up to study it. The drawing was good. More than good. Maybe the best she'd ever done. Sometimes the image would be so vivid in her mind, but what flowed from her fingers lacked the life and detail of the picture in her head. Not this time. The curve of the turrets was shadowed just right, and she could almost feel the cool, damp stones of the castle's facade. Maybe she'd show this one to Mama, even if she didn't like Eryn drawing the same thing all the time.

"Eryn!"

She jumped a little at the harsh whisper. Had she woken Mama? She pulled aside the draping bedcovers to look out. There was a shadowy figure standing at the end of the bed. It took a second to recognize Uncle Bill in the shadows there. He was talking, but his words sailed by her as they often did when she was caught up in her own world. He looked so funny! She pressed her hand against her mouth to stifle a giggle. With his hair all a muss and horror on his face, he resembled a silly cartoon character who'd stuck his finger in a light socket. His face was so white it stood out in the shadows like the glow from her night-light. Maybe he'd seen one of the ghosts living here.

Then he moved away, and she picked up her pencil again to do some more shading. If she was going to show this to Mama, she had to get every bit right. Just exactly right.

"Oh my God, oh my God! What have you done now, you fucking little freak?"

Eryn frowned. Grown-ups weren't supposed to swear, but sometimes Uncle Bill did when he was mad, like he got when Mama sang the funny little rhyme to him. *Silly Billy had a thrilly 'cuz he couldn't control his willy.* The tune drifted across her mind, and she hummed it under her breath. It always made Uncle Bill much madder when Mama sang it, and she'd do it over and over again until he stomped from the room.

She hummed as she sketched rapidly. Almost perfect now. Just a little more . . .

"I said, get up, Eryn. For God sakes, come away from there."

She frowned as she tried to tug away from the hard hand on her arm, but he yanked her to her feet and pulled her toward him. Then he let her go so suddenly she dropped back down on the floor hard enough to make her butt smart. "Put it down. Eryn! Put down that knife!"

Such a silly Billy. She scrabbled over to the sketchpad he'd made her drop so she could finish her picture. But when she raised her hand, there was no pencil in it. Only a knife dripping slow, fat drops onto the sketch, melting together to form a soggy puddle. They were ruining her drawing! She reached back to pull the sheet from the bed to wipe at the sketch. But the drips were coming faster now, a river of blood, like someone had turned on a faucet. The picture was ruined. It was wrecked forever, and Eryn began to sob in frustration.

She knew when things were ruined they could never be put right again. Not ever.

Eryn: Now

The brilliant sheen of the hallway tiles reflected a wavering image of Eryn as she stared down at them. She'd once thought if she stared closely enough she could see what Uncle Bill said the doctors were paid to discover: the inner workings of her mind. Sometimes when the receptionist would come to lead her into Dr. Glassman's office, she'd find Eryn lying still on the tiles, peering closely at her reflection, fiercely summoning the insight that would explain the hollow echoes and dark tangles in her head. It'd been months before the doctor had convinced her the self-awareness she craved would only result from their sessions. She'd been here for most of eleven years, seven months, and sixteen days. And on the date of her twenty-first birthday, she feared enlightenment continued to elude her.

Click click click. Slowly she raised her gaze. Saw the PR woman guiding a couple down the hallway toward her, the sound of high heels tapping against the tiles like a frantic Morse code signal. It was another moment before the woman's muted tones finally made their way into Eryn's consciousness. One thing she'd perfected during her time here was blocking out voices.

"And this is the professional wing of our adult ward. Rolling Acres Resort employs only the most highly qualified board-certified caregivers. We're quite proud of our long-term . . ." The woman caught Eryn's eye then and halted her spiel for a moment. In the next instant, she recovered and smoothly pivoted, motioning toward the nearest of the picture windows lining the area. "As I'm sure you saw on your drive here, Rolling Acres Resort is a jewel nestled in the foothills of the Smoky Mountains. Our property is truly spectacular, the scenery a healing element. If you come with me, I'll show you brochures of the grounds and gardens in full bloom, and I'm sure you'll agree . . ."

Eryn watched them go, amused. Allowing prospective clients to come face-to-face with the crazies on their first visit to the place could leave a very bad impression. Not at all suitable for a high-end mental health facility priding itself on its discretion and security.

The door to the doctor's outer office opened. "Eryn." A smile wreathed Mrs. Becker's face. "You may join the others now."

The others. Her amusement vanished as a boulder lodged in her throat. Another settled on her chest. For a moment, she considered running shrieking down the halls, demanding to be taken back to her room. Maybe even letting loose the panicked screams scrabbling and surging inside her, until personnel came running with the leathers and chemical restraints. She'd only experienced them twice since she'd been here, but for a moment the yearning for the blissful chemical calm was so strong she trembled with the need for it.

"You don't want to keep them waiting." Mrs. Becker's voice was still pleasant, but the hint of firmness in it had Eryn rising from her seat against the wall, walking obediently through the open doorway to Dr. Glassman's office.

But it didn't belong to Dr. Glassman anymore. She was still slightly shocked each time she saw the door with his name removed from the glass and replaced with Dr. Steigel's. To see a young bearded doctor rise to greet her instead of the grandfatherly man who'd treated her for over a decade.

"Eryn." He sent her a grave smile as she entered and waved her to a chair next to the couch where Uncle Bill and his wife, Rosalyn, sat. "It's your big day. How do you feel?"

"Ready." The word was meant to allay the worry in Uncle Bill's expression and lurking behind Rosalyn's overly bright smile. Any doubt expressed would do nothing to alter the outcome, and the couple appeared to have more than enough doubts of their own.

"You and I already went over all the particulars yesterday, and I just filled in your uncle and aunt. As we discussed, I'll give you a couple days to get settled in. You have an appointment Wednesday with Dr. Ashland, who will be taking over your care." To the couple he said, "Eryn and I met with her new therapist last week."

All eyes seemed to turn in her direction. For a moment, Eryn's mind blanked, the way it did when she had to sort through which societal expectation was appropriate. Dr. Glassman's frequent reminder drifted into her mind. *When in doubt, smile.* She did so now, coupling it with a grave tone. "Yes. She seems very nice." The inanity seemed to reassure the other three, and Dr. Steigel nodded slightly, as if she'd passed a test of some sort.

"Your uncle has taken your suitcases to the car," the man went on, "and the rest of your personal belongings are being packed up. They should be delivered this evening."

Her heart clutched. "My paintings and sketchpads."

Dr. Steigel nodded soberly. "I'll leave word they're to be handled with extra care."

Eryn's palms went damp at the thought of strangers touching her work. Perhaps idly flipping through them. "I'll take them with me now."

"The vehicle will be packed full already, Eryn." Uncle Bill's tone bordered on impatient. He seemed to realize it and tempered his next words with humor. "Your clothing and personal items will take up most of the space. We've left room for you, though, don't worry."

"Maybe I can stay and ride with the driver bringing my artwork." Eryn directed the suggestion to the doctor without much hope. He'd only been on staff a few months, and they really didn't have a rapport. Because she refused to let him in, he'd admonished her from time to time. *There's room for more than one relationship in your life, Eryn. Establishing trust with me is not a violation of your friendship with Dr. Glassman.*

"Oh, surely there's a teensy bit of space." Rosalyn's voice suited her exactly. Bright and perky, with a gloss of cheer that often failed to hide the hint of concern in her eyes when she looked at Eryn. "Maybe you could pick out your favorite to bring with you."

She bit back a retort. Pick out her favorite. As if she were being allowed to bring a cherished stuffed animal on a family trip. Anxiety began to clutch and squeeze in her chest.

"Well, Eryn," Dr. Steigel prodded. "We seem to have reached an acceptable compromise, haven't we?"

Compromise. The inflection he gave the word was a veiled reference to their sessions for the last several weeks. They'd focused on strategies necessary for her successful transition home. Ways to defuse any family conflicts as they arose. Plans for quelling the paranoia and depression stress could summon. She needed no reminders that her previous attempts at transitioning from the facility had resulted in miserable failure.

"It's fine." She shoved the burgeoning anxiety aside. "Tonight will be soon enough." The room seemed to exhale with a collective sigh of relief. *Crisis averted. The crazy wouldn't be having a meltdown. Not yet, anyway.*

"Are you sure, honey?" Rosalyn leaned over to pat her knee. "'Cuz we can surely fit in one or two. This is your special day, after all."

This time the smile was a bit harder to summon. A stretch of the lips, parted just a bit to avoid the look of a grimace. To look genuine, it was important to crinkle the eyes slightly too. It was just one of the social norms that didn't come naturally, and one she'd spent years practicing. Although she still didn't understand why she was expected to smile when she wasn't feeling particularly happy. She and Dr. Glassman had spent quite a bit of time on acceptable standards of behavior.

"Well, as long as you're certain." Rosalyn gave her a final pat before withdrawing her hand. "It's fine, then."

But Eryn knew things weren't fine. Rolling Acres Resort had been her home far longer than the sprawling Pullman Estate had. Her childhood home held few pleasant memories. And though she couldn't say she'd been particularly happy in the residential setting here, she'd become content enough.

Dr. Steigel nattered on a bit about change and opportunity. Eryn tuned out because she'd heard it all before. She'd been told leaving Rolling Acres Resort for good—if she was "successful"—qualified as both.

If was the operative word.

◆ ◆ ◆

"Hasn't this drop in temperatures been horrid?" Rosalyn chattered from the front seat. "Of course, one expects November is going to get colder, but my blood just isn't ready for it." She gave a tinkling laugh. "And wouldn't you know, the furnace wasn't running properly, either. Alfred forgot to check to make sure it would be in working order, as if he didn't know how unpredictable autumn can be in North Carolina. You'd think the man hadn't spent his entire life here."

There was more, but Eryn let the words rise and fall around her like the background noise it was. Rosalyn considered silence a void it was her duty to fill, and she'd keep up a running litany for the entire drive. Eryn had faced the window at her side, counting the disappearing landmarks as they rolled by them. Past the bench beneath the drooping willow where she liked to sketch on warm mornings. Down the curving drive lined with crape myrtles and hydrangeas that exploded with color in the summer months. Stopping at the first gatehouse, where Uncle Bill lowered his window to hand a stamped pass to the two employees who'd exited the small structure and conducted a discreet search of the vehicle. Then the car crept by the now-dormant flower beds and the fountains turned off for the winter. They slowed again for another search at the next guardhouse. Her chest hollowed out when the towering iron gates slowly opened to allow their exit. Each successive mile that grew between them and Rolling Acres Resort had bat wings of panic fluttering. The reaction had nothing to do with leaving something precious behind and everything to do with the enormity of change stretching before her.

Seeking distraction—any distraction—she refocused on the conversation in the front seat. When Rosalyn took a breath, Eryn inserted quickly, "I've been wondering . . . when I get home . . . if I could change bedrooms."

The quick glance shared by the couple had Eryn's heart sinking. "Mine is small, and I thought Mama's room would be large enough to serve as a bedroom and studio. Those two big double windows let in the early afternoon light . . ." Her voice tapered off. Eryn's favorite childhood memory had been the time spent in the room for art lessons with Mama. Sometimes they'd both work side by side, Mama with her painting and Eryn with her sketching. The voices in her head were always muted then, and the hours were as peaceful as she'd ever known in the house.

The uneasy silence stretched another moment or two until Rosalyn turned around as far as her seat belt would allow, a cheerful smile on her face. "Well, now you've gone and ruined the surprise. I've just been frantic the last few weeks getting some redecorating done for your arrival. Jaxson even helped me. He's as excited as we are about having you home."

The mention of Bill and Rosalyn's seven-year-old son drifted by her. "Did you change Mama's room?" Again, a surreptitious exchanged look between the two. One of Eryn's hands clenched where she had it resting on the seat beside her. Consciously, she uncurled her fingers.

"We recently updated your bedroom, honey. I didn't get rid of anything," the woman hastened to add. "Just packed things up and put them in the closet for you to go through yourself. I wanted to surprise you with new rugs, comforter, and curtains. Something more suitable for your age. Of course, if there's anything you don't like, it can be changed. I'd welcome a chance for us to go shopping together. Wouldn't that just be the most fun? We could go to Asheville and make a day of it, just the two of us."

Eryn didn't care about the room. In recent years, she'd been allowed brief trips home for holidays and the occasional weekend. Her old bedroom hadn't represented a haven but a curious spot caught in a time warp since her childhood. Eryn was more concerned with what wasn't being said. "But Mama's room would still be free, right? To use as a studio?"

"The thing is, Eryn . . ." Uncle Bill hesitated for a moment before continuing. "Rosalyn renovated the space for her sitting room a few years back. We decided it just wasn't healthy to keep it in disuse. Time goes on, and we have to put the past behind us. We all have to make painful changes to adjust."

A few years back. Eryn mentally reeled at the words. Each time she'd been home, the door to the room had been locked. She'd pressed her face against it, imagining it the way Mama had kept it. The bed neatly made by Mary Jane. The shades raised and the sheer curtains draped back to allow in the sunlight. Mama's current work on an easel near the windows. Her paints on a small, scarred table within reach. A stretched blank canvas leaning against the wall. On a good painting day, Mama would let Eryn look at her progress. But more often than not, she'd be in a snit about her work and she'd whitewash it for Eryn's later use and prepare to start fresh in the morning.

A piercing sense of loss stabbed through her. She wasn't certain she could bear to see the alterations made to the space.

"William, what is that up ahead? What do those people think they're doing? They're blocking our drive."

"I see them." Bill's voice was terse as he slowed the vehicle to a crawl. He uttered an oath and said, "Pay them no mind, Eryn. They're ignorant troublemakers who'd be better off tending to their own business." He picked up his cell phone and spoke quietly and urgently into it as he brought the car to a complete stop.

"Don't let them upset you," Rosalyn added. "Just a few unchristian cranks who should spend more time reading the Bible."

Eryn stared at the small crowd. It was comprised of no more than a dozen people chanting and waving signs. They formed a human wall blocking the entrance to the private drive leading up to the estate's gate.

She couldn't make out the words coming from the group, but her gaze was drawn to the signs like metal filings to a magnet.

AN EYE FOR AN EYE!
KILLERS BELONG IN PRISON!
MURDERERS GO TO HELL!

One woman broke from the group and rushed to the car, pounding on Eryn's window. She shrunk away, as if there wasn't a barrier between them, and the stranger pressed her sign against the window, screaming the words over and over.

MATRICIDE IS MURDER!

The last word had been written with red paint, which had been allowed to drip and run down the sign.

Apparently, Eryn wasn't the only one having trouble letting go of the past.

Ryder

When the jacked-up cherry-apple-red dually truck roared past him doing an easy eighty, Haywood County Sheriff Ryder Talbot flipped on his light bar and accelerated down the blacktop. The driver of the truck was well known to him, and ticketing Frances "Gilly" Gilbert could be considered a part-time occupation for his office. Mostly because Gilly was a congenital dumb-ass, the by-product of a disgracefully shallow gene pool. And when he had a few beers in him, little things like speed limits and noise ordinances completely went out of his head.

The mobile radio crackled from its position on the console beside him. "Ryder, you done with the regional task force meeting yet?" Wilma Young, substitute department dispatcher, asked.

Ryder kept an eye on the truck he was gaining on as he picked up the transmitter. "Been done. I'm on my way back to town after I deal with a speeding motorist."

"Well, if it's Gilly Gilbert, Lord knows he'll keep 'til another day. Everyone's tied up or on the other side of the county, and I just took a call from William Pullman. He's got an ugly situation brewing out at his place. He needs someone for crowd control. Donny's closest, but he's still twenty minutes out."

Crowd control? The Pullman place was in a rural area on the eastern part of the county. The closest thing to a crowd the property would ever see was a group of bicyclists going by. "I'm ten minutes away." Ryder turned off his flashers and slowed, waiting for an opportunity to make a U-turn as Wilma continued.

"It seems some people in the area aren't too happy 'bout . . ."

All too aware of the number of residents in the vicinity with scanners, Ryder interrupted the overly chatty substitute dispatcher. "Fine, Wilma. I've got this." As he headed toward the Pullmans', he reflected this was another reason for the updated encrypted communication system he needed to purchase. It wasn't just nosy civilians wanting to know what was going on throughout the county he had to worry about. Criminals were getting savvier about monitoring the whereabouts of his deputies. Another thing to put on his wish list when it came budget time. Three tours in Iraq and Afghanistan hadn't prepared him for the bureaucratic nightmare of the reams of paperwork that consumed too much of his job.

Of course, it would also help if he could avoid using Wilma to fill in when his regular dispatchers were unavailable. The woman had retired from the office nearly ten years ago and was a product from another era.

He passed a white van with a satellite dish on its roof. Noted the familiar logo on its side. For the first time since he'd gotten the call, trepidation pooled in his gut. Ryder would like to think it was just chance he was heading in the same direction as the vehicle from the local news station. But he'd never believed in coincidences. Unconsciously, he pressed more firmly on the accelerator and wished he hadn't been so quick to cut Wilma off.

The front of the gated property was bordered by blacktop. At the rear of the large estate was a man-made pond a Pullman ancestor had built and stocked, the story went, with largemouth bass and walleyes to indulge his favorite pastime. The same progenitor had later drowned in the pond when he'd toppled dead drunk from his fishing boat. It'd been the first of a series of tragedies to curse the family over the generations.

That hadn't curbed developers' interest in the five-hundred-acre estate. The house was set back a hundred yards from the road, at the end of a winding private drive lined with carefully spaced towering pines interspersed with massive oaks and hickories. The trees effectively shielded the property from the public eye, even in the winter months, which seemed to suit the reserved family.

He slowed to a stop behind a black town car with tinted windows idling at the side of the blacktop. Getting out of his vehicle, Ryder skirted the other car's rear bumper to stride beyond it to the small scattering of people blocking the gated entrance to the drive. At his appearance, they congealed into one group, forming a human chain against the closed wrought-iron gates, shaking their signs while they shouted.

"Murderers belong behind bars!"

"Sheriff, do your job!"

Ryder spotted the reporter making a beeline for him a moment before he noticed the shiny white van parked on the shoulder across the road. An Asheville news station. Swallowing an oath, he scanned the knot of protestors and headed toward the man in the center of them, who was shouting the loudest.

"Sir, you and your group are on private property. Remove yourselves or you'll be arrested for trespassing."

"We have a legal right to protest this gross miscarriage of justice," the stranger bellowed. "You can't deny us our First Amendment rights. Now's your chance to do what your daddy didn't. Lock the young murderer up."

The man could only be talking about Eryn Pullman. Ryder resisted an urge to toss a glance toward the town car. He'd left home before the most recent Pullman tragedy, but he knew the details. Pitching his voice above the man's, Ryder addressed the rest of the group. "As long as you're standing on this drive, all of you are guilty of second-degree criminal trespass. That's punishable by twenty days in jail. You need to move. Now."

A woman with frizzy blonde hair screamed, "You threaten us? A body isn't safe with a murderer running around loose! Think people in these parts have forgotten what the girl did?"

Ryder pulled the handcuffs from his belt and held them up. "I'm not going to tell you again."

"This is what the law stands for round here, looks like." The leader of the group was addressing the television camera rolling behind Ryder. "The rich get special protection while the rest of us have to worry 'bout getting our throats slit in our beds. The sheriff ain't no better at his job than his daddy was before him."

Ryder reached out and, with one hand on the man's shoulder, spun him around midsentence. He cuffed him and steered him toward the department vehicle in a matter of seconds. Over his shoulder he said to the rest of the protestors, "I've got more handcuffs in the vehicle. When I return, anyone still on private property will be wearing a pair."

"I know my rights!" the man sputtered in fury as Ryder propelled him to the county vehicle. "The First Amendment protects my freedom of speech!" They came up alongside the official SUV. Ryder opened the back door. "If you aren't familiar with the Constitution, you don't belong in your position."

"Watch your head." Ryder guided the man inside, securing the door behind him. He went to the trunk for several pairs of flex-cuffs and headed back to the drive. The rest of the people had shifted but still stood on the road, blocking the drive.

"You can't prevent us from protesting!" It was the frizzy-haired woman again, her broad forehead glistening with perspiration. "We're standing right here until we're heard! Something must be—"

"Ma'am, you are currently blocking access to private property. You and your friends can protest to your heart's content." The watery over-head sunlight was stronger than it appeared. Ryder could feel a trickle of sweat beginning to pool at his nape. Stabbing a finger toward the road he continued, "May I suggest you all do it safely from the shoulder of the blacktop or the ditch. I'd hate to see any of you hit by a passing motorist. We've got more than a few careless drivers in these parts." He thought fleetingly of Gilly Gilbert, who probably thought he'd won the daily Pick Three when Ryder had given up the chase.

"We aren't causing any trouble . . ." The woman's words trailed off when he raised an index finger. A pair of flex-cuffs dangled from it.

"Last chance."

It took only a moment for her to decide. "C'mon," she screeched to the others. "Across the road."

"Sheriff, would you care to respond to—"

"No comment." The reporter looked vaguely familiar. Blonde. Plastic face. Practiced sober expression. Maybe he'd caught her a time or two on a newscast. He indicated the area where the group of protesters had re-formed. "For your own protection, you may want to join them over there on public property, ma'am." He walked back a few yards and waved for the driver of the town car to pull into the drive. The gates swung open as the vehicle inched by him. When Ryder turned to watch its progress he almost tripped over the reporter who'd followed him.

"Surely you can't dismiss the fear expressed by these concerned citizens, Sheriff." The reporter's smile warmed, and she lowered the microphone, making a surreptitious gesture behind her back to summon the news crew standing a short distance away. "Anyone would be spooked by a crazed killer returning to their area. You could do your department a world of good and make a statement to your public. Assure them of their safety."

"You want a statement?" Beyond her, he saw one of his deputies pulling up. "I do have a brief public safety announcement." He reached up to remove his mirrored sunglasses. Eagerly the woman raised the microphone again. "Your station's van is partially blocking a public roadway, creating a safety hazard. Please have it moved before it causes an accident.”

◆   ◆   ◆

Ten minutes later Ryder left his deputy to supervise the arrestee and protesters and strode toward the house to join William Pullman where he waited in the open doorway, watching the scene. “I appreciate your assistance, Sheriff.” There was no gratitude sounding in the man’s stilted tones. Leading Ryder down a shadowy marbled hall lined with portraits, William waved him into a spacious office outfitted in gleaming oak and hickory. Closing the double doors behind them, he continued to the inlaid panel desk and then stood next to it, as if uncertain what to do next. Ryder made the decision a little easier by slipping in to a butter-soft leather armchair the color of melted toffee. After another moment, William rounded the desk and sat down in the oversize chair, which matched the other furniture. The chair dwarfed him. The man was no more than five eight, one sixty. If not for the creases beginning to line his face, he’d look like a little kid playing executive.

Ryder surveyed the glassy-eyed row of trophy heads lining the wall above the other man. Lingered on the massive grizzly. “Impressive souvenirs.” He nodded to the display. “Any of them yours?”

William looked blank for a moment before glancing behind him, as if he’d forgotten the decor. “No, my grandfather’s. With my great-grandfather it was fish, but Grandpa traveled all over North America hunting big game. I’m not much of an outdoorsman myself.”

But William, a nonhunter, kept the place just as his grandfather had left it. Interesting.

“Listen, Sheriff . . .” William turned to face him again, his expression growing pained. “As I’m sure you ascertained from the commotion outside, we brought my niece, Eryn, home from the Rolling Acres Resort today. Hopefully for good.”

"Because the doctors say she's cured?"

William seemed to choose his answer carefully. "Her doctors no longer consider her a threat to herself or others. It's our hope a return to her childhood home will provide the necessary tranquility for her continued recovery."

Ryder was less familiar with the residential facility Pullman mentioned than he was with the other structure sharing its property. Miles away from Rolling Acres, carefully situated far from the public eye, sat North Carolina's only federal facility for the criminally insane. Haywood County had one resident there who'd claimed to be possessed by Satan when he slaughtered his entire family twenty years earlier.

"How old was Eryn when she killed your sister?"

The other man's mouth firmed to a thin line. "Nine."

"And now?"

"Twenty-one. She's had excellent treatment. The best. A judge has signed off on her release based on the recommendation of her doctors. What happened today was terribly upsetting for all of us. I hope I can count on your continued support if anything similar occurs again." His fingers were laced together on the desk in front of him so tightly the knuckles shone white.

Ryder gave a slow nod. "Of course. But you need to be prepared for some of the locals expressing a similar sentiment."

William's gaze dropped to his tightly clenched hands. With deliberate care, he loosened them. "That would be unfortunate. My niece's diagnosis remains unchanged. But with continued medical care and medication, she's no threat to anyone."

Unless she refused therapy. Stopped taking her meds. Ryder recognized all the possible pitfalls the man left unsaid. "There's no telling what the news channels will report," Ryder replied honestly. "Knowing how reporters work, I wouldn't be surprised to have a complete rundown of your sister's case on the six o'clock news." The other man swore. "I spoke at more length with the trespasser we arrested. Frederick

Bancroft. Do you know him?" William shook his head. "He's from Crabtree. Affiliated with some fringe church, it sounds like. The kind that shows up at inopportune times to point out how everyone else is going to hell. He contacted all of the others. When I asked how he knew you'd be bringing Eryn home today, he said he'd received a phone call a couple of days ago informing him of the upcoming event."

Ryder watched carefully, but William's expression reflected only bewilderment. "But . . . how? No one outside the family knew about her release. We just finalized the paperwork two weeks ago." He shook his head. "Obviously, the man is lying."

"Anchors from the news stations who showed up today said they'd gotten anonymous tips telling them the same thing. So I hate to ask you this, William"—Ryder leaned forward in his chair, hands clasped between his knees—"but can you be certain no one in your family might have been the tipster?"

"Of course I'm certain." William's tone was dismissive. "There's only my wife, two sons, and the housekeeper. We didn't even tell any of the help until this morning."

Ryder leaned back, instincts humming. "And the facility?"

"The resort has an impeccable reputation for discretion. I'm fairly certain there would be no leaks there, either. They pay their staff well, which ensures a certain amount of loyalty."

Loyalty. Ryder didn't tell him that no matter what the pay was, in most cases loyalty could be trumped by profit. Especially the type that couldn't be traced.

Cady: Two Days Later

"I'll be damned. Like a charm. How the hell do you call 'em?"

"Instinct. Pay up." Without taking her eyes off the man swaggering up the sagging porch steps of Crony's bar and grill, Deputy US Marshal Cady Maddix wiggled her fingers toward the other marshal, Miguel Rodriguez. She closed them around the twenty the man slapped into her palm. The info she'd gotten from DelRay James Woodhouse's ex-girlfriend had paid off. The woman had named half a dozen places the man had been seen recently, most of them duplicates of this establishment. It was barely dusk, but they'd hit gold on the second place they'd tried.

"Looks like a good spot to get ptomaine poisoning," Miguel noted.

She nodded. North Carolina required places serving alcohol to derive 30 percent of their income from food, unless they were private clubs. To get around the law, any place with a grill and deep-fat fryer called itself a restaurant. Cady shifted in the front seat of the minivan to stuff the bill in her jeans, watching Woodhouse step past the window's flickering neon beer sign and through the front door. Only then did she look at Miguel. "And half the assholes in there will be carrying."

"Maybe more. If he has any friends inside, arresting him there could get ugly in a hurry. Maybe we should call in the rest of the task force."

Impatience flickered through her. Fugitive investigations were worked with a group of stakeholders that always included the law enforcement entity that had issued the warrant and frequently other federal agencies as well. The added personnel were often critical, both in the investigation aspect and the arrest. But Woodhouse had eluded authorities primarily because he couch—or bed—surfed. His habit of hooking up with a different woman every few days had made him difficult to track. How long before he left with another one? "By the time it assembles, Woodhouse could be gone," she said finally. "Let me go in alone and see if I can draw him out. Give me thirty minutes or so to work him."

The other marshal's gaze went beyond her to two patrons crossing the rutted lot toward the front of the place. "It's busier than I'd expected for a Sunday. I think it'd be better to follow you inside in five and keep watch from a safe distance. He's not going to notice me behind you when the two of you leave."

"Someone else might. We'll make it twenty minutes."

Miguel's brows skimmed upward. "Confidence. I like it. Okay, twenty it is. If he isn't trailing you out the door like a puppy dog by then, you come out and we'll contact the task force. We could always follow him if he gets lucky before everyone is assembled."

Cady was already sliding out of the vehicle and shutting the door behind her. She lifted her face to the kiss of the cool November air. It was a welcome change from the furnacelike heat in the car. Miguel had the circulation of a ninety-year-old woman. If allowed, he'd counter the outdoor temperatures with a tropical eighty in the vehicle. And since it was her turn to drive, he'd controlled the heat and the radio all day. She felt like she was stepping out of a sauna.

As she walked toward the steps, Cady slipped a hand inside her black leather jacket to unbutton the top three buttons of her shirt. Her weapon was locked in the glove box. She felt naked without its weight strapped across her chest. The steel-toed western boots she wore hid the short sap she'd slid inside. A pair of flex-cuffs were stuffed down the back of her jeans.

The *N* in Crony's lighted sign was out, but she gave the owner props for the apostrophe. She pulled open the door and stepped inside. Its dim interior hid the seediness a more unforgiving lighting would reveal. The place was indistinguishable from a thousand others like it. A long, scarred bar, a few wobbly tables, and nearly twenty thirsty patrons. There'd be a shotgun behind the bar, and the meaty bartender would know how to use it. This far out in the sticks, a businessman had to be ready to protect his own.

DelRay was leaning between two tattooed females at the end of the bar, both of whom were wearing far less than Cady. She weaved in a deliberately unsteady gait to a barstool several seats away from them and assessed her quarry from the corner of her eye. North Carolina was an open carry state, no permit required. When she'd entered, she'd counted eight pistols on the customers in plain view, and she wouldn't be surprised if the ladies packed heat in their purses. DelRay was wearing a tight black T-shirt and black jeans. If he was carrying, most likely his weapon was strapped to his ankle.

"Getcha?"

The bartender slowed his bulk before her, giving Cady an appraising once-over. She wasn't worried about being made as law enforcement. In her experience, there wasn't a male alive who could see beyond a woman's cleavage to the threat she represented. "Jameson Black. Neat."

He moved slowly away, and she half turned, propping an elbow on the bar and scanning the place, letting her gaze linger on DelRay until he looked up, catching her eyeing him. She held his gaze for a second, then unhurriedly surveyed the rest of the interior until she heard the bartender behind her.

"Five dollars."

Cady dug in her pocket for the twenty she'd taken from Miguel earlier and handed it to him. She picked up the shot and pretended to sip, allowing the liquid to trickle onto her shirt. Hopefully, the smell would make her later pretense believable. She shot a look over her shoulder at the lone pool table at the back of the place. From the money stacked on one side, the men gathered around it didn't seem likely to move aside anytime soon.

She slid off the seat. Sauntering toward the old-fashioned jukebox against the wall past the bar, she propped her fists on the machine as she perused the titles. There wasn't a song listed that had graced the country music charts in a decade. Cady took her time selecting two songs for five bucks—a rip-off—keeping her head down as footsteps approached.

"You looking for a dance partner, sweetheart?" The man who appeared at her side sported a hubcap-size belt buckle, only glimpses of which were visible beneath the overhang of his belly. He gyrated his hips. "I'm pretty light on my feet."

"I don't doubt it." She gave him an easy smile and pushed away from the jukebox. "But I'm waiting for someone."

She headed back to her seat, feeling DelRay's gaze on her as she wended through the tables and resettled on her barstool. A few minutes later the two women flanking Woodhouse headed off together to the restroom. Keeping her eyes trained on the shot before her, she felt rather than saw the man slide onto the seat beside her. "Slow as you're drinking, the shot might . . . whatchacallit . . . evaporate before you get to it."

She turned her head, gave him a smile. With the overly enunciated speech of the inebriated, Cady said, "I think I'd be better off if I'd a let the last two or three evaporate instead of drinking 'em." She gave a drunken giggle. "Either I'm gonna hafta sober up, or I'll need to call one of them Ubers to come get me and take me home."

DelRay laughed, showing a missing right-front incisor. "Don't think we're in Uber territory, girl. Where do you live?"

"Outside Weaverville, on Oakdale. It's kinda isolated, but it's a real nice little house. Homey."

"Isolated, huh?" The man's thoughts were transparent. "It might not be safe for a woman living alone out there by herself."

"Oh, I'm not alone." The man's expression stilled. Cady leaned closer, lowering her voice conspiratorially. "I got a cat that went three rounds with a raccoon last week and came out on top. And a Chihuahua who's feared by squirrels countywide."

The man's face relaxed. "Well, now, sounds like you got some fine protection. If you taught either of them to drive, you'd be set."

She laughed hysterically, and he joined in, lifting his left foot to rest it on the step in front of the bar. Cady glimpsed leather above his ankle and knew her earlier suspicion had been right. He was armed.

"My name is Harris. Harris Stevens." It was one of several aliases the man had used before he'd been arrested and charged with armed robbery. Before he'd cut off the electronic monitoring bracelet he'd worn as one of the terms of his bail and taken off for parts unknown.

"Priscilla. Folks just call me Cissy." She pretended to slide halfway off her seat, barely catching herself on the bar. "Oops." Cady giggled again and mentally tabulated the time since she'd come inside. Maybe fifteen minutes. She didn't trust Miguel to wait the full twenty before heading inside to check on her progress. "How much have you had to drink?"

DelRay's teeth flashed again, although his gaze was fixed on her chest. "Not as much as you, looks like."

"Well that's a fact, since I started day-drinking at noon. I'll give you twenty dollars to drive me home. You have a friend you can call to come pick you up at my place?"

His thoughts were as easy to read as a billboard. "I got one or two. You keep your money, though. It'll be my good deed for the day."

She made a show of sliding carefully from the stool, then stumbling against him. "You, Harris Stevens, are a true gentleman."

He slapped a hand to his chest and grinned widely. "It's like you already know me."

Experience told Cady to bide her time. Waiting to take him outside the bar was the easiest way to avoid trouble with any buddies he might have in here. So she leaned heavily on him, positioning her body so the hand he wanted to place on her butt landed on her hip instead. She didn't need him discovering the flex cuffs before she was ready.

"What'd you drive here, sweetheart?"

"Black double-cab pickup with lots of chrome," she lied. The vehicle she described was two spaces over from where they'd parked. "Keys are in the ignition." She batted her eyes at him. "Bad habit of mine."

They staggered out the door. "I wanna hear all about your bad habits." He leered at her as they went down the steps and began to cross the lot. "'Specially the dirty ones."

Cady bent over as if lost in gales of laughter at his half-witted comment. He grinned and turned toward her, giving her the opening she was looking for. With one quick movement, she stepped behind him, sweeping her leg in front of his while she grabbed one of his arms and propelled him forward.

"What the fuck?" He tripped, and she used her knee to force him facedown in the gravel, wrenching the arm she still grasped upward while her knee moved to his back.

"Deputy US Marshal." Cady heard a car door slam as she freed the cuffs tucked into the back of her waistband beneath her jacket and fastened one to the man's wrist before reaching for his other arm. "DelRay James Woodhouse, you failed to show up in court for armed robbery charges." She hauled him to his feet as Miguel jogged up to them. "Weapon in left ankle holster," she said in an aside to her partner.

"Bullshit," DelRay shouted, shooting her a lethal look over his shoulder. "The hearing was postponed."

"Indefinitely, after you cut off your monitoring bracelet and headed out of the county." Cady waited until Miguel had possession of DelRay's gun before guiding the man toward the vehicle. "I'm sure the judge will want to hear all about your decision-making process."

"Keep talking, bitch." DelRay's voice was smug. "Wait 'til I tell my lawyer you arrested me under false pretenses. I'll be a free man by tomorrow."

Miguel opened the sliding door of their vehicle, a white minivan that shouted soccer mom. "This is going to be good," he murmured to Cady.

She put an ungentle hand on the man's head as he got into the back seat. "False pretenses, huh. How do you figure?"

"Entrapment. You were offering sex to get me outside."

Miguel's grin was partially hidden by the fist he raised to cover his fake cough. Cady rolled her eyes. "Yeah, genius, try that with the lawyer when he visits you in lockup while he's explaining there's no chance of bail—or a return of the money—since you skipped out." She slammed the door and opened her own.

Cady buttoned up her shirt before buckling her seat belt. She pulled out of the lot, unmoved by his string of obscenities. "Save it for the judge. It should really sway her at sentencing."

They delivered the prisoner to the Western District of North Carolina federal courthouse in Asheville. After processing him, Cady and Miguel turned him over to the Buncombe County deputies they'd summoned, who would transport him to jail.

Cady and Miguel left the building and headed toward the parking lot. What she'd figured would be another late night trailing Woodhouse had ended far earlier than she'd expected. There was plenty of time to stop by and see her mom before heading home. She'd missed spending

Saturday with her because she'd worked through the weekend. But dropping in at irregular times gave Cady a better feel for what kind of care Hannah was getting from her sister, Alma.

She dug the keys out of her pocket as she approached her vehicle. The Jeep in the lot was the one she usually drove, unless another marshal needed it for an investigation. She sent a sideways glance at Miguel, who was on his phone with one of his seemingly endless string of women.

"I can be there in forty minutes." He listened and then gave a low masculine chuckle. Cady pointed the fob at the Jeep and unlocked it. She opened the door, then paused expectantly, waiting for her partner's reaction. He was so preoccupied with his call it took him a moment to put things together. He halted, looked around with an expression of confusion on his too-handsome face before his head swiveled toward Cady. "I'll call you back," he said hurriedly into the cell before he backtracked and headed her way. She climbed into the vehicle. Started it.

"No. C'mon, even you can't be that mean."

"Mean? Me? I always drive the Jeep, Miguel." The USMS had several vehicles for use by the marshals, and they sometimes traded with each other when one better fit the need of the investigation. Miguel usually drove a pickup equipped like a construction vehicle, but he'd traded yesterday for a lame minivan that would look innocuous in the bar parking lots they'd been cruising while they'd searched for Woodhouse.

"Cady. Please."

She smiled. The charm didn't work on her, but she gave the man points for trying.

"I've got a date! I can't show up driving . . . a van." His tone made the word sound like an epithet.

"You'll have to take it home and get your car, then." She almost felt sorry for him then. Almost.

"That'll take over an hour!"

She managed, barely, to avoid rolling her eyes. "She'll keep. Or you could just use the van. Let her picture you as a future family man." She laughed at the sheer terror on his face and drove out of the lot.

Her amusement faded as she started out of town. Once she'd left behind the Asheville traffic—which, compared to Saint Louis wasn't even deserving of the name—she drove west. Her Aunt Alma's cabin was located in a rural area a few miles west of Waynesville. Cady had spent more time than she cared to recall staying there with her mom, after another in Hannah's string of boyfriends had drank or snorted the rent money. The memories were like bruises, dark and tender. Cady concentrated on the road and tried not to let the familiar shadows drift in. Distance had helped relegate her childhood ghosts to the dusty corners of her mind. Years after leaving North Carolina, she'd thought they'd been banished completely, only to find them still waiting upon her return, a motley army of specters ready to ambush the moment she lowered her guard.

She hadn't seen her mom in four days, and Aunt Alma's updates were notoriously unreliable. Cady had learned that dropping in often and unannounced was the best way of determining her mother's deteriorating mental condition. It wasn't yet nine. Now that Hannah Maddix was no longer able to work, she often stayed up at least until the ten o'clock news came on.

She slowed and turned into the badly rutted lane to the cabin. Her headlights caught another vehicle parked in front of the building. Cady mentally swore when she recognized the rusted primer-gray pickup parked near the home. Like dealing with one asshole today hadn't filled her quota.

She slammed the door to her Jeep and headed toward the shabby porch. The sound of her arrival had the front door opening, and two figures stepped out to watch her approach, looking like twins in the dim light with their long hair and matching black Carhartt jeans and jackets.

Cady didn't extend a greeting. Bo and LeRoy might be her cousins by blood, but she'd mentally excised the relationship long ago. They took up positions leaning against porch posts as she walked up the steps. When she drew even with them, Bo removed the toothpick from his mouth. "Hey, killer."

She slowed a fraction. He could have been referring to the incident in Saint Louis two years ago. Or perhaps alluding to ancient history when she'd given him the scar hidden beneath the ball cap he wore.

But she knew he was referencing neither.

"Bo. Didn't know you were out of county lockup. Did the sheriff get a sudden attack of mercy, or was he just anxious to get rid of you?"

The man spit a wad of tobacco, just missing the toe of her left boot. "Good luck trying to talk to your ma. She was even loonier than normal today." LeRoy snickered. No surprise there. His entire life had been spent as his older brother's stooge.

"Well, she's got early-onset Alzheimer's. What's your excuse?" Without waiting for a rejoinder, she let herself in the screen door. "It's Cady, Aunt Alma."

Her aunt leaped up from the couch where she was lying watching TV. "I swear, Cady, don't know how many times I asked you to call before you come." The woman bustled around, picking up glasses and plates and taking them to the kitchen before hurrying back. "Give a person a warning so I can make the place presentable."

Cady didn't tell her the last thing she wanted was to alert her prior to a visit. She needed to see her mom in the real environment, not the one Alma would present if given the opportunity. "Sorry. My schedule can be unpredictable." She glanced at the empty rocker in the corner. If her mom were awake, that was always where she found her. Frowning, Cady looked at her aunt. "Did she go to bed early?"

The woman's hesitation had Cady's gut tightening. "She had a bad day." Alma shoved her hands deep into the pockets of her housedress. "If'n you'd a called first, I'd a told you to wait until tomorrow."

Without another word, Cady strode toward the tiny bedroom in the corner of the cabin. Alma caught her by the sleeve when she would have turned the doorknob. "She's sleeping now," the woman whispered. "I've been watchin' her real close. Hannah was confused on and off all day, and dizzy. Late this afternoon she got up to go to the bathroom. She musta fell against the wall and rapped her head. She's got a goose egg. I ran her to urgent care in Waynesville and had her checked out, but the doctor didn't think any tests were necessary. Hannah seemed fine. Well . . ." Alma lifted a beefy shoulder. "For her, anyways."

Cady's quick stab of guilt was a reminder that she couldn't protect her mother from the ravages of the disease, even if she'd been here. Then suspicion flickered. "Do you have the receipt from the doctor's office?"

Alma stared at her incredulously for a moment before setting her jaw. She turned and stomped into the kitchen and snatched something off the counter. Marching back toward Cady, she slapped the sheet of paper in her hand. "Think you'd be more trusting of your kin than that."

Cady studied the paper with a flicker of relief. She wished she had more confidence in her aunt as well, but it wouldn't have been the first time the woman had skirted corners to save a dime. "Thank you for taking her, but you should have let me know when it happened." Her mother's declining mental health had been the reason for her seeking a position closer to home. But she was still struggling with balancing the demands of her job with the time needed to properly supervise Hannah's care.

Her aunt's jaw jutted. "I was fixin' to call you later. The boys came for dinner, and I've been on my feet all day. Just taking a minute's rest, is all."

"Uh-huh." It was more likely Alma hadn't intended to tell her at all. "How many other incidents like this have you kept from me?"

"Now just you settle yourself, missy." Alma was a large woman. She'd intimidated Cady when she was a child. But in the last several years, Cady had faced far worse dangers than Alma Griggs. She stared levelly at her until her aunt finally looked away. "I don't follow her into the bathroom. Might be a time when I'll need to, but that time don't seem to be yet. She's just having a bad spell. You remember the doctor warned us to expect them."

Because Cady kept in touch with her mother's doctor in Asheville, she had a good idea of what was in store for Hannah Maddix. The periods of confusion were coming more frequently. And there was no way Cady was going to let Alma know how much the realization scared her.

"Let me know when it gets to be too much." A memory unit in a nursing home would be necessary at some point in Hannah's future. Cady would have to rely on the doctor's assessment as to when her mother required professional care. She couldn't rely on Alma to be objective. The woman received Hannah's entire disability check and a supplemental grocery account Cady had set up at the Waynesville supermarket in return for caring for her sister. Hannah seemed comfortable in the cabin, where she'd lived on and off for over two decades. The situation here wasn't ideal, but Cady was reluctant to uproot her mom before it was necessary.

She was also aware Hannah and Alma would team up to make Hannah's condition appear better than it was.

Easing the door open, Cady peeked inside. Just as Alma had indicated, her mom was in bed, the light off. Sounds of her quiet breathing defused some of Cady's tension. She closed the door quietly. She'd double-check with the clinic doctor, but for now she'd have to take her aunt at her word.

"Tell her I'll try to come by tomorrow." Cady ignored the expression on Alma's face as she brushed by her. Unless something else came up in the next few hours, she'd take some comp time Monday.

"Wait up, now. As long as you're here . . ." She turned at her aunt's voice. "I've been meaning to talk to you about something. I went to the grocery store yesterday, and they wouldn't let me charge everything in my cart. Said you had a cap on the monthly amount."

"You knew the monthly amount we agreed on. We sat down and discussed how much you'd need for the two of you." Cady had a vivid memory of the conversation. It was before she'd moved back. When it had become apparent Hannah could no longer hold a job and shouldn't live alone anymore. Cady had come home from Saint Louis to make the current arrangements for her mother's care.

"Prices have gone up. I need more."

Cady cocked a brow. "You're telling me the grocery money ran out less than halfway into the month? Pretty coincidental, you needing more cash around the same time Bo got out of county lockup." He'd had a job before his sentencing, she recalled. But it wouldn't be waiting for him after three months.

"Now there you go, blaming something on your cousin again for something not his fault. Ain't the first time, either, is it?" Alma folded her arms across her impressive chest. "This has nothing to do with him. It's about you paying enough for me to take care of your mama proper."

Not his fault. The memory summoned by the words seared across Cady's mind. She slammed a mental door before it could take shape.

"I'm not raising the cap." She brushed by the woman and headed toward the door. "If you want to pay for his groceries out of your own money, that's your decision."

"We ain't done talking about this," her aunt called after her.

Yes, Cady thought as she let herself out of the house and jogged down the steps. *We are.* By some cosmic miracle Bo and LeRoy weren't in sight, which, given her current mood, was rare good luck for both men. She put her keys in the ignition and backed up enough to get turned around. She drove cautiously down the pitted drive, unable to escape the most bitter of ironies.

Her mother's problem was not being able to remember.

Cady's was an inability to forget.

She turned her vehicle onto the blacktop, then pressed her foot on the accelerator, wishing it were as easy to leave the tenacious mental images behind. At twelve, she'd already been a wary kid, the trait honed by the revolving door in her mother's social life and the resulting disappointments. So Cady was still shocked her younger self had ever believed her cousins when they'd lured her from the garden by promising to show her a rabbit's nest. The moment she'd gotten down to peer into the thicket they'd pointed out, Bo had been on top of her.

Her palms slipped on the wheel, dampened by sweat. The recollection could still do that to her, even after all these years. His hands tearing at her clothes, loosening his own. Her screaming. Struggling. *Shit, she hardly got no titties!* And LeRoy's donkey bray of a laugh. *She's got a pussy, ain't she?* The panic had lodged in her chest as her fingers searched for something, anything, to use as a weapon. When they'd closed around the fist-size rock, she'd slammed it against Bo's head with all her twelve-year-old might.

She hadn't realized it then, but the incident would mark the end of her childhood.

Cady's eyes burned as they remained on the strip of blacktop. Ancient history. Her past was a bottomless well of insidious remembrances. She'd built a formidable inner wall to keep them from slithering out.

But tonight had scored a chink in her mental armor. Squinting against an approaching vehicle's brights, she worked her shoulders in an attempt to dislodge the tightness there. She already knew the full onslaught of memories would wait until she was asleep to waylay her. Making a sudden decision, Cady reached across the console to her purse. Rummaged in it until she drew out her cell. She checked the time before pressing a familiar number.

"Gabe. Hey," she said when a man's low tones answered. "Sounds like I woke you." It was barely after nine. She'd called later at night. Lots later.

"Might've dozed off." The words were swallowed by a yawn. "Just got home a bit ago from a two-day op." Gabriel Pearson was a special agent with the ATF, stationed at the Asheville office. Like her, he chose to commute to work in order to be closer to family. They'd met on a case a couple of months after she'd moved back. Their occasional after-hours relationship was casual, built on mutual interests and convenience. At least on her part. She assumed it was the same for him. She'd never met a man who was averse to a friends-with-benefits hookup. As evidenced by his answer now.

"But I'm awake now. Want me to come over?"

Something in her chest eased. "Sure. I'll be home in twenty minutes."

"I'll meet you then."

She disconnected and dropped the phone on the console beside her. There was a thin trail of shame trickling down her spine, one she quickly shrugged away. Some people sought oblivion in a bottle, but she'd seen firsthand how destructive alcohol could be. Sex brought similar results, with far fewer side effects.

◆ ◆ ◆

Her cell awakened her. Cady's hand snaked out from beneath the bedcovers in search of the phone on the bedside table. The screen said 1:00 a.m. She'd been asleep less than an hour. "Maddix." She kept her voice low to avoid awakening the man sleeping beside her, but she was already swinging her legs over the side of the mattress.

"Cady, we've got an escape at Fristol Forensic Center in Haywood County." She recognized Supervisory Deputy US Marshal Allen Gant's voice immediately. "The regional task force is being called out. I need you over there."

"Do we have details?" She was already striding to the bathroom, mentally figuring how long it would take her to get to the Fristol property. Five minutes for a quick shower before dressing and another thirty to the facility. Shave ten minutes off that time if she used the dash strobe.

"Samuel Martin Aldeen. Sentenced five years ago for the kidnap, rape, and cannibalization of six children in a three-state area."

The muscles in her gut clenched. She remembered the case. Although she'd been working in the Saint Louis office at the time of his capture, his crimes had made national news. As had the sentencing, when a judge had found the man guilty but insane. "I don't recall him being sent to Fristol." She swung the bathroom door closed and grabbed a towel from the closet before turning on the shower.

"He was in the Bridgeport facility originally, near Greenville, South Carolina," Gant responded. "His attorney filed a hardship plea and got him transferred closer to home. I'm light on details right now, but the Haywood County Sheriff's Office is in charge of the scene. The State Bureau of Investigation is on their way. We're pulling together Aldeen's personal information and making a list of former places of residence, friends, and relatives." Cell still pressed to her ear, Cady stripped with her free hand. "Call in when you get there."

"You got it." Disconnecting, she set the phone aside and then set a record for the world's shortest shower before stepping out of the stall and drying off quickly. Her mind was racing. She'd never had reason to visit Fristol but given its population, she assumed its security measures would be similar to a prison's. Learning everything she could about how the man managed to walk out of the place would give them an excellent starting point.

She pulled her hair back into a ponytail before striding into the bedroom and dressing swiftly. When she walked into the kitchen, she stopped short at the sight of a shadowy figure leaning against the counter. It took a moment for Cady to make the mental adjustment. "Gabe. I'm sorry I woke you."

He took a couple of coffee cups out of the cupboard. "Twice in a matter of hours. Some sort of record, even for you. What's going on?"

Cady filled him in as she strapped on the weapon she'd carried in from her bedroom.

"Aldeen? There's going to be a shitstorm of panic when this goes public."

"Don't I know it." PR wasn't her problem, but public opinion impacted every law enforcement job in a myriad of ways. It wouldn't be the major factor in the manhunt for Samuel Aldeen, however.

Capturing him before he killed again would be.

"I gotta go."

She turned and went to the small living-room closet, pulling out a navy jacket with sheepskin lining. It wasn't until Gabe spoke again as she was threading her hair through the back opening of her matching ball cap that she realized he'd followed her from the kitchen.

"Coffee will be ready in another couple of minutes."

She was tempted, more than she'd like to admit. Regretfully, she shook her head, pulling the gloves from the pockets of her coat and putting them on. "Can't wait. Wish I could." She scooped up the car keys she kept on the tiny oak stand next to the closet door. "Be sure to engage the alarm when you leave, okay?" She backtracked and started toward the kitchen again and its adjoining door to the attached carport.

Gabe caught her arm as she was going by. "You got an extra house key? If I had one, I wouldn't have to wait outside for you like a homicidal stalker the way I did last night before you got home." His tone was light. But his underlying meaning had her squirming.

"Uh . . . can we discuss this later?"

His hand fell away. "Yeah. Sure. Bad timing."

Uncertain how to respond, Cady hurried to the kitchen and out the side door toward her vehicle. Apparently, she'd misjudged him. Exchanging house keys wasn't as casual as she liked to keep her relationships. She cursed mentally. She'd rather race to apprehend a dangerous escapee than navigate sticky relationship waters.

And she knew exactly what that said about her.

Eryn: Then

"Mama says the cake has to look like *The Starry Night*, my favorite painting." Eryn's voice still felt scratchy and raw from last week. She danced with excitement as she watched Mary Jane mix food coloring into bowls of white frosting. She wished she dared sneak a taste. But she already knew the woman would rap her knuckles with the spoon. Mama would've let her have a sample, if she cooked. And if she was in a good mood. But Mary Jane was never in a good mood. Usually the edges of her mouth were turned down like its corners were reaching for her chin. Not today, though. Today her mouth was pinched tight, like she was sucking on something sour.

Eryn didn't care. It was her birthday, her special day. That's what Mama had said. *You're nine today, Eryn. You're growing up. No more doing silly, careless things.* Mama didn't know why Eryn had done what she had last week, and she wouldn't understand. Eryn had told her it was an accident. If she'd told the truth, Eryn would get dragged to the doctor again, the one who liked to hear himself talk. He asked questions she didn't always know the answers to. She knew she couldn't tell him the truth, either, about anything. She'd learned long ago to tell adults exactly what they wanted to hear. Everyone was so much happier then.

Mama was in her room, finishing a painting for Eryn's birthday. It was one of the two of them together. She'd snuck a look at it when Mama had gone to lunch with a friend. She couldn't wait to hang it between the two small windows in her room that faced the pond.

Turning toward the table again, she eyed the bowls of frosting critically. "The yellow needs to be brighter."

Mary Jane sent her a hard look. "How would you like it if I stood over you when you were drawing and told you how to do it?"

Eryn wanted to say Mary Jane didn't know anything about drawing and Eryn did know something about colors. She kept the words to herself. She didn't want to spoil her birthday by arguing. No one ever won an argument with Mary Jane, anyway, including Mama. Not even when she screamed and yelled and slammed doors. Uncle Bill said the older woman was solid steel, and about as warm. But he never argued with Mary Jane. Sometimes he'd say, "Remember who signs your paycheck." And then she'd snap back, "Remember who changed your diapers." And he'd shake his head and lock himself in the office for the rest of the day.

Imagining Uncle Bill in diapers made Eryn smile. "I get to pick where we're eating dinner. Mama's going to take me wherever I want to go." Eryn turned and trailed her hand over the edge of the counters and then over the front of the oven. It was still warm. The cake had just come out a bit ago. "I'm going to ask to eat at Renatta's in Waynesville. I'm going to order lobster." She'd never had lobster before, but she'd seen shows in which the people ate it in fancy restaurants. Mama said it tasted like heaven.

Mary Jane sniffed. "If you ask me, birthday celebrations should be for kids who deserve them. Not for a girl who burned down the boathouse last week, because she's too foolish to not play with matches. Lucky you didn't die of smoke inhalation."

What do you know? Eryn clamped her lips down hard to avoid having the thought turn to words and slip off her tongue. "It was an accident."

"Was it now?" The stare Mary Jane aimed her way had Eryn thinking for a moment she could see right inside her head. But she couldn't. Good thing. "The boathouse and stables are off limits. Have been as long as you've lived here."

It wouldn't do to tell her she had been inside the boathouse lots of times. She liked to balance along the boards of the dock, and sometimes she'd even take off her shoes and dip her toes in the water. It was cool and shadowy inside the structure, and no one ever came to tell her not to play in the boat. No one ever knew she was there.

She'd been in the stables too. Once. She shivered a little thinking of it. It had smelled like old hay and animal sweat and maybe hints of leather. The cobblestone floor had been cold and damp, and she'd gotten splinters from the wood in the stalls.

She'd probably been five the only time she'd been inside. Her cousin Henry had been twelve, and he'd convinced her fairies lived there. But after they'd been inside for a while, he'd locked her in a cold, dark room in back stinking of horses and moldy leather. There were bats swooping low in the shadows, but they weren't what scared her. She'd screamed and screamed until Henry had finally come back and let her out.

Mary Jane took out some table knives and plopped one into each bowl of frosting. "We can't be watching you every minute. You have to start listening and following directions."

Eryn didn't tell the woman that most of the time she'd only gone to the boathouse when the voices had told her to. But she wouldn't be going again. And *they* wouldn't be telling her what to do anymore, would they?

Feeling smug, she waited until Mary Jane went to put away the food coloring before sticking her finger in the nearest bowl of frosting and licking it up with lightning speed. When the older woman turned around again, she smiled brightly. "Do you want me to bring you some lobster from the restaurant?"

Mary Jane snorted. "Most likely thing you'll be bringing from the restaurant is a bellyache. Don't be saying I didn't warn you. Lobster's too rich for kids. You'll probably get sick in the middle of the night, and I already know who'll be called to clean it up."

You should shut the bitch up. Shut her up, once and for all.

Eryn stilled, a sick fear washing over her. *Be quiet,* she thought. *Quiet quiet quiet!*

She's the one who needs to be quiet. See the big knife over there in the block? Just pull it out and ram it right into her chest. That would shut her up right and good.

"You're dead," she whispered, panicked. The voices had been silent ever since the fire. Because she'd killed them there.

At least she thought she had.

"Do I look dead to you, Missy?" Mary Jane said archly. "Standing right here decorating the cake you don't deserve, aren't I?"

But it wasn't Mary Jane's voice she was listening to. It was the ones in her head. The ones she'd thought died in the fire. They said to go to the boathouse, so she'd taken them there. And she'd also taken the matches she'd snuck from the barbecue out back. She hadn't thought the wood would catch fire quite so quickly. Hadn't expected the flames to chase from plank to plank. To lick up the wooden walls and sear across the arched ceiling. *Get out!* That's what the voices had said then. *Save us, Eryn! Save us!*

But she hadn't wanted to save them. With the voices gone, she'd be normal. She wouldn't get the dark moods Mama worried so much about. She wouldn't do bad things, things she knew better than to do. The kind that made the doctor frown and look at her over the top of his glasses. She wouldn't have to take the medicine that made her feel dreamy and not quite awake, even when she was up and walking around.

Eryn had stayed in the boathouse until the fire had gotten too hot. The smoke had been thick enough to suffocate the voices in her head.

Thick enough to kill them. She'd run as fast as she could then, leaving them behind to burn up. She'd had to go to the hospital, because her lungs and throat got hurt.

And when she'd come home the next day, the boathouse was still smoking from the black mass of rubble. And the voices were silent. For good, she had thought.

Until now.

You could creep into her room at night. She squeezed her eyes shut, trying to push the sneaky words away. *Put a pillow over her face while she sleeps.*

A wave of desolation swept through Eryn, followed by fury. *You're dead,* she thought, rage racing up her spine. Her grip on the table tightened and before she even considered the action, she upended it. The cake slid off and the bowls of frosting shattered against the floor, the sound ricocheting and echoing in her head.

Why can't you just stay dead?

Eryn: Now

She came awake at the same time every night, three hours after slipping into bed. Two o'clock. Eryn hadn't had a full night's sleep since she'd arrived home. She wondered if she'd ever sleep normally again.

It was the sounds that were different. Even quiet had its own unique feel. At Rolling Acres Resort, there had always been the soft squeak of the night nurses' thick-soled shoes on the hallway tile. The slight swish of their scrubs as they moved by. The gentle hiss and burp of the aquarium in Linda's room next door.

The noises here felt familiar and foreign at once. The creak of floorboards, as the old house shifted and settled. The whisper of the wind outside the ancient panes of glass in the windows. An occasional bark from the foxes who nested in the arbor every year, despite Uncle Bill's best efforts to run them off.

She could try to lie in bed until she went back to sleep. But Eryn was restless. Wide awake. Slumber wouldn't be revisiting anytime soon.

Rolling to the opposite side of the mattress, she snapped on the bedside table lamp before getting up. The room didn't look anything like it had when she was a child. Rosalyn's renovation was complete. Eryn couldn't fault the woman's taste. The color scheme ran to soft greens and blues with splashes of dull gold. It was tasteful and relaxing.

But it felt as alien as her room at Rolling Acres had been the first night, all those years ago.

She opened the curtains. She selected a canvas from the stack in the corner of the room and set it on the easel in front of one of the windows. She might need to move the lamp, she mused, to provide the necessary backlight to illuminate the scene outside. There was just a glimmer of moon, peeping beneath the hem of cloud cover. It was enough to provide a smudged outline to the landscape below. Darkness had always called to her. It shrouded even familiar objects, making them appear indistinct. Otherworldly. Maybe she felt at home in it because it had always been reflected inside her. Therapy had helped Eryn better understand the shadowy corners of her mind. The right medication had assisted in banishing them, at least to a large degree.

She went to the desk and selected brushes to carry back to the easel, already planning on the colors she'd mix to capture the elongated shadows, the skeletal trees arching their fingers skyward, and the . . .

Eryn stilled, then leaned closer to the window. The dull glow didn't belong on the dusky expanse of lawn stretching between the sprawling home and the pond. Perhaps it could be explained in the summer months, when the fireflies danced and flitted across the yard. Occasionally one would land between blades of grass, its light still visible, though disguised. But it was November. Too cold for fireflies. And this glow, while muffled by the ground, was much too big to be caused by a bug.

Curious now, she watched for several minutes, but the light didn't move. Nor did it dim. With a shake of her head, Eryn crossed the room and eased her door open, moving quietly through the dark house, into the kitchen, and to the back entry beyond it. A room that may have once been a large pantry had been converted to a closet, where the family's outerwear was kept. She shivered in her thin pajamas as she turned on the closet light. Eryn pulled on a coat and jammed her feet into a pair of tennis shoes. Then she went back to the entry and turned on the outside light before opening the door, careful to leave it a little ajar before stepping outside.

Immediately the bite in the air nearly sent her scurrying inside again. Her curiosity about the dim glow in the lawn withered. The wind cut through her thin pajama bottoms and the band of skin bared above the shoes. She could be painting, she mentally castigated herself. But she was here now, so, picking her way carefully, Eryn headed toward the source of the light still visible on the lawn.

The dried near-winter grass crunched beneath her feet. Every few minutes she stopped to get her bearings. She hadn't been out on the property for years. But the gardeners would have put away any lawn ornaments or chairs when autumn had descended. Unless she slid on the frost that slicked the ground in spots, there was nothing to impede her progress.

As she drew closer she could make out a large, dark shape just beyond the light. And almost simultaneously she heard a pitiful whimper. She stopped again, uncertain. "Who's there?"

Silence for long moments. Then came a thready whisper. "Eryn?"

"Jaxson?" She hurried forward. "What are you doing out here? It's freezing."

"I slipped in the grass. My ankle hurts."

As she drew closer she could see the glow came from a small flashlight he must have dropped when he fell. Sinking down beside the boy, Eryn ran her hands along the leg outstretched in front of him. She couldn't find any swelling around the ankle, but his indrawn hiss of pain when she pressed on it was enough to convince her.

"I don't want Dad to see me out here." There was a note of fear in the boy's voice. "Can you help me into the house before he comes back?"

"Back? From where? Pick up your sore foot." She slipped her hands beneath his arms. "When I lift you, don't put your weight on it." With some difficulty, she raised him upright and supported him when he was standing.

"I saw him leaving the house and heading toward the boathouse. I thought maybe he was going for a boat ride. I've never been in the boat at night. Ouch!"

"Don't let your foot touch the ground."

She had him put his hand on her shoulder for balance while she scooped up the flashlight he'd dropped. "Okay, slip your arm around my waist to hang on to me."

"Can't you pick me up?" A whine had entered his voice.

She doubted it. Jax was only seven or eight, but he was sturdy, built more like Bill than Rosalyn. And at a hundred and ten pounds, Eryn didn't trust herself not to drop him, even if she could lift him. "This way is better. Just use me as a crutch and hop on your good foot."

They didn't make fast progress, but it was steady enough. She could feel him shivering next to her. "How long were you out here?"

"I don't know. A long time. I got up to pee, and then when I went back to bed I saw a light outside. That's when I saw Dad."

His pajamas were damp, but his coat wasn't soaked through. Eryn didn't think he'd been outside more than an hour. It would have seemed plenty long to a little kid, trapped and helpless in the dark. She remembered the time her cousin Henry had locked her in the tack room in the old stable. Eryn had been younger than Jax, and it had been daylight outside. But it'd been dark, shadowy, and damp in the room with its cold stone floor and walls. It had seemed an eternity, although she realized now it had probably been only a half hour or so. She felt a stab of sympathy for the boy.

They were close enough to the house now to switch off the flashlight. The outside light she'd turned on illuminated their way. "Eryn? Do you have to tell my mom about this?"

She mentally shied away at the thought of the upcoming drama. And it *would* be dramatic, because Rosalyn could make a fuss over a hangnail. "How are you going to explain your injury?"

"I'll tell her I slipped going to the bathroom."

They were at the back entry. She reached out to open the door. "Whatever you tell her is your business." He wasn't in the clear yet. They still had to get inside and back to his room undetected.

His arm around her waist tightened. "Thanks, Eryn. I can kind of walk on the tiptoes of my bad foot now. Maybe it's going to be all right."

"Let's hope so." This was the longest conversation she'd ever had with the kid, she realized. She wasn't one for small talk. And Eryn wasn't well versed in topics of interest to a little boy. Easing the door shut behind them, she locked it and shut off the outside light before helping him out of his coat. "Wait here." She left him holding on to the doorjamb for support while she hung up their coats and toed off the shoes she'd worn.

"See, Dad's parka is gone. He's still at the boathouse, I guess." Wistfully, Jax added, "I'll bet he *is* taking a boat ride. A long one."

Eryn glanced around the closet. Only a few of the garments were familiar, but she didn't see a parka. That didn't prove the boy was correct. She couldn't imagine why anyone would be outside in the cold or at the boathouse in the middle of the night in November.

She helped the boy back to his room, both of them moving quietly, as his bedroom was next to his parents'. Eryn turned on a lamp and had him sit on the edge of the bed while she set his flashlight on his dresser and rummaged through his drawers for a fresh pair of pajamas.

"I can do the rest by myself."

In the light Eryn could recognize the lines of pain in his face. She squatted down to look at his ankle. There were no signs of bruising or swelling yet. Rising, she nodded. "Does it hurt when you're not standing on it?"

He shook his head. "I'll just kick my other pajamas under the bed. If it starts hurting in the night, I'll call for my mom."

It was clear he was ready for her to go. Eryn was just as anxious to leave. She peeked out his bedroom door and—seeing no one—slipped out of his room and padded silently across the large living room. The huge space split the suites of bedrooms, with Uncle Bill's family occupying those on one side while Eryn's, Mama's, and the guest rooms had lined the other. There was another wing that had been closed off for years.

When she was back in her room, she was more awake than ever. Plucking a newspaper from a small stash she'd been collecting since her return, she spread it over the top of her dresser. There was no other space available to mix paints. She got water from the attached bathroom and brought it back in a cup already flecked with dried paint. Sometime in the near future she'd need to scout a better place to use as a studio. But for now, the desire to create was calling. She mixed the colors she wanted on a palette and carried it back to her easel, with brushes in her free hand. She studied the scene outside her windows again. The sky wasn't quite as dark as it'd been when she'd first awakened. Eryn worked quickly, losing herself in her art. It wasn't until the scene changed that she was pulled from her reverie.

There was a light bobbing in the distance, approaching the home. It was coming from the direction of the boathouse.

She stood frozen, her gaze fixed on the shadowy figure as it drew closer and closer to the house. Up until then, Eryn hadn't totally believed Jaxson's story about following his dad to the boathouse. She couldn't distinguish Uncle Bill's face in the darkness.

But she could make out the oversize hood and long lines of a parka.

Ryder

The Fristol Forensic Center property was lit up like an outdoor stadium on game night. Uniformed personnel swarmed the area. All four county police departments had sent personnel to join the Haywood County deputies. Someone had thought to set up a coffee station on a folding table with large insulated beverage coolers. Ryder stood in front of the table, sipping from the cup he'd filled. The coffee was strong, black, and bitter, but it was hot. Dr. Tom Isaacson, the director of the facility, stood next to him, tilting his Styrofoam cup under one of the cooler's spigots. The man's hand trembled slightly. Ryder was fairly certain tonight registered as one of the worst of Isaacson's life. And the longer Samuel Aldeen remained on the loose, the further the director's day would deteriorate.

Isaacson turned toward him, his gloved hands clenched around the cup. "We're the most secure forensic psychiatric facility in the region." He was repeating himself, as if the fact negated tonight's escape. "It's impossible. I mean . . . I still don't understand. How'd he get through all this?"

He waved his hand toward the property. He'd already given Ryder its history. The structure was only fifteen years old. It'd replaced the three-story building that had been erected at the beginning of the last century as an insane asylum. An attractive brick wall ran in a low arc around the structure, hemming in the outdoor recreation areas, walking trails, gardens, and small pond. The wall was more decoration than barrier. Whereas the old asylum had looked like a prison, its replacement resembled a hospital. But a quarter mile from where they stood was the first of two perimeters consisting of twelve-foot fences strung with razor wire and secured with motion sensors. A gated guard station adorned each of the perimeters.

The building and grounds might be soothing, but the security measures were reminders that the facility housed dangerous, criminally insane patients.

Ryder opened his mouth to answer when Isaacson's cell rang. The man fumbled with it as he took it out of his coat pocket. His face went even more ashen as he read the screen. "It's the governor's office." He turned his back and took several steps away to answer the call.

"Sheriff Talbot." Ryder turned. A bear of a man lumbered up, credentials in hand. "Special Agent Bob Sweeney, SBI." The agent's unbuttoned leather coat with sheepskin lining flapped as he walked. "Took longer than it should have to get here. Damn country roads. My GPS got me turned around twice. Is that coffee? Mind if I grab a cup while you catch me up on your efforts here?"

What Ryder wanted was to get back inside the facility and interview the guard tending the security cameras. But he'd invited the North Carolina State Bureau of Investigation and the FBI onto the case. The Highway Patrol had been alerted, as had the United States Marshals Service and the regional fugitive apprehension task force. His office didn't have the resources to quickly resolve this case on its own.

He ambled alongside the agent, briefing him on the steps they'd taken so far. "The dog followed Aldeen's scent to the employee parking lot," he finished. Sweeney lifted the cup he'd filled to his lips and took a large gulp. From his expression, it was clear he was no more a fan of the taste than Ryder had been. "He lost it in the lot there." Ryder pointed in the direction of the employee lot behind them, with its smattering of vehicles. "We've spoken to the officials in the guard stations and gone through the security feeds from both gates. I think we've got a clear shot of him at the first one."

"You think."

Ryder shoved aside a quick flare of irritation. Everyone here was short on sleep, so he wasn't going to wonder if SBI agents were taught the tone that cast doubt on every other law enforcement officer's decisions or if the agency only hired assholes to whom it came naturally. "He was disguised, but I'm fairly certain it's Aldeen." He pulled out his cell and brought some of the images up on it. In the first was the inmate's ID picture. The next two showed a man with darker, thicker hair and a heavy mustache wearing scrubs under a hooded sweatshirt. A hospital employee ID could be seen hanging around his neck. "Aldeen has been in the infirmary for two days after instigating an altercation with his roommate. Given the level of planning this escape required, I'm guessing the fight was staged as well."

He saw the agent's gaze shift to something over his shoulder and turned. A woman in a dark coat and cap was striding rapidly toward them. Five eight. Midthirties or younger. The cap hid her hair. It wasn't until she got close enough for him to see her pale-green eyes that recognition flickered. The new marshal out of the Asheville office. Ryder had met her a couple of times at regional task force meetings.

"Cady Maddix with the Marshals Service." She stopped beside Ryder. "My colleagues are pulling together all the information they can on Aldeen. Can you update me on what happened here tonight?"

Ryder repeated what he'd just told Sweeney, ending with, "Highway Patrol has a description of the car and is setting up roadblocks in a one-hundred-mile perimeter. They'll be stopping and searching all vehicles, in case he switched to a different one. We've also got two Highway Patrol helicopters doing recon for similar cars from the air. Aldeen had to have help on the inside to make his escape. There's no reason to believe he doesn't have assistance on the outside as well."

"We need a list of all of the center's employees," Sweeney said. He was linebacker material. He'd make two of the marshal. "And tapes from inside the facility."

Ryder nodded. "We're on it. The director is over there in the gray coat. He's already got people in the office working on employee rosters. I've reviewed tonight's outdoor security feeds, and they validate our working theory about how this went down. There are two outside security checkpoints, each manned with an officer who conducts a search of the vehicle. The gates can only be opened by the security guard manning the cameras on the inside. All vehicles are searched upon entrance and exit from the property. Including the one Aldeen drove away in."

"Do you think the guard is an accessory?" Sweeney took another swig of coffee. Grimaced again. "An escape like this? The guy had help. Whose car did he drive out?"

"We're in the process of reviewing more footage. We aren't sure yet whether a worker or visitor parked it there."

Sweeney swiveled to look from one parking area to the other. "Are you saying the guard stations don't have a camera view showing the lot side of the property?"

"Not until the car gets within range of the guard station," Ryder told him. "There are other security cameras situated in front of the building where we're probably going to be able to see some of the parking lot space, though." He hunched his shoulders a bit. A wind had come up, and its chill held a bite. "Every employee at the facility is in a database with their name and occupation, including substitute workers." The officers at the gates had explained that much to him. "The guard monitoring the cameras either has to recognize each person or find them in the employee database and verify their identity through their ID badge and photo before buzzing them through. In the meantime, my deputies are conducting interviews with all other employees on duty." And the process wouldn't be complete until they'd gotten statements from every single person employed by the facility, from the cooks to the professional staff. Ryder was acutely aware that every passing minute meant the escapee was probably that much farther out of reach. "Aldeen's psychiatrist is on his way. Director Isaacson and I just finished talking to Captain Rowland of the Highway Patrol before you two arrived. We've got a press perimeter set up fifty feet beyond the outer security checkpoint."

He saw the question on Sweeney's face and forestalled it. "No sign of a reporter yet, but it's only a matter of time." The cover of darkness likely helped. That, and none of the on-duty employees had had a chance to tip off the press. The small feeding frenzy Eryn Pullman's release from Rolling Acres Resort had galvanized a few short days ago would dim in comparison to the media fireworks Aldeen's escape would elicit.

"Have you viewed the interior security feed yet?" Sweeney took one more gulp of the coffee before dumping the rest of it on the ground beside him.

"No. It's being compiled for me. I'm heading there next. Isaacson has a call in to Aldeen's head unit nurse. She'll put together a list of any employee who had at least occasional access to the escapee."

The SBI agent grunted. "I'd like a word with the director before I go inside." He turned and beelined for the man, who was still on the phone.

"If he got through the gates, he wasn't dressed as an inmate," Cady observed.

Ryder showed her the pictures the SBI agent had viewed earlier. "He passed through the exterior gate nearly ninety minutes ago." And Ryder was all too aware of how far the man could have traveled since then. "The infirmary night nurse reported him missing shortly after."

She nodded. "Highway Patrol is our best chance at this point. But there are also visitor logs and the list of allowed phone contacts, which will give us a place to start. I'd like to sit in for the conference with Aldeen's psychiatrist when it occurs."

"No problem. Follow me." She matched him stride for stride across the parking lot as he spoke. "The director did mention Aldeen has had occasional visits this year from one person on his list. He was transferred here three years ago to be closer to his only living relative, a great-aunt. She lives in Charlotte. Police there have a patrol car sitting on her house, in case that's his destination."

"I'll check it out when I leave here."

Ryder nodded. "Like all patients, Aldeen was required to fill out a list of allowed phone contacts. Only four or five names were on it. They were vetted by security. All were cell phones with the exception of the great-aunt. Hers is a landline."

"We'll check out the names. Here, and those at the previous facility." Cady sent him a questioning look.

"Bridgeport," he supplied. Ryder turned at the sound of an approaching vehicle. The mobile command post had arrived. His chief deputy, Jerry Garza, would be manning it for the time being.

If they didn't catch the escapee tonight, the manhunt would grow exponentially. The thought of the multiple agencies that would be assisting had tension tightening in his shoulders. It was going to require massive organization. Some of their roles would overlap. The task of collecting and disseminating timely updates on leads followed by each agency would be a full-time job in itself.

He returned his attention to the woman beside him. "We didn't find anything helpful in Aldeen's room. Patients spend the majority of their time together in common areas. They return to their personal spaces by nine p.m., and breakfast is at seven thirty a.m. I've got a deputy searching the common areas now, and we'll be inspecting other patient rooms on the unit."

"You think he might have hidden something of note or given it to someone else to hold?"

"It's possible. Since he escaped from the infirmary he would have been unable to carry anything there with him. If, as we believe, Aldeen had an accessory on the inside, he may have had maps. Correspondence. He wouldn't have left either in his room."

"Sounds like you've covered a lot of ground already. How long have you been on-site?" she surprised him by asking.

"We arrived twenty minutes after we received the call." And Ryder was beginning to feel the hour. He pushed the encroaching exhaustion aside. It'd be a helluva lot longer before he'd get any sleep. "We tried to move fast. If it had been a normal escape situation, we'd have a lead on Aldeen already, with the dogs and infrared capabilities in the air." Gravel crunched under their feet as they walked. "The possibility of an accessory changes things. Interviews and physical searches are labor intensive." But they had to be done. And there'd be days of camera images to view. The outside assistance on this case would be imperative for providing the personnel to handle all of the man-hours the investigation would demand.

Cady nodded. "My team is already pulling together all the details we can about Aldeen's history, relatives, and acquaintances. Did the director have any other insights?"

Hedging, Ryder said, "He's given me everything I've asked for." Isaacson was in full cover-your-ass mode, bracing for the shitstorm about to rain down on him. The scrutiny soon to be trained on this facility and its leadership after its first patient escape would be brutal. And given the government cutbacks in recent years that had carved at every department, Ryder wouldn't be surprised to discover Fristol was understaffed. If true, the press would have a field day with the fact.

They showed their identification twice before accessing the building again, and then a guard quickly attached himself to them. Ryder knew he'd accompany them wherever they went inside. Every twelve to fourteen feet the passageway was blocked by a set of locked double doors, with a camera aimed at them. The guard pressed the button on the wall beside them and turned his face up to the camera. "Haywood County Sheriff and Deputy US Marshal Maddix," the man said each time. A moment later, the doors would slowly swing open.

Cady shot Ryder a sidelong glance. "Given this process, Aldeen was allowed through multiple sets of doors by the guard manning the cameras. Is it a one-person job?"

"Two on first and second shift. One on third." He'd run a quick check on Pat Simpson, the man on duty tonight. No criminal record. But they'd be digging deeper into his background, as well as the personnel on duty tonight in the infirmary.

"Any chance I can see Aldeen's room before we head to security?"

Ryder stifled a flare of impatience. He had a mental image of an hourglass with the sand quickly running out. But they'd walk right by the man's unit. It'd take only a few minutes. And it wasn't like they had no capture plans in place. Roadblocks had been erected. The Highway Patrol was out in force.

But he still felt stymied here, and would until he had clear intelligence on how the escapee had managed his Houdini act. He informed the guard of the change in plans, and minutes later they turned off the main hall to the locked unit where Aldeen had been housed. There were six such units in this wing, with ten rooms in each, two patients to a room. A separate wing held female patients. One section housed patients for court-ordered evaluations of their fitness for trial. Other sections were for long-term residents like Aldeen, who'd been found guilty but insane by a judge.

The lighting in the hall outside the patient rooms was set to twilight rather than the harsh overhead glare in the passageway they'd left. The area was quiet. The official accompanying them halted in front of Aldeen's room and unlocked it, swinging the door wide for them. The roommate had been relocated. Two of Ryder's men had gone through the space already. Both of the cots had been taken apart, the mattresses sliced open, the covers removed. There were no pillows. The bunks had been disassembled, the hollow tubes comprising the frames dismantled and examined. Nothing had been found.

Shallow shelved indentations that passed as closets marked both back corners. One space was crowded with personal belongings. The contents in Aldeen's showed the effects of the search. They'd taken some of the man's possessions into evidence. The only things remaining were some clothes and a small stack of books, each bearing the stamp of the facility's library. "He had an MP3 player and earbuds," Ryder said. He stood in the doorway and scanned the small area as she moved around inside it, touching nothing. "He had plenty of money for incidentals and had thousands of songs downloaded on his device. Director Isaacson said IT would have taken care of the downloads, and the payments were subtracted from the patient's account."

She turned around and retraced her steps to the door, clearly having seen enough. He stood aside to let her pass before stepping into the hallway. "Maybe the MP3 player will bear fruit," Cady said. The guard locked the cell behind them as they began retracing their steps to the doors leading to the main hallway. "I once worked a warrant where the guy was obsessed with a country music star. I mean, he had CDs, posters, a matching Stetson . . . even a ringtone of one of his songs. When we heard the star was appearing in concert within a hundred miles of the bandit's last known residence, we blanketed the venue with fugitive apprehension task forces."

Ryder slanted a look at her. "You captured him?"

She smiled. "A marshal ID'd him at one of the entrances, and we caught him waiting in line to buy a T-shirt. Never underestimate the lengths a true fan will go to, to see his idol."

They waited for security to open the next set of doors. "Where'd this happen?"

"Saint Louis." The note of finality in her voice was impossible to miss. *More to the story there,* he mused. Much more.

They arrived, finally, at the three rooms making up the security offices. Simpson, Ryder recalled from their earlier meeting tonight, was in the middle one. The guard accompanying them rapped on that door and announced them. Simpson looked up from a laptop with split screens showing different camera angles. Wariness flickered over his expression when they walked in.

"Sheriff. Ma'am," he said with a nod in Cady's direction.

Because he was looking at her, Ryder caught Cady's slight wince.

"I've been combing through the database I was telling you about earlier." Simpson wheeled away from the laptop he was monitoring to another a few feet away. "Here's the ID of the man in question who I allowed out the doors tonight. And through the gates." He indicated the screen. Ryder and Cady stepped forward as one to look. Aldeen's picture, with phony glasses and a wig, looked back at them. "Carl Mitchell. He was entered into the database for facility personnel a week ago. I didn't recognize him when I buzzed him through the interior doors and gates, but when I pulled up his ID, I figured, hey, he just started. That's why I didn't know him."

"Did everything else about this addition look normal to you?" Cady asked.

"Yes. There's always a photo with the employee badge number, and their job description. He was hired as a substitute orderly. I mean, according to what it said here."

"Who enters the new employees into this database?" Ryder wanted to know.

"Teresa Resling, in human resources. Or her assistant, Tammy Bell. It usually takes a while after a hire to get all the paperwork and training done. But once it is, before a new employee is scheduled for his or her first shift, they're put in this system."

"Who else has access to the database?" Cady asked. Simpson looked confused, so she went on. "I'm assuming anyone working here could bring it up."

"Well, sure, it's meant to be used widely. But the only ones who have editing privileges are people in HR. It's password protected."

"Passwords can be cracked."

Ryder nodded at Cady's remark. "Is the database online?"

The man nodded miserably. "Not the patient records, of course, which are confidential. But this is a federal facility, so we're government employees. All of the personnel employment records would also be on a server somewhere."

A server meant someone on the outside could have hacked into the database. It was possible, but Ryder's focus would remain on the Fristol employees for now. It wasn't an outsider who had left the ID, clothes, and disguise hidden for Aldeen's use.

"Whoever went to the trouble of making a fake work identification badge probably obtained other forms of false ID, as well," Cady pointed out.

Ryder had already figured the same. Aldeen was likely equipped with not only a vehicle but a new identity. Formidable obstacles if the man managed to slip through the law enforcement perimeter they'd erected.

The guard who had accompanied them stuck his head inside the room. "Director Isaacson just radioed. Dr. Luttrell has arrived."

"The psychiatrist," Ryder said in an aside to Cady as he headed for the door. "If anyone can help us get inside Aldeen's head, it'll be him."

Fifteen minutes later Ryder was mentally reevaluating his earlier assertion.

"You understand, I'm bound by patient confidentiality," Luttrell was saying. The stout doctor stroked his gray goatee nervously as they all settled into chairs around a conference room in the treatment ward.

"As such, I can't reveal any specifics shared by Samuel Aldeen, either in group or in individual sessions."

"Let's deal with your clinical expertise for now," Ryder said. There were six of them around the table: Luttrell, Cady, Ryder, SBI agent Sweeney, Isaacson, and Bob Hammill, one of Ryder's investigative deputies. Hammill had a notebook out to document the meeting. "Start with his diagnosis, and what to expect as far as his behavior."

Luttrell seemed relieved at the topic. He removed his dark-framed glasses and polished them with a handkerchief he took from his coat pocket. "In short, Samuel has schizophrenia with paranoia." He held up the glasses to look through them and, seeming satisfied, settled them back on his nose and put the handkerchief away. "When untreated, he suffers from delusions, visual hallucinations, and an inability to separate his symptoms from reality. He also exhibits a raft of sexual deviancies separate from, but impacted by, his mental illness."

"You're saying his medical diagnosis isn't the cause of his compulsion to kidnap, rape, and cannibalize children?" Cady sounded surprised. "He was declared criminally insane. Do you disagree with the court's findings?"

"He was found incapable of telling right from wrong," Luttrell corrected her. "What I meant was his schizophrenia isn't responsible for the parallel fetishes. They may well have existed even if he had no mental illness."

"Like the sexual fetishes are sane," Sweeney muttered.

"His illness didn't cause his paraphilia." The doctor seemed to choose his words carefully. "But it likely hampered his ability to distinguish the acts as wrong. I can speak more freely if I reference only the information found in the court transcripts, which would be available to the public. Samuel has delusions he's some sort of demigod, and that people around him seek to steal his blood or organs to immortalize themselves at his expense. His acts of cannibalism are an attempt to rebuild the strength he believes he has lost through those interactions."

There was a stunned silence in the room as the laypeople digested that. Sweeney spoke first. "I take it back. This guy is seriously warped."

"Any chance he was putting on a show for the judge?" Ryder asked. "You've spent the last—what—three years treating him? You keep records of the time you spend with him, right?"

"Regular progress notes are kept of all sessions." It was Isaacson's first contribution to the conversation. "I think what these people are most interested in, Dr. Luttrell, is the chance of recidivism."

"Is he going to victimize another child while he's free?" Ryder put in. After Luttrell's other revelations, the question took on even more urgency. What was the risk assessment for the public?

Luttrell stroked his goatee, his fingers trembling slightly. "Samuel has been a model patient here. He's well behaved. He's done everything requested of him." The doctor seemed to hesitate.

"But . . ." Ryder prompted.

"I'm not altogether certain he's been forthcoming about the continuing effects of his illness. And I alerted the nurses to do mouth checks after giving medication. Some of our patients are sly about palming the pills or regurgitating them later." The doctor shrugged uncomfortably. "It's tempting to believe my help has been advantageous for him. But therapy is a long game. In the short term, I don't usually see the sort of progress he would have me believe." He snapped his mouth shut, as if already regretting his candor. But his implication was clear to everyone in the room.

"You think he was playing you?" Cady asked.

"Not necessarily," Luttrell said slowly, removing his glasses again. "It would be exceedingly difficult to pretend an absence of symptoms long-term. I noted more than once I thought he was putting up a falsely positive front. Despite our extended time together, I have never come close to the root of his paraphilia. That, of course, is one example of lack of headway. One of the two things I'm most concerned about is he won't have access to his meds on the outside, which keep the symptoms of his psychosis controlled."

The doctor paused, and Ryder's gut clenched.

"The second is my certainty that given the opportunity, Samuel Aldeen will act on his sexual fetishes again. He'll feel compelled to. No child is safe around him."

Samuel

Dawn was tingeing the horizon with pink when Samuel pulled up to the address he'd been searching for. He got out of the car, taking a moment to study the property. The house was as described. Shielded by firs on all sides, with no close neighbors. He closed the car door quietly and approached the structure. It was a bit more dilapidated than he'd expected. Yet another sign of how desperate Joe was for money.

Avoiding the front porch, he rounded the small house and climbed the back steps silently. There had been nothing on the radio about his escape. He wondered if law enforcement had managed to keep it silent or whether the staff at Fristol was so incompetent they hadn't discovered him gone yet. *It would be a mistake to underestimate their progress,* he mused as he reached out to turn the doorknob. Finding it open, he walked into a postage-stamp kitchen with a small table shoved against one wall. It was neat. Tidy. Joe seemed to take his substitute custodial duties seriously at Fristol. His diligence was evident here as well.

Smiling slightly, Samuel walked into the adjoining room. He found the man he was seeking sitting in front of an older model desktop computer next to the TV. "Hello."

Joe started, twisting around, jaw agape as he half rose out of his chair. "You scared the hell out of me. Why didn't you knock?"

Amused, Samuel said, "Why would I knock when you were expecting me?"

The man sank down into his chair, still studying him. "Those aren't the clothes I left for you."

"You're not my only friend, Joe." He walked to the computer. The screen was opened to the offshore account Samuel had taught him to set up. "Did you get checked in to the resort the way we discussed?"

Joe's head bobbed. "I told my employers I wouldn't be available to work for two weeks 'cuz of a vacation. I've already checked in to the cabin. I drove back here after midnight last night. The only loose end is the second half of the payment you promised me."

Samuel grabbed the man's chair and tipped it backward. He had the gun out of his jacket by the time Joe hit the floor. He fired, the bullet shattering the man's knee. Samuel pitched his voice over Joe's blood-curdling scream. "I'm afraid *you're* the loose end. There's been a change of plans. I'm going to need the money back I wired to your account."

"No!" Even while clutching his wound with both hands, the man refused to face reality. "I did everything you asked! The payment will be enough to get custody of my kids!"

"Listen to me." Out of patience, Samuel crouched down beside him. Nudged the barrel of the gun under Joe's jaw. "I want the password of your account. And you'll give it to me, because you also told me all about your kids. Little Joey, a bit old for my tastes, at nine. But four-year-old Annabelle . . ." He licked his lips. Watched the horror wash over the man's face. "You mentioned where they lived with their mama. Leastways, close enough to figure it out. Do you really doubt what will happen if I decide to make their acquaintance?"

He watched the expressions chase over the man's face. Fear, cunning, fear again, until finally . . . acceptance. Joe reeled off the password in a choked voice, and Samuel sat down at the computer. Minutes later, the money transferred, he stood and faced the man. "I want you to know how much our talks meant to me, Joe. You can't imagine the tedium of being locked up in a place like that." Raising the weapon in his hand again, he shot the man twice in the chest. Samuel knelt to search the man's jeans pocket for his cell and took the battery out of it. Then he stepped over the body to go in search of the keys to Joe's vehicle and the room key for the cabin.

He found both sets of keys in the man's jacket, which was hanging on a hook just inside the back door. Samuel set the items on the table and then went back to the computer. He scrolled through the files, opening each to scan them and make sure there were no references to him before deleting the computer's browser history. He'd destroy Joe's phone and throw both it and the battery away when he left here.

Because his "care package" hadn't included food, he went to the refrigerator to study its contents. Taking out some ingredients, he proceeded to make himself a sandwich. A man had to take advantage of every opportunity that came his way.

He ate his first meal on the outside with enjoyment. Five years he'd been locked up. Five years of being poked and prodded, sedated for blood draws and organ sampling. There was no way to be sure how much of his tissue had already been removed. He'd been drained to dangerously low levels, he was certain of that. He'd felt it in the slow seepage of energy before he'd finally mastered the art of puking up the medication after escaping the watchful nurses.

When he finished, he brushed the crumbs into his hand and walked to the corner of the kitchen to dispose of them in the trash can. There was a familiar stirring in the pit of his belly. Even as one appetite was satiated, another was awakening.

Cady

Supervisory Deputy US Marshal Allen Gant's office was close to over-flowing. Cady stood at the man's desk, with three of the other marshals in chairs circling it. Despite the hour, Paul Chester and John Quimby joined Miguel. The two other marshals in the Asheville office hadn't arrived yet. Cady and Miguel were the only two working warrants full-time, while the others split their time between warrant work and court duties.

"Aldeen had only one visitor while he was in Fristol and five phone numbers on his approved contacts list. One of those is his lawyer." Cady stabbed her finger at the sheet she'd laid before Gant. "He's called three of these numbers this year, a couple of them multiple times. The first is his great-aunt's home. Selma Lewis. She's the reason cited for his hardship transfer from Bridgeport to Fristol. In the last year and a half he's called her weekly."

"But no contacts before that? She never came to see him at Fristol?" Gant looked up from the slip of paper and leaned back in his chair, his shaven head gleaming in the glare of the overhead track lighting.

Cady shook her head. "She's eighty-eight. Travel might be difficult for her. I called the Charlotte-Mecklenburg Police Department. They've had a cruiser outside Lewis's house all night. Early this morning the officers went to the door and no one answered. They'll continue surveillance until Miguel and I can get there. Not that I think Aldeen would necessarily head to his great-aunt's house, knowing it's the first place we'd look, but she's one source of information on him. The other will be Sheila Preston, his only visitor. She came by monthly, but they talked by phone more frequently."

"Bet those conversations were interesting." Chester stifled a yawn with one big fist. He was a large man. Wider than most. Taller. And louder than anyone she'd ever known. Even the fist pressed against his lips couldn't muffle his booming voice. "Old girlfriend?"

"If so, their relationship didn't surface in the background check Fristol security ran on her," Cady responded. "She and Aldeen worked together twenty-three years ago at Cisco's, a pizza-joint-slash-bar in Charlotte. She had a pop a decade ago for possession, but charges were dropped. Nothing since then. She's never been married and has two kids, ages four and six. Her most recent employer is Larson's Lumber, in Fletcher, where she lives. She's been there six years. Her last visit with Aldeen was a day before the escape. I called Preston's cell several times, most recently on my way here. It went straight to voice mail."

"What do the security tapes show from her most recent visit?" This from Quimby. He was as thin as Chester was wide, which had likely given rise to the pair's nickname, Laurel and Hardy. Cady didn't use the names, however. She'd been there only six months. Too soon to have that sort of familiar relationship with most of her colleagues. And having been the butt of some less than flattering labels herself as a kid, she'd never apply them to others.

She shrugged in response to the marshal's question. "Too soon to be certain. The sheriff had a lot of assistance on scene, but there are a ton of details to wade through. When I left a couple of hours ago, they'd only gotten through interior and exterior security feeds for the last twelve hours or so. They learned Aldeen had a fake employee ID and uniform, which allowed him to get through the checkpoints. And the vehicle he drove off the property was parked in the employee parking lot."

"Who left the car there?" Gant asked.

"It's too early to say." Cady leaned a hip against the desk. "Sheriff Talbot's office is in the process of viewing the security tapes. But anyone hoping to enter the facility goes through two guard station checkpoints before they get to the lots. Visitors would be to the left as one drives toward the building, employees on the right. There are security cameras mounted in front of the structure, but I'm not sure whether a guard monitoring them would notice a visitor parked in the wrong lot."

"What about the other numbers?" Gant had put on his reading glasses and was studying the list of contacts.

"Aldeen also called his bank in Charlotte a few times and his lawyer twice." She pointed at each number on the sheet in turn. "We'll try to question both Lewis and Preston today. We need more background on Sheila Preston, though. Relatives, friends . . . places she might run to if she does turn out to be involved in this. Were you able to get Aldeen's contacts from the time he spent in Bridgeport?" The man had been arrested and tried in South Carolina, but he'd been linked to multiple murders in three states. He'd likely gotten away with far more.

"I've got a call in. Should have the information for you soon." Gant handed her a slim file folder from atop his desk. "In the meantime, this is what we've compiled so far on Aldeen's history. I'll put Renee Baltes in charge of adding to it this morning. She and Patten had a late stakeout and will be in after they get some sleep. Renee can also follow up on Preston. If she finds something that won't wait, she'll reach out. Media broke the story of the escape right before you walked in. I don't have to tell you the kind of pressure we're going to be up against to apprehend Aldeen before he hurts someone else."

"So the Highway Patrol came up with nothing?" Miguel rose, jamming his arms into his coat and zipping it. The other marshals stood as well.

"Since I haven't heard anything I'm guessing not. Keep me updated on your progress." Gant's voice went dour. "This guy is going to have every parent in the state in a panic. And the longer he's on the loose, the bigger the firestorm is going to get."

◆ ◆ ◆

It was Miguel's turn to drive, which could be a little scary. But it meant Cady wasn't going to swelter in her partner's chosen temperature settings, so that was something. She convinced him to hit a drive-through for some coffees. Once she'd acquired the necessary caffeine, she settled back and plugged Selma Lewis's address into her phone's GPS. As she sipped, Cady opened the file Gant had given to them to peruse its contents.

"Fristol's in Haywood County?" Miguel reached for his cup and drank.

"Right."

"Is the sheriff's office heading up the case?"

Cady scanned the first page of Aldeen's file, which listed his birthplace, family history, and education. "Yeah, so far. But SBI arrived on scene when I did, and it sounds like the FBI will be involved too. It's going to be a multiagency investigation." A case like this could overwhelm the resources of a county office if the escapee wasn't found quickly. Federal agencies brought access to resources and a crime lab that wasn't weeks behind in its caseload. Talbot hadn't seemed like the sort to step back from the day-to-day involvement in the case, though. The amount of information he'd had in hand by the time she'd gotten on scene this morning was impressive.

Charlotte was a couple of hours from Asheville. Cady spent part of the trip telling Miguel about her conversations with Talbot and the discussion with Aldeen's psychiatrist. They fell into silence afterward. She figured Miguel was thinking about the same thing she was. If Aldeen was smart, he'd be hiding out. And if they were all lucky, it would be in a spot where he'd have no access to children.

It was barely 8:00 a.m. when Miguel turned on a tree-lined residential street and slowed to a crawl. They pulled to a stop across from the cruiser parked in front of a white and blue two-story fronted by a screened-in porch. A detached single garage sat on the lot beside it. The houses flanking it were from the same era, 1920s or so, Cady guessed. She felt a faint flicker of recognition when she looked at Selma Lewis's house. It reminded her a bit of her grandfather's in Mount Airy, where she'd gone to live after Bo's attack. His had had a similar porch, where he'd spent the evenings after supper smoking his pipe and making caustic comments about his neighbors. He'd never been a friendly sort, not given to chatting with any of them. But he'd always had plenty to say about their comings and goings.

And in the next moment she wondered if Lewis's home also had a partial dirt cellar with cool, damp earthen walls that leached the warmth from flesh and sucked the air from lungs.

Are you afraid of the dark, girlie? Her grandfather's voice sounded in her mind, the memory tracing down Cady's spine like an icy finger. For a moment she could clearly hear the sound of his footsteps on the stairs. The squeak of the door's rusty hinges. The finality of the lock turning. Then the darkness had rushed in, enfolding her in its chilly embrace.

"Cady." Miguel's voice shattered the mental replay. When her attention jerked to him, his car door was open and he was standing outside next to it, looking at her quizzically. "Are you coming to talk to the uniforms?"

"Yeah." Her voice sounded rusty. Cady unlocked her seat belt and bolted out of her door, drawing in a greedy gulp of air as she walked toward the white police cruiser bearing the blue Charlotte-Mecklenburg Police Department logo. As they approached, the window buzzed down to reveal a young freckled face beneath a crop of red hair. Beside him was a more grizzled officer, a couple of decades older. "Maddix and

Rodriguez, Marshals Service," Cady said. She parted her coat enough to reveal the star clipped to her belt.

"Officers Denby and Sellers. We just replaced the pair who were here last night." The younger cop was doing all the talking. "Last shift did a door knock before we arrived. No answer. We haven't seen anything or anyone around the yard. You guys got this now?"

She looked over the roof of the car toward the house. "Can you give us a chance to see if Lewis is inside before you pull out? She might have been sleeping earlier." Aldeen couldn't have beaten the patrol to this house. But she didn't want to overlook an off chance he'd managed to sneak onto the property sometime while the cruiser was parked outside the home.

Denby lifted a shoulder. "Take all the time you need." His window raised again, and Cady and Miguel walked toward the home.

The door to the screened-in porch was open, so they entered it to knock on the front door. Then waited. "Remember her age," Cady said as Miguel raised his fist to knock again. "It might take her longer to move about."

"Eighty-eight could mean hard of hearing," he countered before pounding loud enough to be heard on the next street. They waited a minute before knocking again, several times, before giving up and heading outside again. They walked to the single-stall garage, peered inside the window. Saw a sedan at least thirty years old.

"Let's split up and hit the neighbors," Cady suggested. Miguel headed for the house on the other side of Lewis's, and she crossed the drive to the next property. This time when she banged on the front door, it was opened by a woman using a walker, who looked close to Selma Lewis's age. The speed with which she answered suggested she'd been watching Cady from her window.

"Hi, I'm Cady Maddix from the Marshals Service." Adopting a more informal tone was beneficial when attempting to elicit information. She managed a slight smile for the diminutive female. "I'm looking for your neighbor, Selma Lewis. Do you have an idea where to find her?"

"Well, she's not home, dear." The woman was stooped, her frail figure dwarfed by a heavy cardigan. "Selma hasn't lived there for—oh, must be over a year now."

"Do you know where she's living?"

"Of course. Wait just a moment." The neighbor angled the walker around and disappeared into the house. It was at least ten minutes before she returned. By that time Miguel was coming up the steps to join Cady. "I found the card. I haven't called her for a while, but she really doesn't remember me anyway. She doesn't remember anyone, I don't think."

Happy Springs Nursing Home. Cady read the name on the card before handing it to Miguel. "You say she's having memory problems, ma'am?"

"Call me Kitty." The woman gave Miguel an appreciative look. "And yes, Selma suffered a fall a few years back and started having a hard time recalling the simplest things. She had home health services for a while but eventually decided she needed a rest home. It's nice to make the decision yourself," she said to Miguel confidingly.

"She had no other family?" *If Kitty is correct,* Cady thought, *Selma isn't going to be much help.*

"Well, she always said not, but her nephew's been in and out of the house since she's been gone."

Cady stilled. "Her nephew?"

"Great-nephew," the woman corrected herself, taking the card Cady handed back to her. "He said he'd moved back from somewhere up north to look over things for Selma. Which was odd, because she'd never mentioned him. As I said, she always claimed she didn't have any relatives. But Raymond admitted he'd been in trouble a lot as a kid. Maybe Selma had washed her hands of him. She can be judgey."

"We haven't been introduced, but I'm Cady's colleague, Miguel Rodriguez." When he smiled, Cady was a little worried the woman would swoon. "When's the last time you saw Raymond at her house?"

Kitty pursed her lips. "Oh . . . last week some time. Thursday or Friday . . . ? Must have been Thursday, because he told me once those were his days off."

"And you've seen him go inside the home?"

The older woman answered Cady's question without taking her gaze from Miguel. "Oh yes. He uses the side door, which is across the two driveways from mine. He has a key."

"Could you describe his vehicle?" she asked hopefully.

Kitty shook her head. "I never saw one. He's always on foot."

"Thank you, Kitty. You've been helpful." Cady half turned away.

Miguel chimed in, "We appreciate your assistance, ma'am."

The older woman simpered, one hand going to her breast. "You're more than welcome, Marshal."

Cady gave Miguel a subtle elbow nudge in warning. The last thing they needed was for the woman to have a Rodriguez-induced heart attack.

They knocked on four more doors, found people home at two of the houses. But only one of the individuals, an elderly man about Kitty's age, verified he'd occasionally seen a young man coming and going from the Lewis house. Like Kitty, he couldn't recall seeing the stranger arrive by car. As they headed back to their vehicle Cady detoured toward the driver's side of the police cruiser again.

"I'm afraid we're going to need you for a while longer." She briefly explained the situation to the officers. "We'll have to talk to the owner of the house and possibly get a warrant."

"We can stay." This from the veteran officer. "We've pulled harder duties."

"I'm sure you have. Thanks."

Cady waited until she and Miguel were in the vehicle before she spoke again. "We've got grounds for a warrant. Lewis is Aldeen's only living relative, and he's been contacting someone at the house weekly for a year and a half."

Miguel started the vehicle. "If the neighbors are correct, Lewis hasn't lived here in over a year. But you don't think Aldeen is in there."

"Lewis is his only living relative, and if he's been keeping up with his great-aunt at all, he'll know the house is empty." Cady was already reaching for her phone. "And that's exactly what I'll tell the Assistant US Attorney."

Miguel glanced toward Lewis's house again. "You think he's headed here? He had access to a vehicle and plenty of opportunity if he could dodge the roadblocks."

Cady powered up the laptop. "My gut says no. Highway Patrol is out in force. With all the back roads and remote areas in the state, I don't see him heading right for one of the most populated areas." The smartest thing for him to do would be to choose a large out-of-state airport, she figured. The farther from North Carolina he got, the less likely there'd be news coverage about his escape. Atlanta, with its international hub, was less than a four-hour drive from Fristol. A plane ticket would necessitate new ID, however.

"We need to talk to the great-aunt." Miguel pulled out his cell and started a GPS search for the name of the nursing home Kitty had shared with them.

"We do." In Cady's experience, the percentage of fugitives trying to leave the country was in the single digits. They usually ran *to* something or someone when running from the law. Girlfriends, mostly. Aldeen's mental diagnosis might make his behavior more difficult to predict, but the majority of the people they tracked went back to something familiar. "Maybe she can give us a lead on the identity of the person who's been answering Aldeen's phone calls to her number."

"The warrant's likely only going to give us restricted access," Miguel noted as he started the vehicle and pulled away from the curb.

Cady waited for the call to go through. Her partner was correct. The warrant would be limited to searching the house for their fugitive in areas big enough to conceal a person. But depending on what they learned from Lewis, Cady was hoping to find grounds for expanding those parameters.

◆ ◆ ◆

"She's with her attorney now. Mr. DuPrey." The nursing home administrator, Sally Hayes, was a woman in her midfifties who looked at them over the top of the reading glasses perched on her nose. "He takes care of most things for her and stops by every month or so. I haven't seen Selma this morning, but she has good days and bad. Sometimes she doesn't remember much."

"Does Ms. Lewis get many other visitors?"

The woman shook her head. "Poor dear doesn't have any living relatives, and at her age her friends are deceased or housebound. There's a lady from her church who comes by once in a while, but Mr. DuPrey is the only one who visits her regularly."

"So you've never known another man to come here to see her?" Miguel asked.

"None that I can recall, but you can ask at the front desk."

But when they talked to two women at the desk, neither could remember anyone else coming to see Selma Lewis. One of the nurses led them to a table in a large common area where Lewis sat. A tall man stood at the table beside her, shrugging into a wool coat before placing a matching fedora on his balding head. He turned to leave. Cady stepped into his path.

"I understand you're Ms. Lewis's attorney."

"I am. Charles DuPrey." He looked from Cady to Miguel suspiciously, especially when Miguel sat down in the chair he'd vacated.

"Let's walk and talk." Cady showed him her credentials as they made their way to the door. "We're in pursuit of a fugitive who escaped from a psychiatric facility early this morning." She kept her voice low. The room was full of residents watching TV, playing cards, and chatting. She didn't want to cause a stir. "He happens to be Ms. Lewis's great-nephew."

The man shook his head. "I'm afraid you're mistaken, Marshal. Mrs. Lewis has no living relatives."

Everyone they'd met today seemed certain of the fact. But Fristol security would have made sure of the relationship between Lewis and Aldeen before allowing him to contact her residence. And their own research had verified it. "Is it possible she had a great-nephew she didn't acknowledge? One she didn't approve of, perhaps?"

"I really have no idea. I can only say she's never mentioned anyone." He halted, his expression concerned. "You don't think he would come here? Is Selma in danger?"

"I don't have reason to believe so, no. But two of Ms. Lewis's neighbors have noted a man coming and going from her home occasionally over the last year or so. One of them claims he has a key and enters from the side door. He's called himself Selma's great-nephew, although that's obviously not the case."

"He has a key?" Alarm sounded in the lawyer's voice.

"The neighbor seemed to think so." She kept the news about the weekly phone calls to the house to herself for now. "I've requested a search warrant to make sure our fugitive isn't hiding in her home. You might want to be present." Cady reflected it was likely the first time in her career she'd issued that particular invitation to an attorney. "If we see evidence someone has been there in Ms. Lewis's absence, in the interests of your client, you should alert the police."

"You can be certain I will." DuPrey dug in his pocket for his wallet, from which he extracted a card and handed it to Cady. "If you'd do me the courtesy of giving me a call when the search begins, I'll be there." He hurried away, looking decidedly more worried than he had before their conversation.

"Very slick." Hearing Miguel's voice in her ear, she turned toward him. Hands in his pockets, he rocked back on his heels, his expression amused. "The warrant is going to limit our movements to searching areas in the house and grounds for Aldeen. It isn't going to give us permission to lift prints from the doorknobs so we can discover who might be entering the home in Lewis's absence. But the attorney filing a B and E report with the police could make that happen."

They fell in step together, heading for the door. "And somehow I think by the end of our search DuPrey is going to be convinced it's his duty to call the police," Cady responded. They paused to punch in a code on the keypad at the entrance to deactivate the alarm and then opened the door and strolled to the parking lot. "I take it you got nothing from Selma Lewis."

"I think I left her more confused than I found her." He opened the car doors with the fob and they both got in before Miguel continued. "After I tried to ask about a great-nephew she went from claiming she didn't have one to thinking she did, and I was he."

Cady was unable to summon an answering smile. The scene he was describing was much too close to what the future held for her mom. How many years would it be before Hannah ended up in a place just like this? How long before she started mistaking strangers for her daughter? Based on the case histories she'd read and the conversations with Hannah's doctor, Cady feared it would be much sooner than any of them wanted to believe. No more than ten years, the doctor had predicted, barring a miracle. Hannah would be sixty-eight years old then, spending the rest of her life surrounded by residents like Selma.

Cady hadn't cried since she was twelve years old. But if she did, the thought would have brought tears.

She checked for missed calls, but there was no response from the Assistant US Attorney's office. Which meant they didn't have a warrant yet. Sighing, she shoved the phone back in her pocket. Much of their job was comprised of waiting, watching, and gathering intelligence. She reached inside her interior jacket pocket and pulled out a pair of sunglasses. Settled them on her nose as Miguel guided the car back toward Selma's house. "Might as well relieve the officers while we wait."

◆ ◆ ◆

It was another forty minutes before the warrant came through. Thirty more before DuPrey and a police officer joined Cady and Miguel for the walk-through of Lewis's house. The sense of familiarity that had struck Cady upon first seeing the Lewis house was even stronger once she was inside it. Old oak flooring with a matching staircase. A postage-stamp-size living room, a dining room, and a kitchen that hadn't been updated in at least six decades. Her grandfather's home hadn't been quite so antiquated, nor shown the signs of disrepair found inside this one. Once he'd been unable to do basic upkeep himself, he'd taught Cady to do it. Those were the only useful skills she'd learned under his roof.

With DuPrey and the CMPD officer he'd summoned waiting just inside the door in the miniscule hallway, Miguel and Cady conducted a swift search of the main floor. When the first floor yielded nothing, Cady headed upstairs while her partner checked the cellar. She drew her weapon and entered the first bedroom. The bed, covered with a fussy coverlet, was neatly made. Because closets were a favorite hiding place for fugitives, she checked there first. The room had clearly belonged to Selma. Although there were a few of the woman's clothes hanging inside it, more were filled with men's clothes, the styles as dated as the kitchen downstairs. Cady looked under the bed and went on to the next bedroom, where she went through the same process.

She didn't find Samuel Aldeen concealed in any of the rooms, but what she did find in one had her going to the top of the stairway. "Mr. DuPrey. Could you come up here?" When he'd joined her, Cady led him to the back bedroom. "I don't know how often you check the house . . ."

"I usually do a walk-through before going to see Mrs. Lewis." The man stood awkwardly in the doorway of the back bedroom she'd led him to. "Mostly I look over the main floor, but occasionally I'll go all the way through it and make sure there are no leaks or signs of mice."

She swung open the closet door. "I don't think this is from a mouse."

He slowly crossed the room to look inside the enclosure. Gasped. The space was filled with overflowing garbage bags stuffed with food wrappers, beer cans, and take-out containers.

"When's the last time you were upstairs?"

DuPrey's mouth was opening and closing like a cartoon fish. "I . . . I don't . . . a few months ago, I suppose. But I don't look in the closets. Just a quick check to make sure everything seems . . ." His voice tapered off.

"Could this have been here while Mrs. Lewis lived in the house?"

The man shook his head from side to side, his gaze never leaving the mess. "She's much too fastidious to allow such a thing. The place was immaculate when she . . ." He broke off, an expression of distaste crossing his face. "This filth is sure to attract all sorts of pests. I'm going to have to see about a cleaning service right away."

"You'll want to have the locks changed too. Today, if possible." Miguel walked into the room and came to Cady's side to look inside the closet. Wrinkled his nose. Selma Lewis couldn't hold a candle to Miguel Rodriguez when it came to fastidiousness. "It stinks. The intruder must have pried off the cellar window. I found the broken frame and glass down there. He replaced it with another. Once inside . . ." He looked at DuPrey. "Would Mrs. Lewis have had extra sets of house keys in the house?"

"Um, I can't be sure. I believe the set I have is hers."

"Have you ever come in the side door?"

"No, always the front. Why?"

Miguel looked at Cady. "The dead bolt on the side entrance looks new to me."

"Oh dear." DuPrey dug inside his coat pocket for a handkerchief to mop his face. "I'm glad you suggested bringing a police officer, Marshal," he told Cady.

"Tell him to have the doorknob of the side entry—and this closet door—dusted for prints," she said gravely. "You might discover the intruder's identity that way."

"An excellent idea. I never would have expected to find someone squatting in here. Why, there's no heat! No water or electricity! I had all of those services turned off when Selma went into the nursing home."

Cady stilled. Of course, he would have. Her eyes were drawn to the twin bed in the corner of the room. It was made, although not as neatly as Selma's. The bed in the third bedroom had been stripped. This one was piled high with covers. "I assume you shut off landline phone services as well."

"Yes, of course. Everything. This is just terrible," he muttered.

She and Miguel exchanged a glance. Bizarre, was what it was. How were weekly calls being made to this home's number if it hadn't been working for a year? "When you have the police department dusting for prints, make sure they do the phone receiver as well."

It was after seven before Cady began heading home. The effects of her early morning call from Gant were beginning to catch up with her. After the search of the Lewis home, she and Miguel had spent the rest of the day running down two of the other contacts on Aldeen's list. Then they'd attempted to track down Sheila Preston, to no avail.

When her cell rang, she glanced at the screen, unsurprised to see the caller's identity. "Sheriff," she said by way of answering, scowling at the driver in the next lane whose vehicle was drifting over the centerline. "Must be important. A call instead of a text." They'd exchanged messages a couple of times throughout the day, keeping each other apprised of their findings.

"I'm on my way home. It's illegal to text and drive in the state of North Carolina, Marshal."

"I think I heard that somewhere." A yawn caught her by surprise. Maybe she was more tired than she'd realized. "Any news?" The Highway Patrol had pulled back on the roadblocks hours ago, he'd informed her earlier. They couldn't be used long-term, given the sheer manpower they required. Not to mention the inconvenience they presented to the public. A criminally insane child killer would be damn inconvenient, too, Cady thought sourly, navigating an exit off the highway. But Aldeen could be holed up somewhere, waiting for the scrutiny to die down before hitting the road.

"Nothing helpful. There are no cameras in the infirmary due to patient privacy, but there are some in the hallway outside of it. We discovered the two nurses on duty had been absent for almost thirty minutes, including during the time Aldeen walked out of there. But after hours of interviewing them individually, they both admitted they were . . . uh . . . sexually preoccupied with each other in the storage closet."

"Convenient timing," she noted.

"Isn't it, though. I wanted to let you know your advice panned out."

Her interest piqued, Cady said, "I don't recall giving you any advice."

"What you said about the MP3 player." Her mind blanked for a moment. He added helpfully, "About how you found your fugitive through his favorite country music singer."

Memory filtered back. "You listened to Aldeen's music?"

"IT had the password, since they took care of the downloads. One of my deputies let it play while he was working with the HR department today. He discovered a lot of the songs started out as music but then switched to speech."

Nonplussed, Cady straightened in her seat. "Like . . . an audiobook or something?"

"Or something." She could hear the weariness in his voice, and she recalled he'd been on scene at Fristol well before she had last night. "At first I thought it was an audiobook with a really boring narrator. Not that I've ever listened to one, but . . . the more I heard, the more it sounded like a doctor talking about a patient. I had Director Isaacson listen to a few minutes of the recording, and he agreed they could be progress notes."

"Like the doctors mentioned today." A moment later Cady braked as a deer with an impressive rack bounded out of the ditch and across four lanes of traffic. She released her breath slowly as she accelerated again. The animals were a constant hazard on rural roads. "Are they notes from Aldeen's sessions?"

"We think not. Although the patient is never referred to by name, a few times the doctor uses the pronouns *she* and *her*. Which would mean Aldeen got his hands on another patient's files. There is a section holding female patients at Fristol. We discovered the audio was narrated by a text-to-speech voice."

Cady digested the information for a moment. It made sense. Paper files were being digitized everywhere. And even if the patient records had still been paper, they'd be easily scanned to a computer and converted to audio.

"I had a duplicate file sent to Isaacson," Ryder continued. "He'll share it with the other doctors to see if they recognize the patient being discussed."

"Someone had to procure those files. If IT was in charge of the downloads, how did the hidden files make their way to Aldeen's MP3 player?"

"How indeed." Ryder sounded exhausted. "I wondered if the same person responsible for the notes and files was also the accessory on the inside. We're looking hard at the employees in the tech office."

"How many of these files are there?"

"We're not sure yet. But it appears to be a lot. If we can figure out who converted them, we might get another lead on Aldeen's whereabouts."

Interesting, Cady mused. But ultimately not helpful until they came up with the name of the patient. Ryder's next words echoed her thoughts.

"But that's not the reason for my call. I wanted to ask if you've found Sheila Preston."

"Ah." She blinked her lights at an oncoming car with its brights on, to no discernible effect. "We struck out. We tried her home in King's Mountain. She wasn't there. We got a warrant to go through her place. Closets and dressers were partially emptied, and there were no suitcases in the house. Her employer says she put in for vacation a month ago and that she'll be off for a week. None of her neighbors and coworkers recalled Preston talking about where she was going. One of her daughters goes to childcare. The other is in school. Both the childcare provider and the school officials said Preston told them she didn't know when the kids would return."

"She may be running. We're slowly getting through the security feed from all the cameras in the days preceding the escape. Preston is the source of the vehicle Aldeen used to get away. She drove the car in, parked in the employee lot, and left a couple of hours later with another visitor."

A spear of adrenaline pierced Cady's exhaustion. "I'd say that puts her at the top of the suspect list."

"We need to talk to her," Ryder agreed. "But Aldeen would have required more assistance than she could have provided. Visitors and patients are closely monitored. I don't see how she could have smuggled a uniform and ID into Fristol. And she certainly wouldn't have had the freedom to access the infirmary. Fristol's background check revealed Sheila Preston's mother lives in Canton. One of us will interview the woman. Maybe Preston headed there. Any luck with the banker or attorney on Aldeen's list?"

There was something vaguely intimate about the rumble of a masculine voice in her ear as she drove, shrouded in darkness. The thought made her uncomfortable. Her relationships were unencumbered. Certainly not the type where she exchanged casual phone calls, as evidenced by the awkward exchange early this morning with Gabe.

"No." Belatedly, her attention returned to the conversation. "They both hid behind the usual wall of confidentiality." Aldeen's last contact with his attorney was shortly after he'd landed at Fristol. The interactions with the banker were more frequent, but nothing in the last couple of months. "Both were advised to call us if they hear from him."

"Sounds good. I'll continue to alert you of the progress on our end. We should be getting a more organized dissemination of investigative results up and running soon. And . . . I'm home." The relief was evident in his voice. "Got a cold beer and a steak waiting for me in the refrigerator. The way I'm feeling, I might forgo the steak."

"Now you're just being mean." She'd be lucky to have time to make a salad before calling it a night, but the beer was tempting. "I'll keep you updated tomorrow."

After promising to do the same, Ryder disconnected, leaving Cady to mull over the information he'd shared for the rest of her drive. Why would Aldeen have someone else's progress notes on his player? It didn't make sense to her. She recalled one class she'd taken in college on abnormal psychology. Everything a deviant offender did reflected *his* wants.

His needs. She puzzled over it the rest of the way home. But as she slowed to pull into her gravel drive, she was no closer to an answer.

Her small bungalow rental was on the eastern outskirts of Waynesville, its location a nod toward the short distance to Alma's cabin and her commute to Asheville. She pulled the Jeep to a stop behind her car, which was parked beneath the attached carport. Grabbing her purse, she got out, locked the vehicle, and headed toward the house.

Its tiny covered front porch had appealed to her when the landlady showed her the place. It at least offered the space for a rocker and a small table when, in warm weather, she got the very infrequent chance to sit outside and enjoy the solitude. The nearest home was a quarter mile away, obscured by the brush and volunteer trees rimming the property.

The security light came on as she climbed the porch steps. She found the key to the house on her key ring and fit it into the lock of the front door. Pushing it open, she stepped inside.

Then stopped still, disturbed by something she could only sense.

Cady drew her weapon and flipped on the light inside the doorway, scanning the area carefully. It wasn't a large home. Two bedrooms. One-story. She studied the adjoining living area, searching for whatever had set her nerves jangling.

The room looked just as she'd left it. The comfortable couch held only a throw she hadn't bothered to refold the last time she'd used it. A book she'd been trying to read lay facedown on the coffee table. Her gaze traveled across the room to the flat-screen TV and to the double set of bookshelves flanking it. She saw nothing out of place.

Continuing through the room, she didn't lower her weapon. If anything, the itch at her nape was getting stronger. The kitchen was straight ahead, separated from the living room by a counter big enough for two stools. She drew closer to it. Stopped and turned around again.

Her gaze settled on the bookcases. They were crowded with rows of books in back, a few pictures and other items arranged in front of them. One of the photos was slightly out of place, as if it had been picked up and then replaced carelessly. A marksmanship award she'd won last year sat a bit crookedly on its stand.

The center rooms were flanked with a bedroom on each side. Cady's room with the attached bath was on the right. She turned on another light, which would illuminate the doorways of the adjoining rooms. Moving toward her bedroom first, she could see through the crack behind the opened door. No one was hiding behind it. With a feeling of déjà vu, she searched it much as she had the Lewis house earlier that day, checking closets, doorways, the bathroom, and under the bed. Then she did the same with the second room before finally drawing a breath and holstering her weapon.

Maybe she'd overreacted. Cady stood in the living room, ill at ease. She was tired. And Gabe had still been here when she'd left. Maybe he was the reason things were out of place.

Trying to put her lingering apprehension to rest, she took off her boots and coat and put them, with her purse, in the tiny hall closet. After locking the front door, she crossed to her bedroom again, already unbuckling her holster. She'd change and then hunt up the beer Talbot had made her thirsty for. If she felt ambitious, maybe she'd make a . . .

It jumped out at her now that she wasn't looking for it. The top drawer in her dresser wasn't quite closed. A small thing, but coupled with the ever-so-slightly displaced items in the other room, her earlier foreboding rushed back tenfold. Someone had been inside her house. It was more than instinct that told her that. One didn't spend most of their childhood living in other people's homes without learning to be freakishly tidy. She'd had to hide her possessions when they lived at Alma's or one of her cousins would have filched them. Her grandfather had regarded untidiness as a character flaw. And punished it accordingly.

She doubted Gabe would have had any interest in her underwear. Cady crossed to the dresser, pulled open the drawer. The disarray was subtle, but apparent. The thought of someone being in her house, touching her things, had a hot flame of anger licking down her spine.

The beer forgotten, she checked the back door in the kitchen. Found the lock secured. On a mission now, she searched the house more thoroughly, focusing on the windows in all of the rooms. In the spare bedroom, she found what she was looking for. Nerves knotted in her stomach.

The inside latch had been unlocked.

Resecuring it, she went to the back door and unlocked it before switching on the security light mounted next to the screen door. She pulled out her cell and turned on the flashlight app before stepping outside onto the small cracked cement porch. She made her way to the window she'd found unlocked and shone her light over the old storm covering it.

The wooden storm was held in place by one-inch clips that had to be turned to a vertical position before removing it. Her grandfather's house had had the same type of outer windows. Years of painting and weather had made them difficult to remove.

She shined the narrow beam of light afforded by the cell's flashlight along the bottom of the window. The clips were in place. But she could see where the old paint had been scraped next to them, as if they had recently been forced into a vertical position before being locked again.

It would be difficult to miss the fresh pry marks at both bottom corners of the window.

She shifted the beam to the ground, but there were no indentations there. No footprints. With daytime temperatures hovering in the forties and twenty-degree drops at night, the ground was too hard to leave impressions.

But she could imagine the scene that had taken place sometime while she was away today. A person standing right in this spot, loosening the storm so it would be easy to remove at a later time. A time of his choosing.

When Cady might be inside the home.

Eryn: Then

"Where's Mama?"

Mary Jane looked up from the floor she was scrubbing. "She's talking to your Uncle Bill. You need to get yourself back to your studies, missy."

Eryn ventured farther into the kitchen. "I'm hungry." She wasn't. Or, at least, only a little. But she was *bored*. She was tired of the pile of textbooks, worksheets, and library books. Sick of the amount of time she was expected to just *sit* there, every day, working alone. There were computer programs, but they didn't interest her right now, either.

"You just had lunch an hour ago. Grab an apple, then shoo. I've got work to do, even if you think you don't."

Eryn went to the pile of fruit in a bowl on the table and selected a piece, then backed out of the room. It was no use to argue with Mary Jane. Mama said she had a will of iron. Eryn didn't know where the older woman hid it. She was thin and bony. Anyone who hugged her would get jabbed by one of those bones, probably. Eryn didn't know for sure because Mary Jane wasn't the hugging type. Mama was, sometimes, when she wasn't sleepy or cross. Especially those times when she was excited about going out for the night or away for the weekend. Then Mama always hugged, squeezing tight so Eryn could tell how good she smelled. Sometimes she danced Eryn around the room for a few steps, laughing.

Dragging her feet, Eryn headed back to the study where she had school. Not the big gross one Uncle Bill used for his office, with all the animal heads staring down with their dead glass eyes. That room gave Eryn the creeps. She thought maybe spending too much time in it might be the reason Uncle Bill always had the pinched, worried expression he wore a lot of the time. He seemed to have the look a lot more since Henry's mom was letting him spend more time here. Probably because Henry was mean and a jerk. He should worry everyone.

Her classroom was in the other wing. The rooms there didn't get used much. Her pace slowed. It was time for art class. Almost, anyway. And she didn't want to wait. She'd have to, if Mama stayed cooped up with Uncle Bill for too long.

Eryn came to a stop. Then she backed up until she could see the closed door to the office. With a quick glance around she saw she was alone. She wondered what Mama and Uncle Bill were talking about in there. Stupid grown-up stuff, probably.

Maybe they're talking about you.

She shook her head impatiently. *No, they're not,* she mentally argued. She'd learned long ago not to answer the voices out loud. People looked at her strange when she did. Kids at school had made fun of her. The teachers had gotten scared eyes.

I bet they are. Why don't you check? Use your special place.

Eryn cast another look about and then walked quietly to the small room on the other side of the office wall. At least Mama said it used to be a room, a long time ago, but Eryn's grandparents had turned it into a closet. The knob was cold beneath her fingers when she pulled it open and slipped inside. Even with all the coats and shoes and boots, there was still plenty of room in it. And it wasn't dark. Not really. There was a large vent in the back corner where she could crouch on the floor and listen. Two strips of light shone, one under the door, and the other through another vent, high on the wall. Henry had locked her inside once, but it hadn't been scary because it was daytime. He'd gotten in trouble for it, though, when Eryn had told Mama. She smiled a little at the memory.

Making herself small in the corner, she pressed her ear against the vent.

". . . Bill, honestly." Eryn could hear Mama clear as a bell. "You're going to lecture me on money while you squander it on not one, but two women? What a hypocrite."

"I have responsibilities, Aurora. You . . ."

"Oh, is that what you call your mistakes?" Eryn always got scolded for interrupting adults, but Mama just did it. "First Eileen, and God knows, at least Mother and Daddy had the sense to make her sign a prenup. Otherwise the nasty little bitch would have ruined us. And now Rozzie, your new little piece. A drugstore clerk?" Mama laughed. "Bet she thinks she's in high cotton now, catching the eye of a Pullman heir. Don't think I don't know you sneak her into your suite some nights."

"Leave her out of this."

"Silly Willy had a thrilly . . ." Mama started in with the teasing singsong Uncle Bill hated. Eryn clapped her hand over her mouth to stifle a giggle. Then Mama stopped, and her voice went hard again. "If you were so worried about money, Henry doesn't have to go to a private university when he graduates high school. Tuition will cost twice what UNC would."

Eryn was glad Henry would go away to college someday. She wished he'd go now. She hated thinking of him being around for a few more years.

". . . and you hated every minute at UNC, remember?"

"Not every minute." Mama gave a full throaty laugh. "There were moments. Mostly outside of class, of course. I would have preferred art school in New York City, but our parents didn't indulge us like you do Henry."

"Can we return to the subject at hand? The last time you went to Raleigh, you ran up five thousand dollars on credit cards for clothes. The same thing happens whenever you go to the city. It's irresponsible, Aurora, and it has to stop. You need to . . ."

Eryn grew bored with the argument. She'd heard it, and others like it, too many times to count. Mary Jane said Mama and Uncle Bill bickered just to hear themselves talk, like when they were kids. Mary Jane had been here forever, so she would know.

Eryn turned to crawl out of the closet, remembering to pick up her apple first. She was hungry now and didn't want to leave it behind. Maybe she could knock on the office door and ask Mama to join her for art class, real polite-like. Otherwise who knew when this bickerfest would be over.

She stood, placing her ear against the closet door, listening for any sounds outside it that would mean someone was near who might see her creep out. The only ones who could be were Mary Jane or Elsa, who came in to clean once a week.

Then she stopped in the next moment, her attention jerking back toward the vent. She was too far away from it to make out the words, but she'd heard one. Her name.

She got down and scrambled on all fours back to the corner.

". . . you dare talk about my daughter like that!"

"Oh, but it's fine for you to bash Henry every chance you get. God knows, he's a bit mixed up. There are reasons for his behavior, but Eryn . . . good God, Aurora, you still haven't come to terms with how sick the girl is. She needs help. It's not normal for her to have those screaming fits in the middle of the night and wake up the whole damn family."

Eryn bit her lip, hard. Her free hand curled tight into a fist. She couldn't help it. She couldn't! It wasn't the same nightmare every time, but they were all alike. She was somewhere alone. Somewhere dark, and cold and damp. There was a door, but she couldn't get out, no matter how much she screamed and yelled. It was Henry's fault. Her night-mares probably started when he'd locked her in the stable's tack room.

"She has night terrors." Mama's voice had risen. "Which Dr. Freeman says is common in children. You weren't there for most of Henry's childhood, except for every other weekend. You don't know a damn thing about raising children."

"I know you're blind to what's going on with yours. You thought her talking to people who weren't there was normal too."

"Oh my God." Eryn couldn't see Mama, but she knew she was throwing up her hands the way she got when she was at the end of her rope. "She had imaginary playmates, for heaven's sake. Which she's outgrown, by the way. You've never liked her. Never cared a whit for your own niece, and that's really what this is all about. It's fine to spend money on your child, but anything for mine is a problem."

"Get off your damn high horse," Uncle Bill snapped. Eryn shifted position because one of her legs was going to sleep. But she wasn't ready to leave the closet. Not even when the conversation was making her stomach hurt like it did right before she threw up. "Your spending habits don't have a thing to do with Eryn. Although I don't think the so-called therapist you're taking her to has done a damn bit of good."

"Dr. Freeman says she's making real progress."

"Dr. Freeman is a quack. An expensive quack. Eryn's eight, for God's sake. She doesn't need play therapy, she needs treatment! She isn't a little kid anymore, although this odd behavior of hers was apparent even then. Remember what she did to Henry's cat?"

That wasn't fair! It wasn't! Eryn gritted her teeth so hard they hurt. The cat wouldn't stop talking to her! Or so she'd thought at the time. She'd been too young to realize the voices came from her head. Not from the cat. Not from the trash can in the school classroom. Or from the drawer of the teacher's desk. Uncle Bill was a mean old jerk! Just like Henry.

"She's high-strung, like I was. You don't understand the creative mind, Bill. You couldn't. And it's taken a while for Dr. Freeman to land on the right diagnosis. What looked like attention deficit disorder is actually depression. And this new medication will help."

"I've heard that one before." Uncle Bill's words were so low Eryn could hardly make them out. But she didn't care. She didn't want to hear him anymore. He was mean and horrible, and . . . and . . . an *asshole*!

"Eryn may be a freak, but she's *my* little freak, got it? Butt the fuck out."

She couldn't move away then. The word rang in her ears, rattling inside her head. *Freak.*

Eryn drew her knees up, burying her face against them as she clutched them tightly with her arms. She didn't want to leave the closet now. Maybe not ever again.

A hot tide of anger and shame worked through her, rising and rising until Eryn felt like she was choking on it. She hated Uncle Bill. She wished he'd get hit by a car. She wished he'd fall in the pond and drown. Or that someone would shoot him dead.

And sometimes—like right now—she hated Mama too.

Eryn: Now

"I don't have to go to school today," Jaxson announced when Eryn came into the kitchen for breakfast. He sent her a wide-eyed innocent look, and she read his intent clearly. She smiled to herself. She was being warned by a seven-year-old.

"Really? Why not?" Mary Jane was nowhere in sight, but there were covered dishes on the counter and she went to them now, lifting the lids off one after another. Sausage gravy and homemade biscuits. Eryn had learned to skip the dish when it was served at Rolling Acres because after the first couple of tries she'd realized it wasn't ever going to taste like Mary Jane's. She took a plate from the set table and served herself before sitting down and settling a napkin on her lap.

"Because this little man somehow managed to twist his ankle going to the bathroom during the middle of the night." Rosalyn bustled in with an ice pack in her hand and knelt next to her son. "There now, sweetie, just put your leg up on this chair."

"It's cold."

"It's straight out of the freezer. The cold will keep it from swelling." She rose again and sent Eryn a rueful smile. "Did you ever hear of such a thing? I'm wondering if he was sleepwalking. I'll be sure and ask the doctor. It's not uncommon for children, I understand."

"I wasn't walking in my sleep, Mom. I just had to pee."

"What have I told you about that kind of language?" But there wasn't a hint of reproach in Rosalyn's voice. She kissed his blond head. "I'm calling for an appointment just as soon as the doctor's office opens." She whisked away the plate set in front of him and put it away before bringing him a bowl. "I don't know why Mary Jane can't seem to remember you prefer cereal in the morning." Rosalyn set the dish in front of him and went to the pantry, coming back with a box of sugary cereal. Jaxson's eyes went round. She saw his reaction and smiled. "Just for special occasions. Because you've been so brave about your sore ankle."

Happily, Jaxson sat back and allowed his mother to pour the cereal and cover it with milk before diving in. His mother smoothed his hair back, then smiled brightly in Eryn's direction. "You haven't said how you like your room."

She swallowed before answering. "It's nice. Thank you." It was lovely, yet somehow impersonal. Maybe because Eryn hadn't selected the paint, bedding, and curtains herself. Not that she had any experience in interior decorating. She was twenty-one years old, and the most decorating she'd ever done was to hang paintings or prints on the walls of her room. She wouldn't even have known where to start. What stores to go to. She only knew her taste as far as artwork went.

Which could be said about almost every aspect of her life. "Maybe you can help me again," she said. "I was going to talk to Uncle Bill about this—but I'd like to fix up a room to use as a studio. There's an entire wing not in use. Surely I could repurpose one of those spaces."

Rosalyn's smile became set. "I'd just love to help in any way I can. You talk to your uncle about it and let me know what he says."

As a kid, Eryn hadn't been adept at picking up on social cues. Which was only one of the reasons elementary school—for the limited time she'd attended—had been such a nightmare. But she'd come a long way since then, enough to recognize the unspoken words behind Rosalyn's smile. Eryn returned her attention to her breakfast, her appetite diminishing. She was an adult, but still dependent on a relative she barely knew for . . . everything, she realized sickly. She and Dr. Glassman—and later, Dr. Steigel—had talked a lot about how to adapt upon her return home. They'd never discussed how she'd support herself.

"Eryn, you aren't eating the rest of your breakfast."

Her gaze rose slowly to Rosalyn's face. "I guess I'm not as hungry as I thought I was."

"Pretty girls don't eat, Mom." When Rosalyn and Eryn looked at Jaxson, he shrugged and continued shoveling cereal into his mouth. "In the cafeteria, Bentley—she's the prettiest girl in school—she doesn't eat hardly anything because she says she doesn't want to get fat. That's how I know."

"Well, buried in the disturbing Bentley story is a compliment, Eryn." Rosalyn laughed. "Jaxson thinks you're pretty." He squirmed in his chair.

"Pretty amazing," Eryn deadpanned, and he grinned.

"You're all right."

"High praise, indeed." Rosalyn glanced at the clock on the wall. "Now eat up, young man. I want to be ready to leave the moment I can make a call to the doctor."

Eryn rose and took her plate to scrape it into the garbage disposal, then rinsed it and put it in the dishwasher. She'd painted for hours last night and had risen later than normal. She knew from experience she'd need to get to work now, this morning, because the medication made her tired by lunchtime. It was going to take a while to get used to being able to set her own schedule and not adhere to a strict lights-out-at-11:00 p.m. and breakfast at 8:00 a.m. policy.

She was returning to her room when a stray thought occurred. Retracing her steps, she went to the coat closet at the back of the house

Cold Dark Places

and surveyed its contents carefully. Everything was neat and organized. Eryn figured Mary Jane saw to that. There was a tall box for sporting equipment. Tubs for hats and gloves. Plenty of space to hang up coats and jackets. A man's parka was among them.

Troubled, she returned to her room. Last night she'd wondered what would have taken her uncle to the boathouse at night. She was no closer to an answer this morning. The easiest way to find out was to ask him.

Her mind skittered away from the idea. There'd been a furtiveness in his movements as he'd approached the house last night. And really, what business was it of hers? For all intents and purposes, she was a guest in her uncle's home.

Seeking a distraction from her pesky thoughts, she looked at her canvases with a critical eye, studying what she'd accomplished last night. Eryn wasn't the painter Mama had been. She despaired of ever being so talented. But she'd worked for years to perfect her technique. And, she admitted to herself as she turned away to pick up a sketchpad, she'd always hoped at some point in her life—a hazy, nebulous *someday*—that she'd have the opportunity to take lessons from a teacher who could help her improve.

Now she was questioning if it would ever happen. *How* it would ever happen.

A small sound had her stilling. A moment later she walked swiftly to the adjoining bathroom and opened the door.

Mary Jane turned away from the sink and brushed by her, but not before Eryn noted a dull flush crawling up her cheeks. "What are you doing in here?" she asked bluntly.

"I brought some laundry into your room and put it away. You're welcome, by the way. Fresh towels in your bathroom."

Eryn's gaze went to the towels hanging neatly on the rail by the tub. "Why were you looking in my medicine cabinet?" Because that

97

had been the noise she'd heard, she realized now. The magnetic click of its door closing.

Then comprehension filtered in and she felt a rush of impatience. "I don't need you checking up on me. I'm an adult. I'm capable of taking my medication without someone second-guessing me."

The older woman sent her an arch look. "Are you, now? Took it without supervision in Rolling Acres, did you?"

Eryn caught her lip in her teeth. Staff at the residential facility dispensed medication to patients individually, regardless of their recovery status, as a matter of legal protection. "I'm not a child."

"No, you're not." Mary Jane studied her long enough to have Eryn fidgeting. "You look like her, you know. Your Mama. She'd have been a bit younger than you when she left for college. She was twenty-six when she came back, with you in tow." She gave a little shake, as if dislodging the memory. "What are you planning to do now?"

In answer, Eryn held up the sketchpad she still had in one hand.

"I mean with your life."

She'd managed, in her blunt, callous way, to put her finger directly on the worry throbbing inside Eryn like a bruise. "I don't know."

Mary Jane pursed her lips. "Just don't bury yourself in this place. Pullman Estate has a way of sucking people in and never spitting them out again."

A measure of Eryn's earlier concern rose to the surface. "How am I supposed to do anything else? I don't have a job. Even if I got one, I don't know how to drive. I've never been in a store alone. I've never bought my own groceries or cooked a meal on my own. How am I supposed to get on with my life when every normal experience passed me by while I was locked up?"

Her outburst brought an arrested expression to Mary Jane's face. Her response was slow in coming. "Never thought about it much, I guess. But you have some time to make up, rightly enough. I'll take you with me next trip to the grocery store. And you'll come, even if it means putting away your paints for a while. As to the other, well, you'll have to tackle one thing at a time. Maybe speak to Mr. William about driving lessons, first off."

"I don't like feeling beholden to him for everything." If this was how it was going to be, Eryn had only stepped out of one restrictive environment into another. On some level, she knew she was worrying too soon. She'd just come home a few days ago. But the fact she required "lessons" in how to be independent seemed an insurmountable hurdle.

"Well, it's not like this place isn't just as much yours as his." Mary Jane continued to the bedroom door. "You inherited your Mama's share, and now you're twenty-one, you'll have a hand in the decisions, I expect. But that's between you and Mr. William." She disappeared through the doorway, leaving Eryn staring after her, jaw agape.

She'd inherited Mama's share? Her knees weak, Eryn dropped down on the bed. She would have never, in a million years, even considered such a thing. A trickle of revulsion snaked down her spine. It didn't seem right. Not after what she'd done. Not when Mama was dead because of her.

Her chest went tight, her heart beginning to pound with what she knew were the signs of an imminent panic attack. She bent at the waist, hauling in deep breaths, pushing all thought aside as she concentrated only on drawing oxygen in and releasing it from her lungs. Baby steps, she cautioned herself when she'd finally calmed her breathing. But Eryn didn't miss the irony in her own reaction.

One minute she was moping over her lack of experience and freedom. The next, she was hyperventilating at the thought she might have the means to independence after all. Among other things, she'd always been a study in contrasts.

"Can I speak to you for a moment, Uncle Bill?" Eryn eased the door to his office open after her knock. Saw him glaring at a laptop screen open on his desk. He closed it and looked up, managing a pinched smile.

"Of course. What is it?"

Although he hadn't issued an invitation, she went farther into the room, her gaze going to the array of animal heads high on the wall. This space had seemed creepy to her as a child. But now she had a movie image in her mind of powerful cigar-smoking men retiring to a dark paneled room to sign documents and declare war. Bill hadn't updated the room in her absence. Hadn't brought in a huge TV screen to turn it into a man cave. She wondered why.

In that moment, the memory of last night flashed into her mind. She looked at him now, at the impatient expression on his face, which was showing the signs of middle age. In the daylight hours, it was even more difficult to imagine a reason for him sneaking out to the boathouse in the middle of the night.

"Uh . . . I was thinking. I'd like a bigger place to use as a studio. And I was wondering . . . you have all those empty rooms in the unused wing . . ."

"We've turned off the heat to those rooms." His brows drew together. "As much as I could manage, at any rate. Perhaps you should ask Rosalyn to help you move the furniture around in yours. Or try one of the other bedrooms."

"There's not enough natural light in them." The nicest rooms in this wing had already been claimed. One large suite was occupied by Uncle Bill's family; the other had once been used by Eryn and Mama. Mary Jane had a small bedroom, and there were two guest rooms. None of them was suitable for her purposes.

"Well, sometimes we have to make do with what's at hand, Eryn."

Her earlier courage was draining away. Before she lost the last remnant of it, she added in a rush, "I'd also like to learn to drive."

His expression turned thoughtful. "I think that's probably a good idea. In due time."

Irritation stiffened her spine. "When is in due time?"

"As head of this household, I'll make the decision. Perhaps in the spring."

She waited, but he only lifted the lid of the computer again, began staring at the screen. "What did Mama's will say?" She watched the tension settle in his shoulders before he looked at her again.

"Why do you ask?"

"I've been feeling . . . grateful," she said hastily, ". . . but uncomfortable, thinking I was encroaching here."

"Eryn, you've just gotten back . . ."

"I know." She trailed her fingers over the butter-soft leather of the winged chair next to her. "But I think I'd be more comfortable if we had a conversation about where things stand."

"Very well." She could feel him watching her, but she couldn't meet his eye. Not yet. Most of the adults at Rolling Acres had been professionals of some sort. While she'd managed a modicum of ease with her peers there, it was still easy to be cowed by grown-ups. They held all the control. They made the rules. She wondered how long it would be before she identified as a bona fide adult herself.

"Your mama and I were equal inheritors of our parents' estate." He rocked back in the desk chair, his mouth held as though he'd tasted something unpleasant. "I've always managed the finances of the various Pullman properties and businesses. Most of the profits from them are plowed back into the companies. Some, a fairly significant amount, are used for the upkeep of this property. The remainder has been split between Aurora—now you—and me."

Absorbing this for a moment, Eryn said, "When do I gain control over my share?"

His lips flattened. "*Control* probably isn't the best term, but under ordinary circumstances it would come upon your twenty-first birthday, which has passed. Your doctor will be called upon to attest you're equipped for the responsibility. But," he waved a hand dismissively, "we're rushing things. You need to give yourself some—" His cell rang, and he fumbled for it before drawing it out of his trouser pocket.

"Rosalyn, what is it? You only left a minute—" He stopped talking, shooting from his chair as if launched. "What? Where?"

Eryn could make out Rosalyn's voice, but not the words. Her hysterical shrieks, though, were unmistakable.

Uncle Bill rounded the desk and bolted from the room, shouting over his shoulder, "Eryn, stay inside!"

Trailing behind him, she watched as he ran to open the front door, slamming it behind him. Had there been an accident of some sort? Her pace quickened until she reopened the door. Stepped through it. She followed her uncle down the circular drive in front of the sprawling house. Her gaze traveled beyond the expanse of lawn, brown now with winter's approach, past the spiked wrought-iron fence to the other side of the road.

A figure was mounted on a tall pole. Flames were climbing upward, engulfing its feet.

"Eryn! Get back in the house!"

She heard the sound of her uncle's voice, but his words didn't register. Eryn wasn't even aware she'd left the drive and was crossing the lawn, drawn as if by an invisible force. The figure, a mannequin she could see now, had long light hair. A wig, maybe. Eryn's hand rose of its own volition. Fingered a strand of her own straight blonde strands. At the top of the pole a large sign was displayed. She stopped only when she was close enough to read it:

KILLERS BURN IN HELL!!!!

Ryder

The fire truck might have been overkill, but Ryder had been concerned about having a ditch fire on his hands by the time he got out to the Pullman Estate. A concern that had been warranted, because when he'd arrived, ten minutes ahead of the fire department, the flames had spread beyond the base of the pole and were racing through the ditch.

He'd used the extinguisher in his trunk on the effigy, which had mostly burned itself out before his arrival. And only when the firefighters seemed to have the ditch fire contained did he leave his chief deputy, Jerry Garza, in charge while he headed toward the Pullman house for the second time in only days.

The gates were open this time. William Pullman was standing in the drive, hands shoved into the pockets of his leather jacket. There was a girl beside him. *No, not a girl,* Ryder corrected himself as he drew closer. *A young woman.* The one who'd been in the car the last time he was called. Eryn Pullman. She wore no coat, but someone had draped a blanket around her shoulders. The boots she was wearing looked too large for her.

"Thank you for coming, Sheriff."

"I'm glad you called. This fire could have spread to several acres, as dry as it's been." And he had a few names that jumped to the top of the suspect list for today's stunt. Every single person who'd been here last week, all of whom had to be ordered off the Pullman property.

"Let's go inside." William turned, and, with a hand on Eryn's arm, guided her back toward the house. With a feeling of déjà vu, Ryder followed them to the office he'd been shown to days earlier.

"You said on the phone that your wife noticed the fire first." Ryder pulled a notebook and pen out of his coat pocket.

"Yes." William Pullman slipped out of his jacket and hung it on the back of the desk chair before dropping into the seat like dead weight. "She had my son in the car. He's seven. She was taking him to the doctor and he had to see . . . that."

"It was me."

Ryder looked at Eryn. It was the first time he'd heard her speak. She remained huddled in the blanket, as if the warmer temperatures inside hadn't chased away the chill that enveloped her. "I mean, it was supposed to represent me."

"I'm sorry," he said grimly. Like the girl—he had to stop thinking of her like a kid—the *young lady* didn't have enough on her plate. "I'll be interviewing everyone who was here the day your uncle brought you home. The perpetrator has broken several laws, not the least of which is harassment. The wording of the message is similar to those on the signs wielded by the crowd blocking your gate a few days ago. But I don't want to get tunnel vision on this. Can you think of anyone you came into contact with in Rolling Acres who might be responsible?"

"What are you implying?" William demanded. "You just guessed it was probably the same people who were here earlier this week."

Eryn turned her head slowly in Ryder's direction, seeming to focus on him for the first time. Her eyes were the palest blue he'd ever seen, like a winter sky.

"No. The professionals wouldn't have any reason to do this, and the residents . . . well, they're still locked up."

"Maybe you had an altercation with someone, recently or in the past." A former patient. Or even a current resident could have reached out to a friend or relative to do their bidding, much as Aldeen had done from Fristol.

She shook her head definitively. "There's no one." Eryn stood abruptly. And when she spoke again, her voice was almost childlike. "May I go now?"

"Why don't you have Mary Jane make you some tea and lay down?" William suggested.

Without answering she went to the door. Then paused. She turned her head to look at Ryder over her shoulder. "What I did when I was a child was horrible. People don't understand it. They think I'm a monster, and if I were them I'd probably think so too. But you need to stop them. I might deserve this treatment, but my uncle and his family don't." Then she glided silently from the room like a quilt-covered ghost.

When Ryder glanced at Pullman, the man appeared shaken. "This can't continue." He wiped a hand over his face and his jaw squared. "My niece is still in a fragile state, and this is a critical transition period for her. She doesn't need the constant turmoil."

"None of you do. What time did your wife notice the fire?"

"Um . . . it would have been about forty-five minutes ago. Only a minute or two before I called your office."

"Have you had any other incidents since you brought your niece home?" William shook his head. "No trespassers? Strange phone calls?"

"No. We don't have a landline. We all use cells."

Ryder asked several more questions, but it soon became apparent William had no more information to offer. Finally, he stood. "I'll contact you after I've conducted some interviews." He'd start with the guy they'd hauled in a couple of days ago. Frederick Bancroft. The man had spent a day in lockup and still faced charges for multiple misdemeanors.

"Thank you, Sheriff." William sounded weary.

Ryder nodded and headed for the front door, letting himself out and jogging down the steps to rejoin his deputy, who was still outside the gate. The fire looked well in hand. He spotted Jerry speaking to Bruce Mayer, one of the firemen, and strode in their direction.

"Ryder." Bruce's greeting was friendly. They'd played on the high school football team together, although Bruce was a year older. "I haven't seen you around in a while. We're gonna have to get together and relive our glory days over a beer."

"I'm up for the beer, but I have a feeling the memories will be more exaggeration than fact."

"It's all in the tellin'." The other man winked. "We'll wait until the origin of the fire cools off before taking it down and packaging it for shipment to the state crime lab."

Ryder nodded, but he didn't hold out much hope he'd see results anytime soon. The fire wasn't linked to a high-profile crime, and finding evidence that had withstood the flames and could be traced back to a suspect would be dicey at best.

When his cell rang, he stepped away from the duo to answer it. "Ry, it's Patterson." Cal Patterson was one of his deputies who was finishing up interviews of Fristol personnel. "We've covered just about every employee or sub who worked the week prior to the escape with the exception of seven. All of them are currently out on sick leave or on vacation. Security tapes show only one of those in the vicinity of the infirmary in the last several days, though. Joe Bush. Last month he signed up for a two-week vacation to begin two days before the escape. No one seems to know where he was headed, but he isn't answering his cell. We contacted his ex, and she had no idea, either."

"Do you have an address?" Cal reeled it off for him. With one eye on the fireman who had peeled away from Garza and walked back toward the ditch, Ryder said, "We'll check it out. By the way, I had a message from Dr. Isaacson this morning. None of the doctors on staff recognized the patient referred to on Aldeen's audio files. Are you still listening to them?"

"Finishing as we speak," the deputy said sourly. "That voice could double as a sleep aid. I haven't heard anything that would give me a clue about the identity of the patient. The only other weird thing I've run across is an entire file that contains nothing but laughter. Five minutes and eighteen seconds of it, to be exact."

"What the hell?" Ryder was nonplussed for a moment. "Was there any background noise? Maybe it was recorded at an event of some kind." The crime lab could probably do something with the file if that were the case. Mute the laughter. Turn up the other sounds. Maybe they were from a place Aldeen had visited.

"I'm not an expert, but it didn't seem that way to me. It sounded like it could be different clips spliced together. All of little kids laughing."

Everything inside him stilled. The hair on his nape raised. Children. Of course. In the next moment another thought slammed into him. "Cal? I want you to contact administration at the Rolling Acres Resort." There would be kids there, although he wasn't sure how young. And there would be progress notes on all of them. "We'll need another warrant like we had at Fristol for patient records. Take it and a copy of Aldeen's audio files and ask if they can ID the patient." Rolling Acres shared the same property as Fristol, although miles separated the two facilities.

"Rolling Acres? Huh. Joe Bush worked there part-time, too, according to his employment records. I'll get right on that."

Garza's brows rose as Ryder disconnected. "What was that all about?"

Ryder filled him in on the conversation while he scanned the scene, his mind already elsewhere. "The fire department seems to have things well in hand. We're going to drop by Joe Bush's house. He hasn't been interviewed yet, and I have plenty of questions to ask him."

"Might be a waste of time if he's supposed to be on vacation. But if he showed up on the security feed near the infirmary recently, maybe he's our guy."

There was a kick in his veins telling Ryder the same thing. They got into the cruiser, and as Ryder pulled onto the blacktop, the deputy asked, "Is anyone else from the task force meeting us at Bush's?"

Ryder shook his head. He'd been on his way to the local community center, which they had set up to be a command center to accommodate all the agencies involved in the case, when he'd received the call from Pullman. "Let's wait and see what we learn at Bush's."

They drove a few miles in silence before the older man scratched his craggy cheek. "This case, along with the Pullman thing, raises all kinds of interesting ancient history. From back when your daddy was sheriff."

As always, just the mention of Butch Talbot had tension creeping up Ryder's spine. Most of the employees in the sheriff's office had been hired by Ryder's dad. Many had worked alongside him for decades—Jerry perhaps the longest, since the man was well into his sixties and showing no inclination for retirement. "How so?"

"Well . . ." Garza settled his weight more comfortably in the car seat. "Take the Pullman girl, who killed her mama all those years ago. You would have still been in the military then, but our office—your daddy—handled the investigation. Sad state of affairs. The judge said the kid was crazy, and she's been locked up until recently."

Ryder wasn't at all sure being in and out of Rolling Acres Resort met the traditional definition of "locked up," but he understood the sentiment. Tragedy was blessedly infrequent in the county. The memory of it by longtime residents would be fresh.

"And then you have that Deputy US Marshal, Cady Maddix, on the Aldeen task force. Funny sort of coincidence."

The introduction of the marshal seemed a non sequitur. "Maddix? I don't see the connection."

"Well, I'm not saying there's a connection, just a coincidence, given her childhood." When Ryder only looked at him, Jerry shook his head. "I keep forgetting you'd a just been a kid yourself at the time. Shit, that makes me feel old. You'd a been no more than seven or so. No reason you'd remember. But when Cady Maddix was just a mite—four or five, I think—one of her parents left a loaded handgun on the table. The girl picked it up and it went off. Lonny Maddix was all kinds of a son of a bitch and a wanted man, at that. Not many were sad to see him go, but it was a helluva thing when his little girl shot him dead."

◆ ◆ ◆

Joe Bush's home was just outside the Waynesville city limits. Rimmed by timber, it offered seclusion and not much else. The surrounding property was unkempt and—except for a narrow patch on which the house sat—unmowed. It boasted a detached garage several decades newer than the house. The place looked deserted as Ryder and Jerry got out of the vehicle and approached the front door.

"Maybe he's around," Jerry suggested as they climbed the peeling steps to the front porch. "If Bush lives like this, he probably can't afford to be off on some luxury vacation."

"Maybe he can afford a vacation *because* he lives like this." Ryder pounded on the rickety screen door. He waited a minute and then repeated the action. When the third try brought no response, the men turned as one and made their way down the steps again. "Let's try out back." *Plenty of places a guy could go to get away from it all without spending a ton of money,* Ryder reflected as they rounded the house. He was partial to fly-fishing himself. No better way for a man to relax than heading for a mountain stream and soaking up the solitude.

The back porch was in the same state of disrepair as the front. But as Ryder approached it his pace slowed. The interior door was standing ajar. They might have gotten lucky and caught Bush at home.

He knocked on the screen door, to no avail. Shifting position, Ryder tried to get a better glimpse of the interior. The first space was clearly a kitchen, one with cracked vinyl flooring. It opened onto another room, of which he could only see a sliver. Something caught his eye then, and he stilled. "Stand right here," he murmured, moving aside to allow Jerry to crowd closer. "What do you see beyond the kitchen? On the floor?"

The deputy pressed his face against the screen, squinting. "It looks . . . oh damn. That's a bare foot." As one they drew their weapons. "Mr. Bush!" Ryder called out. "Haywood County Sheriff. We're coming in!"

With Jerry on his heels, Ryder walked through the door. He was only two steps inside before the smell hit him. The unmistakable scent of decomposing flesh. He followed it through the doorway of the kitchen into the next room.

Joe Bush had been a tall man. The bare foot they'd seen from the porch was attached to a long leg encased in denim, topped by a plaid shirt, which was now marred by the sort of blood loss associated with massive trauma.

The deputy carefully skirted the body and did a check of the rest of the rooms. Ryder crouched near the corpse. Two bullets had caught the man center mass. Another had likely shattered his knee. He'd seen enough dead bodies to gauge this one as no more than two days old. A spear of frustration stabbed through him. None of the questions he'd wanted to put to the man were going to get answered now. He rose and radioed it in and then summoned the local coroner before putting in a call to SBI Agent Sweeney at the command center, where the task force members gathered. He knew the man would already be there.

The agent came on the line. "Where are you? When I came in this morning, they said you hadn't arrived yet."

"I got a call that had nothing to do with the Aldeen case." He took a few steps away from the body and acknowledged Garza's wave when he came back into the area. The deputy had cleared the premises. "Then

I followed up on one of the Fristol substitute employees we hadn't interviewed yet. He was supposed to be on vacation. We found him at home, with a couple of bullets in his chest. He's probably been dead less than forty-eight hours."

The agent cursed. "Is there any sign of a connection to Aldeen?"

"Not yet." Spying the computer on a nearby table, Ryder crossed to it and pulled a latex glove from his pocket to don before touching the space bar. The screen lit up. He went to the history, and his brows came together when he saw it'd been cleared.

"Call me if you find a link."

Promising to do so, Ryder disconnected. He was feeling slightly more friendly toward the agent than he had the first few hours after they'd met. The agencies joining together for the task force brought a mixture of personalities. Ryder focused on getting results, and the extra manpower was helping achieve them far faster than his office could have done on its own.

"Type up the paperwork," he told his deputy. "Besides the search, we'll need warrants on his cell phone, financials, and electronics. I'm going to take a look around the property." Their entry would qualify as exigent circumstances, since they'd seen the body inside the home.

Jerry followed Ryder out of the house, and they parted ways at the base of the steps. The official vehicle held the laptop the deputy would need for typing and submitting the requests. Ryder studied the back of the home. The half-open back door signaled something entirely different than their initial assumption. It was probably how the killer departed. Ryder slowly circled to the front without finding any signs of forced entry. Which suggested Bush knew his attacker and let him in.

Ryder crossed to the single-stall garage. It boasted a small window on both sides. When he pressed his face against the panes, he could make out the shape of a vehicle but not the make or model. He went back to his car for a Maglite and headed back to the garage with it. The beam lit up the interior of the structure. A jolt went through him.

He didn't know what kind of vehicle the substitute custodian drove. But the one housed inside this building looked an awful lot like the one Aldeen had driven off the Fristol property.

◆　◆　◆

"It's the car Aldeen used for his escape," Ryder informed Sweeney and FBI Special Agent Quinn Tolliver as they donned latex gloves and joined him in the garage. In an odd sort of synchronicity, their arrival had almost exactly coincided with the warrants. Once Ryder had the paperwork in hand, he'd called in his criminal investigation deputies. The medical examiner had come and gone in the intervening time. The body was on its way to the morgue. "Bush drove a ten-year-old Impala. His plates, and those on Aldeen's original vehicle, are there." He pointed to the pile in the corner of the garage where they'd been discarded.

"So the escapee has Bush's car with a third set of plates on it." Tolliver put words to the obvious.

Ryder nodded, careful to keep his frustration in check. The state troopers had a description of the vehicle used in the escape, but they wouldn't have stopped a matching car if the plates didn't match the BOLO.

"Dumb to leave the plates for us to see. He could have had us chasing our tails looking out for two different licenses. Now we know we don't have the plate number he's using on Bush's vehicle," Agent Sweeney said. He sipped from a go-cup he must have picked up on the way over.

"Dumb? Or showing off?" This from Tolliver. "Each would say something different about the inmate."

"He was smart enough to avoid capture for at least six violent crimes for years," Ryder said shortly. Regardless of Aldeen's mental illness, he possessed the skills to pass as normal in public. He'd done just that for too long before justice caught up with him. It'd be a mistake to underestimate him. "Based upon what his psychiatrist told us, the man's IQ is well above average. He's thumbing his nose at us, I expect. Just a little reminder we have no idea what his resources are." Ryder stared at the plates as if they held some answers. "The working assumption now is he had two accomplices, Preston and Bush. But there's another guy figuring into the equation. One Aldeen probably doesn't realize we know about."

"The one who hacked the old lady's phone."

"The mysterious Raymond." Ryder had looked the vehicle over but found nothing of interest in it. Preston's fingerprints might eventually be discovered, but they already had a video image of her driving the escape vehicle onto Fristol property. And they knew Aldeen had escaped in it, so finding his prints or DNA would be superfluous.

A thought occurred then. "Maybe Aldeen had an ulterior motive for leaving the licenses. They announce his presence here, and why would he want to tie himself to a dead body? Because by doing so, he also wraps up Bush and Preston in a nice neat little bow for us as his two accessories. 'No need to look elsewhere, folks. I'm giving away my coconspirators right here.'" *Downright insulting, is what it is,* Ryder mused. But it meant they were a step ahead of the escapee in one way. They knew about the stranger who'd pretended to be Selma Lewis's great-nephew. And it was looking like Aldeen was shielding the man.

They needed to figure out why.

"Damn coincidental that Preston and Bush both took vacation just prior to the escape," Tolliver noted.

"If they thought that gave them plausible deniability," Sweeney said as he pulled open a car door and stuck his head in, "they'd be wrong."

The FBI agent looked thoughtful. "So Bush could have smuggled the contraband inside Fristol. Everything Aldeen would need to walk out. The uniform. Shoes. Jacket. ID."

"Someone else had to convert the audio files," Ryder said. "There's no equipment inside Bush's house to do so." They needed a deeper dive into the custodian's background. His friends, contacts, skills . . . the list of tasks continued to grow while answers remained in short supply.

"Maybe Preston was responsible for the files," FBI Special Agent Tolliver suggested. "We know she supplied the vehicle. And Aldeen had to get the gun and a change of clothes from someone."

"Or perhaps the mystery man who hacked into Lewis's phone line provided the necessities. He had to have been the one speaking regularly to the inmate." Which told Ryder whoever Raymond was, either he couldn't get clearance to be on Fristol's patient contact list or he didn't want to leave evidence of his link to Aldeen. The man could have been the one who'd gotten Sheila Preston involved.

Tolliver approached the car to peer into the open trunk. "You found nothing in it?"

Ryder shook his head. "I've got my investigative team inside the house. They'll comb the vehicle, but I didn't see anything. I'm betting it's a rental, so it shouldn't be difficult to trace the company and find out who obtained it."

He was already laying odds the person would be Sheila Preston.

◆ ◆ ◆

Ryder was just pulling into Canton's city limits when Deputy Logan Middleton called. He'd dispatched the man to follow up on Frederick Bancroft, the ringleader arrested a few days ago for trespassing on the Pullman property. Ryder had gotten phone calls from not one but two county supervisors in recent days, both reminding him of the importance of Pullman Industries in the area. Which was why he'd dealt with the fire this morning himself. But with the Fristol escape pulling him in too many directions, he had to delegate.

"Hey, Ry, it's Logan."

"Did you touch base with Bancroft?" Ryder slowed as he entered the town, glancing at the GPS on his dash to guide him to Cindy Preston's home.

"I did. Not a likable guy."

A brief mental image flashed into his mind of the combative Bancroft, pugnacious jaw jutted as he'd shouted hateful remarks. "Nope. You're saying spending the night in jail didn't accomplish an attitude adjustment?"

His deputy chuckled. "None I could see. He spent the first ten minutes complaining I had no right to talk to him. The next ten he recounted all of the reasons the effigy was justified, and the final few minutes claiming he had nothing to do with it. Short story . . . he's alibied. I got the feeling he made sure of it before this all went down. He was attending a funeral in Cruso. I'll follow up, of course, but I'm guessing he had someone else from his church do the dirty work."

"Okay, verify his alibi. Then call the office and get the contact information for everyone who was protesting Eryn Pullman's arrival home."

"I'll interview all of them," Logan promised.

They disconnected just as the GPS was announcing Ryder's arrival at his destination, a 1960s-era ranch-style home painted an unattractive dark brown. He walked swiftly to the front door and knocked. But he was saved from repeating the action by a man coming out of the neighboring house.

"Nobody home," he called out to Ryder helpfully as he dragged a garbage container toward the end of his drive. "Cindy would be at work. Johnson's Motor Supply on Main Street."

"Thanks." Ryder paused. "Does Ms. Preston live alone?"

"She has as long as I've lived here, so at least for ten years." Concern filtered through the man's expression. "Is anything wrong?"

"Nothing to worry about." Getting back in his car, Ryder pulled away from the curb. He shouldn't need GPS to find Main Street in a town of forty-two hundred. Twenty minutes later he was sitting across a table in the store's employee lounge from Cindy Preston, a sixty-something woman with improbable red hair and heavy makeup. She was peering uncomprehendingly at Ryder through a spiderweb of false lashes.

"I don't understand? You said Sheila is okay? But you're looking for her?" The woman's inflection made every statement sound like a question.

"As far as I know, she's fine," Ryder assured her. He unzipped his jacket. The room was like an oven. "But I need to speak with her. She may have knowledge of a crime my office is investigating."

Something flitted across the woman's expression, there and gone too quickly for him to identify. She sat back a little in her chair. And when she spoke next her voice was decidedly cooler. "My daughter had some trouble with the law a while back. I'm not going to deny it. But she's moved on. Her kids are her life now. She wouldn't do anything to put them at risk."

"Sheila took a week's vacation a couple of days ago. She pulled one child out of school and the other from day care." He could tell by Cindy's widened eyes she hadn't known that. His gut tightened. They weren't going to find Sheila Preston hiding inside her mother's home.

The woman recovered quickly. "Well, I guess a person has a right to go on vacation when they want."

Ryder held up a hand. "Ma'am, we need to speak to her. If you know where she is—if you have any idea at all—you can help her by helping us."

Cindy dug in her oversize purse for a tissue. Dabbed at her eyes. "I'm sorry, I don't. I talk to both of my girls once a week, and Sheila never mentioned a thing about a vacation. Now that I think about it, she's been a bit stressed. She said there's been a lot of pressure at work."

"Maybe she confided in your other daughter."

"Julie? She's married and lives in Mecklenburg. Near Charlotte? But I can't believe she wouldn't have mentioned anything to me if she knew.

You leave her alone. I don't want her dragged into some problem with Sheila. It's not fair to Julie or her family."

"I think she'd want to help her sister if she could, don't you? I know my sister would." Ryder gave her an encouraging smile. "If she thinks I have the tiniest problem, she's on her white horse, galloping to the rescue. Bossing me the whole way too."

Cindy chuckled a little and with a final swipe at her eyes she replaced the tissue in her purse. "You're exactly right. Julie's the oldest. Stuck her nose in Sheila's business something awful 'til she got a family to focus on. Maybe . . . if Sheila had reached out, Julie would have tried to help."

Ryder was betting on the same. He left Cindy Preston looking far more worried than he'd found her. Getting into his vehicle, he scrolled through the emails from his deputies updating him about their progress before finding Cady Maddix's number.

Jerry Garza's words flashed across his mind. *It was a helluva thing when his little girl shot him dead.*

Ryder's fingers paused on the phone. What did such an early trauma do to a child? Maybe it all depended on how the adults around her handled it. He had a mental image of Cady at their first meeting. Cool. Competent. Closed off. She'd impressed him with her professionalism in his dealings with her so far. She'd obviously managed to put the early tragedy behind her.

But he knew from experience traumas were never forgotten. They had a way of hanging around, ready to ambush when you least expected it.

He finished putting the call through. Started his car and pulled away from the curb. There was a task force meeting in less than an hour. He couldn't miss it.

She answered on the third ring. "Maddix."

"Ryder Talbot."

"I have caller ID," she noted dryly.

He grinned. She didn't suffer fools gladly. A trait he appreciated. "So you've got me in your contact list. I'm touched."

"You just might be." Her tone gave his words a different meaning. His smile grew wider. It'd been a long damn day, and there was no end in sight yet. "Do you have news?"

"You might consider it that." Ryder filled her in on the events of the day, ending with his conversation with Cindy Preston.

There was a moment of silence when he finished before Cady said, "Aldeen obviously doesn't think we know about the man calling himself Raymond."

She'd cut right to the heart of the matter. "It gives us an advantage. Have you heard anything on the latents left in Selma Lewis's house yet?"

"You'll know when I do. Aldeen probably didn't plan on the guy chatting with the neighbors, or living there—at least some of the time—since Lewis went to the nursing home."

"The escapee might be protecting him. But if we get Raymond's real name through his print, we might get the best lead yet on our fugitive."

"They're promising me later this afternoon or tomorrow at the latest for the results," Cady said. "Not that I've been pushing."

He smiled again. "Push away." Passing the city limits, Ryder pressed on the accelerator. "Sheila Preston's mother thinks she might have confided in her sister."

Interest sounded in Cady's voice. "She's next on our list. We went by Sheila's house and her place of employment again this morning. Talked to a few neighbors, and to some of her coworkers. Didn't learn much."

"Hopefully you'll discover more from the sister than we did from Bush."

"I saw on the updates you found him dead this morning." Her voice was grim. "Aldeen has been a step ahead since he escaped."

"Bush was a loose end. We still might get something from his phone, computer, and financials, but it's going to take a while." The man's phone had been password protected. The search of his house hadn't turned up as much as a bank statement. Most people did their banking online these days. They'd be waiting on the state crime lab to retrieve all the information. "The sooner we track down Preston the better." Ryder's imagination might be working overtime, but he didn't think so. "The ME estimated Bush has been dead thirty-six to forty-eight hours. Preston has been missing for at least as long."

"You think she's dead too?"

"If she isn't now, she still might be in danger. She could have taken off because she knew we could link her to the car Aldeen used to escape. Or . . ."

Cady finished his thought. ". . . she may suspect someone will be coming for her."

A buzz sounded. "I have another call coming in."

"No problem. Miguel and I will head to Mecklenburg."

As Cady hung up, Ryder answered the incoming call. It was Cal again. "Ryder, I won't need to send a copy of that audio file to Rolling Acres Resort after all. I talked to a Dr. Patchett, who's in charge over there, and played him a short clip. He recognized the patient right away, just from the content. Said he'd gone over the progress notes recently, prior to the patient's release. He identified her as Eryn Pullman."

Samuel

Samuel stepped outside his cabin and drew in a breath of fresh air. Most people didn't realize freedom had its own smell, taste, and feel.

It started with sleeping as long as he wanted. Going to bed whenever he pleased. But the ability to move about, circumspectly, unsupervised . . . the wonder of it couldn't be taken for granted.

Not to mention being liberated from the crew at Fristol who attempted nightly missions to whisk him off to a private room to steal blood and tissue samples. Fighting them off had been exhausting. He'd thwarted them by napping during the day in the common room with witnesses all around him and remaining vigilant at night.

He carried a mug of coffee brewed in the small kitchen tucked in one corner of the structure. Sipping from it now, he leaned a shoulder against one of the timbers used as porch posts. It was chilly outside without a jacket, but he didn't mind. He could go in and fetch one. He could go for a hike in the surrounding woods. Although Samuel had never considered himself much of an outdoorsman, the isolation added to his newfound sense of liberation.

His mind felt the clearest it had in years. He'd perfected a way to dispense with the mandatory meds in Fristol, but his method hadn't been foolproof. The enemy had watched him so closely. They knew the medication weakened his ability to see through their disguises and ward them off effectively.

He brought the mug to his lips and sipped, then froze. The breeze carried a distant noise on its wings. Lyrical and sweet. He strained to hear it more clearly. And when he did, a warm flush crawled through his body.

Children nearby. *Laughing.*

There was no more precious sound in the world than that of children at play. The music of their laughter warmed something inside him that had been forced into dormancy for too long. A long-suppressed hunger stirred. Wouldn't be denied.

He abruptly turned and reentered the cabin, setting down his mug and grabbing the lightweight jacket from a peg inside the door. Then he exited again and started walking in the direction of those sounds.

Cady

Cady's cell rang as they were approaching the Asheville city limits. Seeing Ryder's number on the screen, she answered with a slight frown. "I'm beginning to think I have a stalker," she joked. Miguel sent her a quizzical look from the passenger seat.

"Where are you?" he asked without preamble.

"About fifteen minutes from the office. We're stopping in there briefly before heading to Mecklenburg." They needed to make a courtesy contact to the Charlotte USMS office to let them know she and Miguel had a case in the area. Or better yet, they could talk Allen Gant into making it for them.

"We just ID'd the patient on Aldeen's audio files," Ryder said tersely. "Eryn Pullman, recently released from the Rolling Acres Resort, where she'd been treated since she killed her mother at age nine."

Cady's fingers clenched once on the steering wheel, a single involuntary response. "How old is she now?"

"Twenty-one. Her home is close to the eastern Haywood County border." He rattled off the address. "I'll be sending some men to search the property. It's several hundred acres. But I'm just walking into the task force meeting and can't get there myself right now."

"Sounds like we're close enough to swing by," she said immediately, noticing Miguel's *what-the-hell* gesture. "Any known connection between Aldeen and Pullman?"

"Not that I'm aware of."

She nodded, wincing a little as Miguel reached forward to turn up the temperature in the vehicle. "We'll find out."

"I appreciate it. She lives with her uncle and his family. I'll call William Pullman and let him know you'll be coming by and why."

When the call ended, Cady filled in Miguel about the conversation. He immediately straightened in his seat. "How does Talbot think the fugitive and this girl are linked?"

"He doesn't know. That's what we're going to find out." Julie Preston Neve could wait another couple of hours. Cady swung onto the exit that would take them west. Toward the young woman who might be their strongest connection yet to Aldeen.

And one whose past had more than a little in common with Cady's.

◆ ◆ ◆

They turned through the open wrought-iron gates of the Pullman Estate and continued up the drive. It was several more minutes before the home came into view. Miguel craned his neck to look out the window. "Not exactly the Biltmore, but not too shabby. I think my entire house would fit inside the garage."

Silently Cady agreed. The place was massive. According to Ryder, the property was comprised of several hundred acres. Was money the reason Aldeen was interested in Eryn Pullman? Kidnap and ransom would be powerful motivators to those with a criminal bent. She said as much to Miguel as she slowed to a stop in front of the house.

"Kidnapping is in his history," the man agreed. "Ransom isn't. Neither is an interest in victims over the age of eight."

"Well, Joe Bush might be Aldeen's first adult homicide victim," she responded as she parked and grabbed the case file off the console. They got out of the car and headed toward the home's entrance. "He appears to be broadening his horizons."

The front door opened, framing an unsmiling middle-aged man who watched their approach. "Mr. Pullman?" Cady walked up the tiled steps and stretched out her hand. "Cady Maddix and Miguel Rodriguez. Deputy US Marshals. I believe Sheriff Talbot called to let you know we were coming."

His handshake was unenthusiastic. "He did. I still can't wrap my head around his news. I have no idea how a depraved criminal could be in possession of my niece's therapy notes. But I can assure you we have nothing to add to your investigation."

"Do you mind if we come in, sir, and discuss this a little further?" Miguel's smile had noticeably less effect on Pullman than it had had on Selma Lewis's neighbor yesterday. The man seemed to be weighing his options. After a moment, however, he stepped aside and waved them in.

"We won't take up much of your time," Cady promised, surveying her surroundings as she trailed behind him. The sprawling estate was easily ten thousand square feet, with passages spoking off from the main hallway to parts unknown. The hall they were in could pass for a room itself, with carved tables and pairs of chairs dotting the area. Gilt-framed, dark oil paintings punctuated the walls. The overall impression was not so much antique as dated.

That perception wasn't altered when she entered a room adorned with heads of animals and trophy-size fish. She took a brief moment to wonder whether Pullman ever got the creeps from all those vacant glass eyes looking down on him. When he motioned them to chairs in front of his desk, she was hard-pressed not to look up at the row of sentries above.

Rather than sitting down, Cady opened the file and selected two photos, stepping forward to set them on the desk Pullman had seated himself behind. "Samuel Aldeen and Sheila Preston. Do you recognize either of these people?"

William Pullman studied them in turn. With a note of relief in his voice, he said, "No. I've never seen either of them before. I assume the male is the man Sheriff Talbot called about."

"Yes," Cady affirmed. "Preston is wanted in connection with Aldeen's escape."

William's gaze met hers. "She assisted in it?"

"We believe so, yes."

Collecting the two pictures, William handed them back to her. "I'd never heard of either of them before Sheriff Talbot called earlier. Well . . . ," he corrected himself as Cady took the images and sat in a chair next to Miguel, "he only mentioned Aldeen. Of course I've heard the news reports since his escape. But I can honestly say there is nothing connecting either of these people to my family."

"Except for your niece's progress notes being in an audio file on Aldeen's MP3 player," Miguel put in.

"I can't begin to predict how the man's mind works, but given the man's perverted proclivities, I'm sure any child would do."

Cady inclined her head. "That's possible. Obviously someone stole the computer files for him and made copies, adding text-to-speech. But we can't overlook the possibility that Eryn was selected specifically. Maybe she would have an idea why. May we speak to her?"

"No," he stated baldly. "You may not. She's had a traumatic day. We all have. A group has been harassing us since Eryn got home. Today they burned an effigy in her likeness across the road. Sheriff Talbot can give you the details. I assume you've heard about the tragedy here over eleven years ago." He barely waited for Cady's nod before going on. "She was nine when she was court-ordered to a forensic psychiatric facility, and she's recently returned home. The only people she met were employees and patients there."

"I'm sure they had outings," Miguel said patiently. "Or perhaps when she was a child . . ."

A young woman appeared in the doorway. "Uncle Bill, Rosalyn asked me to bring you your . . ." Her voice trailed off as her gaze skated from Cady to Miguel. "I didn't know you had guests."

This had to be Eryn Pullman. Unconsciously, Cady rose and took a step toward the young woman. With long blonde hair and a slender figure, she had an ethereal air about her. For the first time, she gave credence to William's protectiveness. Maybe the girl was too mentally fragile to speak with them.

"Are you with the fire department?" Eryn asked curiously as she crossed to hand her uncle his phone.

"No. Eryn, these are deputy US marshals." There was a note of resignation in William Pullman's voice as he slipped his cell into his pocket.

"I'm Cady and this is Miguel. We came to ask your uncle—and you—a few questions." Cady went to her chair and picked up the file folder she'd brought in. When she glanced at William, he definitely didn't look happy, but he didn't object. Reaching inside the folder, she brought out the same two photos she'd shown William earlier and crossed over to show them to Eryn. The young woman took each of them out of Cady's hands and studied them intently before looking up at Cady again.

"Who are they?"

A band of disappointment tightened in Cady's belly. "Samuel Aldeen and Sheila Preston." There was no answering recognition on Eryn's face when she handed the pictures back to Cady.

"Why did you want to talk to us about them?"

"Aldeen escaped from custody a few days ago." Cady chose her words carefully. "Preston helped him. He had copies of your progress notes on an audio file. We're trying to figure out why."

The young woman looked more puzzled than shocked at the revelation. "I can't imagine why anyone would want them." Her tone went wry. "Believe me, the sessions were boring enough to take part in. Even I wouldn't listen to those recordings."

A measure of tension seeped from Cady's muscles. The girl didn't seem as fragile as she'd first appeared. "Maybe he's someone from your childhood. A family friend, perhaps."

Eryn looked doubtful. "I don't know. I was born in Charlotte, but Mama and I moved here when I was about three. And I don't ever remember her bringing anyone to the house. She always went to the city to meet friends."

Feeling a bit deflated, Cady managed a smile. "What was your mother's name?"

"Aurora Pullman." The note of finality in William's voice said better than words that the discussion was at an end.

"Thank you both for speaking with us." She glanced back at William. "I'm sure Sheriff Talbot discussed his security plans with you?"

"Yes." The brevity of the man's answer left her with no doubt he didn't want to discuss it any further in front of his niece.

When Miguel rose, the two of them left the room. Cady was surprised when Eryn accompanied them to the door.

"This is a huge home," Cady remarked as they retraced their steps down the long, dimly lit hallway. "Do you ever get lost in it?"

"I've never been in most of it," the young woman surprised her by saying. "There's an entire wing not in use anymore. And the farthest I ever went outside was the gazebo, the gardens, and the pond. And the stables, but once was enough. My cousin traumatized me when I was a kid by locking me in a small room in the back. I'm not a fan of small, damp, enclosed places."

Her words had Cady's steps faltering. *I reckon you'll lose some of that sass after a little time alone.* The sound of her grandfather's tread on the stairs. The slam of the door. The shooting of the lock. And the darkness enclosing her like a gritty, frigid fist . . .

". . . suppose I should be embarrassed to admit that now that I'm grown."

"Not at all." Cady shook off the memory and looked the younger woman in the eye. "I feel exactly the same way."

◆ ◆ ◆

"Eryn said she was born in Charlotte." Miguel broke the long silence that had stretched between them for the last hour of their drive to Mecklenburg. "Where was the restaurant Aldeen supposedly worked at with Preston?"

"Charlotte," Cady responded. She should have been thinking about Eryn Pullman's connection to Samuel Aldeen as well. But her thoughts kept returning to the odd parallels between the young woman's past and her own. Both of them had killed a parent. A hideous, tragic event in anyone's past. Each had grown up without loved ones near. Eryn had been locked away in a mental health facility. Cady had been imprisoned with a bitter old man.

"So maybe the connection is really between Aldeen and Eryn's mother."

Cady nodded. Miguel was right. "We need to dig further into Aurora Pullman's past. But first . . ." She slowed to a stop in front of Julie Preston Neve's home. The neighborhood was several income levels above her sister's. Cady surveyed the house as she and Miguel exited the vehicle. Large lawn, four-stall garage. The dwelling would swallow up three of Sheila's with room to spare.

There were no signs of life around the place as they walked up a bricked path to the front porch, past a discreet sign warning guests the house was protected by a security company.

The sign was an unwelcome reminder of last night. "What do you think a security system costs?" She'd never had reason to buy one before. Her home in Saint Louis had already had one installed when she bought it. Cady had done a little research before leaving for work this morning, but the sites she'd looked at required phone calls and visits for quotes.

"Installed? Several hundred dollars, I'd guess."

Her partner pressed the doorbell. Melodic notes sounded in the home. "They have ones now with a video option. It automatically calls you if there's a disturbance."

Video. She mulled the idea over as they waited. Maybe she could rig up something above the window the intruder had used at her house. At least she could capture an image if the bastard came back. But the price Miguel had quoted had her balking at installing a complete system. It seemed a waste for a rental and enough of an expense to strain her budget at the moment. She had the monthly payment on her house in Saint Louis that still hadn't sold, as well as the stipend she was paying Alma for groceries.

"Of course, you could go the simpler route and do what I did." Miguel reached out a hand to ring the bell again. "Get a dog."

The thought wouldn't have occurred to her. She knew nothing about caring for a pet. She worked long hours. It didn't seem fair to have an animal around.

But it appeared her options were limited.

A slight noise sounded. Cady cocked her head, looked at her partner. She could tell from his expression he'd heard it too. Not of approaching footsteps. But perhaps the scrape of a shoe on the other side of the door.

"Ms. Neve," she called. "We're from the Marshals Service. It's critical we speak with you about your sister."

The ensuing silence held a hint of eeriness. Cady couldn't shake the feeling they were being watched. Looking around, she spotted a small camera discreetly located above the door. She pointed it out for her partner while she said, "She may be in danger, ma'am."

Miguel shifted subtly so that he was positioned more fully in front of the camera. "Ms. Neve, you wouldn't want it on your conscience if something happened to Sheila and you didn't try to help her. We're not going anywhere. If you don't talk to us now, we'll be waiting at the curb for your husband to come home in a few hours. I imagine you want to handle this discreetly."

Maybe it was fear of the neighbors observing them. Perhaps they'd struck a nerve in the woman. More likely it had been the mask of sincerity stamped on Rodriguez's too-handsome face. Whatever the cause, a moment later the heavy cherry door swung inward and an expensively coifed and clothed woman in her midforties stood before them.

"I have nothing to say to you." Her fingers clutched the necklace she wore and twisted it, an outward sign of distress at odds with the dispassionate mask on her face. "You need to leave. You're causing a disturbance."

"We have a warrant for Sheila's arrest, and you're aiding and abetting her." Cady's voice wasn't without sympathy. If she had a sibling, she'd probably go to similar lengths to help. "Your sister could be in grave danger right now. The longer you keep her from us, the greater the chance the wrong person is going to get to her first." It might have been an overstatement. They had no specific knowledge Aldeen would go after Sheila Preston. But one accessory to the fugitive's escape was already dead. It wasn't beyond the realm of possibility Preston could be next.

"Aunt Julie! Aunt Julie!" The childish voices sounded in unison. Small running feet could be heard in the tiled hallway. "Sydney cheated! Come and see! She moved your piece and . . ."

Julie Neve turned her head to address the kids—two girls, Cady saw now—and when she did her voice was bright with false cheer. "Sydney!

Am I going to have to get the tickle monster after you? Go on, back to the game and I'll get some cookies for all of us."

"Yay!" As quickly as the duo had approached, they vanished. Julie watched them go and then faced Cady and Miguel, opening the outer glass door and stepping out onto the porch.

"Sheila's terrified." The woman's voice was low, her words coming quickly. "She showed up on my doorstep three days ago with Sydney and Selah in tow. I don't know what she's gotten herself into, but she's frightened someone is going to hurt the kids. She was paranoid, thinking she was being watched. She dropped the girls off—I didn't have much choice but to take them. I've never seen her so scared."

"Where did she go?"

The other woman shook her head. "I asked, but she wouldn't say. I'm not sure she even had a plan. She said something about staying safe until he was caught." Julie's mouth quivered before she firmed it. "I don't know who *he* is. She wasn't making much sense. I thought at first she was talking about her ex, but he hasn't been in the picture for a couple of years. He went to Texas the last I heard and doesn't send money. Doesn't talk to the kids."

"And his name?"

"Dennis Fastbinder. They never got married. Not a bad guy, at least so I thought at first. But no ambition and not an especially great dad, even before he took off. Lousy boyfriend too." Her fingers never stopped fidgeting with the necklace. "So I guess I'm not such a great judge. I wanted him to turn out okay. I wanted Sheila, for once, to catch a break."

Maybe Fastbinder was the mysterious Raymond who had been living in Selma Lewis's house. Cady made a mental note to run a background check on the man.

"Where would she go, ma'am?" Julie Neve's attention shifted to Miguel. "If she's that frightened, she probably has reason to be. You have to help us get to her before someone else does."

"I don't know!" Julie's eyes glistened with tears. "I think she'd want to hide . . . from whatever or whomever she feared. But she isn't answering my phone calls. They go straight to voice mail. I've been going out of my mind with worry."

For good reason, Cady thought. Because it was looking more and more likely the woman was in just as much danger as they'd feared. "What was she driving when she dropped the kids off?"

"Her car." Julie blinked away the tears and straightened, as if her spine had been reforged with strength. "A 2012 silver Prius. We helped her buy it. She needed something reliable and gas efficient. She's paying us back. She's never missed a payment. Sheila's made some dumb decisions in her life, but since the kids . . . she's really changed. She's tried so hard . . ."

A Prius. That was the vehicle listed under her name when they'd run the check, Cady recalled, sliding a glance at Miguel. The one they'd gotten local law enforcement to run a BOLO on, with no results as yet.

"What about Sheila's friends? Is there anyone she'd call for help?"

Julie was shaking her head before Cady finished the question. "The people she ran around with back in the day . . . she's avoided them since her arrest for drugs. She's never mentioned anyone since then. I mean, first she was head over heels for Dennis. A woman sometimes neglects friends when a man's involved. I think she just sort of kept to herself after he left. She's focused on providing for her girls. It's not easy, being a single mom."

"Can you think of a place she would have known? Maybe one you went to as kids. Or one she'd visited and spoke to you about?"

Julie considered for a moment and then shook her head. "Not really. We never vacationed much when we were young . . . Oh!" Her face brightened. "There was a spot we went once. My dad was a gambler. Not a great provider most of the time, but one time he won several thousand dollars. He was talking big about taking us all on this great vacation. We got there and it wasn't nearly as wonderful as he'd made it out to be. But we were kids, right? First time ever away from home. There was a pool with a slide and a big playground. We stayed for a weekend and had a blast." She fell silent for a moment. "I don't even know if it's still there. The Freebird Motel, in Charlotte. It was my only time in the city until my twenties, believe it or not."

"When did Sheila say she'd be back for the kids?" Miguel asked.

"I know she has a week off from work, but I'm not sure when it ends." Her hand dropped to her side, as if she became belatedly aware of the death grip she had on her necklace. "She was indefinite. A few days, she said."

"Thank you for your time, Mrs. Neve," Cady said, digging in her pocket to come up with a card to hand to the woman. "If Sheila calls, please give her the number on the bottom there. We can assist her. Convince her to call us."

Julie Neve stared at the card as if memorizing it. "I will. I promise I will." Her gaze rose. "But I don't know if she'll contact me. You need to find her. You need to be sure she's safe. I . . . I gave her cash. Five hundred dollars. It won't last long. I'm scared for her. Now more than ever."

"We'll do our best, ma'am." This from Miguel, delivered in his best "trust me" somber tones.

As they walked down the steps and toward their vehicle at the curb, Cady muttered, "I'm getting less and less certain we can get to Preston before someone else does."

"We might be the ones she's running from," Miguel pointed out. "Maybe she's just avoiding arrest. She had to have known she'd be caught on camera delivering that car to Aldeen." He rounded the car to get into the driver's seat.

"What are you doing? My day to drive, remember?" Cady had learned early she had to maintain clear ground rules with the man. "It's your turn to overheat the car and choose crummy music channels."

He gave her a look of exaggerated patience. "True. But if we're tracking Preston around the city, you're better at it than I am."

"That sounds suspiciously like a cop-out."

His smile was beatific. "It does. It also happens to be true."

Disgruntled, Cady tossed him the keys and climbed in the passenger seat. Buckling her seat belt, she resumed their earlier conversation. "She could be running from the law. It's equally possible Aldeen, or maybe even his buddy Raymond, is after her. Joe Bush proved Aldeen doesn't believe in loose ends. Disappearing might have been the smartest thing the woman ever did. At least it buys her some time."

"Until what?" Miguel started the vehicle. "She has to know she can't hide forever. What's she hoping might change in the next few days?"

"Guess we'll ask her when we see her."

Because nothing in their job was ever easy, there was no listing for the Freebird in Charlotte. With a little digging, Cady found the address where the business used to exist. They decided to head there anyway. *It's doubtful Preston would remember how to find the place,* Cady thought as she began making a list of cheap motels in the Charlotte metro area. The woman would have been too young when she'd gone there. But she'd also lived in Charlotte for a time, according to the background check Fristol security had done on her. She could have grown familiar with the city then. Meaning there could be other places in the area she might run to.

"What's that?" Miguel took his eyes off the road long enough to peer at the notes she was taking on her phone.

"A depressingly long list of dive motels in the Charlotte metro area. We know Sheila Preston worked at a place called Cisco's with Aldeen about twenty-three years ago." She did a quick check and discovered the place was still in business. "We have her former address when she was living here, also courtesy of the background check. So I say we get a city map and make a grid around the addresses of her home and work, looking at cheap motels in the area."

"As good an idea as any. We should try Cisco's as well. Maybe someone's still there who would remember her."

The possibility was no less remote than the chance of finding a single woman in a city of eight hundred thousand. Cady released her seat belt and reached over the seat for the briefcase holding the laptop and printer. When she'd settled it on her lap and resecured her belt, she turned on the computer and, finding the same city map she'd brought up on her phone, proceeded to print it and mark the motels she'd found.

Thirty minutes later Miguel's words had her lifting her head from her task. "This is it. Or rather, the spot the Freebird used to sit on."

Cady looked out the window at the place he was indicating. A small strip mall sat in place of the motel, with a nail salon, chiropractor, Chinese restaurant, and bedding store taking up the storefronts. "Okay. The place Preston used to live at is about ten miles from here. Cisco's is two miles from her former residence. We'll check all the motel addresses between here and there and then concentrate on those in the vicinity of where she resided and worked."

"How many is that?"

"Believe me, you don't want to know."

"All right," he grumbled. "But if I see a sandwich place along the way, I'm pulling in. Unlike you, I need regular meals."

Cady was well aware of the fact. Miguel's temperament was usually sunny to a fault. Deprived of food, however, it notched down to hangry in a heartbeat.

They hit five motels on her list in the next hour. For each they did a slow drive through the parking lots, looking for Preston's car. After striking out at all five, they grabbed a quick bite before starting again. They were getting closer to the grid she'd drawn around Preston's former stomping grounds.

"Seems to me she'd seek isolation. Maybe something on the outskirts of town."

"Perhaps. But if it were me, worried someone is on my trail, I'd figure they have a description of my vehicle. So I'd find a place out of sight. Which meant I'd need restaurants nearby I could walk to. More than one. So people wouldn't remember me."

"Because you have a devious mind."

"Part of my charm." Cady directed him to the next address. Their progress was hampered because pedestrian traffic was heavy as they got closer to the heart of the city. Miguel pulled in to the address she'd given him, and they did a slow roll by the cars in the lot. The rooms were situated in an L shape, the office fronting the longest section. An alley adjoined the back of the lot, behind the shortest chain of rooms. Seeing nothing in the parking area, Miguel turned into the alley and then cursed as untrimmed denuded branches of thick brush scraped at the Jeep on both sides. He stopped. Prepared to reverse.

Cady leaned forward abruptly. "Wait. Keep going."

"Not a chance. The only things back here are thickets and brambles."

"There's another parking lot behind those bushes on the other side of the alley. And I see a glimpse of silver."

He swung the car into a wider arc to inch along the passageway. "Yeah, okay." He was craning his neck as they drew closer. "Of course, there're thousands of silver vehicles in the city."

Cady was already unbuckled and set the briefcase at her feet before she unlatched the door. "I'll check."

She jumped out and walked closer to the overgrown brush. Dropping to her hands and knees, she grasped some branches and pulled them apart to make a space she could see through. There. Right there. She squinted at the Prius's license plate. It was a match for Sheila Preston's. She backed out, one arm raised to shield her face until she was out of reach of the brambles.

Miguel was rounding the hood to join her. "It's hers." Cady allayed his question. She looked over the surroundings carefully. The motel lot had been hemmed on both sides by an office building and a cell phone store.

Instead of parking her vehicle in the motel lot, Preston had hidden it in the one across the alley behind more bushes. That area was likely used by the two old brick businesses flanking it. She walked a little farther down the alleyway. There was another access connecting the alley to the street in front of the motel. Other than these two entrances, one would have to go to either end of the block and around to turn into the passageway.

"Let's check inside at the desk," Miguel suggested. They both got in the Jeep. They had a warrant for Preston, so whoever was on duty would be compelled to answer their questions about the woman. *But,* Cady thought as her partner did a slow retreat down the alley before turning into the motel lot again, *it'd be better if one of us was stationed outside, keeping the rooms and lot in view.*

This close to the woman, Cady wasn't about to take the chance of letting her slip away.

She let Miguel go into the office while she positioned herself outside their vehicle. Ten minutes later, he was out again and heading to their car.

"She didn't sign in under her own name, but the clerk recognized the picture I showed him," he said when he drew even with her. "She registered as Stella Pappas. He tried to claim the motel doesn't have a policy about needing a credit card to ensure against damages. I figure he's lying. Maybe Preston gave him money or something else to avoid showing a card. The clerk said she's in one of these back rooms and has been for two days."

They both got in the vehicle and prepared to wait. Although surveillance wasn't Cady's favorite part of the job, a thread of adrenaline unfurled along her spine. They were close. And there was no way they weren't going to take Preston down soon. Whatever the wait, it would be worth it.

As it turned out, the delay wasn't as long as it could have been. It was no more than fifteen minutes before Miguel murmured, "Here she comes."

Cady's head snapped up. Sheila Preston, wearing sunglasses, a hoodie, and jeans, was dodging traffic as she hurried across the street from a fast-food restaurant. She was headed for the lot where they waited.

Cady straightened, never taking her eyes off the woman. Even with the hood up, her face down, it was easy to be certain of Preston's identity.

Neither Cady nor Miguel moved. She was certain of it. But when the woman reached the sidewalk in front of the parking lot, she raised her head sharply. Pausing, she surveyed the cars in the lot. Then she abruptly turned toward the office. Began walking rapidly.

Cady and Miguel jumped out of the Jeep. "Take the access to the alley on the right. I'll go left. She's headed toward her vehicle." She tossed the words over her shoulder as she began to run. Miguel began jogging after the woman. Cady raced toward the entrance to the alley they had vacated only a short time ago.

She reached the short section of motel rooms and rounded it too quickly, getting caught on the needlelike branches of the brush lining the back of the rooms. Cady pulled violently away. Heard the rip of fabric. She could already see Preston emerging from the opposite entrance and sprinting toward the car in the lot behind the motel. Yanking herself free, Cady ran in the same direction. "Sheila Preston, stop! Deputy US—"

The rest of her words were lost as an explosion ripped through the air, a smoke-capped fireball mushrooming toward the sky. The blast lifted Cady off her feet, hurtling her backward until her body slammed into something solid. She was dimly aware of debris raining down on her. Then everything went black.

◆ ◆ ◆

"You decent?"

"Yeah." Cady reached for her jacket. She gingerly pulled it on over the T-shirt one of the ER nurses had found for her. The curtain around her cubicle was pulled aside and Miguel appeared, accompanied this time with Allen Gant. Twin gazes bored into her.

"Jesus, don't get up." Allen sprang to her side as Cady cautiously slid off the side of the hospital bed and stood, taking mental inventory.

"I'm fine. You didn't need to make the drive over here." A bit woozy, she tried and failed to zip her coat. It took a moment to realize there was no longer a zipper in it. The muscles in her legs and back were screaming. A troop of demented drummers had taken up residence in her head. But she was upright. And alive. She didn't have to be told she'd been damn lucky.

"I said earlier I hoped she felt a helluva lot better than she looks. She assured me she did."

Cady directed a glare at Miguel with the eye that wasn't swelled shut. The single gauze bandage on his forehead somehow managed to look rakish. A reward for being a slower runner than either Cady or Sheila Preston.

"Shit, Cady." Allen sounded horrified. "You look like hell."

"And here I dressed up for you." She'd taken one look in the mirror an hour ago and didn't figure her appearance had improved in the intervening time. "It looks worse than it is, which is why I'm being released. Any change on Preston?"

Miguel shook his head. "The doctor said it could be days before we can interview her. But she's out of surgery, and they're cautiously optimistic she'll recover. She was a lot closer to the vehicle than you were, so she has burns they're dealing with as well."

"The CMPD bomb squad won't have answers for us for a few days, either," Allen said. "But preliminary details validate Miguel's and your guess. There was some sort of incendiary device wired to the vehicle."

"I told the detective who came to talk to me Preston never touched the car," Miguel said. "She didn't get close enough to it."

"That means a remote trigger," Cady murmured. It was tempting to reach out to steady herself by laying a hand on the bed's side rails. She refrained. She wouldn't show weakness in front of her supervisor. He'd mother hen her into taking sick leave. She wasn't going to. Now, more than ever, they had to redouble their efforts on this case. "Preston had been at the motel for two days. If the bomb was on a timer, he wouldn't have waited long to detonate it. Which means the person responsible was out there somewhere watching the vehicle, waiting for Preston to get near it." Maybe he was overeager if he'd been out there for two long days and nights. That would explain why he prematurely detonated the bomb before Preston actually got in the vehicle. The woman wouldn't have survived if he'd waited a minute longer.

"CMPD isn't ready to publicly call it a bomb before their investigation is complete." Allen raised a hand to stem Miguel's and Cady's words. "Privately, the bomb squad commander says your assessment is plausible. But bottom line is, they're in charge of that investigation. They did agree with your suggestion to post a guard outside Preston's door. You contacted her family?"

Cady nodded. Her supervisor pulled something from inside his wool coat. A file folder. "In the meantime, we got a name from the latents lifted off the doorknob and phone receiver inside Selma Lewis's house. David Sutton, last known address in Greensboro."

"Since you got a hit I'm assuming he has a sheet." Surreptitiously, Cady shifted until her back was against the bed rail. She was less steady than she wanted to admit, but that could have been from whatever they'd shot her up with prior to the stitches in half a dozen places. Or from the jackhammering in her temples.

"He does, indeed. Two arrests for aggravated assault. He received ten years for possession with intent and served eight. He was released almost two years ago."

Allen handed her the folder and she flipped it open. Miguel crowded to her side to look. The mug shot images of Sutton showed an attractive man with dark hair and a one-inch scar on his cheek. The report beneath the pictures identified Sutton as thirty-six years old, six foot two inches, with blue eyes. "His last known address was from six months after his release," she noted.

"We'll start diving into his background. Family and acquaintances. In the meantime, I don't want to see either of you at work tomorrow."

"Hey!" Miguel's objection drowned out Cady's. "I'm fine. A few scratches."

"And the doctor told me I was okay to return to work," she put in. She didn't bother to share the ER doctor's acquiescence had come only after a prolonged argument.

But Allen was going to be a lot harder to convince. The man pointed at Miguel. "I don't want you at the office before noon." He turned to Cady. "If I see you before the day after tomorrow, I'll have you escorted out of the office." He stemmed her protest with one upraised hand. "Making forcible contact with a twelve-foot wooden fence in a torrent of debris at least constitutes the need for one day of rest."

"I could stay in the office. Research Sutton."

"We'll take care of it. Final word, Cady."

The subtle nudge from Miguel was meant as a warning. Releasing a sigh, she subsided. It'd probably be wise to see just how she felt tomorrow before she got too far ahead of herself. With one suspect in the Aldeen escape dead and another currently occupying a hospital bed in this facility, Cady was anxious to get a handle on David Sutton. He might be another accomplice in the escape. Someone had to have hacked Lewis's phone line. And his prints on her phone receiver made him the likely culprit.

Despite her brave words to Gant, Cady was fairly certain she was going to collapse as soon as she reached home. She used the commute to call her landlady. Dorothy Blong was in her midseventies, a perennial ray of cheer whom Cady usually enjoyed for short durations. When she reached the woman, Dorothy regaled her with a rundown of her day, the properties she'd shown, the houses she'd had to clean, and the lovely substitute postman she'd met. The moment Dorothy paused to take a breath, Cady said, "The reason I'm calling is because I'm wondering if you have a policy about pets." If there'd been one included in the contract, Cady couldn't recall it.

"No-o-o," the older woman said. "Not specifically. You do have a wonderful fenced-in property, and it would be perfect for a dog. Any damage incurred by a pet would, of course, be deducted from your deposit."

Cady's mouth quirked up. The woman was getting on in years, but she was a masterful businessperson. "Of course. I don't recall seeing gates for the fence."

"Oh, I'll deliver those tomorrow. I still have them in the shed. The last tenant didn't want to bother with them."

If they were in as poor condition as the rest of the fence, Cady could imagine why. The rusty expanse consisted of three-inch square holes and equally corroded posts. Tomorrow she'd check it for sturdiness, since she was going to have some time on her hands.

"I'm glad you called. I've been contacting all my tenants, but I hadn't worked my way to you yet."

Cady steered the car to hug the other side of the road when she met a semi pulling an extrawide load. "Is there a problem?"

She could picture the woman on the other end, a cloud of soft-looking white hair fluffed around her round face, fluttering a hand as she responded. "Much to-do about nothing, I'm sure, but I had a break-in the other day. Kids, probably, and oh, what a mess they made of my office! Why, I was all day cleaning up and talking to the police. They broke into my desk and filing cabinets . . . even the case I keep the spare keys in. Scattered things all over the room. I still haven't found all of them."

A chill worked over Cady's skin. "What night was that?"

"Saturday evening. Or rather, early Sunday morning. The police discovered it and called me to come look. I apologize, dear, for not letting you know sooner. I had to make a list for what's broken or missing. The nice policeman who came said a lot of businesses were being burglarized, and it might be someone looking for drugs. Can you imagine me, having drugs at the office?" The thought apparently flabbergasted Dorothy more than the break-in itself.

"I'm going to call a locksmith tomorrow," Cady said. It was clear now how her intruder had gotten inside her house. She weighed whether to tell the woman the story. Decided against it. Dorothy would blame herself, and there was nothing to be gained in the telling. Whoever had lifted the keys had more than burglary in mind when entering Cady's home. Her mind flashed to the window that had been left unsecured. He—or she—had left themselves an entry should she change the locks.

"Oh well . . . whatever you think, dear. That's why I'm letting everyone know, so they can make the decision for themselves." She prattled on for a few more minutes, but Cady was no longer listening.

The break-in at Dorothy's office could be exactly what the policeman had called it—a person looking for drugs.

It also could be someone who'd gone to a lot of trouble to target Cady directly.

She'd go to some lengths, as well, to arrange a few surprises for her wannabe stalker.

◆ ◆ ◆

Relieved to finally be home, she gingerly reached under her seat for the Maglite she kept there and got out of the car. The simple movements took far more effort than they should have. Cady wondered how easily she'd be moving tomorrow. Flipping on the light, she drew her weapon and did a perimeter search of the house, spending a few minutes at the back window looking for signs her intruder had returned.

She saw nothing out of place. At least, not until she headed to the front again. Rounding the back corner of the house, she caught sight of a beam, smaller than hers, heading toward her. "Hands in the air!" she shouted, shifting her light to the figure's face. "In the air! Now!"

"Cady, it's me. Gabe."

She recognized his voice at approximately the same time she'd identified him with the aid of her Maglite. Irritation worked through her. "Sneaking around outside someone's house is a good way to get shot."

"When I pulled in, I saw your light going around the house. Figured you might have a trespasser and . . . good God. What happened to your face?"

This explanation is going to be a fun icebreaker for the next several days, she thought sourly as she holstered her weapon. "Car explosion. Not mine. It belonged to a person of interest. I'm fine. It looks worse than it is."

"It looks pretty damn bad," he said as they walked toward the front porch, with its lone security light ablaze. "Now I know why you didn't answer any of my phone messages."

"Sorry." She juggled the flashlight to another hand so she could search for her keys in the pocket of her ruined jacket. "I turned it off in the hospital, and when I got released I made a call but didn't think to check for messages." The pounding in her skull was interfering with her thought processes. She unlocked the door and reached inside to flip on the interior lights before pushing it completely open.

"Easy to see why. I took the chance you might be home." Gabe held up the bag he had in one hand. The barbecue smell emanating from it had Cady's stomach churning. "Ribs." He frowned as he got a look at her in the light, but to his credit, he said no more about her appearance.

"Much as I wish otherwise, I'm not sure I can eat. Too many painkillers on an empty stomach."

He set the bag on the counter. "I puke my guts out when they shoot me full of that stuff." A grin crossed his face. "Doesn't dampen my appetite, though." He opened her cupboards to search for dishes. Cady was slightly ashamed at the relief she felt when he withdrew only one plate. Then he took containers from the bag and dished up some food with the plastic silverware included with the order. "If you can't eat tonight—and you look pretty dead on your feet—this will keep for tomorrow. Did they put you on mandatory leave?"

"Only for a day." She took off what was left of her jacket and surveyed it. The back fabric was half torn away, revealing the lining beneath. One sleeve was just as shredded, and the tears and stains on the rest of the coat didn't bear close study. Her pants were in similar shape. Her boots, she noted, looked no worse for wear.

She stuffed the coat in the waste can. When she turned around, Gabe was rewrapping the rest of the food and putting it back in the bag.

"Were there any other injuries?"

"The suspect we were chasing is in bad shape. Some people were injured from the nearby motel. They're all still hospitalized. Miguel's guardian angel worked overtime to ensure he suffered only scratches."

Gabe grinned. He knew her partner too. Cady hitched a hip on the opposite counter and concentrated on remaining upright.

"You need to get on better terms with your guardian angel."

"I think mine gave up long ago." *Or maybe,* she thought, *one only gets so many lives.* And she'd used most of them on the warrant that had gone south in Saint Louis. Many marshals went their entire careers and never discharged their weapon. She hadn't been as lucky. But she'd walked away from that incident too. Maybe she had a celestial being looking over her after all.

Gabe seemed to take an inordinate amount of time refolding the top of the bag. When he spoke, there was an unfamiliar glint in his gray eyes. "I'm glad you're okay. I came by tonight because I didn't want to leave things weird. I didn't mean anything when I mentioned exchanging keys. Just thinking of convenience. This thing between us . . . keep it casual, right?"

"Right." Although she was discomfited with the conversation, her gaze never left his. "That's all I'm up for."

"Okay." His piece said, he picked up the bag and headed to the door. "Get some sleep. You probably know tomorrow you're going to be feeling muscles you didn't know you had."

"I'm feeling them already," she admitted as she pushed away from the counter and followed him to the door. "Thanks for the food."

He gave her a half grin over his shoulder. "Thanks for not shooting me."

"I get that a lot."

He laughed but was already on his way out the door. He was probably as anxious as she was to put this conversation behind him. "Let me know how you're doing, okay?"

"I will." She locked the door after he exited, wondering if he'd heard the lie in her promise. Something inside her had started backpedaling the moment he'd hinted at taking their relationship to a different level. She recognized the need to put distance between them, even if she couldn't identify where that need stemmed from. Her system was doing a fast backward shuffle, and she knew she wouldn't be calling Gabe again. Would make excuses if he contacted her.

With one hand on her weapon, she went to the window in the second bedroom and examined it for signs of tampering. The inside was still locked. The pots and pans she'd located beneath it were untouched. Weariness rocked her then, and Cady had to pause a moment for the wave of fatigue to pass. When it did, she collected some glasses from the cupboard and lined them up inside the front door. If her intruder returned before she could get the locks changed, she'd at least be warned if her house was breached.

When she'd finished the task, she placed cellophane over the food Gabe had left and put it in the refrigerator. First a shower and something for the headache. Probably also a change of bandages, which she'd left in the Jeep.

But as Cady walked into her bedroom she experienced a flashback of the moment the bomb had detonated. Until now, she'd deliberately refrained from considering there would be few to mourn her death if things had turned out differently. A mother losing a battle with Alzheimer's. Some colleagues. Precious few people she called friends, because Cady didn't do long-term relationships.

She refused to consider that sad. Her circle was small because she'd chosen to make it so. She'd learned early in life a person could only rely on herself.

Cady sat on the edge of the bed to remove her boots and then made the mistake of stretching out. Just for a moment.

She was asleep in seconds.

Eryn: Then

Eryn opened her bedroom door. It still squeaked, even though she was being super quiet. She stood still in the doorway, waiting for an adult to wake and scold her for getting up in the middle of the night. But no one did. Not even when she snuck down the hallway to the kitchen, past Mary Jane's room. The house was old with a lot of creaks and groans. Eryn knew there were ghosts here too. Mama had said so once, and sometimes, when Eryn was very still, she could hear whispers and rustling of the long-ago people who lived here before.

She wasn't afraid of ghosts. They couldn't hurt anyone. Not like people.

Eryn got a glass out of the cupboard and went to the refrigerator, taking out the milk. She poured herself a glass and sat at the table drinking it. The wind was whistling against the windows. It almost sounded like a girl crying. Almost. When Eryn was finished, she rinsed out the glass and dried it before putting it back in the cupboard. She screwed the cap on the milk and replaced it in the refrigerator. No one would even know she'd been out of bed! Starting back toward her room, she hesitated.

There were ice cream bars in the refrigerator freezer. She'd seen Mary Jane put them there when she came home with the groceries. Without another thought, she snuck back to the freezer and opened it.

A little light came on inside it and she hurried to find the box, open it, and take out a treat.

But she didn't want to eat it in the kitchen. What if someone came in? She scurried to the coat closet by the back door. No one would see her there. Eryn sat in the corner and took her time enjoying the ice cream. She could still hear the ghost crying. But now she could hear words too. *She'll never let us be together.* Maybe it was a kid ghost. Two of her kindergarten classmates had cried and cried when they'd discovered they wouldn't be in the same class for first grade. They'd been so mad at the teacher! Eryn had thought that was dumb. What difference did it make who was in your class? She hadn't liked many of the kids at school. And she didn't miss any of them now that she didn't have to go anymore.

In the next moment, she wondered if the voice was real. Maybe it was Henry begging to live here full-time. The thought made the ice cream turn sour in her mouth. School had been terrible. Having Henry around more would be worse.

But if Uncle Bill knew how bad Henry was, he'd never let him move here for good.

So when she was done, she got up and tucked the ice cream wrapper so it half stuck out of Henry's jacket pocket. And then, smothering her giggle with a hand to her mouth, she hurried back to her room. When Mary Jane saw that someone had snuck an ice cream bar, she'd be on the warpath. And Eryn was betting she'd find that wrapper.

◆ ◆ ◆

"Eryn, I . . ." Mama stood still in the doorway to Eryn's bedroom, her voice turning hard. "Who are you talking to?"

Silently, she motioned to her stuffed bear and doll, seated at the miniature table in the corner of her bedroom. She was supposed to be in the classroom. But she'd gotten tired of reading and waiting for Mama to come start art class, so she gave herself recess.

Mama came farther into the room, her hands on her hips. "And what are the bear's and doll's names?"

Eryn's mind raced. "Gizmo and . . . Bernadette," she lied. Bernadette had been a girl in Eryn's class before Mama took her out of school this year. She'd been nicer than the other kids. And Eryn hadn't meant to push her down, but she was such a tattletale! After she had, Bernadette hadn't been nice anymore. She hadn't talked to Eryn again.

It was the voices in her head that got her in trouble. Mostly it was Uncle Arlo's fault. He had all the bad ideas, whispering them over and over until sometimes Eryn did things, said things he'd told her to and then got in trouble. Mr. Timmons got mad at him, too, and sometimes shouted at Eryn not to listen to him. They made a racket in her mind, like the echoes when Eryn and Mama went to Lookout Ridge in the Smokies and called out hello.

Mama's pretty face was cross. "You remember what we talked about. You're a big seven-year-old girl. Too old for imaginary playmates."

"I can't play with Gizmo and Bernadette?" Something in Eryn wanted to smile when Mama looked unsure.

"I don't want to hear you talking to yourself. Or to imaginary friends. Or toys. People don't understand that, Eryn. And they don't like things they don't understand."

"Like the gallery didn't understand your paintings."

"You're exactly right." Mama gave Eryn a quick hug. "Sometimes people just aren't clever enough to know what they don't know."

She wasn't sure what that meant, but Mama had stopped being cross, and Eryn hadn't gotten yelled at for not doing her schoolwork. "Is it time for art class yet?"

"We'll have it tomorrow. I just stopped in to tell you I was going to Asheville to meet friends."

This morning Mama had said art class would be this afternoon. *Because she's a liar,* a familiar voice in her head said. *You get in trouble for lying, but she can lie whenever she wants. Lie lie lie.*

"I want to have art today."

"You work on something special to surprise me with, okay?" Mama was already leaving the room. "Then tomorrow we can look at it and talk about how to make your drawing even more special."

Eryn wasn't going to work on her sketches. She wanted art class! Stomping over to the stuffed bear and doll, she threw them back in her toy box. Swept the plastic dishes off the little table and kicked them under her bed. She didn't even care if the noise made Mary Jane come in and get all scoldy-faced and make her pick things up.

But Mary Jane didn't come. Neither did Mama. Eryn threw herself on her bed and listened to the sounds that meant Mama was getting ready. And after a while the front door closed. And things got very quiet.

"What are you doing? Pouting?"

Eryn scrambled off the bed when Henry wandered in the room. Mama said not to listen to him. Not to trust him. She watched him carefully as he went through her room, casually touching her things as if it were okay. Eryn never went in his room and got into his stuff. She never would. She wanted to stay as far away from Henry as possible.

"You're not supposed to be in here." Mama had said so. Eryn didn't know if he'd gotten in trouble for the ice cream bar she'd eaten, but if he had, he'd be mad. He didn't seem to be, but she couldn't tell with him.

"Yeah, well, I'm not supposed to be home, out of school, either, but here I am." He turned and grinned at her. "Got suspended. That's what happens in middle school if you get caught smoking. Think you'll ever get to high school, or are you going to stay home and pretend to be homeschooled for the rest of your life?"

She shrugged. Eryn didn't care if she ever went back to school. "They have dumb rules there."

He laughed loudly. "No doubt." He trailed a hand over her dresser. Picked up a snow globe from it and shook it while he crossed to the window. Hooking a finger in the curtains, he pulled them all the way back. You might think Henry was okay if you didn't know him. He had a nice face. But his eyes were mean sometimes. And *he* was mean a lot of the time.

"I caught a mermaid in the pond yesterday. Did your mama tell you?"

For a moment, Eryn forgot what a liar he was. "You did?"

He looked back at her. "Yeah. It's a baby one. My dad wanted me to let her go, and your mama wanted to paint her. I said I released her, but she's tied up at the end of the dock."

She sat on the edge of the bed and watched him. Henry made things up, like when he told her he'd take her on a boat ride and then locked her in the boathouse. The boathouse wasn't scary. Not like the stable. She'd climbed in the boat and pretended to drive it until he'd come and let her out. Mary Jane had said she didn't know what got into the boy.

But Eryn thought maybe he had an Uncle Arlo and Mr. Timmons fighting in his head too.

"I don't believe you."

He shrugged. "I don't care. Maybe your mama will let you come watch when she paints the mermaid. Or maybe I'll go down to the pond tonight and cut her loose." He tossed the snow globe to her as he left the room. It bounced on the bed beside her. Eryn listened for the sound of footsteps leaving. Sometimes he waited outside her doorway and scared her when she came out.

When she was sure he'd gone, she got off the bed and ran to the window. She could see the boathouse from here, and the dock to the side of it. Henry was probably lying. Eryn had seen *The Little Mermaid*, but she knew mermaids weren't real because the movie had been a cartoon. She wondered now if maybe there were other movies that showed real mermaids.

She watched for a long time, but Henry didn't go down to the dock. Eryn wasn't supposed to, either, but if Mama had cared about her going to the pond, she should have stayed home. Eryn poked her head out of her room and looked down the hallway. When she didn't see anyone, she snuck into Mama's bedroom. It had those double windows Mama painted in front of. On nice nights, she opened them to let the breeze in. Eryn knew, because sometimes she crept in there when Mama was asleep.

She pushed one of the windows open, easy-peasy, and jumped down to the ground. Mary Jane or Uncle Bill wouldn't know a thing, because they wouldn't hear a door close.

Eryn skipped across the lawn. It was a long, long way to the pond. She hurried by the stable without looking at it. Then past the line of crepe myrtles that hadn't bloomed yet. The pond was even farther. Eryn was out of breath by the time she got to it. She looked over her shoulder but couldn't see Henry. She smiled and ran out onto the dock.

The boards creaked beneath her tennis shoes. There was a rope tied to one of the posts at the end.

You should go back. You're not supposed to be here. Mr. Timmons' voice was stern, the way Uncle Bill's got when he was mad at her. But she wasn't hurting anyone. No one even had to know she'd left the house. Eryn got down on her belly and stared into the pond. But it wasn't pretty and clear like Ariel's ocean. The water was cloudy and green. It was hard to see through, no matter how hard she looked.

She found the rope tied around the post and tried to pull on it. But whatever was in the water was too heavy. Eryn stopped tugging and sat on her haunches, staring into the pond. Maybe there *was* a mermaid down there!

"Do you see her?"

She jumped up and whirled around. Where had Henry come from? Eryn looked in both directions wildly. Mr. Timmons was right. She shouldn't have come.

"Uh-huh." She edged her way by him. There was no other way to run home without having to walk by Henry on the dock. To her shock, he let her pass and then continued toward the rope tied around the post, swinging a pail in his hand.

"I'm going to feed her. She'll eat minnows, and I've got some in this bucket." Eryn looked at the expanse of spring grass and then back at her cousin. And her feet made the decision for her. Slowly, she retraced her steps as Henry got down on his stomach, much the way she had earlier. He held the bucket below the dock at water level, and he was taking something out of it. Dropping it into the pond.

"You have to get down on your belly to see her." Henry's voice startled her a little. He must have heard her on the dock coming closer. "I'm going to toss in another minnow. Get down close to the edge if you want to watch her eat it."

Caution forgotten, Eryn crouched down. And then his hand came up lickety-split and pushed hard at her back. And she toppled headfirst into those dark-green depths.

She swallowed a bunch of water when she went in. And when her head popped up, she was choking, the icy water burning her throat and lungs. Henry was laughing and laughing. Eryn could feel herself begin to sink again and started to panic. But she could swim. A little. She dog-paddled until she could grasp the edge of the dock. "You're a . . . big . . . fat jerk!"

He stepped on her fingers and smiled when she yanked them away. "It's not nice to call people names, Eryn. Didn't those voices in your head ever tell you that?"

She tried to grab the dock in another area, and he stepped on her fingers again. And then again. Finally, she wrapped her arms around one of the fat posts. It was slippery with yucky green stuff.

"You're going to get in trouble." Her teeth were chattering so hard she could hardly get the words out. "Way more trouble than you got in for smoking. Uncle Bill will send you to the pep school he's always talking about."

"It's *prep* school, you little freak." His smile was nasty. "Is the water warm? You look like you're enjoying it."

Maybe she could just swim a little to the next pole, and then the next until she got to the grass again. Shivers shook her body as she counted, and her stomach dropped. Ten poles to the shore. Less to where it got shallow. Her hands slipped on the slimy post she clung to, and she adjusted them. Held tighter.

"When Mama asks how I got wet, I'm going to tell her."

He stared at her for a moment. "Okay." His sudden change of heart made her wary. He stuck a hand down to her. "I'll help you out of the water. C'mon."

Eryn stared at him. She didn't trust him. Why would she? But she was getting really, really cold. It was harder to hold on. And she didn't want to spend another minute in the pond. She stretched out a hand. He grasped it and pulled her up onto the dock. Water streaming off her, Eryn hugged herself and rubbed her arms, trying to get warm. Henry grabbed her by the back of the neck and hauled her close.

"You slipped and fell in. Got it? You slipped, and I helped you out of the water. If you tell your mama any different, I'll do a lot worse to you. Do you want to get locked in the stable again?"

Cold, damp walls closing in around her. Smells hurting her nose and making her eyes tear. And a door that didn't open except by someone you didn't want inside there with you. *It's chilly in here, isn't it? But I can keep you warm . . .*

"No," she shouted hoarsely, her body quaking, her heart galloping. "No! No!"

"Shut up," he hissed. Henry pushed her in front of him and then, with a hand to her back, kept her moving up the dock, back toward the house. "Better keep your mouth shut, then. You fell in the pond and I helped you out. It's not like you didn't deserve it." His hand left her back then and grabbed her neck, under her wet hair. His fingers squeezed. "Consider it payback for trying to frame me for stealing the ice cream. And for what you did to Whiskers."

Eryn: Now

"I have to go to school today," Jaxson told Eryn glumly when she went into the kitchen. His backpack was on the floor next to the table. His coat hung on the back of his chair. "And because of my foot, I can't go to recess or PE, which really sucks. What's the point of school without recess?"

"Staying in from recess will give you time to finish the assignments you missed yesterday," said Mary Jane tartly, moving efficiently as she unloaded the dishwasher and put dishes away. "Learning is the whole point of school, not running around outside like wild Indians."

Jaxson rolled his eyes, and Eryn nearly laughed out loud. He was the third generation of Pullmans to have a similar reaction to the woman. "It was fun staying home yesterday and watching TV and playing video games." His face brightened. "I beat you pretty bad in *Minecraft*."

"Well, considering I'd never played before you should have beaten me worse." Eryn picked up a plate and trailed over to the covered pan on the stove. French toast. Heavenly. Sitting at the table, she watched Jaxson rub a piece through a pool of syrup and lift the bite, dripping, to his lips.

"You'll only get better if you keep practicing."

"Don't talk with your mouth full." Mary Jane never paused in her task. "Table manners aren't just for company."

"I guess I have to continue playing with you to get the necessary practice, huh?" Eryn was onto the kid. He'd roped her into competing with him yesterday and before she knew it, two hours had slipped by.

"Life rewards those who work hard at it," he said solemnly.

Recognizing the words she'd heard many times from Mary Jane, she laughed, earning them both a dark look from the woman. The dishwasher door slammed shut with a bit more emphasis than necessary. "You'd be wise to apply those words to your schoolwork and your chores rather than video games."

Jaxson gave Eryn a conspiratorial smile, and something warmed inside her. Before she'd returned home she probably hadn't exchanged more than a dozen words with the boy. But he was turning out to be an unexpected bright spot in the home.

"Eryn, I'll be driving you to Asheville to your doctor's appointment, looks like." Mary Jane's tone was dour. "Everyone else is too busy doing who-knows-what. Gives us a chance for you to help me shop, though, like we talked about. You'd better see your uncle about taking some money along if there's anything you're wanting to pick up."

The thought of talking to her uncle about money again had Eryn's stomach tightening. She had a sudden memory of yesterday's effigy across the road. What would they find when they left the property today? Trepidation rose. A part of her wanted to stay away from windows and hibernate in her room with her sketches and paints.

Rosalyn bustled into the room, buttoning a pretty pink wool coat and pulling on matching gloves. "Jaxson Beauregard Pullman, you'd better be done eating because it's time for school."

Eryn cut her eyes at the boy, who had a piece of French toast on his fork and was swooping it in loop-de-loops before dive-bombing into the copious syrup again. "I like riding the bus better anyway."

"Until your ankle is healed I don't want you going up and down the bus steps and making your way through a crowded aisle to your seat." She stopped long enough to send Eryn a strained smile. "Your uncle wants to see you before you and Mary Jane leave."

All earlier remnants of humor fled. Arrangements for Eryn's appointment had apparently been discussed with every adult in the place before being shared with her. The realization made her feel not much older than Jaxson. The sensation would likely continue until she acquired more independence. She picked up another piece of toast and chewed slowly. Found it impossible to swallow.

"Oh, and Mary Jane?" Rosalyn bent to help Jaxson zip his coat. "Please set another place for dinner this evening. William says Henry will be eating with us. Maybe you can shop today for something special for the meal." She rose and bustled the boy out the kitchen door.

The news ruined her appetite. Henry. She hadn't seen or talked to her cousin in years. He was another part of her childhood she tried very hard not to think about. As Eryn got up to rinse her dishes, Mary Jane said, "Be ready to leave in thirty minutes."

"Okay." The appointment would put some limitations on the upcoming conversation with her uncle. And Eryn was all right with that.

But when she walked into Uncle Bill's office, he was donning an expensive-looking trench coat over his suit. Looking up at her arrival, he said, "Good. You're here. I'm headed out to a board meeting for Pullman Properties. Mary Jane mentioned you were going shopping after your appointment." He gave her a strained smile as he took out his wallet. "Hopefully, you'll get farther than the grocery store." Taking some bills out, he rounded the desk to press them into her hand. "Maybe the two of you can even have lunch. Make a day of it."

Eryn looked uncomprehendingly at the cash she held. Five hundred dollars. She'd never seen so much money at once in her life. She'd never held over a hundred dollars . . . ever. "Is this my allowance?"

"No, of course not." But a dull flush rose to his cheeks. "We haven't discussed an amount for your monthly stipend yet. We'll do so later when we have time to analyze your budgetary needs. I can have our lawyer draft an agreement, if you like. Later on, perhaps you'll want to consider allowing me to remain in control of your share of the Pullman trust, while getting regular payments from it."

The bills felt crisp and foreign in her fingers. But his last statement had a niggle of concern rippling through her. "Shouldn't I have a meeting with the lawyer first so he can explain the trust to me?"

"Eryn," Uncle Bill said chidingly, "I can do that." He searched in his pockets for gloves. "I have to go. Enjoy your outing, but dress warmly. Temperatures dropped overnight."

She stared at him then. The black coat he wore over his suit had her blurting, "Maybe I'll buy a warmer coat. Maybe a parka like yours."

He sent her an odd look as he pulled on his gloves. "It would certainly be warm. I don't wear mine much, but it comes in handy during those winter cold snaps." He walked out of the room, leaving Eryn to stare after him. It'd been chilly two nights ago but certainly not wintry. But maybe that's not why he'd worn the parka. The oversize hood had concealed his face.

A thought struck her then, one she should have considered before. She and Jaxson had seen a figure wearing the coat. But there was really no way to be sure who the person was.

◆ ◆ ◆

"How are you feeling about the transition home after the first few days?"

"Fine."

Dr. Ashland's tone was friendly, but her gaze was knowing. "That's the fourth 'fine' I've gotten from you. Let me rephrase. How are you filling your days since getting back home? What have the stressors been?"

Eryn watched the doctor impassively from a chair beside her. They sat in a cozy little grouping, two armchairs arranged near each other in front of the picture window in her office. She shrugged. "I paint and draw. My room is nice, but small. I've asked my uncle about turning another into a studio, but . . ." She paused to recall the conversation exactly. "He didn't seem to approve."

"Why do you think that is?"

Eryn stifled a mental sigh. She liked the doctor better than she had Dr. Steigel. But therapy was therapy. She tired of the endless questions. The constant reflection. "He seems to be very concerned about money."

The doctor nodded and smoothed a crease from her pant leg. "Since your uncle is an accountant, I suppose that's to be expected."

Surprise filtered in. Her uncle was an accountant? It was odd the psychiatrist was aware of the fact and Eryn had had no clue. It was yet another reminder of how little she knew about her own family. How much she'd missed by spending her formative years locked away.

"When will my transition time be up?" She'd mentally practiced this conversation during the near-silent ride here with Mary Jane. It had occurred to her the doctor might be able to provide some answers to help her fit together the bits Uncle Bill had revealed about the trust.

"Well, of course that depends on many different factors," Dr. Ashland started.

"But in summary . . ."

Her lips firmed at Eryn's prodding. "Overall, a ninety-day adjustment period is what we'll use to evaluate the success of your transition before making our final recommendation to the state regarding your mental health. Why do you ask?"

Perhaps she should have found the doctor's words ominous, but she preferred knowing what she was dealing with. The thought of spending more time at Rolling Acres didn't bother her particularly. Imagining another failed transition did. A thin trickle of unease threaded down her spine just thinking of a return of the paranoia, dark moods, and bursts of mania.

A return of the voices.

"I was just wondering. My uncle suggested I give him permission to continue to control my share of the family trust. I'm thinking I should wait before making such a big decision."

Dr. Ashland frowned slightly. "Because it would be a stressor for you?"

"I'm not ready to agree to anything right now." She couldn't put her finger on the source of the unease Uncle Bill's suggestion had created in her. Eryn still felt like all she had were crumbs of information and until she knew more, she was unwilling to commit to something she didn't fully understand. She said as much, adding, "That's part of being an adult, right? Gathering all the facts before making an informed decision?"

"Yes, of course, you're correct." The ticking of the antique clock on the table between them sounded unnaturally loud in the short silence. "Are you experiencing any changes in your thoughts or behavior? Depression? Manic states?"

She shook her head. None of that described how she'd been feeling for the last couple of days. She had some trouble sleeping, but Eryn chalked it up to the recent changes she'd undergone.

"Remember your past history with tachyphylaxis. If you have any indications your medications aren't working, or aren't working as well, you need to let me know."

"I will." It was Dr. Glassman who had diagnosed her with the condition and attributed it to her less-than-successful transition to the group home a couple of years ago.

"Are there any other stressors you've faced since returning home?"

Her gaze flicked to Ashland's. The woman knew. Eryn didn't know how, but she did. "A small group of individuals has been bothering us." At least she assumed the persons responsible for the effigy were linked to the protestors at the gates on her first day home. The sheriff mentioned they might be related. She was unwilling to go into more detail, although the mental image of the fiery effigy was branded on her brain. The flames chasing down the pole and skipping across the dry-as-tinder weeds in the ditch. A little preview of the hellfire the protestors had said she was doomed to.

The doctor gave a nod of satisfaction. "Your uncle called and informed me yesterday. He worries you'll find the events disturbing, which would certainly be understandable. He said there have been crude sayings on other signs as well. We need to discuss that, and your reaction to them, Eryn. If the situation escalates, it might serve as an emotional trigger for you. How did you feel when you read the sayings on the signs they were wielding on your first day home?" She picked up a small notebook with scrawled notes on it. Read aloud. "Matricide is murder. Murderers go to hell." Then she lowered the notebook and gazed at Eryn expectantly.

The tightness in her chest seemed to spread, like the eddy of ripples in water. "I can understand on some level why my release would anger people," she said carefully. "But they're strangers, and they don't know me. They don't understand mental illness. So, I'm really not bothered by it."

Dr. Ashland simply nodded approvingly, as if she'd given the correct answer to a trick test question. Eryn knew better than to tell her the truth she hid away, deep and secret in the recesses of her mind. If she told her, it'd bring a frown to the woman's face. She might scribble on her pad, and in future sessions they'd discuss it ad nauseam.

It wouldn't be helpful to share that on some level Eryn thought those screeching strangers with their wild eyes and red faces were probably right.

◆ ◆ ◆

"And what about if I bought four of them at this sale price?" Mary Jane demanded, thrusting one of the soup cans she was holding closer to Eryn's face. "How much would I save then?"

"A dollar fifty," she said, without much interest. "And right now, without the soup, you have items totaling fifty-eight dollars and nine, no," she corrected herself, "ten cents in the cart."

Mary Jane reared back a little and sent her a considering look. "Hmmph. Didn't get that math sense from your mama. Nothing she hated more than working with numbers." She put the cans in the cart and continued pushing it down the aisle. "She never cared much about any subject outside her beloved art. I always told her if she ended up selling a painting, she'd be mighty interested in math then."

For some reason, Mary Jane's words brought a pang. They reminded her the older woman had decades of memories of Eryn's mother compared to the handful Eryn had had time to form. Alone in her room in Rolling Acres, sometimes she'd take out each and every recollection she had, reexamining it with an objectivity tinged with longing. If things had been different . . . would they still be living in the home they'd shared with Uncle Bill? Had her mama been happy? There had always been a subtle air of . . . discontentment layered beneath even her happiest moods. But it was impossible to be sure, because her memories were those of a child.

Eryn had once read that every time we recall a memory, it is altered in some way. The recollection couldn't be analyzed without considering it through the lens of new experiences and situations. The memories were cast with the child and now reevaluated as an adult. She doubted she'd ever be able to view them dispassionately.

The grocery store was more crowded than she'd expected for a weekday. Eryn had taken part in regular outings at Rolling Acres. Concerts in the park. Trips to the mountains. Library readings. Movies. It had always felt like the residents in her group were on display. The transit van they'd used had no logo on the side. Their supervisors wore no identifying clothing. But people couldn't help but notice their group and wonder about them.

She was enjoying herself right now more than she'd expected to. The sheer normalcy of walking beside Mary Jane, two women engaged in the most mundane of activities. Not so very different from the other customers inside the store. There was nothing to make them stand out. Nothing to make people stare. She could understand the appeal of big cities, she mused, as Mary Jane stopped the cart again to compare the price savings between two brands of crackers. The thought of drifting anonymously among a sea of people held more than a bit of allure. No preconceived ideas to confront. A comforting blanket of obscurity, where no one was aware of her past.

"Henry always loves my fried chicken," Mary Jane was saying. They stopped in front of the meat counter so she could peer at the display there. "Fried chicken, mashed potatoes, and gravy made from the drippings." Eryn scanned the aisle around them as Mary Jane spoke with the man behind the counter before making her selection.

There was a pretty woman with sleek auburn hair several yards away staring at them. Eryn realized she'd noticed her before, sneaking looks over her shoulder as she'd passed them in an aisle. Eryn turned away, pretending an interest in the wrapping of Mary Jane's chicken. Asheville wasn't the major anonymous city she'd been thinking about minutes earlier, but it may as well have been because Eryn didn't know a soul in it.

She trailed Mary Jane down the next aisle. "I won't have time to make a pie from scratch for dinner, but I could probably manage a pan of brownies." The older woman glanced at her. "Wouldn't hurt you none to know a bit about cooking, neither. You could help out in the kitchen and learn how to make some basic meals."

"Did you teach Mama to cook?"

The other woman snorted. "Your mama wasn't interested in household—"

"Excuse me."

Eryn looked up at the interruption. Saw the red-haired woman stop her cart beside them, raking them with her avid gaze. But it was Mary Jane she directed her question to. "Is this your daughter?"

"No." Mary Jane followed up her abrupt response by moving her cart farther down the aisle.

But the other woman kept pace with them. This time she addressed Eryn. "I'm not usually so rude. I must seem like some crazy stalker lady! But you're the spitting image of an old friend of mine. I just can't get over the likeness. Aurora Pullman. You wouldn't happen to be a relative, would you?"

Nonplussed, Eryn looked from the stranger to Mary Jane. There was a warning in the older woman's eyes. In her pinched tight mouth. "I . . . yes."

"I just knew it!" the other woman crowed. She smiled then and edged her cart closer so nearby shoppers could get around her. "The resemblance is just too strong. I remember Aurora had a brother . . ." Her words tapered off as comprehension filtered in. "You're not . . . Eryn?"

Was it paranoia to believe the stranger's tone was tinged with horror? Eryn had a sudden violent urge to turn and sprint out of the store. To race across the parking lot and dive into the car to cower there until Mary Jane caught up with her and they could race back to the house. It'd never occurred to her that her past could ambush her this way, that a random meeting in a grocery store could drag her back to face the most devastating of truths.

"Yes." Now it was she who was moving down the aisle. Not running. She refused to allow it. But . . . she needed escape. Her lungs were on fire, strangling the breath there. There was an anvil on her chest, crushing her lungs.

But the other woman stuck to her like a burr. "I'm sorry, I thought you were still . . ." She swallowed the rest of the statement and tried

again. "I just didn't expect . . . it to be you. I don't know how I'm supposed to feel about it, but I'm a good Christian woman." Her smile
made something inside Eryn wither. "It's God's place to judge and my
place to accept. I'm Madeline Grayson, by the way. I mean, Madeline
Grayson Carson. Mad Dog Maddy, Aurora used to call me." A wistful
smile danced at one corner of her mouth before it disappeared. "I was
your mama's roommate in college. A few of us used to get together
every month or so, even after she moved home." She considered Eryn.
"It's just so uncanny. Her hair was different, of course, when she was
your age, but the color, your features . . ." She shook her head. "It's like
looking at a ghost."

She seemed to realize what she'd said a moment later. Or maybe it
was the expression on Eryn's face. "Oh, I didn't mean . . ."

"Eryn," Mary Jane hissed. And this time she heeded the older woman's veiled message and moved away, walking blindly down the aisle,
aware of nothing but the pounding of her heart. The roaring in her ears.

She turned a corner, not even waiting to see if Mary Jane was following. And a stray thought occurred then, drifting across her mind like
a thread of gossamer on a playful breeze. Maybe Madeline could give
her details about her mother. She could help fill in the nearly empty
tapestry of Eryn's memories of her.

But as anxious as Eryn was to acquire the independence to grapple
with her future, she suspected she still didn't possess the courage to
confront her past.

◆ ◆ ◆

Eryn excused herself from dinner as soon as she was able. She felt off-
kilter, a result, no doubt, of the day's events. Even after the awkward
meeting in the grocery store, Mary Jane had been determined to pro-
ceed with her other plans for their day. There'd been a trip to the local
mall, where Eryn had finally bought a purse and a pair of jeans, if

only to placate the woman. Then they'd moved on to a department store. Mary Jane had a list for it, too, and Eryn had found a paint-by-numbers book of video game characters. She'd bought it for Jaxson, with paints and brushes, despite the sniff her purchase elicited from the older woman. "Boy's got more toys and games already than he knows what to do with."

But her selection was neither, and when she'd given them to the boy, he'd seemed generally enthusiastic. She'd been reminded again how dissimilar her cousins were.

There was a knock on her bedroom door. Somehow Eryn already knew who'd be standing on the other side of it even before she opened it to find Henry framed in the doorway.

He took her lack of response as an invitation and brushed by her, looking around. "Must be safe, since they let you out. I guess you can be trusted with scissors now, right?" After a moment, he gave her a twisted smile. "Okay, bad joke. It's good you're home. But you didn't have more than two words to say at dinner. What's the matter? Not excited about the prodigal's return?"

"Not especially." The stress of the day had stripped away any vestige of politeness.

He looked at her over his shoulder from his stance at her window. "Well, you're honest, at least. Probably the only one in this house with the trait." He leaned against the window frame. "Not that I gave you much of a reason to miss me. I was a bit of an arrogant asshole back in the day."

"I don't know about the arrogant part."

After a moment, he let out a bark of laughter. "Still have a bite, don't you? In my defense, I was dealing—not well, I admit—with an alcoholic mother who had a habit of bringing her drinking buddies home to spend the night in her bed. Best thing my dad ever did for me was to fight for custody. Life in this place was never any prize, but considering the alternative . . ."

She'd had no idea of his history. How could she? Eryn had been a kid at the time. Henry looked much like he had as a teen. Still good-looking. His hair had darkened in the intervening years. He'd put on weight, and the jaded look in his eyes was new. The vague air of disgruntlement was not.

"Let me guess." He gestured to the room. "Rosalyn's doing?"

"Yes."

He nodded, shoving his hands in his pockets. "I recognize the insipid look. She did mine, too, when I got out of college. I honestly think it drove me to join the army." His smile was twisted. "Learned there are a helluva lot worse things in the world than insipid."

"So." Her mind scrambled for a topic of conversation. Hopefully one that would lead to him leaving her room. "What are you going to do now?"

He took a few steps to sit on the corner of her bed. "Haven't you heard? Dear ol' dad hasn't exactly approved of the way I've been spending my time—and his money—since I got out of the army. He closed the purse strings, so I ended up back home, exactly where he wants me." It would be difficult to miss the bitterness in his tone.

"You're going to live here?" Bat wings of panic fluttered in her chest.

"God, no." He looked as appalled as she felt. "I have a place in Asheville. I'm being put to work at Pullman Industries, learning the lumber business from the bottom up. My life's ambition."

His sarcasm was difficult to miss. "You don't have to do it if you don't want to. There are jobs around. In Asheville. Charlotte."

"But they wouldn't be close to the money, Eryn. In this family, it's always about the money."

Finally, a subject that interested her. "Do you know about the trust?"

"The one keeping us all chained to this archaic estate? Of course. And little ol' you is the only thing standing between a trust set up fifty years ago and freedom for all of us." He waggled his eyebrows at her. "Bet you never knew you had so much power."

Her mind raced, but she simply didn't have enough facts to comprehend his meaning. "I don't understand."

Henry's expression went sly. "You don't know anything about the family finances, do you?"

She shook her head. "Not really." It was the only reason she was prolonging this conversation. Despite the passing years, her cousin still made her uncomfortable.

"Our grandparents set it up long before they were killed in a small plane crash. Nothing on this property changes—ever—except for modernization and upkeep. The boathouse you burned down? It had to be rebuilt because of the trust, despite the fact it was rarely used. The trustee has to approve all changes. And nothing can be sold." His expression now was amused. "At least not until after our grandparents had been dead ten years and then only with joint permission of both beneficiaries."

"Sold?" For a moment, the thought filled her with alarm. The family property might be dated and secluded, but it was at least familiar. She couldn't imagine where she would have gone when she'd left Rolling Acres if this place didn't exist.

"Plenty of people have been sniffing around here in the last half a dozen years or so." Apparently growing bored with the conversation, he rose again. "There are developers who have this grandiose idea for turning the property into one of those fancy golf club developments, ringed with overpriced homes. Dad doesn't have the power to sell even if he wants to. He was just the guardian of your share of the trust until you turned twenty-one. Now, if you manage to stay out of the nuthouse, you have equal say."

Something about the expression of barely restrained glee in his voice reminded her of when they were younger. "It's going to be damned entertaining to see how this plays out."

Ryder

The unincorporated town of Crabtree was an unlikely location for Frederick Bancroft's Life's Hope Church. North of Lake Junaluska on the Pigeon River, there wasn't much there to draw the fifty congregation members Bancroft had boasted when he'd been arrested at Pullman's.

Ryder got out of the car he'd parked on the street in front of the church and the small white house next to it and surveyed both properties. There were a couple of places in town on the historic registry, but neither of these properties would make the list. The tiny brick building with the church sign out front didn't look large enough to hold even thirty people, so he figured Bancroft had embellished his numbers. The man had to be drawing church members from outside the area. The town, such as it was, wasn't big enough to supply them.

Ryder had made sure to get here at first light, before Bancroft would be leaving for his shift at a Waynesville molding shop. He got close enough to the church to read the framed sidewalk sign next to the front walk. In black plastic letters it proclaimed, "God hates Jews, fags and freaks." Beneath the words, smaller letters said, "Worship with us Wed. nights and Sun. at 8."

He looked up when he heard the door close at the house. Saw Bancroft coming down the front steps. The man's step faltered when he saw the sheriff's car out front, and his gaze quickly found Ryder.

"This is private property, Sheriff." The stout man marched across the patchy lawn to confront him. "And you're trespassing."

The irony in the words wasn't lost on Ryder. "It's not trespassing when I'm here on official business."

"And what might that be?" Bancroft was bundled up in a black parka and a red stocking hat. "I already talked to the dumb-ass deputy you sent out here. Told him I didn't know nothing about the fire at the Pullman place. It didn't stop him from hassling several of my church members, though. This kind of harassment won't be tolerated."

Ryder indicated the sign he'd just read. "Nice sentiment you've got displayed there. What is that? Corinthians?"

Bancroft shoved his fleshy face closer to Ryder's. "It's called righteousness. And you're still trespassing."

"I just came by to give you a friendly heads-up. I'm glad I did, so now I know when your services are," he responded, jerking his head at the sign. "I'll have a deputy stationed across the street during services from now on. It'll give him a chance to jot down license plate numbers." He observed the matching flags of color flooding the other man's cheeks. "We patrol the unincorporated towns, too, and it's always nice to show a presence. Crime deterrent. I hope it won't keep your members from attending services."

"You can't do that! It's intimidation!"

Ryder gave a slow nod. "You'd probably know. The flames on the effigy spread to the ditch and beyond. Burned fence line and at least two telephone poles before it was put out. Whoever's responsible broke several laws in the process. Your alibi checks out, but you could say those others with you at Pullman's several days ago are prime suspects." He turned and started back toward his car.

"I know what you're up to," Bancroft hollered after him. "But I'm not ratting on any of my church members."

Ryder stopped. "Assuming you have any members left after we camp out here for a few weeks."

The man appeared to mull Ryder's words over. Finally, he said, "Listen, like I said before, I keep getting phone calls from someone about the Pullman girl. And I don't disagree with the message. She deserves to burn—"

"Who's the caller? What's the number?"

The other man—Ryder couldn't bring himself to call him a pastor—pulled a flip phone out of his pocket. Then ponderously looked through his contacts before reeling off the phone number. Ryder pressed it into the note function on his cell before focusing on the man again. "Is it a man or a woman?"

Bancroft shrugged his beefy shoulders. "Hard to tell. The voice is muffled. Like maybe someone is trying to disguise it."

"How many calls in all?"

The man checked his phone again. "Three. Two a couple of days before Pullman got released, and another two days after. You have to realize, we're not the only ones upset by the release of a cold-blooded killer. We represent the vigilant ready to do God's work when the law refuses to protect us."

Before the man got wound up again, Ryder gave him a nod. "Thanks for the information." It was more, far more, than Bancroft had given when he'd been arrested. Ryder turned toward his car, calling over his shoulder, "We'll see you at services tonight."

"What?" The pastor sounded incensed. "I just cooperated! I helped your investigation!"

"And if you want to stop the patrols in front of your services, you'll give us the name of the person responsible for the effigy." Ryder opened his car door and slid behind the wheel. When he pulled away, Bancroft was still standing there, steam all but emanating from him.

Once the man faded from his rearview mirror, Ryder forgot about him. The pastor would eventually break once his church participation numbers began to dwindle. In the meantime, the phone number Bancroft had given would be run so they could determine the caller's identity.

As if on cue, his cell rang. He drew it out of his pocket and answered it, slowing to a stop behind an unmoving school bus. "Talbot."

"Dr. Isaacson, Sheriff. I hope this isn't too early to call you."

"Not at all." The bus's stop sign arm was retracting. After another moment, the vehicle began to move.

"I wondered if you'd had any luck identifying the doctor and patient on Aldeen's audiotape. If not, I believe I may be of some help if you want to reach out to the administration at Bridgeport, the facility where Samuel was housed before ours."

"We did get an ID, thanks." His deputies had arrived to search the Pullman Estate shortly after the marshals had left but found no sign that Aldeen was hiding anywhere on the outside property. William Pullman hadn't been especially pleased at Ryder's decision to have two deputies parked on the road in front of his home for the foreseeable future. But their presence served a twofold purpose: to ensure the escapee didn't get close to Eryn Pullman and to discourage any future protestors at the estate.

"I do have one question, Doctor." Once the bus had lumbered away, Ryder pressed on the accelerator again. "There was a file on Aldeen's player that held nothing but children's laughter. What do you make of that?"

"Oh God." The man sounded genuinely distressed. "Dr. Luttrell expressly asked if anything similar was contained in the audio files. This is terrible. We go to great lengths to avoid allowing the patients access to anything that feeds their paraphilia."

"You're saying Aldeen got off on the sound." Ryder's jaw clenched.

"According to Luttrell, it's one of his triggers."

"Well, we knew Aldeen was a sick fuck," SBI Agent Sweeney said as he sipped from the always present go-cup of coffee in his hand. "No telling how long the bastard was secretly jerking off listening to happy kids."

FBI Special Agent Tolliver nodded. Ryder had never noted the man drinking anything other than water. He was twirling a plastic bottle of it between two fingers now. "He'll gravitate to a place with access to children. Unfortunately, it could be anywhere. Parks. Schools."

"He snatched two of his victims from their yards." Ryder missed the fancy coffee maker his mother had given him for Christmas. Because he spent more time in his office than his house, he kept it there. As long as he remembered to program it before he went home each night, he had a fresh pot waiting for him every morning. They'd installed multiple commercial-size coffeepots at the command center. The brew left a lot to be desired.

"How much longer before the lab is finished with Grafton's computer?" he asked. Morris Grafton was the Fristol IT employee who would have been in charge of downloading Aldeen's purchased musical files. He'd have had the skills to cover his tracks if he'd done something illicit with Aldeen's device.

"This case has high-priority status. If they'd found something in their first pass at it, we'd have heard by now. Going deeper will take a bit longer." Tolliver drank from the bottle again. The man had taken charge of searching through Bush's computer files and history when the warrants had come through yesterday. But even with data recovery software, he'd struck out retrieving Bush's browsing history. The only thing of interest in Bush's files had been the records he'd kept of his personal finances; careful spreadsheets of monthly income and expenses going back ten years. It'd been clear Joe Bush had been in dire financial straits since he and his wife had separated. He would have been especially vulnerable if Aldeen had offered money for aiding his escape.

The monthly expense records had also provided them with the name of Bush's cell phone provider, which was helpful since no cell had been found.

As if plucking the thought from Ryder's mind, Tolliver asked, "How about Bush's cell phone and financial records? Have they come through yet?" He tossed his empty bottle in the waste can in the corner.

"Not as of six thirty this morning." Ryder checked his email on the laptop he'd brought from the office. A hum of adrenaline lit in his veins when he saw one of the messages in his in-box. "I spoke too soon. No financials yet, but we've got phone records." He opened the email's attachment and hit Print, getting up to collect the sheets being spit out of the printer in the corner of the room.

"I'll have a couple of deputies track down the numbers on it." Ryder couldn't contain a tiny thrum of excitement. Aldeen's trail had fizzled at Bush's residence. Maybe, just maybe, they were about to get their first lead since they'd found Joe Bush's body.

Two hours later they'd identified most of the callers and call recipients from Bush's phone. The numbers appearing most frequently were linked to personnel in charge of employee scheduling at Fristol and Rolling Acres, and the voice mails were job related. There had been several text messages shared between Joe and his estranged wife, who'd been apprised of the man's death yesterday. When contacted, she'd tearfully informed them the two hadn't spoken in person since she'd moved out. A few numbers belonged to take-out places and two people professing to be friends of Joe. Ryder had Jerry Garza running background on both individuals.

One number appeared three times. When Ryder called it, the phone went directly to an out-of-service recording.

He checked the dates against the calendar on his desk. The first time that caller had contacted Joe had been a few days before Aldeen's escape. The final contact was a received call from Pine Ridge Cabins on Jonathan Creek in Maggie Valley.

Bush had told both Fristol and Rolling Acres he'd be on vacation for two weeks. Maybe he'd planned to use the time to hide out at a mountain retreat during Aldeen's escape, establishing an alibi for himself.

Ryder contacted the place three times and got no answer. But finally, on his next try, someone picked up the phone. "Pine Ridge Cabins," a male voice said.

"This is Haywood County Sheriff Ryder Talbot calling. Your number showed up in cell phone records obtained in the course of one of our investigations. Joe Bush is the individual the phone belonged to. Can you tell me the nature of the call you made to him?"

"It was probably to follow up on an online inquiry he'd made about a reservation, Sheriff."

Ryder stilled. "Did he end up making a reservation with you?"

"Yes, sir. He arrived here . . . let's see." There was a moment of silence. "Last Saturday."

Saturday. Ryder's mind raced. That would have been the day before the escape. "How long did he stay?"

"He's still here. At least, I assume so. I just had a conversation with someone from his party."

Everything inside Ryder slowed. Lungs. Breathing. Heartbeat. "Can you describe the man you spoke to?" Sweeney's and Tolliver's gazes fixed on him.

"Average height, I guess. Not as tall as Mr. Bush. I checked him in myself. And I have to say, he never let on there'd be more than just him staying in the cabin. We do ask for the names of everyone in the party, but Joe mentioned he'd be alone. This fella has a shaved head and the start of a beard. He's a writer, he said. Steven Bennet is his name."

"Any idea how long he's been there?"

"Two days at least. I was talking to him today about a complaint some other renters had about him. They said he approached their kids yesterday, and when the children told their parents about him, they didn't like the sound of the conversation the kids relayed. They thought he was a bit inappropriate. I spoke to Bennet this morning and just warned him he probably shouldn't be approaching any of the children staying here. Actually," the man corrected, "these are the only renters who brought kids. Most would be in classes, but the father told me they were homeschooled."

"You didn't happen to notice what sort of vehicle was parked at the cabin, did you?"

There was a pause, and then, "I didn't see one. Since there was no sign of Mr. Bush, maybe he drove it somewhere."

"Thanks for your time."

Ryder had barely replaced the receiver on his desk phone when Sweeney said, "Do we have a sighting?"

"Possibly." The word did nothing to quiet his growing certainty that Bush had made the reservation for Aldeen. "Whoever is there approached a couple kids yesterday. Their parents were concerned." As one, the three of them turned to exit the room. "Let's get a tactical team assembled."

◆ ◆ ◆

Ryder had left the majority of the tactical team members at the base of the drive leading up to Pine Ridge Cabins' main office. There was intelligence to gather before they attempted entry at Joe Bush's rental.

Ryder, three of his men, FBI Special Agent Tolliver, and SBI Agent Sweeney were surveilling the place from each side. Since Tolliver had provided the high-tech Range-R device, Ryder had been happy enough to have the man come along. His office didn't have the budget for the equipment the feds and staties could afford. The mechanism sent out radio waves to detect the slightest movement through walls, including breathing, from as far as fifty feet.

Like the owner had noted, there was no vehicle anywhere around the place. The cabin fronted Jonathan Creek, so Ryder was across from it, in a lightly wooded area with plenty of trees and boulders to take refuge behind. He'd had the high-powered binoculars trained on the cabin for half an hour, with no sign of movement near it.

They had the cabin surrounded. Agent Tolliver was operating the Range-R device to determine whether there was anyone inside the structure. The slightest sound had Ryder's muscles tightening with tension. Twice he'd noted movement nearby. First he'd spied an older woman with a walking stick and a large dog, and the other time it had been a female hiking with two kids. He watched the children toss rocks into the creek. They must have been the ones the man calling himself Steven Bennet had spoken to.

The radio clipped to his belt sounded. Ryder brought it up to his ear. "The cabin is empty." It was Tolliver's voice. "Whoever was inside could still be in the vicinity. Do you want to wait or enter immediately?"

Ryder's gaze sharpened as he saw a figure moving toward the front of the cabin from farther down the creek. Raising the binoculars again, he murmured, "We've got a man heading toward the front door."

"So we wait."

"For now." Watching the figure stride confidently to the building, Ryder could feel his system slow. The height could fit Aldeen's description, but the man sported a beard, which may or may not turn out to be fake. Right now, it was the rifle he carried that was of more interest.

They didn't have ballistics back yet on the weapon used on Joe Bush, but the ME had guessed the wounds were inflicted with a large-caliber handgun at close range. That didn't mean Aldeen didn't have access to two different weapons, though.

He reached for the radio. "The man approaching is armed."

"I've got visual," Deputy Garza's voice sounded.

"So do I," Sweeney said.

The stranger walked up the two steps to the wooden porch running in front of the building and pounded on the door. He waited before banging again, hard enough this time for the noise to reach Ryder's ears. "Hey! Come on out of there! I got something I wanna say to you!"

Ryder scanned the area. The older woman was out of sight. So was the family he'd seen. The man didn't give up easily. He pounded and called to the cabin's occupant several more times before finally retracing his steps.

It could have been an elaborate pretense. Bennet—or Aldeen—could have made them and was engaged in a farce to bluff his way out of the situation.

"Take him," Ryder whispered into the radio. Moments later the deputies and Sweeney swarmed the man, shouting commands until he dropped his weapon and laid on the ground, hands behind his head.

His gun raised, Ryder came out in the open, wading across the creek to meet them. But when Deputy Fornier turned the bound stranger over so Ryder could get a good look at him, frustration lodged a giant knot in his throat.

He had Aldeen's features committed to memory. Whoever the stranger was, he wasn't the man they sought.

◆　◆　◆

The ten-year-old boy looked from Ryder to his father, Ian Molitor, who was now uncuffed and sitting on the porch next to him. "Go on and answer the sheriff, Danny," Molitor urged.

"I don't know. The man was nice at first. He showed us how to find the best rocks to skip across the creek. But then he said we needed to go where it was deeper, so there was enough water to make them skip better."

"And we weren't supposed to go far from our cabin," piped up blue-eyed Jenny. "Mom said to stay where we could see the porch. But Danny said we could, for just a little way."

Ryder could tell from Ian's narrowed gaze that the boy would have some explaining to do once they left. "So how far did you go?"

The boy pointed at a large rock on the edge of the creek well past the cabin Bush had rented. "Just to there. Then I stopped. He started to say weird stuff. It kind of creeped me out."

"What kind of stuff?"

Danny didn't meet Ryder's gaze. "Like how he liked the sound of our voices. He said he hadn't been around kids for a long time. I told him I'd been collecting a bunch of cool rocks since we got here, and he told me to go back and get them. He said how he and Jenny would wait for me."

Ryder pulled out his cell and brought up some pictures of Samuel Aldeen and showed them to the family. Danny looked at the image critically. "The man we saw didn't have hair."

"And he had a little beard," Jenny added. "Not a fluffy one like Daddy's."

Ryder showed the picture to the parents, but both of them shook their heads. "I never saw him," Ian said.

His wife piped in, "And I only did from a distance. I wasn't close enough to really see his features. Was he . . ." She hesitated and looked across the creek where two of the team members were searching the area. "Is he dangerous?"

"We're interested in talking to him," Ryder said noncommittally. Aldeen's escape was still in the news every day. Tensions were running high in the nearby communities already. The tip line they'd established was full of mostly useless so-called sightings of the man. The revelation that he'd been seen in the area would be handled with finesse. They didn't want to cause a public panic.

The owner of the cabins—the one Ryder had talked to earlier—had ID'd pictures they'd shown him of Aldeen as being the man he'd spoken to. But even if he hadn't, the kids' description of the stranger's behavior would have been compelling. It sounded very much like he'd been trying to separate the young girl from her brother.

Ryder looked at Jenny, who was climbing up into her dad's lap, and a chill prickled at the base of his neck. Near misses. If Danny hadn't refused to leave his sister . . . if Joe's cell phone records had arrived a couple of hours earlier . . .

They appeared destined to remain a step behind Samuel Aldeen. Ryder tamped down his rising frustration and thanked the family. Walking a short distance away, he used the radio to confer with his team, who were spread across the property and beyond.

They'd search the area more thoroughly, but they hadn't found a vehicle yet. Ryder was willing to bet they'd missed their chance at the fugitive.

Mingled with his disappointment was a flicker of curiosity. Aldeen had obviously had the means to leave the county. Or even the state. Ryder found himself hoping that Eryn Pullman wasn't what was keeping the man in the area.

Cady

The nightmare was a montage of disconnected movie clips, one melding with the next in a Technicolored display. Cady's mom, one hand to her bloody mouth, huddled on the kitchen floor in the nightgown that matched her daughter's. Her husband standing menacingly over her, his features blurry and indistinct. Cady's fingers closing around the grip of the gun. The weight of it in her hand. The explosion of sound. The spattering of crimson.

She tossed in the bed as she attempted to claw her way to consciousness. The image gave way to another. Bo chasing her to the cabin, one hand covering the wound she'd inflicted. *You fucking whore! I'll kill you!* And then her grandfather appeared, shoving her struggling body down the cellar steps to the waiting well of darkness. *You get what you deserve in this life, girlie. Next time you'll think twice about taking something don't belong to you.*

Eryn Pullman's face superimposed over the scene. *I'm not a fan of small, damp, enclosed places.*

Cady opened her eyes, heart hammering, lungs heaving, the smell of dirt and mold still in her nostrils. She raised a hand to her head and winced when it grazed her eye. The events of yesterday filtered back. When she struggled to sit up, the action brought a synchronized chorus of pain. She gave herself a minute to adjust, beating back the remnants of panic still fluttering in her chest.

She stood gingerly. In a masterful understatement, the ER doctor had told her to expect some stiffness today. He hadn't mentioned that all the muscles in her body would stage a minor rebellion at the slightest movement. Gritting her teeth, she shuffled to the bathroom and adjusted the shower to a temperature just shy of hellfire and let the scalding spray pummel her muscles into submission.

Arms braced on the shower walls, Cady tried to empty her mind as she waited until the water began to chill before she stepped out and dried off. She caught a glimpse of herself in the mirror then and stared in horror.

Well, shit. She patted her face dry cautiously. She could open her right eye only to a slit, which was a modicum of improvement over yesterday. The deep red welts on her face had begun changing to blue by last night and had completed their metamorphosis to navy and purple by morning. She looked like she'd gotten in the ring with a prizefighter and narrowly crawled away with her life.

Which, she thought darkly as she cautiously toweled her hair, *isn't such a stretch.*

Dressing and breakfast required a bit more time and care, but by eight she was up and carefully walking to her car, her face partially shielded by sunglasses.

Three hours later she was heading home from Waynesville with a three- or four-year-old German shepherd mix sharing the front seat with her. It would be difficult to say which of them was warier.

"Okay, the locksmith is due any minute. I'm probably going to have to chain you up while he's here, but not every day. You've got a big fenced-in yard." *Or will have,* Cady thought, *after I install the gates Dorothy promised.*

The dog stared at Cady with what looked an awful lot like doubt. She heartily reciprocated the emotion. What did she know about caring for a pet? Her mom had struggled to keep a rented roof over their head, and too often they'd ended up living with Alma. And later on, after she'd been foisted on a grandfather she barely knew, Cady hadn't been in the habit of asking for favors.

When she pulled up to her place, her good eye widened. Dorothy had not only had the gates delivered; she'd had them installed. Although the fiscally frugal landlady would undoubtedly charge her for the service, Cady's muscles wept with gratitude.

She pulled over to open the gates—which was going to be a big pain in the butt on a daily basis—and then got into the vehicle again. Drove through them and stopped to close them behind her.

The Jeep was under the carport. She parked behind it, got out, and went to the passenger side to open the door for the dog. He just looked at her. "Really? This place looks worse than the shelter I rescued you from? C'mon." She took hold of his new collar, complete with tags attesting to his shots, and guided him from the vehicle. Leaving him to check out his new home, she unlocked the front door and did a walk-through to ensure the intruder hadn't returned in her absence. Then she hauled in the supplies she'd bought for the animal, who didn't seem as happy as one might think about being released from a three-by-four cage.

The property was a beehive of activity for the next couple of hours. On the heels of the locksmith was the delivery from the store from which she'd bought the doggie Taj Mahal. The doghouse was roomy and heated, with a piece of canvas over the door to keep out the wind and chill. She'd gotten two beds and dog dishes, one for outdoors and the other for inside. Just as it wasn't fair to keep him locked up all day, Cady didn't figure it was right to make him spend all of his time outdoors. Unless his manners dictated otherwise. He'd proven his watchdog capabilities by incessantly barking and lunging as far as the chain would allow while strangers encroached upon his newly marked territory.

While keeping her only good eye on the action, she texted Miguel. What's going on today? Minutes later his reply appeared. You're on leave all day so what does it matter?

Smart-ass. Heading to Cisco's in Charlotte this afternoon. Meet me there at 5. She'd made a few phone calls on the way home from town. The pizza place where Preston had claimed she'd worked with Aldeen twenty-three years earlier remained under its original ownership, and the owner appeared most nights from five to eight.

You mean tomorrow. Because you're not on duty today. Gant's orders. Duty? I'm going for the pizza.

There was no response, but Cady didn't need one. Once the locksmith and doghouse guy were finished, the canine—who really needed a name—would be released from his chain and given his first opportunity to protect the property in her absence. Allen Gant might have ordered her off official duty today, but he couldn't control where she ate.

Cady was unsurprised to find Miguel waiting for her at the door to the restaurant. Although it was barely five, several tables were already filled. A cheerful middle-aged woman led them to their table and handed them menus, promising a waitress would be with them shortly. Cady looked across the expanse of the red-and-white checkered tablecloth at the other marshal. "How was your day, dear?"

"Getting blown up didn't make you funnier." He was already perusing the menu selections. "Yelp reviews on this place are great. I've never been here, and I'm a pizza connoisseur."

"Being a human garbage can doesn't elevate you to connoisseur status."

He looked affronted. "I eat very healthy. My body is a temple."

"Given the tales of your social life, I'd guess more of an amusement park."

"Time off has not been good for you," he observed, considering her more closely. "Although those sunglasses probably are. If your eye is the shade of the rest of those bruises, do all these diners a favor and don't remove them."

"It is and I won't." The walls of the place caught her attention then. Rows and rows of framed photographs seemed to cover every square inch of them. She got up to get a closer look.

There were celebrities shaking hands with the owner, often with a compliment written beneath the frame. She recognized a few athletes and a couple of singers, but there were more pictured people whom she didn't know, which wasn't surprising. She didn't keep up with popular culture or local politics.

Cady was intrigued to see the same man appear in each of the photos. The owner of the place, she assumed. In the progression of images, his hair turned from black to peppered to full gray and then white. Several photos depicted what she imagined were family celebrations. Cady only turned away from them when the waitress showed up at their table. She returned to her seat to place her order for a soft drink.

"Fast service."

"She probably thought you were a terrorist." Miguel was still studying the menu.

"Whatever works." When the waitress returned with their drinks, Cady smiled and asked, "Is the owner in tonight?"

"He is," the girl answered. She couldn't have been more than sixteen, with a talent for hair and makeup that still eluded Cady. "Poppa Cisco is here for a few hours most days. Are you a friend of his?"

Laying her credentials on the table, Cady said, "No, but I'm sure I'll be part of his fan club after we sample his pizza. We'd like to talk to him about some employees he had a long time ago."

"Um . . . I'll tell him." She rushed away.

"Why'd you have to scare her before we put our order in?"

"She'll be back."

Cady's prediction proved prophetic. Not only did the girl return in under ten minutes, she did so with an older man in tow. Cady recognized him from his appearance in most of the pictures on the wall.

"You are with the Marshals Service, my granddaughter tells me." The man was small and compact, with an enviable full head of white hair. "I am Francesco Romano. Like the cheese."

She and Miguel smiled, as they were supposed to.

"Here, though, I'm Poppa Cisco. What is it I can do for the Marshals today?"

"We'd like to ask you a few questions, if you can spare the time."

His gaze shifted to the kitchen behind him. "If they can't survive without me for a few minutes, I haven't trained them well." He pulled out a chair and sat down, looking from Cady to Miguel quizzically.

"I have a couple of pictures to show you of people who worked for you twenty-three years ago," Cady said.

The man's bushy eyebrows rose. "Now you're testing my memory. The employees . . . they come and go. So many college kids back then. As my grandchildren got old enough I mostly hired family for many years. Now Bella"—he nodded at the girl who had waited on them—"she's the youngest. Perhaps I will soon have to hire the great-grandchildren. But let's see."

Cady had printed recent pictures of Aldeen and Preston before she left the house. She reached into her coat now and withdrew them to put in front of the man, who pulled glasses from the pocket of his white shirt and settled them on his nose. He studied the photos for a moment before shaking his head. "Maybe yes, maybe no. It's hard to tell after not seeing them for so many years. What are their names?"

"Samuel Aldeen and Sheila Preston."

Romano's lips tightened. "Those I recognize. He's the horrible man who hurt those children years ago. I remember her name only because I was contacted once by the security people from where this man was locked up. I had to verify they had worked here so she could be allowed to visit him. I ask you, who would want contact with a monster like him?"

"How were you able to verify they worked here?" Miguel asked. "It was quite a while ago."

"You see my walls." Cisco waved to the array of photographs. "Life is people and people are memories. I keep my memories close by taking pictures, you see?"

A flicker of excitement lit in Cady's veins. "Did you ever take pictures of your employees?"

"Of course. We had Christmas parties, and there were many photos." His chair scraped as he rose. "They wouldn't be on the walls. I keep them in scrapbooks. That's what I had to consult when security called. Let me fetch them."

Cady watched him go and then looked at Miguel. "I almost forgot to tell you. I had a voice mail from Ryder Talbot. The Haywood County sheriff." She must have missed his call in the midst of the commotion at her house this afternoon. "There was a sighting of Aldeen this morning."

Miguel nodded. "Highway Patrol is out in force looking for the car he stole from Joe Bush's house." He'd obviously read the task force updates. "SBI sent a forensic artist to work with the witness. They're currently deciding whether to release it to the public."

Weighing the benefit to the case was always tricky. "Supposed sightings will quadruple." And probably overwhelm the staff monitoring the tip line the task force set up. On the other hand, if Aldeen was still in the area, the information couldn't be kept from the public. "Do you have a copy of the forensic sketch?" It hadn't been attached to the message she'd received.

Her partner nodded and brought it up on his cell and then held it out to her. Cady studied it. The escapee had made minor changes. Shaved his head. Begun to grow a beard. He would have altered his looks again by now, so if the sketch was released, it would no longer match the man's appearance.

But there was only so much to be done to disguise facial features. Obviously, the witness who'd seen Aldeen hadn't recognized him. Others might.

"The sheriff's department and local police departments are all over the surrounding area where he was last seen. Allen sent Chester and Quimby." Miguel's expression was resentful. "I had to spend the afternoon in-house."

Cady stifled a tiny flare of professional jealousy thinking of the other two marshals being in the middle of the action. "So the million-dollar question is, why is Aldeen still in the area?" The question had niggled at her ever since she'd read Talbot's text.

"It was Bush who made the arrangements for the cabin. Another way Aldeen used the man. Maybe he figured he wouldn't get far if he ran so he holed up until the search was scaled back."

"Or maybe," Cady said slowly as she spotted Cisco coming from the kitchen with an armful of scrapbooks, "there's something keeping him in the area. Something undone or a payoff of some kind he's waiting for." Her stomach twisted. She hoped like hell that "something" didn't include Eryn Pullman.

The older man reached their table, out of breath, and set the books down heavily. They were dusty. Cady wondered where he'd kept them.

"Twenty-three years, you said." He thumped the book on top. "That would probably be this one, although I brought them all just in case. It spans a five-year period, but the pages are marked with names and dates. Some of the employees were just here to collect a check and then . . ." He made a dismissive gesture. "Others became like family. We were invited to their weddings, their children's baptisms . . . life is people."

Cady felt a slight pang. He was the sort of man who would embrace strangers. Treat them like family. She could count her living relatives on one hand. And she was close to none but her mother. The contrast plucked at a cord buried deep inside. Something she didn't care to contemplate.

He flipped open the book and turned a few pages until he came to the one he was looking for. "Some stayed more than one year," he murmured, putting his glasses on again to examine the dates under the pictures. "A few worked for us the entire time they were in college. Not all were students, of course, but at the time we were very popular with the college crowd. We were open all day back then. Not now. Momma and I are too old. They used to start filing in at noon. They'd eat lunch and then stay to study or drink."

Cady and Miguel dragged their chairs closer to the pages he had open. She recognized the restaurant in the photos, festively decorated in the trappings of the season. As she studied each picture intently, her gaze arrowed on a familiar face. It wasn't one she'd expected to see.

David Sutton. The man who had been seen at Selma Lewis's house. The one who'd intercepted the calls to her number from Aldeen.

Cady caught Miguel's eye and pointed to the handsome, smiling man. Sutton's face was split in a wide grin, his arm wrapped around an equally attractive blonde. Scanning the rest of the people in the picture, she spotted Aldeen and Preston among a few other faces.

"Did David Sutton work here too?" She tapped his image.

The owner followed the direction she was indicating and stared at the man's face for a moment. "Not for long. Not that one. He didn't like to take direction. Always wanted to do things his way. Like the girl." Romano moved his gnarled finger to the blonde. "The parties were for employees only, but he brought his girlfriend. She hung out here all of the time while he worked for me. She brought a lot of her friends too. Good for business. But lots of drama. You know the type?"

Cady did. "Do you mind if I take a picture?" When Cisco shook his head, she snapped a few photos on her cell, then indicated the woman with Sutton. "Do you know her name?" It didn't appear beneath the photo. Likely because, as Cisco had said, the woman hadn't belonged there.

It all seemed a little too cozy. If Preston was on visiting terms with Aldeen and if Sutton was still friendly enough to be communicating with him through Lewis's hacked phone line, perhaps the unidentified woman would be entangled in Aldeen's circle as well. At the very least, she may have information leading them to Sutton.

"Hmm. Now you really test me." The restaurant owner closed his eyes. Pursed his lips. "There was something . . . later . . . something awful . . . but yes!" He snapped his fingers, his eyes opening as the memory he'd sought materialized. "She was murdered. It would have been a few years after this picture was taken. I can't quite remember all the details. But her family was well off. It was in the papers. Pullman, that was her name. I don't recall the rest of it."

Shock blazed through Cady. They'd struck out yesterday questioning William and Eryn Pullman about a possible link to Aldeen. Now here it was. Eryn's deceased mother would have known most of the players in their investigation. Samuel Aldeen. Sheila Preston. And David Sutton.

Miguel said, "Thank you. You've been very helpful."

The man gave them a shrewd look. "Why the interest in these people? Aldeen is locked up, and these others . . . I haven't seen or heard from them since they stopped working for me."

"It's been in the news." Cady managed to keep her excitement from sounding in her voice. "Several days ago, Samuel Aldeen escaped from the facility where he was being held."

Cisco recoiled. "The evil man who preyed on children?" At their nods, he did a quick sign of the cross. "Then I will pray he is caught soon. Before he hurts anyone else." Something across the room caught his eye then. "I must get back to the kitchen. Please, if you need more, send Bella to collect me. I am happy to be of service."

"You have been," Cady assured him. "Thank you."

He gathered up the scrapbooks he'd brought and rose, looking far more troubled than he'd been when he'd first stopped at their table.

They sat in silence for a moment, Miguel appearing as stunned as Cady was. "So this explains the link between Sutton and Aldeen. They have a history together as well."

"Sutton was in prison himself when Aldeen was sentenced," she mused. "He wouldn't have been allowed to get in touch with him. But their mutual acquaintance Preston could. Maybe Aldeen was already planning his escape when he sought a transfer to Fristol."

"Looks like it." Miguel took a drink from his water glass. "But an initial contact between Sutton and Aldeen had to come from someone else. How did Sutton know to hack Selma Lewis's phone line so he could learn what it was Aldeen wanted him to do?"

"Maybe Joe Bush delivered a message for him." Conjecture was all they had at this point, since Bush was dead. "Someone had to, in order to get the ball rolling. And Aurora Pullman has to figure in Aldeen's interest in Eryn." Cady thought for a moment. "Aurora still used her maiden name. You don't think . . . Sutton couldn't be Eryn's father, could he?" Her next thought was almost too awful to contemplate. "Or even . . . Aldeen?"

Miguel drummed his fingers on the table in thought. "God, I hope not, for her sake. Twenty-one years ago? Or maybe closer to twenty-two? I'd have to check the file. I thought Aldeen's address around that time was somewhere in South Carolina."

He was right. Cady remembered now. It didn't mean Aldeen couldn't have traveled to Charlotte to see an old friend. According to their research, he'd been a trust fund baby with a spotty employment history. With the man's lack of relatives, it'd been hard to pin down where and how he'd spent his time.

"I did a deep dive into Sutton's past today," Miguel was saying. "All of his arrests took place in Charlotte or the surrounding metro area, so maybe he never left the area. But there were no employment records for at least two years before his last arrest. And even then he gave no permanent address." He caught the waitress's gaze and gestured her over. "How do you feel about a meat-lover's pizza?" Miguel asked.

"Enthusiastic."

He ordered that, with a side of garlic bread. After Bella hurried away, he picked up on his earlier thread. "I discovered Sutton's mother is dead now, and there was no father on record. Grandparents are deceased, and Sutton was an only child. The only relative I could find was an uncle in Alaska, who said he hadn't seen Sutton since he was about ten. There were no cousins."

Cady felt a flare of frustration. With Preston in the hospital and Pullman dead, they were running out of leads on the man. "What about cellmates?"

"Way ahead of you. Three are still locked up, and all of the rest live out of state."

"College? High school?"

"Apparently, Sutton and his mother bounced around the state a lot. I found some online yearbooks with him pictured. I'd started making calls to some former classmates of the school he graduated from before I headed here."

"Maybe Aurora's brother knew him." Given Eryn's age when she'd moved from Charlotte, it was unlikely she'd remember the man. Did the Pullman business interests extend this far east? Cady used her cell to do a search and waited impatiently for several results to start filling the page. None of the resulting hits mentioned any business interests in Charlotte. She continued reading until the garlic bread arrived. Each of them put a piece on their plate, but she continued skimming articles as she ate.

Cady clicked on a sensationalized-looking headline about Aurora Pullman's death and scanned the story. Her throat went tight.

"Aurora was stabbed to death by her nine-year-old daughter." There was a fist-size knot in her chest. A spreading pressure. Ryder had said only that the girl had killed her mother. He hadn't hinted at the details. She wondered what Eryn remembered about the incident. Cady's memory of the scene with her father was grainy and incomplete. She'd only been four at the time. She couldn't be sure whether the memories were hers or what she'd been told. Or whether they were a by-product of the news articles she'd read when she'd gotten old enough to do the research herself.

Her gaze lifted to Miguel's. His expression was impassive, but that didn't mean he was unfamiliar with her background. It'd be in her personnel file. And the gossip was too juicy not to share, regardless of their profession.

"We need to talk to the Pullmans again. William might have known about Sutton's relationship with his sister. Maybe the two men even met." She reached for another piece of bread.

Seeming unimpressed with her suggestion, he snagged another slice of bread too. "Waste of time, probably. He's a few years older than she would have been. If you asked me about anybody who dated any of my sisters, I wouldn't have a clue."

Cady lifted a shoulder, unable to shake some of the details in the stories she'd read. A psychotic break, the mental health professionals had called Eryn's dissociative amnesia of her mother's death. What had that been like for the child, she wondered sickly, whose only explanation of the life-altering event came from what others told her? She could imagine too well. The similarities to Cady's own experiences were haunting.

Noting Miguel's gaze on her, she picked up the bread on her plate. "You may be right about Pullman, but it's still worth checking out. I could swing by there tonight on my way home and fill you in tomorrow morning. I called the hospital on the way here. They still aren't allowing anyone to question Preston."

Miguel's face lit up when the steaming pizza was set on the table. "You were pretty busy for someone who was on leave today."

"On leave, not dead." She immediately regretted her choice of words. A few yards closer to Preston's vehicle and things could have ended differently. Her cuts, bruises, and aches could have been lost limbs. Or worse. Cady slid a piece of pizza onto her plate. Her partner, never shy about such things, took two.

"CMPD still has a guard outside Preston's hospital door, but it'll be tomorrow or the next day before we can talk to her. Word from the bomb squad is the device was crude and wired to the ignition. Probably homemade."

Her brows rose. "Since she hadn't made it to the car, are they thinking remote start or cell phone detonator?" Preston had been closer to the vehicle than Cady had been, but not inside it.

"The working premise is she had the fob in her hand and started the engine remotely. Detectives also recovered a piece of what they think might have been a GPS tracking device."

"Which explains how Sutton made sure she was doing exactly what she'd agreed to." Pizza forgotten for the moment, Cady considered the information. A GPS tracking device and an IED that wasn't remotely triggered. Both meant the person responsible didn't have to be in the area when the bomb went off. He just had to be able to locate the vehicle and wire it. The spot where Preston had parked the car would have afforded him some degree of privacy, especially if he'd done it at night.

"I talked to Julie Neve, since she'd said they'd bought her the vehicle," Miguel was saying between bites. "She confirmed it had a remote start."

"It ended up saving Preston's life."

His face was grim. "From the sounds of things, she's got a rough road ahead of her. At least two surgeries, not to mention skin grafts for the burns."

And the medical implications, Cady reflected when they fell into silence as they ate, didn't take into consideration the legal ramifications for the woman's part in Samuel Aldeen's escape.

An hour later Cady and Miguel parted. When she got to her vehicle, she put in a call to William Pullman. She was anxious to question him about David Sutton, if not tonight, then tomorrow morning. She didn't doubt that she could wrangle an invitation to stop by.

When motivated, she could be very persuasive.

◆ ◆ ◆

Three hours later, William Pullman held the door open for Cady and stared. "Good heavens," he said faintly. "I hope you haven't been in an accident." As if belatedly recalling his manners, he ushered her down the hallway toward the office she'd been in yesterday.

"Something like that. But I'm fine. I won't take up much of your time."

"I'm going to hold you to that." He waved her to the chair she sat in yesterday. "It's my son's bedtime. We have our ritual." Rather than sitting next to her, he took a seat behind the desk again. "After you left yesterday the sheriff searched the property. Although I didn't think it was necessary, he's posted deputies on the road in front until he has a better idea of the escaped prisoner's plans."

She'd spoken to the men before continuing up the drive to the estate. "It may prove to be unneeded, but it doesn't hurt to be cautious." She took out her cell and found the pictures she'd taken of the photos Cisco had shown them earlier and got up to show each of them to William. "We found another individual I'm hoping you could provide some background on."

Shock flickered across his face as she swiped through each of the images.

"Good Lord. Where would you have gotten that picture of my sister?"

She provided a quick explanation, ending with, "Do you recognize the man with her in the photos?"

William shook his head. "I'm afraid not. The restaurant was in Charlotte, you say? Aurora went to UNC Charlotte. Well, we both did, but I was seven years ahead of her. I was back home by the time she attended. I really know very little about her college life or her friends from back then."

Disappointment slammed into her. Coming here was likely another dead end, as Miguel had predicted. "You don't know any students she graduated high school with who might have also gone to UNC?"

"I'm afraid not. My sister and I grew closer when she returned home, but she wasn't one to share confidences about her college days, even then."

"Perhaps other members of the family might know more."

"I doubt it." He looked in the direction of the grandfather clock situated beside the door. "Rosalyn and I didn't marry until a couple years after Aurora's death. And Eryn, of course, would have been much too young."

"As long as I'm here, could I talk to her again?" Cady smiled easily. "You're probably right, but one never knows what might jog loose a memory."

He hesitated, clearly reluctant. "Eryn goes to bed fairly early. Her medication makes her sleepy. But I can go check her room."

"Thank you." He left the room and she prepared to wait. But when she heard voices in the hallway, Cady got up and went to the door.

"Why were you coming out of our suite?" William was addressing Eryn.

"Jaxson wanted me to look at a picture he'd painted today. I bought him a book of paint by numbers when I went to town yesterday."

"Yes, well . . ." William looked over his shoulder. Caught sight of Cady standing there. "Deputy US Marshal Maddix is back again. I don't think you can help her, but if you feel up to it . . ."

Eryn never took her gaze off Cady as she trailed behind her uncle. "What happened to your face?"

"Eryn," her uncle said, his voice pained. "Please remember your manners."

"It's fine." Cady smiled at the young woman as she dropped into the chair beside her. "There was an . . . accident yesterday. I look like the walking wounded, but I'm okay." At least she would be, she hoped. Soon. "We found a picture today of your mother with someone we recognized."

"May I see it?" Eryn's voice was as polite as a schoolgirl's.

"Of course." Cady brought up the photos she'd taken again and handed her cell to the young woman. Eryn took the phone from her and stared at the first picture intently.

"She looks . . . happy."

Her comment struck something inside Cady. "You don't remember her that way?"

"Sometimes. Sometimes she was." She handed the phone back to Cady. "When was the picture taken?"

"Twenty-three years ago. She would have been attending college in Charlotte at the time."

"Do you know the name of the man beside her?"

Cady nodded. "His name is David Sutton. Does he look familiar? Do you recall your mother ever mentioning his name?"

"I already told you," William said impatiently, "Eryn would be too young to recall."

As if to validate his assertion, she shook her head. "I don't remember meeting any of Mama's friends. Oh." The hand resting motionless on her lap twitched, the fingers curling into her palm. "I met someone in the grocery store in Asheville yesterday when we went shopping. She said she knew Mama from college." Her voice was flat. As interested as she'd seemed in the picture Cady had shown her, meeting with her mother's friend hadn't elicited the same pleasure.

"Did she give you her name?"

"Madeline Grayson Carson. She said she and Mama had been college roommates. That she and some friends had gotten together with her monthly . . . before."

Before she'd been murdered. Cady couldn't help but feel a dart of pity for the young woman. "You've been helpful, thank you." She rose, her gaze going to William's. There was a frozen look on his face, as if he'd gone somewhere else. Thoughts of his sister probably summoned a host of painful memories.

Eryn surprised her by asking, "Will you come back and tell me . . . if you find out anything about my mother?"

William frowned. "Deputy US Marshal Maddix's job does not entail . . ."

But the entreaty in the young woman's eyes tugged at something inside Cady. Something impossible to ignore.

"I was a kid," Eryn said. "I only have a few years of memories of her. I gather snippets. Of what people say. How they mention her. But it's hard too. I want to know more, but facing the past is like getting a chance to pet a dragon. Who wouldn't be tempted to get near enough to see one? But there's always a chance if you get too close, it could devour you whole."

◆ ◆ ◆

The dog's ferocious barking brought Cady instantly awake. Struggling to sit up in bed, she reached for her weapon in the drawer of the bedside table. The dog threw itself at her bedroom window, barking and growling wildly.

She stifled a groan of pain as she rolled from the bed and joined the canine at the window. "What is it, buddy? What do you see?" With her free hand, she lifted aside the curtain, studying the scene outside the window.

A blanket of black shrouded the property. Not a sliver of moon provided illumination. The dog turned suddenly and raced out of the room, never letting up its yelping.

Cady followed it to the front entry. She donned a coat and boots as quickly as her protesting limbs would allow before unlocking the door. The animal tore down the steps in front of her. Her heart rapped rapidly as she trailed it around the corner of the house to see the dog snarling and jumping toward the roof of the doghouse.

Hands steadying her weapon, Cady ran closer until she could see the small shadow crouched there, growling and hissing.

The adrenaline that had shot through her veins only moments earlier dissipated. "Congratulations, pal." She lowered the weapon and used her free hand to grab the dog's collar. Yanked him away. "You've saved us all from a villainous raccoon."

The dog continued barking and lunging as she led it away. A crunching sound could be heard behind them. Realization dawned. Cady hadn't considered that leaving the dog's food outside was going to attract other creatures as well. So would the warmth of the doggie Taj Mahal. Tomorrow she'd find something to block off its entrance each night when she brought the dog inside. *With* the food dish.

Her bare legs chilled quickly in the cool night air. But since they were already outside, she did a perimeter check of the yard. The dog paused to sniff a few times but alerted at nothing else. It was as good a barometer as any for gauging whether a two-legged pest had been out here.

Satisfied, Cady waited while the dog relieved himself, and then they went back into the house. She resecured the door. Habit had her checking the rooms, flipping on the light to the spare bedroom where the pots and pans still lined the floor beneath the window. She made sure it was locked before returning to the kitchen, where the dog was lapping up water as though it had fought off a battalion of masked marauders. She smirked, thinking of the coon. Maybe in tall doggy tales of exaggeration, it had.

The animal lifted its head and looked at her. It was likely her imagination that its eyes were filled with pride.

"Yeah, my hero," she told it, amused. "Were you warning me of danger or just pissed off the raccoon was eating your food?" The canine shook itself and then, circling the nearby dog bed three times, sank down on it. Settled its head on its paws and looked up at her. With effort, Cady sank to her haunches, stroking its head. "Is that your name? Hero? As good as any, I guess." She should follow the dog's lead and go back to bed. But she was wide awake now. She had a feeling any attempts at slumber would be futile.

She set the gun on the floor and carefully sat down next to the animal, still stroking it. Better to remain awake than to suffer from another nightmare like she'd had this morning. Cady let her head rest against the wall. She could go weeks without experiencing the recurring dream. Almost getting blown up yesterday would have been enough to trigger it.

But she knew it was more than that. The similarities in her and Eryn Pullman's pasts were eerie. It was difficult to understand the vagaries of fate that landed one of them in a psych facility and the other in the US Marshals Service.

Eryn: Then

Screams tore from her throat, a steady stream of frenzy. Eryn flailed on the bed. Shudders shook her body. Her throat went raw and hoarse, but still the shrieks came, flowing around her, a wordless voice for the terror gripping her. "Mama! Mama!"

The sound of running footsteps didn't stem her cries. She was wrapped in a horror she couldn't put into words. It was dragging her back. Back to something she couldn't quite remember, except for the sense of horror.

"Eryn! Wake up!" Arms tightened around her and at first Eryn fought them. The arms with their clawing fingers would return her to a place she didn't want to see again. Never wanted to see, ever.

"Wake up, Mama's here. Sh-h, now. Sh-h." Eryn choked back sobs as she was rocked, shaking so hard it felt like her body would break in half. "It's all right now, everything's all right. Sh-h." Mama stroked her hair and Eryn snuggled closer, shivering. "Tell me about your dream, baby. Tell me all about it."

Eryn shook her head against Mama's chest. Even now the nightmare was fading into the distance, like the balloon she'd once let go of at a parade. It got smaller and smaller until she could no longer see it.

But the fear remained. Even when the dream was over, the way it made her feel lingered.

"Want to come to bed with me for a while?" Eryn felt herself being lifted and carried down the hall. It was a rare treat to be allowed in Mama's bed, but all she cared about now was Mama holding her close. Whispering that nothing would ever hurt her again.

Eryn knew the words were a lie. But she needed to believe them. That was easier when she could stay clutched in Mama's arms until she went back to sleep.

After a long time, her eyes shut again. She could no longer answer Mama's whispers in her ear. She felt the arms loosen around her, which was okay. She was still in Mama's bed, where it was snuggly and soft. Eryn felt herself begin to drift. Everything was quiet except for the whispers nearby.

"So what's wrong this time?"

"What's wrong? She's *five*, Bill. You saw the information the doctor gave me about night terrors."

"Did the doctor have any idea how many years this is supposed to go on? Maybe she should be trying to get at what's causing them."

Their words floated around Eryn, preventing her from fully falling asleep.

"I think I already know. It's my fault. All of it."

Something in Mama's voice had Eryn lifting her head from the pillow. She sounded like she was about to cry. Uncle Bill had his arms around her. "Stop. You don't know that. It doesn't help to blame yourself."

"Even if I deserve it?" Mama sniffled. "It all went wrong so fast. And I was so busy trying to fix it, I didn't even consider Eryn was part of it too. Do you think she remembers?"

"No." It was the voice Uncle Bill used when he didn't want you to argue anymore. "She was too young. Life happens. We deal with it."

"Someone has to be there for her, Billy." Mama rested her head on Uncle Bill's shoulder. "I just wish Eryn had a big brother to look out for her like you did for me."

Eryn nestled into the pillow again. They were talking about boring stuff. She didn't want a big brother. Henry was bad enough. Except . . . she yawned and pulled the covers closer. If she had a brother, maybe he'd beat up Henry when he was mean.

Or maybe he'd beat up Eryn. People didn't always act the way they should. Not even grown-ups. Sometimes the people who were supposed to protect you from monsters were monsters themselves.

◆ ◆ ◆

Everyone was always extra nice the day after Eryn had bad dreams, even though she was fine when she woke up. When she overslept, Mama said she didn't have to go to school that day. Eryn was happy. She didn't like kindergarten. They had fun books and paints there, but she couldn't use them all the time. Only when the teacher said. The other kids were mean sometimes and didn't share the paint. And when Eryn hit them to make them share, she was the one who got in trouble.

Even Mary Jane made her favorite breakfast. French toast. She ate it all, and when the woman wasn't looking, she licked the leftover syrup off her plate. Somehow Mary Jane knew, though, and scrubbed Eryn's face with a smelly dishcloth.

"Where'd Mama go?" she asked, pulling out of Mary Jane's grasp.

"She went back to bed. Why don't you get your paints out and make her a nice picture? I'll get you some newspapers."

Eryn skipped to her room and pulled the containers from beneath her bed. She took off the covers and removed the paints, stacking one on top of the other until she had a rainbow of colors. Mary Jane bustled back in and laid newspapers on the floor beneath Eryn's easel. "Make a mess and I'll put all your paints away," the woman warned before leaving the room again. Eryn made a face behind her back before carefully carrying the paints over to the shelf on the easel. She made Mama lots of pictures, but even after she was done, Mama was still asleep.

Bored, she went back to her room. Mary Jane had brought in a lot of newspapers, and some were still folded in a pile on the floor. Eryn went to get scissors and tape from another tote under her bed. She'd make some paper dolls. Then she could get construction paper out and make clothes for them.

You're not supposed to use scissors without an adult.

"Shut up," she muttered. Mr. Timmons was always so, so bossy. It was like having a Mary Jane in her head all the time.

Bet Henry would be surprised if you snuck in and cut up the clothes in his dresser.

She pressed her lips together. That would be bad. Very bad. Lots of times Uncle Arlo had naughty ideas. If she listened to him, she often got in trouble.

But sometimes they're fun ideas. And Henry deserves it after locking you in the stable.

A shiver crawled up her back. She didn't want to remember the cold, damp room in the stable. Eryn was scared when Henry locked her in there. She'd screamed and screamed. Henry had gotten in trouble, but not enough.

Sneak by Mary Jane so she doesn't hear you. You can be in and out lickety-split. All of Henry's clothes, in pieces!

"They'll know it was me. You should be quiet."

"Eryn?"

She turned around, shoving the scissors down at her side so Mary Jane couldn't see. "What?"

The woman was standing in her doorway with a basket of dirty clothes. Twice a week she collected them from everyone's hamper to do the wash. The way she was looking at Eryn right now made her think Mary Jane could see right into her head. "Who are you talking to?"

Hunching her shoulders, Eryn muttered, "No one."

"I heard you, so don't lie to me, missy."

"Mr. Timmons and Uncle Arlo."

"You know, your mama had an imaginary friend when she was little."

"She did?" Eryn's gaze shot up.

"Yes, ma'am. By the name of Scarlett Mooseberry. She used to insist I set a place for her at the table."

"Mr. Timmons and Uncle Arlo don't eat." They just chattered all the time, arguing mostly. Telling her what to do. Their voices filled her head and made it hurt.

Sometimes they made her scared.

Mary Jane took a step into the room. "Your mama knew her friend was just pretend. You know yours are, too, right?" She had a look on her face Eryn had seen from adults before. The doctor lady said it was normal for kids to have imaginary friends. They could feel very real. But everyone got weird if they heard her talking to them. Eryn tried not to do it. But sometimes she forgot.

"I know."

The way Mary Jane stared at her made Eryn feel small and afraid. But the woman finally moved away. When she was gone, so was Eryn's good mood.

Go away, she silently commanded the voices. *Go away go away go away!*

It's all right, Eryn. Just listen to me and everything will be fine.

Nosy old bitch. You should stab her with the scissors. Teach her to mind her own business.

Put the scissors away now.

Use them. Use them like I said. And maybe the next time you see Henry, you should . . .

"Shut up!" Eryn brought both hands up to clap them over her ears. She accidentally grazed her face with the scissors. "Ouch!"

Put them down, Eryn.

See what I mean? Use them use them use . . .

"I said shut up!" She knew whom she should use the scissors on. How she could get rid of the voices for good. Eryn pulled her hand way back and then brought it forward to ram the pointed scissors into her ear.

Eryn: Now

"You were up late." Rosalyn's voice lacked its normal cheeriness as she stuffed Jaxson's limp arms in the sleeve of his coat.

Eryn thought that at seven Jaxson was plenty old enough to dress himself. But his mother zipped him up before fetching his lunch box out of the refrigerator. "I couldn't sleep." She'd dragged out a fresh easel and painted until she tired. And then she'd gotten on her laptop and looked up some information for today.

"I know." Rosalyn smiled before leaving the room, reappearing a few moments later with Jaxson's boots. "I was reading until after midnight and saw your light. I peeked in on you. Do you feel all right?" At Eryn's look, her smile dimmed. "I mean . . . Dr. Steigel said if the medication isn't doing its job, sometimes difficulty sleeping is one of the side effects."

Rosalyn's words brought a sliver of concern. One Eryn doused by saying firmly, "Everyone has insomnia sometimes. Even you, apparently."

"Oh, I was sleepy." The other woman lifted her sluggish son out of his chair and nudged him toward the kitchen doorway. "The book was so good, I just had to finish it. I'm paying for it now, though."

"Rosalyn." Once Eryn had the other woman's attention her courage shriveled. She forced herself to continue. "Have you ever noticed lights shining on the property? I saw some last night. I couldn't figure out where they would be coming from."

"I've seen some before, too," Jaxson piped up.

Rosalyn gave him a light shove. "Go to your room and get your backpack. Quick, like a bunny." His pace qualified more as a trudge. When he was out of hearing, his mother looked at Eryn with a frown. "Please don't fill his head with crazy ideas. He already has the wildest imagination. Why, just a couple of weeks ago he was certain he heard noises in the attic after we put him to bed. He wasn't satisfied until your uncle had gone upstairs and looked all through the place and assured him there was no one hiding up there."

Eryn could attest that Jaxson had seen lights outside at least once, but there was no way she was going to rat on her young cousin. She nodded. "I'll try to be more careful around him. But I wasn't imagining things. I caught glimpses of a light several times last night."

"Well." Rosalyn sent a harried look in the direction her son had gone. "We could get you some room-darkening shades, I suppose. Once in a while we do get a car using the drive in front of the gate to back up in. Maybe you saw headlights. Or it could have been the deputies, looking around again. I'll be glad when they're gone." She broke off as Jaxson reappeared. "All right, young man, let's get you to the car."

Eryn stared after her aunt as she hurried her son to the large living room. Headlights wouldn't account for the lights she'd seen over the course of at least an hour. And maybe she was asking the wrong person, in any case. Because when she'd first seen the light last night, Eryn had gone to the coat closet and looked for Uncle Bill's parka, the same one Jaxson had discovered missing when he'd gone outside hoping to meet up with his dad.

It'd been missing.

◆ ◆ ◆

When her cell sounded, Eryn read the text and then set the note she'd written on her neatly made bed. Pulling her coat on, she moved quietly toward the front door. Rosalyn hadn't yet returned from dropping Jaxson at school, and Uncle Bill's office door was closed. She hadn't seen Mary Jane this morning, but she knew from experience the woman could appear when one least expected her.

Eryn slipped out the door, ran down the drive, and saw the strange vehicle idling outside the gates. The sheriff's car sat almost directly across the road. The deputy in the driver's seat was watching her. It added to the niggling sense of paranoia that had lodged inside her, summoned by Rosalyn's words. The tachyphylaxis condition required her to remain hypervigilant about monitoring her symptoms on a daily basis. But she'd been on her current cocktail of pills for over a year without a problem. Just because she'd had trouble sleeping for a few hours didn't necessarily mean her medication was losing its effectiveness.

But tossing and turning waiting for sleep was different from the industrious hours she'd spent last night. The long stretch spent painting, followed by hours researching on the web.

She pressed the button to allow the gates to swing open and walked through them, closing them behind her before slipping into the black sedan.

"Hi. You Eryn?"

"Yes. Thank you for coming." She immediately felt silly. An Uber driver was paid to take her where she wanted to go. Eryn had discovered that much in her research last night. She'd used the credit card Uncle Bill had set up for her years ago to charge incidentals at Rolling Acres. The ride to town would be the first thing she'd ever charged without supervision. The thought was simultaneously thrilling and depressing.

If the older woman behind the wheel found anything odd about her words, it didn't show in her expression. "No problem." She checked her phone. "It's a beautiful day for a drive. You're wanting to go to Haywood County Private Driver's Instruction in Waynesville, correct?"

"Yes." Eryn repeated the street address to her, and the car slowly pulled onto the road. Nerves jittered in her veins. The plan she'd formulated last night now felt hasty and ill advised. But she had to start taking control of her life at some point.

This was a baby step toward that end.

◆ ◆ ◆

Eryn stood hesitantly in the doorway of the driving school she'd found online. "C'mon in." The fortyish man rose from his desk chair and strode to the doorway to shake Eryn's hand. "I'm Gary Atwood. This is the premier private driving school in the county." That's what the online ad had proclaimed. "You look like you're having second thoughts. If you do, I don't want you close enough to escape out the door."

He chuckled and she managed a slight smile. Arranging for private driving lessons would constitute the first independent act she'd taken outside of Rolling Acres. She didn't want to spend time considering the fact. It would give this moment a weight disproportionate to the act. She wiped her palms on her pants. Tried to quiet the rapid pounding in her pulse.

"Are you here for yourself or someone else?" Atwood dragged a chair over to a small table and gestured her toward it before fetching himself another.

"Me."

"Okay, that's all right. Not everyone gets the opportunity to learn in high school. And some people aren't ready in their teens." Atwood had no more sat before he bounced out of his seat to grab a brochure on his desk and came back to hand it to Eryn. "The best thing about private instruction is the individualization. We work around your schedule and can design the program to your expectations. You actually chose an excellent time to make arrangements." He had the swift and smooth patter of a natural-born salesman. "Everyone needs instruction in winter-weather driving. And in another few weeks, winter's gonna be here, whether we like it or not."

She nodded silently, anxious to get this part over. "Can I sign up now?"

Surprise flickered across his face, but Atwood quickly recovered. "Absolutely. Let me get a contract." He jumped up again to cross to a filing cabinet. Pulled open a drawer and withdrew a file folder. "We don't have to get into all the specifics right this minute. You'll want to consult your schedule, and then I can try to match it up with one of my drivers." He came back, taking a paper out of the folder and handing it to her with a pen. "We can start with your name and contact information." Eryn carefully filled out the lines he was indicating. When she'd finished, he took the sheet from her. "Rather than making you complete all this, we'll just have a conversation and I can fill it in. First off, what are you hoping . . ." His voice broke off as he stared at the paper. When he looked back at her, his expression had closed.

"Eryn Pullman. Don't tell me you're Henry's wife?"

God, no. "He isn't married."

The man nodded, then rose and ripped the contract in half. "Sorry. I misspoke earlier. We aren't accepting new students, after all."

"But you just said . . ."

"No new students." He crossed to the door and held it open. His meaning was unmistakable.

A hot wash of shame flooded her when she realized what was happening. Without another word, Eryn got up and walked stiffly toward the car waiting for her.

"Well, that was fast!" The woman—who'd asked to be called Lucy— took one glance at Eryn and then snapped her jaw closed.

Eryn yanked open the car door and practically dove inside the vehicle, slamming the door behind her. She bent forward, arms wrapped around her waist, wishing with all her heart the ground would swallow her whole. After meeting Madeline Carson yesterday, how had she failed to consider something similar could happen the next time someone recognized her name? Tears pricked her eyes, and she swiped them away furiously. She wanted nothing more than to be back in her room so she could curl up in a ball and lick her wounds. What was so damned special about being able to drive, anyway? Her meds could make her super sleepy. She'd have to be extra cautious each time she got behind the wheel.

"Honey, I don't know what happened in there. But Atwood's isn't the only private driving instruction outfit in town."

Eryn drew a deep breath. Forced herself to sit upright. "It's all right."

"Maybe it is." Lucy was watching her in the rearview mirror. "But something seemed important enough for you to come here this morning. Does it matter enough to check somewhere else?"

She wanted to say no. But the burn that had taken root inside her last night flared just as hot this morning. If she could drive, she could sign up for some college classes. Go to scenic areas for inspiration. The only way she was ever going to improve her painting was by furthering her instruction.

After a long moment, she said, "Can you take me to a different one?"

Lucy's smile was wide. "Give me a minute to search online."

◆ ◆ ◆

Ike Masterson had twenty years on Gary Atwood, and it was soon clear his driving school was a one-man show. Eryn sat woodenly through his spiel, steeling herself for a repeat of the earlier scene.

"How much?"

If he was surprised by her abrupt question, it didn't show. He stroked his bearded jaw and quoted her a price. "I require a four hundred dollar down payment."

"I don't have that much with me." She'd spent some money when Mary Jane had taken her shopping. The woman had steered her to the sales racks with the admonition never to pay full price for anything if she could help it. "I can give you two hundred today."

Ike looked amused. "You drive a hard bargain."

She reached into her coat pocket for the cash Uncle Bill had given her. Peeled off two hundreds and handed them to him.

"Looks like we're in business." He got up to rummage in a desk drawer. "I've got a contract in here somewhere. Nothing much to fill out, really." Smiling, he handed her a slightly creased paper and a pen.

He has a nice smile, Eryn thought numbly as she stared at the contract. She was unable to return it.

"How much experience do you have?" Ike asked.

"None."

"Not a problem. No bad habits to unlearn."

She only half heard him. Her eyes were fixed on the contract. NAME. The first line jumped out at her, while the other print faded. She set the pen to the paper. Couldn't manage more than the *E* before she stopped again.

"My name is Eryn Pullman," she said defiantly. There was no use filling out the contract if it was just going to be torn up like the last one.

There was a flicker of recognition in the other man's eyes. "Okay. Would you prefer I did the writing for you?"

Eryn stared at him, nonplussed. Family tragedies like hers might fade from memories, but she'd seen the television vans outside their drive on her first day home. Although she hadn't tuned in, she was certain her history had been splashed all over screens in the area. Even people who didn't personally know her family would recall their name.

"When you get done filling out the contract, go ahead and turn it over. Write your schedule on the back." Ike's teeth flashed. "Pretty sure I won't have a problem accommodating you, but if we have a conflict in our schedules, I can work something out most days."

"I only have appointments on Wednesdays." That was the day she went to Dr. Ashland. She quickly filled out the contract and then wrote her appointment days on the back. "How many days a week are the lessons?"

"Up to you. We're required by the state to provide a certain number of contact hours. The quicker we get them done, the faster you can apply for a license."

A thread of excitement entered her veins. She was in charge of determining how long it would take to be permitted to drive a car. The knowledge was heady. "Can we try for two days a week? In the mornings?" Mornings were the best time for painting, before the medication kicked in. She was decidedly more sluggish by noon.

But the road to independence was going to take sacrifice.

"Did you put your cell number down?" Ike peered at the paper before nodding in satisfaction. "You might want to put mine in your contacts, in case you need to reschedule." He recited it for her. "How about Mondays and Fridays? Is ten o'clock okay?"

"All right." Dizzy with relief, she smiled at him. "I'll see you tomorrow."

She got up and strode to the door, anxious to get to the car, but for a different reason this time.

"Coincidence, you coming here."

She stopped, his words acting like a dash of ice water on her enthusiasm.

"Some time back, I did driving instruction with your mama."

Warily, Eryn met his gaze. He was smiling again. And the kindness she saw in his eyes had a bit of her tension seeping away. "She'd been mandated to attend driving classes. These days they'd just yank your license for too many moving violations, but back then you could avoid losing it by taking part in remedial driving instruction." He lowered his voice conspiratorially. "Your mama had a lead foot."

"She did?"

"Yep. She had a sparkle about her. Drew people in, you could say. I still remember how her face would light up when she talked about you. Proud as punch, she was. If people round here get you down, maybe it'll help to just hold on to that."

Ryder

Laura Talbot set a steaming mug of coffee in front of Ryder before sitting next to him, cradling another cup in her hands. He took a sip, wincing at its temperature, but appreciating the flavor. The coffee maker in his office was pretty great, but nothing matched his mom's brew.

"Heck of a thing when I have to bribe my only son with coffee to get a visit these days," she teased. It wasn't six yet, but she was dressed with her hair and makeup done. No one saw Laura Talbot before she had her face on for the day. Her habit of early-bird mornings was a standing joke in the family.

The hour suited him fine. In twenty minutes, Ryder would head to the office and take a stab at the mountain of county matters unrelated to Samuel Aldeen. By seven fifteen he'd be at the community center room they'd confiscated for a command center, which he'd left shortly before three this morning. At this point, he may as well move in a cot.

"I've been keeping long hours. Hopefully it will end soon."

His mom's pretty face sobered. "I know you have. It makes me feel better knowing you're in charge. People in town are getting mighty jumpy with that murderous pervert on the loose."

Ryder gave a wry smile. "We've got so many alphabet agencies gathered to assist in this thing, I can't say for sure who's running what." SBI.

FBI. The regional fugitive task force. USMS. And after they'd found Bush with a couple of bullet holes in him, the ATF had joined the team. Coordinating the actions of all the groups was a staggering task.

"Your sister is planning to bring the kids for a few days this weekend." Seeming oblivious to Ryder's expression, his mother sipped from her mug. "Seems like forever since I've seen Ronda and the boys, even if it's really only been a few weeks."

"Why don't you go there?"

His mom's mug paused mid-descent. "What? Why?"

"I don't want the kids here while Aldeen is still free." The odds were stacked against the man ever being within miles of this home. But the fugitive had been riding the wheel of Lady Luck since he drove out the Fristol gates. There was no way in hell Ryder's nephews were going to be anywhere close to this area. He realized his fear was more emotional than logical. But caution cost them nothing.

"You're right," she sighed. "Of course, you're right. I'll call Ronda later today and ask if she minds switching plans."

He almost regretted his words when worry replaced his mom's smile. But not enough to rescind them. He didn't mind knowing his family would be safely away on the other side of the state.

"You're certain he remains in the area, then?"

The question was like touching a bruise. The fugitive's best chance at leaving the state had been right after he escaped. Ryder couldn't figure what was keeping him in the vicinity. The manhunt grew more focused by the hour. As yesterday had proven, it was only a matter of time before he was recognized.

Ryder's mood darkened when he thought of how the new sketch of Aldeen had come about. The next time he tried to entice a child, there might not be a smart ten-year-old brother in the vicinity to stop him.

His mom smiled. "Your mind is already on the case. Go on, then. Go out and save the world."

"My cape and tights are with my other uniform," he deadpanned. But with another look at the clock, Ryder took a big gulp of coffee before rising. A familiar band of tension was forming across his shoulders. It was one he wouldn't shake until Aldeen was in custody again.

His mom stood, too, and he kissed the top of her head. Easy enough to do; he'd been a foot taller than her since eighth grade. "I'll call you before you leave for Cary," he promised.

"Uh-huh. Heard that one before too." She smoothed a hand down his shirt and smiled up at him. "I'll never get over the sight of you wearing the same uniform your daddy did. He would have been so proud, Ryder."

His answering smile was tight. Butch Talbot's idea of pride had usually taken the form of unrelenting pressure and unrealistic expectations, followed by ridicule and belittlement when those expectations weren't met. He'd treated Ryder's mom like she was wrapped in gossamer, which was perhaps his only redeeming quality. Ryder had never doubted Butch's love for his wife. But that was negated by his history of being a serial cheater. As far as Ryder knew, his mom had never discovered her husband's sexual proclivities. God willing, she never would.

"Thanks for the coffee." He headed for the door.

"Thanks for the suggestion," his mom called after him. "I'll pass it on to Ronda. But you know your sister. She's stubborn."

Ryder did know. But if it came to it, he'd call his younger sister himself. He waved to his mom as she watched him from the window. He didn't ask his family for much. But it'd be nice if they'd give him some peace of mind until this case wrapped up.

◆ ◆ ◆

Ryder had gotten exactly thirty minutes of peace before there was a rap at his office door.

"Come in if you're bearing doughnuts."

Cady Maddix entered, her mouth curled into a smile. "Sorry. I'll have to remember for next time."

Ryder stared. "Holy shit." Not especially eloquent, especially when addressing a female. But damn. Instead of the ponytail she'd sported the other times they'd met, she was wearing her hair loose, probably in an effort to shield the brilliant bruising along one side of her jaw. He winced a little at the explosion of color there. He could only imagine what her sunglasses were hiding. "Was that from flying debris, or did you hit something in the blowback?"

"Both, I think." She moved, rather stiffly, he noted, and sank into a seat across from his desk. "Do you have time for a quick update, or are you going to make me wait for the official one later this morning?"

He leaned back in his chair. They had a team of people working on a twice-daily coordinated dissemination of information. It was essential to let all the different law enforcement entities involved with this case know what the others were doing. But he appreciated the way she'd sent him quick summaries on her daily results. Didn't mind doing the same. "You heard we missed Aldeen again." At her nod, he continued: "He had a ninety-minute head start on us. We don't have a license plate number, but Highway Patrol is doing a stop and search on all similar vehicle make and models. Every law enforcement entity in the area has the same information."

And so far, it had yielded jack shit. The quick flare of frustration was familiar. The Highway Patrol helicopters had spotted a few matching vehicles, but none of the sightings had panned out. After the news alert, the tip line had been overwhelmed. There'd been close to a thousand reported sightings of Aldeen scattered throughout the surrounding states since his escape. Hundreds since yesterday. But while the task force was following up the most credible tips, so far they'd all fizzled.

"He has to know the vehicle he's driving is no longer viable," Cady said thoughtfully.

Ryder tapped the stack of paper on his desk. "Which is why we're collecting stolen car reports." He was wishing now he'd brewed a pot of coffee when he'd come in. His caffeine fix hadn't been satisfied with the single cup at his mom's. "We got word of a home burglary report outside Gatlinburg. The witness who called it in described a car that might match Bush's but couldn't give much of a description of the intruder, other than the guy was wearing a hat. We sent some people to check it out. Aldeen would have had time to get there, but . . ."

"Why would he have chosen now to leave the state?" Cady wondered. "He's had plenty of opportunity."

He shrugged. "The cabin wasn't safe for him any longer. He had to go somewhere." He stifled a sudden yawn with his fist. "On another note, ATF reports are back on the ballistics from Joe Bush's homicide. The gun had been used in a shooting in Charlotte in 2017. The ATF team on the task force is tracing the lead. And . . . I think that catches you up." He straightened in his chair. Reclining even slightly would put him to sleep. "Did you discover anything else linking Aldeen to the Pullmans?"

In answer, she took out her cell and scrolled through some pictures before leaning forward to set it on his desktop. "Samuel Aldeen, Sheila Preston, and David Sutton worked together at a restaurant-slash-bar in Charlotte twenty-three years ago. It's still in operation and the owner has pictures."

Ryder picked up the cell and studied the photo closely. "Okay. Who's the blonde on Sutton's lap?"

"His girlfriend from the time—Aurora Pullman." His expression must have reflected his shock. Cady gave a slow nod. "Yeah, that was our reaction too. It's our first clue as to why the fugitive showed interest in Eryn Pullman's progress notes. He knew her mother."

"But not Eryn. At least not then." Ryder handed the cell back to her, his mind racing. "Anything that links Aurora Pullman to either Sutton or Aldeen after Eryn was born?"

"Not yet." Cady slipped the phone in her coat pocket. "But when I spoke to the Pullmans again yesterday she mentioned the name of one of her mother's friends from the time. We'll talk to her today." She stretched her legs out and crossed one booted foot over the opposite ankle.

It was totally inappropriate and undoubtedly due to lack of sleep that he noticed just how long and slender her denim-clad legs were. "Maybe William Pullman . . ."

She was already shaking her head. "He claims he didn't know much about his sister's life when she was in Charlotte. He hasn't been a lot of help. And the daughter, of course, was too young at that time to remember much of anything from her time there. Have you cleared the IT employee at Fristol yet?"

A dull throb started in Ryder's temple. "I sent his computer to the feds, and they didn't find any trace he uploaded those patient progress notes disguised as audio files. I should hear about Joe Bush's computer today." Sutton. Preston. Bush. The help with the audio files probably originated with one of the three known accomplices. He got a text message then and picked up the cell on his desk to read it. "I'm afraid I'm going to have to go." Rising, he shoved the reports he'd been going through in a file folder and rounded the corner of the desk. "The new shift is starting to roll in at the command center."

"Okay." He noticed the caution with which she moved as she straightened and shoved out of the chair. "I had a personal reason for stopping, if you can spare another minute."

Something in her tone alerted him. "Sure." Ryder backed up a step and hitched his hip on the desk.

"There was a break-in at Blong Rentals a few days ago. Just outside of city limits, north of Waynesville."

Intrigued now, he nodded. "Okay. We've had a string of burglaries of local businesses." He vaguely recalled seeing the Blong report, although the break-in had been crowded from his mind by the Aldeen investigation.

"I was wondering if your officers took prints."

"Yes, and they've been submitted to the state crime lab. Maybe we'll get lucky and they belong to the same person. Preferably one in the system. But with the lab's backlog and no suspect in the burglary, it'll be a low priority."

Cady nodded. "Okay. If you get a suspect, let me know."

He eyed her shrewdly. "What's this about?"

"Someone broke into my home. Well, not broke in," she corrected herself. "Waltzed in, more like. I found out later keys had been stolen at Dorothy's place. It would explain how the intruder entered. She said the keys were in a cupboard on hooks with the addresses above them. Maybe you've had other break-ins at some of her other rentals."

"I can look into it, but I don't recall offhand." He pushed away from the desk to grab his coat from the rack by the door as she started moving in that direction. "No reason we can't print your place, too, if you want. Was anything taken?" She shook her head. "You've changed the locks?"

A smile flickered across her lips. "One benefit from being forced to take the day off yesterday. Got a dog too. The way he carried on last night about a raccoon in the yard, I'm pretty sure he'll be a deterrent."

"Both are good ideas." If other rental keys had been taken, the most likely explanation was Blong's burglar intended B and Es of the rental properties. But an intruder who hadn't taken anything when he or she had the chance put the idea to rest. And left a far more serious one.

Cady could have been targeted by someone she'd arrested. Or someone who thought a woman living alone was an easy mark. But she was a Deputy US Marshal. And he took possible threats to law enforcement damn seriously.

His hand on the knob, he looked at her. "Give me your address. I'll send a patrol past your house a couple of times each shift."

She seemed like she was about to object when her gaze fixed on something across the room. Her expression stilled.

Turning, he looked in the direction she was staring.

"The man in the picture . . . he's the former sheriff?"

Ryder winced mentally as he looked at the side-by-side formal pictures of him and his dad. Stepping into the sheriff's position in his father's posthumous shoes had been a delicate situation when it came to staff. Butch had been respected by his employees. Change had to be instituted incrementally. After two years on the job, the only remaining photo of the man was in here. And Ryder wasn't sure how much longer diplomacy would have him waiting to take the final picture down.

"Butch Talbot."

Her eyes jerked to his. "Your . . . father?"

"Yes."

"You don't look like him."

There was a note in her tone he would have liked to explore further. She'd seemed shocked when she saw the photo. But there was something else in her expression too. Something he didn't have the time to probe.

"I favor my mom." He opened the door and she moved through it faster than she'd entered. In a few minutes Ryder was going to be neck-deep in the newest details of the investigation again.

But a part of him was going to keep puzzling over Cady's reaction to Butch Talbot's picture.

Samuel

The car door opened and David Sutton slid inside, two fast-food sacks in one hand.

"You took your sweet time," Samuel noted. Too many hours on the outside had been spent waiting on the man for one reason or another.

The other man reached for the controls to the heater. "Jesus. It's fucking freezing in here. It took me a while to find you. Your directions weren't the greatest."

"I can only run the car for a few minutes at a time to warm up. I'm practically out of gas. And I haven't eaten since yesterday afternoon." Samuel grabbed at one of the bags and dug into it. He'd taken some food when he'd packed up his things, but the supplies hadn't lasted long.

David gave a nasty smile. "Guess you didn't figure you'd have to live in ol' Joe's crappy car for a few hours."

"A few?" The temper that had simmered in him since yesterday threatened to bubble over. After the owner of the rentals had come to talk to him, Samuel had known he'd have to move quickly. What he hadn't figured on was waiting nearly twenty-four hours in this shitty abandoned farmyard for Sutton to get here. "I could have walked across the state in the time it took you to follow a few simple directions."

"It took a while to make all new arrangements. We figured on you staying in the cabin for the duration. What happened?"

"Someone recognized me. I got out before the cops could arrive." Samuel unwrapped a cheeseburger and bit into it.

"Okay, so I used my false ID and one of my cards to get you the rental." David nodded at the two-year-old sedan vehicle he'd parked. "I found a secluded set of cabins in the Bryson City area. Farther into the mountains. I still think a motel would have been better. They might be looking at cabins in this part of the state since finding your place yesterday."

"I'm not worried about it." The first sandwich gone, Samuel began eating some fries. Food was fuel, but he knew it wouldn't bring him back to full strength. It was impossible to know how much of his blood and organs had been removed while he'd been locked up. He could only be certain that the Takers had used the stolen material to strengthen themselves at his expense. That's what he called those who would prey on his strength for their own purposes. Law enforcement officers were their helpers, which was how he'd been put away. His enemies would stop at nothing to rob him of his superior DNA. And there was only one way to rebuild it.

Wadding up the sandwich wrapper, he asked, "Did you bring it?" At David's blank look, Samuel mentally sighed. The man had never been a genius. But it was his habit of thinking he was smarter than he was that was truly annoying. "My new ID. You said you used yours to acquire the rental." He pointed to the car parked next to them.

"What? Oh yeah. I had to get my hands on some fake cards since you still won't allow me access to the money you paid me."

The man's whining was as annoying as a mosquito's buzz. Samuel didn't necessarily trust him, but he understood him, and that was equally vital. Their monetary arrangement had been much like Samuel and Joe's. The money had been put in an overseas account for David, but he couldn't get at it until Samuel supplied the password. In return for David's patient waiting, Samuel had provided other information David had long sought. But David was wrong if he thought their partnership was an equal one. "I'll ask again. Did. You. Bring. It?"

"Your passport and ID?" David reached into the second bag and pulled out a sandwich. "I've got it in a safe place. I'll give it to you when you've upheld your part of the deal. I've busted my ass for you. It's time for you to show your gratitude."

"David." Samuel gave the man a chilly smile. "You're my oldest friend. Where's the trust?"

"I've been your errand boy for months now. I'd say I've done my part."

"The cabin Joe rented was nice." David looked confused by the change of subject. "Rustic, but peaceful surroundings, as promised. Details are important, don't you agree?"

The other man took a huge bite of the cheeseburger. "Yeah. Sure."

"I appreciate a friend who follows instructions specifically. It's unfortunate you aren't as keen on detail as Joe was."

David had always had a hard time controlling his temper. "Fuck you. I've done every damn thing we agreed on. You wouldn't be sitting here if not for me."

"If that were true, Sheila Preston wouldn't be lying in a hospital instead of in a grave."

David looked like he was having a difficult time swallowing. "Bullshit. The explosion was all over the news. She's dead, but her kids are at her sister's. A sweet little twofer for you."

"Sisters." Samuel allowed himself a moment to contemplate the treat before tucking the fact away. "The idea is delightful. But your sloppiness isn't. Preston isn't dead. You should have made sure. You know how I feel about loose ends."

"What the hell? The bomb I wired to her ignition was crude, sure, but there shouldn't have been anything left of the bitch but pink mist. As soon as she turned the key in the ignition . . ."

Samuel sighed and reached into the bag on his lap to withdraw the remaining sandwich. "Either it malfunctioned or she had a remote start. You have some unfinished business to take care of. She's at Charlotte Memorial. I'm a cautious and meticulous man. You should be as well."

"How hard could it be to sneak onto her floor in the middle of the night and hold a pillow over the bitch's face? She'll be taken care of."

"I hope so." The second sandwich gone, Samuel held out a hand silently. Watched the silent war in the other man's expression before he handed him the uneaten one from his sack.

"Tell me about the new arrangements."

"I got a second rental from a different company. It's parked at the motel I've been staying at. As for the other . . . a few more days and we'll be ready to move."

"Not a few more days. *Two* days."

"I can't be ready that fast."

Samuel unwrapped the sandwich and bit into it. He chewed and swallowed before replying, "Forty-eight hours and then I'm out of this state and out of the country." That should have been his first move once he was free. However, having to depend on others for assistance meant he wasn't totally in charge of the timeline. "If you're not ready by then, I'll be . . . displeased."

David took a long time to reply. "Yeah. Okay. I'm going to have to move fast, but maybe that isn't such a bad thing. They've got an army looking for you." He smirked. "I gotta protect my investment. I'll drive you to the cabin I rented for you and then walk back down to the road and call an Uber. Using one of my burners and a fake card, it should be safe enough. I'll have them drop me at the casino and head to the motel room on foot."

Samuel frowned as he dug in his bag for a napkin and wiped his fingers carefully. "After we part ways, make sure you walk a few miles through the woods before you find a road. If someone recognizes you, I don't want you anywhere near where I'll be staying." His mood lightened when he saw David's hand curl into a fist. The man's temper had often gotten ahead of his good sense. But Samuel wasn't concerned. David had too much to lose to cross him now.

"All right, then," David managed finally. "Let's get going before it's full light."

Cady

It helped to concentrate on the road. To remain focused on the drivers and the passing scenery. Then Cady wasn't thinking about the picture hanging in Ryder's office. The one he'd said was his father. Butch Talbot.

A name to go with a face in the snippet of memory that occasionally surfaced in her consciousness before receding, as if withdrawn by an invisible tide. Another flash from the past. Cady was never sure if they were real or imagined.

But the emotions accompanying those bits of recollection were genuine enough. Confusion. Fear. And . . . shame? For what, she'd never been certain. But seeing the image had hurtled her back to her childhood. She'd been five or six. Padding out of bed when she heard a noise. She could still feel the cold plank floor beneath her bare feet. Cady could see the girl she'd been standing in the doorway of the kitchen. It was a different house every year, it'd seemed like, but the details remained the same. Cracked linoleum. Sagging countertops. A refrigerator that didn't keep much cold.

And that night, a man sitting in one of the kitchen chairs, with her mom on his lap. His shirt was partially unbuttoned, and his hand was inside her mom's shirt. Shock had held Cady rooted in place.

Her mom had tried to rise. The man's arm tightened around her, preventing it. "Go on back to bed, baby." Hannah had brushed the hair back from her face and tried to smile. "Get, now. I'll see you in the morning."

But she hadn't moved. Couldn't.

"You heard your mama. Get."

The man's rumbling tone had held a command, one the child in her recognized and obeyed. She'd run back to her bedroom and dove under the covers.

Her subconscious had long mimicked the action. Every time she'd remembered the scene, the man's features had been blurry. Indistinct. She recalled a uniform of some sort. But a bolt of familiarity had twisted through her when she saw the picture in Ryder's office. The stranger had Butch Talbot's face.

That troubled her on some level, although she wasn't sure why. Cady slowed until she could pass the driver in front of her, who was moving with the dedicated speed of a tortoise. There had been other men. Hannah Maddix was the type of woman who'd needed someone to lean on. And the times when there wasn't a man in the picture often corresponded to those periods they'd had to live at Alma's.

The thought of the time they'd spent at her aunt's had Cady's mind shuttering. She wasn't up to examining those memories. One jolt from the past was enough for the day.

There were few things in her childhood she really cared to dwell on.

◆ ◆ ◆

"Gracious, this is just so exciting!" Madeline Grayson Carson showed them into a sleekly furnished living room. Cady sat gingerly on a white sofa decorated with throw pillows in black and scarlet. The space looked like something out of a home decorator magazine. Although their background check revealed Grayson had two children, their immaculate house showed no signs of them.

Since Carson lived in Asheville, Cady and Miguel had decided to stop here first before proceeding to the hospital in Charlotte in the hopes of talking to Sheila Preston. Somehow Cady didn't think Preston would be as excited to see them as Madeline appeared to be.

The other woman sank on the edge of the sofa and clasped one knee. "This is a coincidence. I just ran into Aurora's daughter in the grocery store yesterday. It was such a shock." The woman's hand fluttered to her chest. "She's the picture of her mama. I had no idea they'd allowed the girl to go free."

"She's the one who gave us your name. How long did you know Aurora Pullman?"

"We met a few days before college classes started our freshman year. But we'd been communicating the whole summer. The university gives roommates each other's name so they can start to get acquainted, and we hit it off right away." The woman smiled. "All of my favorite college memories involve Aurora. Except for the ones involving college boys." This was accompanied with a sidelong glance at Miguel.

Cady managed, barely, to avoid rolling her eyes. She and Rodriguez had worked together long enough to recognize which of them was the more likely to elicit information from their subjects. And it was pretty clear he was up in this situation.

"Did you room together all four years?" he asked the woman.

"We did. Aurora's parents died when we were sophomores. She was absolutely devastated, but it was their demand she live in the dorms. After they passed . . ." Madeline lifted a shoulder. "We moved into a house near campus with two other girls. And Aurora got a bit wilder. Maybe we all did. She was sort of the sun in the group. We moved in her orbit."

"Is that when she met David Sutton?"

Madeline leaned toward Miguel conspiratorially. "I don't recognize the name. Aurora went through men like tissues. I never bothered learning their last names, because none of them were around long enough to make the effort worth it."

Cady took the picture she'd run of the photo from Cisco's and handed it to the woman. "This is Sutton." She tapped his image.

Madeline sent her a sidelong glance. Good manners kept the woman from asking about Cady's face. But she hadn't been able to conceal her avid curiosity. She leaned closer, comprehension dawning in her expression. "Oh, the hunk. Romeo, we all called him. Aurora fell hard for him."

"How long were they together?"

The woman pursed her red-slicked lips. Cady couldn't help but think it was for Miguel's benefit. "They started dating our senior year sometime. And then we graduated, and I moved to Asheville. Aurora stayed in Charlotte, at least for a few years. She'd gotten hooked up with the art community there. I know she and this guy—Sutton—broke up for a while, because every time I visited her she had someone new on the line. Then, once when I saw her, they were back together, and she was head over heels again."

"Is he Eryn Pullman's father?"

Madeline shrugged at Cady's question. "Truth? I don't know if Aurora could be sure. Like I said, her and guys . . ." The rest of her words trailed off. "But I don't think so. She got pregnant several months after we graduated, and they'd broken up then. I'm still close with our friends from college. None of us really knew."

"Do you remember any of David Sutton's acquaintances?" Cady took Aldeen's photo out of her coat and showed it to her.

Madeline's eyes went wide. "Not the man who escaped a few days ago? No, heavens, of course not. Why would you even ask?"

"Because we have reason to believe the two men were friends." Miguel took over again. "And since Aurora dated Sutton, she probably knew Aldeen."

The woman shuddered. "I hate to even consider that. But I certainly never met him."

"What about other friends of Sutton's?" he pressed.

"I didn't really run in the guy's circle. I only saw him when he and Aurora partied with us."

This was going nowhere fast. "Why did Aurora move back home?" Cady took the picture the woman held out, folded it, and put it back into her coat. "You said she was involved in the art scene. Why would she leave?"

"Well . . . Aurora said it was to provide Eryn more structure. But I wondered myself. She hated that house. She always said it. But maybe it was different without her strict parents there running her life. I sort of thought . . ." Madeline hesitated for a moment. "Something happened in Charlotte. I don't know what, but it scared her, and believe me, Aurora Pullman didn't scare easily. I talked to her on the phone every couple of weeks. But I never saw her after she moved back for at least a month, which was weird. We didn't live far apart. And when we did get together she seemed . . . rattled. Same old Aurora on the outside, but nervy under the surface."

A few more minutes of questioning didn't elicit any further details, so after writing down the names and contact information for Aurora's other closest friends, Cady and Miguel took their leave.

"I can't help but believe we can interview every single one of these women"—Cady shook the list she held in her hand—"and we still won't be any closer to a lead on David Sutton." Reaching the car, they both slipped inside it.

"I'm too much of a gentleman to say I told you so."

"When did that change?" she muttered, buckling herself in. "Let's hope we have better luck at Charlotte Memorial Hospital."

Cady's boots rang hollowly on the hospital's polished tile floors. The policeman stationed outside Preston's room wore the CMPD uniform. "Maddix and Rodriguez." They showed their credentials. "What's the latest on Preston's condition?"

The cop, Tom Lockhardt, according to his nameplate, shook his head. "Doctors have made their rounds but didn't say a word to me when they left. I heard the nurses mention Preston's condition had improved, though."

Cady and Miguel exchanged a glance. This might be the only chance they were going to get, at least for the foreseeable future. "We need a few words with her."

"So does the department. More than a few." Lockhardt looked toward the nurses' desk. "You'd better make it quick."

Cady slipped inside the door, then stopped dead when she caught sight of the woman in the hospital bed. Only when she felt Miguel bump into the back of her did she remember to move.

Machines surrounded the bed, all hooked to its occupant. Bandages swathed Sheila Preston's eyes, cheeks, and arms. Cady could only imagine the rest of her body bore similar injuries.

The sight of her made Cady's bumps and bruises pale in significance.

"Who's . . . there?" Sheila's voice was little more than a rasp.

"Cady Maddix and Miguel Rodriguez with the Marshals Service." Miguel held up a finger. Cady nodded. They might not have more than a minute. "Do you know who did this to you?"

"I saw you." The words sounded as if they hurt to utter. "I was coming across the street after eating and you . . . you were in your Jeep. By the office. I was careful to check for different vehicles in the lot. When you got out, I knew you were cops of some sort. I ran."

Cady winced. Yes, Sheila had run. And the action had nearly cost her life.

Footsteps sounded outside in the hallway. Cady's tone went urgent. "Who would have wanted you dead?"

"Sutton. David Sutton. The son of a bitch ruined my life." Sheila's words were choked. "He approached me. I hadn't seen him in years, but one day I came home and he was on my porch. I sent the girls in the house. He wanted me to do . . . some favors. When I refused, he got ugly. He'd always had a temper. He said if I didn't help he'd hurt the girls. Sutton knew where they went to school and to childcare. I believed him when he said he'd kill them. How could I not?"

There was a low murmur of voices outside the door. Cady could feel the remaining time slipping away. "The favor was to go see Samuel Aldeen in prison?"

"Monthly. Sometimes Sutton gave me information to share with him. Usually . . . I just sat there with that horrible man while he whispered about my girls. He said he had pictures of them in his room. I don't know how he could have. He said . . . lots of things." A visible shudder shook the woman's body. "I did what I was told. I brought a car there. I'm not stupid. I knew what it was for. But what was I supposed to do? Let my girls die? I figured . . . they'd catch him quickly. No way he would even get off the grounds. Then my family would be safe. I was going to move out of state. Find a different job. Maybe change our names. But he wasn't caught." Sheila released a long sigh. "Unless he's been captured?"

"Not yet. What do you know about David Sutton?"

Sheila shook her head slowly. "Nothing. We worked together for a bit, but that was two decades ago."

"Did he say anything to give you a clue where he lived? Did you see his car?"

"No. He only issued threats. And . . . the one time he came to my house there was no car out front. I remember looking. After that he called me. He'd made me give him my number. I only saw him once."

They'd had her phone number from the contact list from Fristol. But when they'd had the company ping it, it'd come back as out of service. "You have a new phone," Cady said grimly.

"I used one he'd given me to call Fristol. He . . . he said to make sure I got rid of it after."

"Do you remember a woman Sutton dated named Aurora Pullman?"

"No. But he always had women."

"How about Aldeen?" Miguel put in. "Do you recall anyone he dated from back then? Anyone he was friends with?"

"Not really. He seemed nice enough. I mean, I was shocked when I'd read what he'd done. I would never have guessed it. But I didn't socialize with any of them outside of work."

The door opened behind them. "What are you doing in here?" Cady turned to see a nurse with a fierce expression on her face. "Visitors have to check in at the nurses' station. And no more than one at a time. Five minutes maximum each hour."

"I . . . can have . . . visitors? Did you call my sister?"

"And your mom." The nurse's voice gentled as she went to Sheila's side, checking the readout on the screen above one of the machines. "You two," she said over her shoulder. "Out."

"One more minute." Ignoring the nurse's glare, Cady said, "Sheila. Was there anything else you did for Samuel Aldeen?"

The woman's lips quivered. "Yes. Once. About eight months ago, Sutton gave me an address and told me to go there and pick up a package. Then I had to drop it off somewhere else. I wasn't supposed to look in it, but I did. If it had been drugs, I wouldn't have done it. But it was just an MP3 player."

"Where did you pick it up?" Miguel shifted closer to the bed.

"Here in town. I don't remember the address, but it was a gray house on Eighth and Tulip. There was an old swing set in the front yard. I remember, because it's odd not to find them in back of the house."

"Who gave you the package?"

She shook her head slightly. "There were several people in the home. One of them called him Philip. I didn't talk to him much. Sutton gave

me his address and told me what time to be there. I gave the man—
Philip—my name and he handed me the package. That's all."

Interest piqued. "Did you smuggle it into the facility?" Cady could
tell from the nurse's stance her time was running out.

"No. I took it to this run-down house several miles past Waynesville.
I was told there'd be a red ribbon tied around the back porch and I
should leave the package there. So I did."

"Minute's up." The nurse gestured to the door. "Out with you
both."

Cady reached into her pocket and took out a card, laying it on the
table next to the bed. "If you remember anything else, I left my number.
We'll let you get some rest now."

"Marshal?" They'd only taken a couple of steps before Sheila
stopped them. "How much trouble am I in?"

"I don't know," Cady answered honestly. "You aided and abetted a
federal inmate's escape. But the fact you were coerced will be a consideration. You need to get an attorney."

She pushed open the door, and she and Miguel stepped into the
hallway. Lockhardt looked up. "Sorry. I held the nurse off as long as I
could. Did you learn anything?"

"We appreciate your efforts." Miguel propped his shoulder against
the wall next to the officer. "She verified our suspicions about who was
behind the attack, although she couldn't place the man at the scene of
the explosion."

"There's not much doubt he's responsible," Cady put in. "And he's
used threats before to get her to cooperate." She let Miguel relay the
woman's connection to Aldeen.

"Some lawyer is going to see she skates for her part in the escape,"
Lockhardt predicted. From his tone it was clear he regarded the possibility far differently than Cady did. "With our luck, she's gonna get
off on coercion."

Cady said nothing, but she hoped he was right. From what she'd seen in the hospital room, Sheila Preston had already paid enough.

She and Miguel didn't speak until they were outside the hospital. "A first name and part of an address. That's more than we had when we walked into the hospital room." Miguel unlocked the car and they got in, with him behind the wheel. Given her aches and pains, she hadn't argued when he'd suggested driving.

"Damn straight." Cady fastened her seat belt. Maybe this one would be the link they were looking for.

"Do you think she told us everything she knew?" He started the ignition.

"She's got to be on massive amounts of painkillers. They might be the reason for her loosened tongue, but I don't think the woman could have kept her story straight if she wasn't telling the truth. I figure she delivered the MP3 player to the home of the substitute custodian from Fristol. Joe Bush." At least they finally had the answer of how the progress notes had been converted and embedded in the audio files: Bush smuggled Aldeen's MP3 and the notes out. Either he or Sutton delivered them to Philip. Sheila finished the loop by getting it back to Bush, and he likely got it to Aldeen. The remaining mystery was the reason behind the fugitive's interest in Eryn Pullman.

While Miguel backed out of the parking lot and headed for the exit, Cady pulled out her cell and punched Eighth and Tulip into the GPS. "Maybe this Philip will lead us to David Sutton."

"I'm getting tired of chasing maybes. We need something solid," he grumbled.

Cady silently agreed. They had a whole lot of suppositions. A couple of near misses.

And two dangerous men still on the loose.

"This has to be it."

Miguel slowed in front of a dark-gray house that—like the rest of the neighborhood—had seen better days. The skeleton of a rusted swing set sat off-kilter in the front yard.

They got out of the car and approached the structure. A board was missing from the second step. When they stepped over it, Miguel remarked, "Wonder how many times someone comes out at night and puts their foot right through the hole? Good way to break a leg."

Cady didn't answer. There'd been times in her childhood she'd lived in similar places with her mom. Only when she'd gone to school had she realized how dire their circumstances were compared to her friends'.

When she knocked at the scarred front door, a woman with a baby opened it, eying them suspiciously. "You cops?"

"Cady Maddix and Miguel Rodriguez with the Marshals Service." The door was swinging shut before she got the words out. "Looking for Philip," Cady called before it could slam in their faces.

It remained open a crack, the woman still staring suspiciously through the small space. "There's no Philip here."

"How long have you lived at this address?"

"Six months, and it's just me and my baby."

"Maybe he was the previous tenant," Cady suggested.

The woman opened the door wider. "Could've been." The baby began to fuss, and she bounced it a little as she spoke. "I got some junk mail in someone else's name at first. Philip . . . N something." She shook her head. "Don't remember the rest of the last name. Sorry." The baby let out a wail, and the woman backed away a step.

"Not a problem." The door was closed before Cady had completed the sentence.

"Now we've verified a former address and part of a name." There was a bounce in Miguel's step. If Cady weren't so stiff maybe she could match it. "We've got enough to check with the post office and see if the former tenant here left a forwarding address."

◆ ◆ ◆

"Philip Nieman's moved up in the world," Miguel observed as he did a slow roll by the man's new address an hour and a half later.

Cady surveyed Nieman's new digs. It was nothing fancy, but the neat single-story boasted vinyl siding and shutters, with a detached double garage and the remains of a neglected lawn. It represented leaps rather than steps above the last place the man had lived.

"Three cars in the drive." Miguel passed the house.

"The curtains in the front picture window are closed, but there's a garbage container on the curb." When the house was out of sight, Miguel turned the corner to round the block and take another drive by. There was no activity outside the house. But given the multiple vehicles in sight, someone was at home.

"Let's split up. I'll go to the front door. You hang back and cover the side and rear exits."

Cady didn't protest. Given her appearance, Miguel would draw far less attention than she would. She settled sunglasses on her nose while he parked halfway down the block. When he turned the engine off, Miguel shrugged out of his coat to reveal a long-sleeved T-shirt. Twisting, he reached over the seat and snagged a hooded sweatshirt. Shrugging into it, he pulled a baseball cap out of the pocket and used the rearview mirror to settle it on his head.

"Did you really just check yourself out?"

"Nothing wrong with making sure I look the part."

"And which part will this be?"

"Pizza delivery."

She nodded. It was a tried-and-true gambit to get an otherwise recalcitrant person of interest to open the front door. They got out of the car, and she waited for Miguel to retrieve the pizza boxes they carried in the trunk as props. "Let me get in place before you ring the doorbell."

Cady started walking to the house three doors down from Nieman's. She passed through the adjoining yards to get to the rear of the properties. Although she saw a curtain twitch at a window in one of the homes, no one came to the door. At Nieman's yard, she dropped to her knees and crawled below window level. There was a small wooden back porch and concrete steps leading to the side entrance. Situating herself between the porch and the driveway, she prepared to wait.

They'd run Nieman after they got his name from the post office. The man's record showed a few drunk and disorderlies and a ninety-day sentence in the Mecklenburg County Jail thirteen years ago. He'd been clean ever since. Maybe Nieman was simply skilled with electronics. There was nothing inherently illegal about the work he'd done on Aldeen's MP3 player.

His association with David Sutton, however, raised suspicions.

"Pizza delivery." Cady heard Miguel's voice. A moment later, someone must have come to the door.

"Who the hell ordered pizza?"

"The bill says Philip Nieman. Got a pepperoni and a taco," Miguel said.

A woman's voice sounded. "I could eat. Give him some money."

"That's bullshit. Shut the fucking door." Cady tensed as the third voice sounded.

"Just pay him, Phil, who the fuck cares?"

"Philip Nieman? Deputy US Marshal. Get down on the floor. Get down! Runner!"

Cady drew her weapon when she heard Miguel's shout. A moment later the back door burst open and a man vaulted over the railing of the small wooden porch and sped in the direction of the drive. He skidded to a halt when he saw Cady.

"Deputy US Marshal," she shouted, training her gun on the man. "Down on the ground. Hands behind your back."

He wheeled and ran in the opposite direction. Biting off a curse, Cady took up pursuit, holstering her weapon as she ran.

Normally, she'd outpace the man, but her muscles were still stiff. She chased him down the alley and through another yard. He leaped over a small hedge, knocking over a row of metal garbage cans in the process. Cady attempted to hurdle the bushes and failed. She struggled through the clawlike branches. He threw a look over his shoulder and, seeing her falling behind, headed for the adjoining yard with its tall wooden fence.

She knew exactly what he was about to do. Cady turned back and picked up one of the empty toppled cans and ran around the hedge after him. It took the man two tries, but he jumped up, his fingers grasping the top of the fence, and began hoisting himself over it. She ran closer and raised the garbage can over her head, hurling it with all her strength, smashing the stranger in the back of the legs. He clung to the fence a few moments longer before sliding to the ground.

Her muscles sang a chorus of complaints as she reached his side, weapon ready. "On your stomach. Now."

He was already on the grass. He rolled over. "Fucking cop. You fucking broke my leg. I'll sue your ass."

"And I'm going to arrest *your* ass." She holstered her gun to put the cuffs on him and hauled him to his feet. Although he did limp a bit at first, by the time she was nudging him inside Nieman's front door, he was walking fine, although still bitching bitterly.

"Sit." She pressed a hand on one of his shoulders, and he slid down the wall she'd guided him to.

"I've got a couple of CMPD units on the way." Miguel's brows rose when he saw her torn jeans. "These three have quite an operation going here. It was in plain view when they opened the front door."

"I told you before, it's not my operation." This from another man sitting against the opposite wall, arms cuffed behind his back. Cady recognized him from the background check they'd run. Philip Nieman.

"The hell it isn't. You hired us both." This from the lone woman in cuffs.

"Shut up, Debbie," the runner snarled.

Cady scanned the area. Four folding tables formed two rows in the front room. Atop them sat several computers, each with a device attached. *Magstripe readers,* she realized. If that wasn't a giveaway of an illegal operation in plain sight, the stacks of credit cards on one of the tables would have been. She walked over to pick up a few. She read different names on each of them before looking at Miguel.

"Have you advised them this sort of op is considered a felony in the state of North Carolina?" The crime was simple. Steal the cards either by swiping wallets or purses, then run them through the devices. The information contained on the magnetic stripe on the back displayed on the computer screen. The crew filled out credit applications with the victim's personal identification, changing only the address to a drop box or vacant home.

"Are you selling them on the deep web or using them yourselves?" She directed the question to Nieman. He turned his face away. *Probably both,* she figured. They had only to order big-ticket items. Electronics were the favorites. Then they'd pawn them or sell them online for instant cash.

"Philip admitted he met David Sutton a long time ago in county lockup."

Damn. Cady felt a spark of annoyance at Miguel's words. They'd spent a lot of time looking at Sutton's cellmates when he was in prison and had even run down some old high school classmates. They hadn't worked their way far enough in the man's background. Not enough to level the same scrutiny at anyone he might have met while in jail for prior arrests.

"Did you make any cards for Sutton?" Cady walked slowly up and down the aisle between the tables, studying the computer screens before shifting her gaze to Nieman.

Sirens sounded in the distance. The woman emitted a low wail, but Nieman's expression turned calculated. "I didn't do David's. He made them himself. He's the one who turned me on to this venture."

Adrenaline kick-started in her chest. "And do you have a list of the names and numbers he used?"

"Lady, like I was telling your buddy here, I have a list of *everything*. But the only way you get it is if I face no charges."

◆ ◆ ◆

"We'll tell the prosecutor you're a cooperating witness in a major investigation." Miguel raised his hand to stall Nieman's objection. "We just need to make a phone call before going through these computers ourselves. You've already told us the information we want is on them. You don't have a lot to deal except saving us some time."

Maybe it was the sight of his accomplices being hauled away by uniformed officers, but the man finally jerked his head in a half nod. "You gotta unlock the cuffs. I'll need my hands free."

Five minutes later the man had his skinny frame perched on a folding chair, and he was opening up a file and rapidly scrolling through it. "Sutton was running this scam on a smaller scale back when we met in county lockup." The man had gingery-colored hair with a matching patch on his chin, and the quick, furtive moves of a rodent. "I suggested some improvements. I mean, hey, plenty of room for more than one guy running the same scheme. We worked together for a while until he got himself sent to prison. I didn't hear from him again until about a year ago. I figured he was going to try to claim I owed him some of the business, but he just wanted some favors done now and again."

"Like embedding some narration into audio files."

Nieman gave a quick bounce of his shoulders. "It was an easy job. I didn't even charge him. Sometimes he wanted to borrow my car. But a few weeks ago, he wanted in on the operation. As partners."

"Partners. I thought you said this wasn't your business."

Nieman stopped scrolling to look over his shoulder at Cady. "It was and then it wasn't, you know? Sutton is the one calling all the shots now. I still get paid the same, so why do I care? It ain't worth pissing off a guy like him." He pushed away from the screen. "These are the credit cards he kept."

"Print it," Miguel ordered. The man turned back to the computer to obey.

Cady smiled. "You're a good record keeper." He'd scrolled through dozens of pages. She was fairly certain they'd find files on the computer to incriminate all four involved in the operation. But the possibility paled in comparison to the find they'd made on Sutton's fake cards.

They'd run the financials corresponding to them. With any luck, the man had used one of the cards recently, and they'd be able to use the records to nail him.

◆ ◆ ◆

They'd no more than stepped into the office when they were summoned to Supervisory Deputy US Marshal Allen Gant's office. "Close the door," the man directed. "I figured you'd want to hear this right away. The task force in Haywood County was tipped off about two men outside Robbinsville resembling Aldeen and Sutton."

"What?" Cady sank into a seat. "When?"

"A couple of hours ago. The guy was going down a gravel road and got suspicious when a car pulled out of a farm drive on an abandoned site. He got a good look at the vehicle and passengers before he pulled onto the property to check for damage. He thought they might be vandals. He found Bush's vehicle behind the barn and recognized it from the newscasts. They've got a BOLO out on the car the men left in and a perimeter around the area."

"Well, that's good news."

Gant gave Cady a wry look. "Try to contain your enthusiasm. Chester and Quimby are taking part in the manhunt. I'm getting regular updates."

Chester and Quimby. She knew without glancing at Miguel he felt exactly the same way she did. Cady wanted Aldeen and Sutton arrested. But there wasn't a person on the fugitive investigations unit who wasn't a bit of an adrenaline junkie. To be relegated to the sidelines for the capture burned more than a little.

"Somehow, running Sutton's fake card numbers doesn't seem quite as exciting as it did fifteen minutes ago," Miguel muttered to Cady as the two of them left Gant's office.

She couldn't disagree. Not then. And not during the hours it took to receive the information and pore over it. She was at first surprised to discover Sutton's earliest transactions were less than two weeks old. But then it made sense. Why else would he have been using Selma Lewis's house when the utilities were turned off? He must have been broke. If she remembered correctly, his parole had only ended weeks ago. It hadn't taken him long to return to criminal behavior.

"What'd you find on the addresses to correspond to the cards?"

"Some are fake." Miguel wheeled his chair from his desk to Cady's and showed her a list he was making. "We know from Nieman's computer files they were using anonymous mail drops to send and receive the applications. According to Google Maps, a few of the addresses on the applications don't exist. I'm guessing the others are vacant houses." He showed columns of notations he'd made correlating online purchases and the addresses given for delivery.

"All it takes is sitting down the block from the address, wait for the delivery, and scoop the packages up," she murmured.

"A bit more than that. He still has to set up the channels to sell the merchandise, but yeah. Easy money."

Miguel picked up a few more of the sheets on the pile in front of her and took them back to his desk. Cady scanned the transactions quickly on the remaining records. Some cards hadn't been used yet. She put those statements in separate files. Her gaze landed on the date on the next one in the stack. She stilled. "Look at this." She rose and went to his desk, slapping the statement down in front of him. "A rental car. With yesterday's date."

Excitement shot through her veins. She strode back and grabbed the remainder of the pile of statements and returned to his desk with them. Rifling through them, she honed in on the dates on each. "Hotel rooms." She spread the statements bearing the transactions in front of Miguel. "Apparently, Sutton got sick of the accommodations at the Lewis house." She glanced down at the next statement she held and felt the floor rock a bit under her feet. "Two days ago." Cady shoved the sheet she held to Miguel. "David Sutton made a motel reservation in Cherokee and a cabin rental in Bryson City." She flipped through the other statements before another transaction jumped out at her. "And here's a second car rental. Made the same day as the first one." She wheeled around and went back to her desk, scooping the statements into file folders.

Miguel was already doing the same. Without exchanging a word, they strode to Allen's office, folders in hand. There wasn't a doubt in Cady's mind they'd just discovered a vital lead in the whereabouts of David Sutton. And this time, she and Miguel weren't going to be shut out of the manhunt.

The Kozy Room Motel on the outskirts of Cherokee bore more than a passing resemblance to the place where they'd found Sheila Preston.

With sections of connected rooms detached from the main office, it was a sensible choice for anyone trying to keep a low profile.

A plainclothes female deputy from Swain County had entered the office and radioed the rest of the team, secluded in a large perimeter surrounding the area. Sutton's room was at the far end of one long row. The plate on the dark-gray compact in front of the room corresponded to one of Sutton's rentals. They'd already shared the plate number of the second vehicle Sutton had acquired with the task force watching the cabin rental in Bryson City.

A dozen personnel had been reassigned to the motel. They had people situated on benches and inside parked cars keeping track of the license numbers of passing vehicles. All were equipped with radios on the same frequency.

Cady and Miguel were outside the back of Sutton's motel room. She pressed the radar device against the siding and depressed the buttons to begin the analysis. Seconds later, she read the screen. Stifled a feeling of frustration. Shaking her head at her partner, she reached for her radio. "There's no one inside. Wait for entry."

The two of them ran to the front of the motel room, where two other members of the team waited. Like them, the others were outfitted in tactical gear. Miguel used the key the deputy had gotten from the motel clerk. They entered as one and spread out across the space.

There was a laptop sitting on the bed. Cady booted it up, but it was password protected. She set it aside. Miguel was going through a duffel bag in the closet. "TracFones." He held up a handful of the cells, all still in their plastic packaging. The other team members were checking the dresser and bathroom. Cady lifted the mattress. She spied a plastic bag and pulled it out. Checking inside, she said, "And here are the rest of the credit cards."

"What is this, and why would it be in the bathroom?" The deputy came out holding a portable black device.

"It's a magstripe reader." Miguel briefly explained how it worked. It looked an awful lot like the ones they'd seen in Nieman's house. "As for why it's in the bathroom . . ." He shrugged and got down to look under the bed. "Apparently, Sutton is the paranoid type. He doesn't want to keep all his goodies together in case his room gets tossed."

"He's going to be disappointed then," the deputy observed. She set the device on the desk and continued the search.

Cady smiled at Miguel's expression of distaste when he rose, brushing at the knees of his trousers. "Anything of interest under there?"

"Only to the department of health."

She pulled open the single drawer in the bedside table. It was empty except for a battered Bible. Flipping through its pages, she found a sheet of paper folded into a square. Smoothing it out, she saw a list of addresses. Some seemed familiar.

She held it up, catching Miguel's attention. "Sheila Preston's address is on this."

He came over and scanned it. "I'm pretty sure one of those addys belongs to her sister."

The others weren't familiar, but Cady wondered if one might belong to Preston's mother. Or the girls' school and day care. She turned the paper over and frowned. There was a rough drawing on the back consisting of little more than measurements and Xs. A map of some sort, perhaps. At the bottom of the page, a line of text was written in block letters.

REVENGE IS COMPLETE WHEN THE ENEMY HAS LOST EVERYTHING.

It was nearly dawn when Cady pulled up in front of the gates to her house. Sutton hadn't returned to the motel yet, which worried her. Given the possessions he'd left behind, it was certain he'd planned to come back. The cover of darkness would have been the most likely time to do so.

Where the hell was he? And where was Aldeen? Despite the miles-wide search in place, there'd been no sign of either of them near the Bryson City cabin.

Exhaustion hazed her vision. They'd taken up surveillance of the motel from a used car lot across the street. Even when the next shift came to relieve them, Cady had still had the task force's emailed updates to go through before she'd headed for home.

The dog came racing across the lawn as she got out of the car to open the old gates. She stooped to give him a quick pat and grabbed his collar, walking him to the passenger door and letting him in the vehicle. It was starting to be their routine.

She drove inside the gates, got out to close them, and passed the area where her car was parked on the grass to park under the carport. "I hope you didn't have to battle it out with a raccoon while I was gone," she told the dog. A pang of guilt stabbed through her for leaving the animal outside overnight. The clerk who'd sold her the doghouse claimed it was a balmy seventy degrees inside the structure, but . . .

"What's that?" As weary as she was, it was the first time she'd noticed Hero was holding something in his mouth. Turning off the car, she flipped on the interior light and reached for the object. The dog didn't release it, but Cady felt the object. It was fabric of some sort, thoroughly wet. He'd been chewing on it for a while.

"Drop it," she ordered. Slightly surprised when the dog obeyed, she picked up the small jagged piece of material and held it up to the light. Dark colored with visible stains on it. They looked an awful lot like blood.

She slanted a look at the animal. "Where'd you get this?" But Cady was certain she already knew. Grabbing the Maglite beneath her front seat, she got out. The dog scrabbled to her side of the vehicle to follow her.

The security light turned on as she went past the house and rounded the corner. She stopped to put the food and water dishes inside the doghouse and blocked the entrance with the piece of plywood she'd found in the basement. Then she continued to the back of her home. The door was locked. She directed the beam of the flashlight toward the window as she headed to it. Her step faltered.

The bottom two clips were turned to a vertical position.

She trained the light on the ground beneath the window, squatting so she could see better. It'd rained a bit around 3:00 a.m. The ground was still damp but not soggy. She could see partial footprints mixed with paw prints. And more fabric. Dark threads, mostly, with a bit of material clinging to them. Hero put his nose down and started sniffing the ground. A low growl sounded in his throat.

Cady put her hand on his fur to calm him. But she was feeling rather feral herself.

Eryn: Then

Eryn's eyes fluttered open. She looked around at her small room in their apartment, then settled back into her bed. Her Nemo night-light was still on. The matching lamp on the table by her bed wasn't. Mama always crept back in when she was asleep and turned it off. But even with the night-light, it was too dark in her room. There were big, scary shadows in the corner. The closet door was open a little. She didn't like that. Mama said there were no monsters there. But Eryn wasn't sure.

Her gaze darted to the door to her bedroom. Closed. Panic started to flutter in her chest. Mama always left it open. Always, always. She started to call for her and then closed her mouth again. Mama didn't like to get woke up. Eryn pushed the covers back and started to slide out of bed. She could open the door. She wasn't scared. Or, only a little.

The crash had her jumping. She turned and ran back to bed.

"Get out! Get. Out!" Eryn froze. Mama's voice didn't sound like her. It was loud. And very scared. It made Eryn scared too.

"Don't even think about using that on me." A man was talking. Low and mean. Something hit the floor, and there was a crack. Like the sound when Mama swatted Eryn's bare butt. Crack! Crack!

"Stop it! You lunatic, get out! I never want to see you again!"

"When are you . . ." Thud. ". . . going to . . ." Thud. ". . . learn?" Another crash.

Tears streamed from Eryn's eyes. "Mama! Mama!" But she didn't come. There were just more scary noises. Yelling and then screaming. Bad words. Very bad words. Smash! Crash! Thud! And then there were no more screams. But Eryn heard crying.

She scrambled out of bed and slid underneath it, sobbing softly. She pressed her hands over her mouth so no one would hear. Something bad was happening. Something terrible. A monster was hurting Mama. She should go help.

But Eryn was scared of monsters too. "Mama," she moaned. "Run." It was the only way to get away. Run fast, so the monster can't catch you.

Maybe this was a bad dream. The kind Eryn couldn't wake up from. She pressed her hands over her ears. She didn't like it here. She didn't like this big old house with different people living in parts of it. She hated the smelly basement where they did their laundry. Eryn was crying so hard, she couldn't get her breath. And still the loud noises didn't stop.

Eryn tried to go far away. Away inside herself where the monsters couldn't follow. Where princesses lived in beautiful castles. No one could hurt them. If they did, the dragons would breathe fire and kill them dead.

She shivered and whimpered for a long time. Until she finally took her hands away from her ears. And all she heard was quiet.

Eryn stayed under the bed, too frightened to cry anymore. She didn't know why the quiet was scary, too, but it was. "Mama?"

It took a long time for her to be brave enough to wiggle out from under the bed. Then she crept to the door. Listened. Someone was moaning real soft. Eryn made herself reach for the knob. Turn it. She pulled the door open just a crack and peeked out. There was no one in the hallway. She tiptoed to Mama's room. Pushed the door open.

But there was no one in there.

Tears squeezed out of Eryn's eyes. Her stomach felt sick. Her feet didn't want to move anymore, but she had to find Mama. Quietly she continued down the hall until she got to the kitchen. She caught her breath at the sight there.

Broken glass. Chairs tipped over. A big, big mess. Eryn's belly knotted as she stared. Then she saw someone's leg on the floor. "Mama!" She ran the rest of the way and started to cry again. Because Mama was dead. She wasn't moving. And there was blood all over her.

"Eryn." The word didn't sound like it came from Mama. And she didn't lift her head. "Listen . . . to . . . me. Bring my phone. In my purse."

She hesitated, little bubbles of fear filling her. Eryn wasn't supposed to touch Mama's phone. Or her purse. Not ever.

"Now."

She looked around the kitchen. It was such a mess. She couldn't see the purse. Eryn went to Mama's bedroom. Sharp pieces of glass bit her bare feet, but something inside her made her hurry. The purse was on the carpet. She dumped it out. Finding the cell phone, she ran back to the kitchen. Then she stopped and tiptoed back to Mama. "Here it is."

"Press the green . . . button." Mama still didn't lift her head. Her voice sounded thin and far away.

Eryn knew her colors. She knew green. She found the button with a little bit of green on it. "Okay."

"Find . . . one. Number . . . one."

Eryn knew her numbers too. One, two, three, four, up to twenty! But she found the one. Pressed the button. "Okay."

"Tell . . . to come . . . help."

Eryn: Now

Eryn lay in bed and tried to sleep. Her eyes were closed, as if she could summon unconsciousness through sheer force of will. But despite all the relaxation techniques she tried, she was too wired. She was itching to get her paints out and start another picture. Not of the night shadows and watery moonlight this time. But of the image in her head of the scenery when she'd looked out over the Smokies with Mama. It was one of her final memories of her mother. And this time, the picture would be perfect. Better than the last time she'd tried to capture the scene. Better than anything she'd ever done before.

The thought had her eyes coming open, worry stabbing through her. It was normal to have trouble sleeping after her transition. It didn't have to mean anything. Just like the pile of finished canvases in the corner of the room weren't a bad sign. Despite her lack of sleep, she was being productive, that's all.

It didn't prove she was becoming manic. She shook her head back and forth on the pillow. She hadn't needed a medication adjustment in over a year. The rainbow-colored cocktail of pills was finally the exact correct balance. It was paranoid to think a few nights' trouble sleeping meant a regression.

Paranoia was a symptom too.

Frustrated with herself, Eryn sat up. She'd get out of bed, but only to get the log the doctor had told her to write in. She'd been avoiding noting how she felt each day. Just being forced to do so was a constant reminder that she wasn't normal. She'd never be normal.

But it was the only way to analyze patterns in her thoughts and feelings. And she'd worked too hard for the day when she was finally living outside the walls of Rolling Acres Resort.

Sitting up, she swung her feet over the bed. Eryn had once gotten to the point where she didn't care whether she left Rolling Acres or not. The longer she'd been there, the more fearful she'd grown about what awaited her outside those walls. It had been easy to convince herself it didn't matter much where she lived.

But yesterday had changed that. She'd taken the first step toward doing something she couldn't have accomplished if she was still at the facility. Learning to drive put a host of other independent acts within reach. Getting a license. Enrolling for college art classes. Improving her technique. It was a dream that had once seemed out of reach.

Eryn got the notebook out of the drawer of her bedside table. She settled back against the pillows and opened it, removing the pen she'd tucked inside.

Trouble sleeping, she wrote. Then she tapped the pen against the page. She started to write down the days she'd been home so she could note her sleep patterns for each. But something caught her eye, and she raised her gaze without thinking.

A light was bobbing in the distance.

She set the notebook down and went to the window. The glow was heading to the boathouse. And this time Eryn didn't even hesitate. She picked up her cell and went to her closet. After jamming her feet in a pair of tennis shoes, she tiptoed out of her room to get a coat. As she pulled on her winter coat, her gaze scanned the others hanging there. She didn't recognize all of them, but there was no parka among them.

And when she turned the back doorknob, she knew whoever was outside was someone from the house.

Because the knob wasn't locked.

She switched on the cell's flashlight app and quietly let herself out into the biting night air. Eryn hurried across the lawn toward the pond. A long way, she recalled. Longer than it looked. There were two lights now, both angling toward the boathouse, and she began to run. This time she was determined to put an end to the mystery.

The lights disappeared before she was close to the structure. She got a stitch in her side, and slowed, but continued on until the dark, hulking shape of the building loomed in front of her. She'd never been inside the one they'd erected after she'd burned down the other. She put a hand out, felt the cool siding against her palm. The other boathouse had been wood. She'd lit the timbers on fire and the flames had spread so quickly, it was a wonder she'd gotten out alive.

Eryn made her way around to the side, surprised to see the new building had a door there. The only accesses to the old one had been from the water or dockside. She paused in front of the door and placed her hand on the knob. It turned easily in her hand. Was it usually locked? She had no idea.

Silently she pulled the door open and stepped inside. Twin rays shone in the interior, highlighting two figures. She directed the beam of her flashlight app toward them. Both people jerked around to face her. Eryn's heart plummeted. One of them was Rosalyn clad in Uncle Bill's parka.

Standing very close to a man who was definitely not Uncle Bill.

Eryn lay in bed long enough for the rest of the house to rise. For breakfast to be served and then cleared away. Only then did she get up. Rosalyn would be gone taking Jaxson to school. With any luck, Eryn could be gone before she got back. She was in no hurry to face the woman.

She showered and got dressed, keeping an eye on the time. It was Friday, which meant it was her first day of driving instruction. There was a quiver of nerves in her stomach. She was uncertain whether they were due to the events of last night or the upcoming lesson. Eryn put on a pair of shoes and ordered an Uber to take her to town. She'd be early for the lesson. Having to wait for a bit was a better alternative than chancing a conversation with Rosalyn. Eryn couldn't avoid the woman forever. But she was anxious to delay the conversation as long as possible.

She went to the kitchen and grabbed a banana from the bowl of fruit on the counter. Mary Jane was nowhere in sight. She peeled the banana and leaned against the counter to eat it.

Rosalyn's appearance in the doorway had Eryn choking as she swallowed her first bite.

"Eryn." The woman rushed into the room, a distressed expression on her face. "I wanted to talk to you. I wanted to explain . . ."

"I have to go." Eryn walked out of the room's other entrance, grabbed a coat from the closet, and headed for the door.

"Wait!"

Rosalyn ran to catch up, positioning herself in front of Eryn and blocking her way. "You need to listen. It's not what you think."

"I don't think anything," Eryn said truthfully. Because she didn't know what to make of the scene she'd witnessed. Possible explanations had buzzed in her mind all night. She'd shoved them aside, unwilling to consider any of them.

"I told William I was sick this morning." Rosalyn was still in her pretty printed robe. Her fingers fiddled with the belt securing it. "He's taking Jaxson to school. And I sent Mary Jane on an errand. I wanted us to have some time alone to talk."

"I'd rather not," Eryn said bluntly.

"Please." Rosalyn reached to lay a hand on her arm. "I've been faithful to your uncle." She managed a tremulous smile. "He's the love of my life. You can't know what I've sacrificed . . ." Her smile faded, and her hand dropped away. "But I have trouble with anxiety. The doctors don't understand. The man you saw . . . I used to work with him at the drugstore a long time ago. He helps me manage my nerves."

Comprehension dawned. Of all the possible explanations for last night's scene, this had never occurred to her. "He's giving you drugs?"

"No, of course not. I mean . . . I'm not an addict. It's medicine. You understand the difference."

She understood there often *was* no difference. She'd seen too many patients who'd treated their symptoms by self-medicating before they went to Rolling Acres. Or turning to illegal drugs and alcohol once they'd left, which only exacerbated their underlying conditions. It was just as dangerous as patients who didn't follow through taking their prescriptions after treatment.

"I think that's a bad idea." She inched toward the front door. Eryn didn't want to have this conversation. She didn't know Rosalyn. Not on any more than a surface level. She didn't welcome the woman's confidences, and Eryn didn't want to be put in a position of having to keep them.

"You're right. And I'm going to tell your Uncle Bill about it tonight." A surge of relief swept over Eryn. "Good idea."

"Last night . . . it made me see what I was doing to myself." Rosalyn tightened her robe and gave Eryn a brave smile. "There's no one stronger than your uncle. I should have asked for his help earlier. I just want to thank you for hearing me out."

Longing for escape, she said, "You're welcome."

Rosalyn reached out to give her arm a pat. "And where are you going this morning? Is there an appointment we forgot about?"

Eryn's cell sounded. She knew without looking it was the Uber driver. She edged toward the door. "It's all right. I have a ride outside."

"Really?" The other woman followed her to the front entrance. "Who is it? Where are you going?"

"I called for a ride. I'm going to Waynesville. I'll be back soon." Eryn slipped out the door and ran toward the gates where the driver was waiting. And tried not to feel like she was fleeing.

◆ ◆ ◆

Four hours later Eryn returned home with a residual glow of satisfaction. Her first driving lesson hadn't exactly been what she'd expected. Ike had turned out to be a stickler about her learning all the parts of the car and engine before beginning some preliminary lessons on driving laws. They'd watched a video on the dos and don'ts of the road, and Eryn had to admit most of it had been new information. He'd promised that on Monday they would go to a parking lot and she'd get some time in the driver's seat. Eryn couldn't wait. He'd sent her home with a booklet to study. It'd help her pass her state driver's test, when it came time. And with a wink, he'd promised she'd know the regulations backward and forward before they were done.

She'd been so flushed with excitement afterward, she'd asked the next Uber driver to take her to a restaurant. For the first time in her life, Eryn had eaten out in public, alone. No, she hadn't spoken to anyone but the waitress, but the experience had been heady. She was still smiling when she got home and let herself back into the house. Up until the moment when she passed the open door of her uncle's study and heard her name. "Eryn."

She took a breath and turned to see Uncle Bill approaching the door. "Where have you been? Rosalyn said you went to Waynesville. Your next session with your doctor isn't until Wednesday."

"I know. It was a different appointment." When the man waited, she straightened her spine and said, "I had my first driving lesson." The expression on his face was as gratifying as her day had been.

"Come in and sit down."

She trailed him into the room and sank into one of the leather chairs. When he headed for his desk, she surprised them both by saying, "Why don't you sit next to me?" When he froze, she continued, "I always feel like I'm in the principal's office with you behind your desk."

His mouth twitched. "You did spend some time there." But he retraced his steps and seated himself—somewhat gingerly—on the chair beside her. "Tell me how you happen to be taking driving lessons. I thought we agreed to wait."

"We didn't agree. You just said it." The words were out of her mouth before Eryn could temper them. Unease stirred. She was usually quieter. More reserved. Another notation to make for the doctor?

"Well . . . yes. But I would have preferred to make the arrangements. I haven't checked out the most reputable places . . ."

"I researched driving instructors. And I set things up yesterday when I went to Waynesville." When his mouth gaped, she said, "I use Uber. I don't like having to rely on people here for everything. I need to learn to do things on my own."

"Well, of course," he sputtered. "In . . ."

". . . due time?"

He snapped his mouth shut. Considered her for a moment. "I'm sort of feeling my way here, Eryn." It was her turn to be surprised. "This is new territory for me. My first inclination is to follow your doctor's instructions specifically. But I also know you have to start acquiring more experiences. And yes, more autonomy. Why don't you share what you've done this week with your doctor next Wednesday? When we have our family session with her, we can discuss it further. In the meantime—"

"In the meantime, I need to pay the instructor. I gave him some cash up front, but the total cost is due after the second lesson. Next week. I didn't have enough money for the down payment, so I negotiated a lower price." Bill was staring at her again. "Mary Jane says to always look out for bargains if we can find them."

He cleared his throat. "Not bad advice. It appears I've been remiss. You have the credit card I set up for you to charge necessities while you were at Rolling Acres. But we'll open a bank account too. I'll deposit some money in it each month. And I'll be monitoring your transactions, Eryn, to see how fiscally responsible you are."

And he was likely to report the information to Dr. Ashland via the family appointments. Eryn didn't mind. Her needs weren't great. And at least her uncle wasn't bucking her on the steps she'd taken so far.

The scene she'd stumbled on last night flashed across her mind then, and she found it difficult to meet his gaze. It was between Rosalyn and him. The woman had promised to discuss it with him, but either way, Eryn wasn't going to insert herself in the middle of it.

"I was wondering . . . whatever happened to Mama's paintings?" She steeled herself for the answer. Eryn wasn't quite certain what she expected. When she was a kid, her mother had hung her work everywhere, arguing with Uncle Bill when she'd replaced the family portraits that had been on the walls forever. *We need to brighten up this place!* Eryn could hear her mother saying. *It's like living in a morgue.* But on Eryn's visits she'd noted those old portraits back on the wall. And now with the remodel of her mama's room, it was like her mother's very memory had been erased.

Uncle Bill looked away. His throat worked for a second. And Eryn had a flash of panic that he was going to say they'd been destroyed. "They're in the attic. It was hard to see them every day. I had them put away. You're certainly free to look through them. As Aurora's heir, they belong to you now."

It was difficult to see them . . . The guilt that had lived inside Eryn most of her life carved furrows in her gut. For the first time, she saw her mama's death in terms of what it had meant to Uncle Bill. Aurora's paintings had been put away because they were too difficult to face. Like her murder had been.

With a piercing sense of pain, Eryn wondered what it was like for him to live with the person who'd caused his loss.

◆ ◆ ◆

Eryn had never been in the attic before. Uncle Bill had to tell her how to access it. She'd expected a cramped, dusty space with discarded possessions stored away to be forgotten. Instead she found a vast area that must run the length of the house. The ceilings were slanted, so she couldn't stand up straight in some areas. But it was well lit. When she found the light switches and snapped them on, she realized there was little dust to be found anywhere.

She peeked beneath one of the sheets in a corner and discovered the space was filled with unused furniture. There was a pile of old pictures, still in their frames, and she looked through some of them. More long-dead relatives, she figured, and turned away in disinterest. She supposed she should care about where she'd come from, but Eryn found it enough of a struggle to learn how to live with the relatives she knew.

The bags she'd emptied after arriving home had been added to a neat pile of suitcases. Eryn didn't even know who'd put them there. Mary Jane, probably. The household couldn't run without her.

Eryn spied the canvases she was seeking in an opposite corner. She crossed to them, glad she hadn't discarded her coat before coming up here. The space was unheated, and the wind seemed to creep through the paned windows.

There were at least seventy canvases, of all shapes and sizes. Eryn was shocked at the number. While Mama had been prolific, she'd also been a ruthless critic of her own work. She'd painted over some of her pictures that hadn't gone to plan, but she'd destroyed more canvases than she'd tried to reuse. Eryn now knew why. The paint never went on a recycled canvas in quite the same way.

She spent the next hour pulling out the pictures and setting them against the walls to look at. Studying each in turn, she realized she could still learn from her mother. Some of her techniques had been out of Eryn's reach when she was a child. Surely she now had the experience to duplicate them.

She worked faster, placing the canvases upright in rows along the walls. It took a lot of space. When she finished, she would begin at one end of the paintings and survey each critically. Perhaps she'd be able to see the progression of her mama's talent.

The task took longer than she'd expected, because she couldn't help lingering over some of them. A few Eryn recognized. Most she didn't. While a handful were titled, the majority weren't. There was only the familiar lowercase *a* in the circular space of the *P* in the right corner of each.

Many were scenic. Wild, crashing ocean waves. Serene beaches. The beauty of North Carolina's forested mountains. And others pictured nothing at all. They were a collection of color, bold and vibrant or soft and dreamy. Tilting her head, Eryn tried to analyze the use of light before moving on. When she saw the lone portrait in the bunch, she stopped.

It was her as a young child. She was maybe one or so. Her hair was only short white fuzz. She had a toy in her hand, and she was gazing at it with utmost absorption. The depth of detail had Eryn's throat going tight. And she knew she'd be taking this work back to her bedroom.

She set the painting aside and continued to set up the rest. But the next time she paused to stare at one, it wasn't because it inspired softer emotions.

It elicited a primitive fear.

The canvas was huge. She recognized the destroyed room it depicted, but she couldn't place it. A kitchen. A body on the floor.

Blood spattered . . . everywhere. Eryn shivered. Art was supposed to evoke strong feelings, and this one did. Terror. She wiped her damp palms on her pants. The pounding in her chest sounded in her ears. Eryn's muscles tensed, as if readying for flight. It was like she'd walked right into the painting and become an unwilling participant.

She forced herself to look more closely at the body on the floor. A woman, her features obscured by a tangle of blonde hair. There was nothing distinguishing about her, but Eryn knew somehow it was Mama. She knew she'd seen the scene before. She'd been *inside* it.

Sinking to the cool wooden planks, Eryn never took her eyes from the canvas. There was a reason it summoned such a visceral reaction from her.

And she wasn't leaving until she figured out what it was.

Ryder

When his cell rang, Ryder answered without a pause in his stride. The task force had divided into teams over the last couple of days. At first light, he'd joined one walking grids within the perimeter they'd established after the marshals had discovered rental transactions on Sutton's phony credit cards. It'd rained a little last night, the first precipitation this part of the state had had in weeks. The ground was still damp. They'd found no sign of Aldeen around the cabin near Bryson City. The rental had been empty, and no one had appeared even after darkness had fallen. Today the Highway Patrol helicopters and troopers would again search for the vehicle Sutton and Aldeen had been spotted in yesterday.

He tried to push away the fear that the men had slipped away again. They could be hemmed in within the human shield the team members had erected and afraid to take to the roads.

"Ry, it's Logan." The voice of one of his deputies sounded in his ear. "I just got around to tracking the number Bancroft gave us. The one he said belonged to the caller who tipped him off about Eryn Pullman's release. It's a pay phone. I traced it to the Handy Mart in Waynesville."

Of course he had. There were only two of the relics in town, as far as Ryder knew. The other pay phone was outside the bus station. But the convenience store had cameras. Whoever had contacted the pastor hadn't broken the law, but Ryder wanted to speak to the person anyway.

"Check the cameras there for corresponding dates and times of the calls."

"Will do. You want me to get my spiritual lift on Sunday by parking outside Bancroft's church again?" Logan had run all the plates from Wednesday night services and was following up with each of the church members. Many of the drivers had taken off when they'd seen him idling near the parking area. That hadn't prevented him from recording their plates. Ryder wondered how many of the church members would return.

"Yes." A branch cracked beneath his foot, reminding him to pay closer attention. In November, there weren't snakes in the woods to worry about, but the thick cover of leaves on the ground could hide any number of obstacles.

"Talking to all of the owners of the plates and checking out their alibis for the day of the effigy burning is going to be a lot more labor intensive."

"I'm hoping Bancroft will break when he sees how few people come to service on Sunday. Keep following up." The ground began a gradual slope beneath his boots as the call ended. Ryder tucked the phone away again. There were large outcrops of boulders dotting the area. They occasionally concealed the task force members who were walking grids parallel to Ryder's.

A mound of large rocks loomed ahead of him. As he drew closer to the boulders he heard the distant sound of running water. The map they'd consulted when parceling out search territory hadn't depicted a river in the area, but there were plenty of streams crisscrossing the territory.

Ryder's hand went to his weapon as he approached. The huge pile of boulders would provide excellent cover for someone hiding behind them.

He paused for a moment when he saw a glint near the boulders ahead. A flash that was there, then gone again. Drawing closer, he could catch a glimpse of metal.

Ryder rounded the heap of stone cautiously, looking for signs of anyone in the vicinity. When he had half circled the pile, he drew his weapon. There was a silver vehicle on the other side matching the description of the car the fugitives had been seen in yesterday. It looked empty. But the men could be lying down. Asleep. He detached the radio from his belt. "Position twelve." He reversed direction and stood where he had a view of the rear of the car. "The car has been located." Ryder described his location and waited for other members of the team to arrive. He could see the rutted hiking trail leading near the spot before it veered away to the nearby creek. His gut clenched with disappointment even as he could see other officers hurrying to join him. He wanted to remain positive. But Ryder was very much afraid the vehicle would be empty.

Samuel

Samuel was feeling a great deal more upbeat as they traveled the rural gravel roads heading east. It had been his idea to hide out in the forest until dusk yesterday before approaching the cabin. But they'd seen a sheriff's car concealed in the brush a half mile away from the drive leading to the rentals. That had been enough to convince him Sutton had fucked up again. Somehow law enforcement had discovered the cabin. And when David had tried to argue that it was impossible, Samuel had been very close to putting a bullet in the man's head.

Only the fake ID Sutton was holding for Samuel had saved him. Samuel's mood hadn't improved when he'd had to spend yet another night in the fucking woods with no food.

But as usual, the gods had been looking out for him. It'd been just before dawn when a late-model double-cab navy pickup truck had lumbered up the same path they'd taken. An older man had gotten out and hauled fishing poles, a backpack, and a tackle box out of the bed before starting toward the creek. All the while he'd sent suspicious looks toward their vehicle over his shoulder. It'd taken very little discussion to reach agreement: they needed the truck, so the stranger would have to die.

Samuel was now lying in the truck's back seat, finishing off part of the fisherman's lunch. He blew air into an empty baggie and popped it, laughing out loud when David jumped and cursed loudly.

"Son of a bitch! Everything's a fucking joke to you." He worked his shoulders. "My back is killing me. That bastard weighed a ton, and you insisted on carrying him for a mile."

"Quit being a drama queen." Samuel dug through the rest of the stranger's backpack, but there was no more food hidden away. They'd dumped him between two fallen logs and then dragged over more to pile on top of him. "The longer it takes the cops to find his body, the longer it'll take to ID him, and his missing vehicle."

"You're the only one who thinks the cops are dragging the area near the cabin for us," David muttered.

"Then apparently, I'm the only one with brains." It was growing tedious having to explain himself to David, who'd never win any awards for his intellect. "But by all means, if you're so certain your fake credit cards are good, I'll take the truck and drop you off in Cherokee. You can walk to the motel room you rented for yourself." A thought occurred, and Samuel straightened in the seat. "Tell me you didn't hide our new IDs in that motel room."

"Of course not. I've got a friend holding a package for me. When we're ready, I'll grab it from him and we'll both head out."

"Let's do it now." Samuel didn't know how much time they had before the dead guy was found and ID'd. He'd feel better if he had the new credentials on him, in case something went wrong later. "I'm not going anywhere or riding in anything you used one of your fake cards to rent." He returned to the point he'd made earlier. "Not the room. Not the rented car. Not the fucking Bryson City cabin."

He saw David's fingers clench on the wheel. Didn't particularly care that he'd infuriated the man. His friend couldn't understand how stressful it was to constantly watch for an enemy more fearsome than the cops. Samuel had looked over the stranger in the woods carefully and only approached him when he'd realized he wasn't a Taker. But they were around. Always looking for the right moment to steal more organs and tissue from Samuel. He needed to . . .

His attention fixed on a sheriff's car passing them in the opposite lane. *Oh my.* He twisted in his seat to look out the back window. The vehicle wasn't slowing. It wasn't turning around.

Not yet.

"That was too close. After we're finished we'll settle up. Like I've said before." Samuel stretched out on the seat again. "It's time to finish it. I'm not spending another night in the forest. Get us in the vicinity of where this is going down. We'll hide out there until after."

"What are we supposed to do when they ID this vehicle?"

Samuel thought for a few minutes. Then he said, "Do you know anyone in a surrounding state? Virginia? Tennessee? Kentucky? Preferably someone who owes you a favor?"

It took a while for David to answer. "Maybe. Got a guy who ripped me off for about ten thousand when I was dealing. Bad debt. I tracked him to Pigeon Forge, Tennessee. I was going to settle up with him later."

"Call him. Tell him to get three friends in three different towns near there to call the tip line and report they saw us in this vehicle. Give him a good description. None of the friends can be related. We don't want any connections when the police follow up."

David's reply was grudging. "That might work. I'm not wiping out all his debt, though."

"Negotiate." Did he have to script everything? "It will take the pressure off us while we finish our business."

David didn't argue. He turned onto a poorly maintained gravel road while Samuel folded his hands under his arms. Everything came to a close tonight. He closed his eyes and thought about David's promise.

Sisters, he'd said.

Cady

Cady only slept a couple of hours before she was awake again, that piece of fabric still on her mind. She eased out of bed and went to the kitchen. The dog got up and followed her, its nails clicking on the bare floors. Last night she'd had the idea to soak the scrap of material, and she checked the sink now. The water she'd filled it with was pink. The stains had been blood.

She picked up the piece of fabric and wrung it out, narrowing her eyes as she rubbed it between her fingers. Black denim. Nothing in particular to identify it. But before Cady headed back to the stakeout at Sutton's motel, she was going to do a different sort of investigative work on her own.

She showered, dressed, and gulped some coffee before donning her coat. Hero bounded out the door Cady held open for him. She followed at a more sedate pace after securing the door behind her. The stop she was going to make wouldn't take long. And she was already certain of her welcome there.

Gracious Estates was a grandiose name for the rows of shabby trailers filling a square dirt lot that hadn't been graveled in a generation. The mobile home Cady parked in front of was no better or worse than its neighbors. Meaning it ranked slightly above shithole status. She climbed the stoop and began pounding on a screen door, which threatened to fly off under the assault. She didn't stop hammering until a voice sounded inside.

"All right, all right! I'm coming. But I'm telling you right now, fucker, you better . . ." The expression on her cousin LeRoy Griggs's face when he pulled open a splintered wooden door and saw Cady outside it would have been amusing. But her sense of humor had gone dangerously absent last night.

"Put some pants on, LeRoy." Without waiting for an invitation, she pushed by him. "No one wants to see your junk."

"Who asked ya?" But he grabbed a coat off the hook by the door and pulled it on. As if its length were going to cover his tighty-whities.

"I see you have a guest." Cady stopped next to the sagging couch. Smiled as Bo struggled to sit up. "Looks like you boys tied one on last night." The group of beer bottles could have just as easily been collecting for days. Neither of them had inherited their mother's tidy habits. But given the bleary-eyed look on both of their faces, she didn't think her earlier guess was too far off the mark.

"I'm not going to lie, Bo. You look like shit." Unlike his too-bare brother, Bo had a quilt covering him. He clutched it to his neck like a virgin in a gothic movie.

"Me? Looks like you got your ass kicked good." He smirked. "Just sorry I wasn't the one to do it. That can change, though, if you don't get the hell out of here."

"Your lack of hospitality wounds me deeply." There were scratches on his bare arm. Deep furrows already scabbing over. And the black Carhartt jeans crumpled on the floor next to the couch looked as though they'd seen better days. "I just stopped to pass along some information you might find interesting. Seems like there's been a rash of burglaries in town. Even my landlady's place was broken into."

"Who gives a shit?" Bo belched loudly.

"Probably whoever matches the prints the cops lifted in each of the places." Bo flicked a glance in his brother's direction. She shifted a bit to keep both of them in sight. She'd learned long ago not to let a Griggs boy behind her. "Since my house got broken into, too, the sheriff is sending someone out to dust for prints there. I'm not going to lie; the state crime lab is backed up. But in a few weeks, if the burglar is in the system, we'll have a match."

Bo's eyes had gone flat. "Well, thanks for the crime bulletin. Now get the fuck out."

"There's one more thing." She lifted her booted foot and brought it firmly down on his covered legs. His howl of pain verified the suspicion that had bloomed last night. "Shoot, Bo, are you all right?" Cady reached down to grab the end of the quilt by his feet and yanked it upward. Bloody bandages were affixed to one of his calves. More scratches and puncture wounds marred the other leg.

She smiled beatifically. "I see you've met my dog."

Her cousin's suggestion was anatomically impossible.

"Bo got his leg caught in a trap when we was hunting last night." Always the loyal brother, LeRoy rose to Bo's defense.

"He got caught in a trap all right," Cady said meaningfully. "What were you hunting?"

"Wild pigs."

"Funny. Me too."

"You don't got no call to come in here and try to cause trouble. But then," Bo's smile was nasty, "you always was a troublemaker. It's why you got sent away."

Her hand clenched. "Hell of a thing, wasn't it? Me getting banished to live with our grandfather because you tried to rape me?"

Bo flipped the blanket back over his legs. "Shee-it. You couldn't take a joke back then any better than you can now. Calling a little wrestling match rape is what they call gross exaggeration."

Her fist clenched. Exaggeration. A mental snippet flashed across her mind of the last time her grandfather had locked her in the cellar. She'd been prepared. She'd hidden a screwdriver there. A flashlight. A thermos of water. She could still recall the priceless look on the old man's face when he'd awakened from his nap in his recliner to see her standing in front of him after taking the cellar door off its hinges.

I'm no one's victim. If you try that again, you'll be the one locked down there. For good.

It'd taken a moment for the man to give her something resembling a smile. *Well, you got more grit than your mama. At least that's something.*

It took a second to swallow the bile rising in her throat. Looking at the scar on Bo's forehead she'd inflicted made her feel a modicum better.

"Course even then you landed in clover. Got to live a cushy life in Mount Airy. The old man never had nothing to do with us. Bet you got treated like a fourteen-carat princess."

"Sounds almost like you were there." She and her grandfather had reached an uneasy truce of sorts, but she'd spent the remainder of her childhood with an embittered, taciturn old man who'd never uttered a kind word she could recall. Cady realized now Hannah had protected her the best way she could. But lack of money hadn't been the only thing keeping her mother from visiting very often. Elmer Griggs had probably been even worse when he'd been raising his daughters.

"Maybe that's why you're here now." Bo's gaze narrowed. "Maybe you want another 'wrestling match.' Me and LeRoy would be happy to oblige." He sat straighter against the pillow.

"I'm just here to warn you. The next time you come for me, I won't be using a rock to defend myself," Cady said grimly. "Better get your leg looked at. Hero's had his shots, but dog bites can be dangerous." She walked out of the room. "I'd hate for you to die of infection before those latents return from the lab."

◆ ◆ ◆

"You're quiet today," Miguel observed.

"You're chatty enough for the both of us." They were back in the lot across from Sutton's motel after catching up with the latest info dissemination from the command center.

"So what's your guess?" Miguel had the passenger seat moved back as far as it would go to accommodate his outstretched legs. "Does the news of the abandoned vehicle and the dead fisherman make it more or less likely Sutton will return here?"

She took a moment to consider. "It depends." Whoever was stationed on the sidewalk bench across the street already looked chilled. The parked car from yesterday sat in the same place. But the people occupying it were different. She couldn't make out any of the other team members' positions. "Philip Nieman's phone is being monitored. If Sutton had reason to call it, he might get scared off if it isn't answered by Philip."

"Sutton and Aldeen will need another car." Miguel raised the binoculars in his hand to his eyes as a car rolled by them. Then he lowered them and continued. "The minute Talbot's crew IDs the dead body, we'll know the make and model of the vehicle they stole, as well as its license plate number."

"The odds are against Sutton realizing we have his credit cards. And that we're stationed outside his motel. Remember the stash we found inside there? There's no way he's leaving until he recovers it. I think you're right. He'll be back." But it wasn't the credit cards and phones the man had left behind bothering Cady most. It was the message on the paper he'd stashed between pages of the Bible.

REVENGE IS COMPLETE WHEN THE ENEMY HAS LOST EVERYTHING.

"What if payback is what's keeping them in the area?" she asked. An old woman with a trio of yipping dogs walked slowly on the sidewalk in front of them, pausing to allow the canines to relieve themselves on the tire of a used car.

"You mentioned it yesterday." Miguel sounded half-asleep. She slanted a glance at him to make sure his eyes were open. "Again, revenge for what? Aldeen has no contacts in this area we know of. And Sutton blowing up Preston's car was just cutting a loose thread. Like Aldeen shooting Bush."

She'd spent enough time debating the issue in her head. Miguel had just articulated the counterarguments she'd already considered. But still . . .

"Keep your eyes open," she advised, a sudden thought striking her. Cady turned and reached into the back seat and rummaged through the case notes she'd brought with her. Settling back behind the wheel, she looked through the file until she found the notes on Sheila Preston. Something was niggling at the back of her mind. Something she'd missed earlier.

A half hour later she found it. "Remember the drug arrest on Preston's record?"

"For possession." He didn't take his gaze off the scene across the street. "If you needed a reminder, you could've just asked."

"And the charges got dropped. The date of her arrest was three months before Sutton's. And he spent a long stretch in prison after his trial."

Miguel's brows raised. "I'm waiting to be illuminated."

"What if"—Cady pounded her fist lightly on the wheel—"Sheila Preston lied to us yesterday?"

"An accomplice to a dangerous felon's escape was untruthful. I don't think I'll ever recover from the shock."

"No one likes a smart-ass, Miguel."

"You would certainly know." He was silent for a moment. "What'd she lie about?"

"She said she hadn't seen Sutton since they'd worked at Cisco's. We're expected to believe he just happened to remember someone he worked with for a few months twenty-three years ago? David Sutton collected women back then, from what we've heard. But Preston wouldn't have been the type to catch his eye. Not flashy enough."

Miguel sat up straighter in his seat. "So they got reacquainted in the intervening time."

"Yeah, they did. Charges can get dropped for a number of reasons. Being a cooperating witness against a dealer is one of them."

"Okay. She didn't reveal that because . . . ?"

Verbalizing her supposition just made Cady more certain. "The arrest is still on record, but so is the fact that the charges were dropped. Sheila's free to spin an explanation to friends. Her employers. Coworkers. She can claim the police learned the drugs weren't hers. A case of mistaken identity." Cady waved a hand. The possibilities were endless.

"Yesterday at the hospital you said you thought she was telling the truth," he pointed out.

"I thought she was credible. But when you tell a lie long enough it becomes your reality. Do you think she's going to tell her girls what really happened?"

"Maybe it's not a lie." Miguel reached for the water bottle in the holder nearest him and unscrewed the cap. Took a swig. "We don't know yet why the charges were dismissed. Where are you going with this?"

"The revenge phrase on the back of the map we found." The more Cady considered her argument, the more convinced she became. "And the addresses. I looked them up. Sheila's house. Her sister's and mother's. And an Outer Banks beach property listed in the Neves' name." The last revelation had Miguel freezing in the act of lifting the bottle to his lips again. "Revenge explains what's keeping Sutton and Aldeen in the area."

"Your theory only implicates Sutton."

Cady grabbed her cell and began searching through her contacts. "As far as we know, they're still together. And we might be overlooking the specific reason for that."

Forty minutes later, she disconnected her call. Bureaucratic red tape was real even for federal agents. She could only imagine how bad it was for regular citizens. "The Mecklenburg County prosecutor who handled Preston's case just confirmed it. Sheila Preston gave evidence against Sutton. He went to prison. She continued on with her life."

Miguel grabbed the file still spread on her lap. "Do you have Julie Neve's contact information in there?"

"Let's hope so." Cady glanced out the window as the owner of the car lot walked by, making a Hollywood-worthy production of not looking in their direction. "Because she has to be warned. She needs to get her nieces to safety."

◆ ◆ ◆

"Yes, Marshal, I'm at the hospital." Julie's voice was low. "What's wrong?"

"Who's watching your nieces?"

"My husband. Why?"

Cady slid a glance at Miguel. "Are they at your home in Mecklenburg?"

"Yes."

"I don't want to alarm you unduly. But until we have David Sutton in custody, I think it would be best if your husband took them somewhere no one would think to look for them."

There was a silence. Then . . . "Just a minute." Cady could hear the murmur of voices in the background. A distant beep of the machines they'd seen near Sheila Preston's bed. After a few moments Julie was back. "I needed to leave the room. I don't want to upset my sister. The doctors just left." She sounded as though she was fighting back tears.

"She has to have immediate surgery. Something ruptured and there's internal bleeding . . ." A sob erupted. "I have to be here. But the girls need someone too. That's why Andrew stayed home."

Cady's voice softened. "I'm sorry to hear about your sister. You're right. She needs support right now. Can I get your husband's number?" Sounding rattled, the other woman recited it. Cady wrote it on the front of the file still on her lap. "I want you to text him and tell him I'll be calling." Most people didn't pick up a call from an unfamiliar number. Even fewer when USMS showed in the caller ID.

"Yes. I'll do it now." Julie's voice sounded stronger. "I'll text you afterwards, so you'll know I've made contact."

"Thank you. I hope things go well with the surgery."

"So do I. Her little girls need their mom."

When they'd disconnected, Cady relayed Julie's side of the conversation to Miguel. His mouth flattened when he heard of Sheila's condition. "If it's revenge Sutton is after, sounds like he's already exacted it."

"Possibly." But it was equally likely the man wouldn't be satisfied until the woman's entire family was destroyed.

It was nearly an hour later before Julie Neve got back to her. The call was short. It was hard to miss the underlying panic in the woman's voice. Afterward, Cady told Miguel, "They're taking Preston into surgery now. Julie's husband hasn't answered her texts. I'm going to contact the CMPD to send a car to their house."

Miguel was silent for a few moments. When he spoke, it was with a note of resignation in his voice. "You want to go to Mecklenburg, don't you?"

"Neve's husband could have taken the girls to the park. His phone might be dead." There were any number of reasons for the man to not answer his wife's calls.

"Exactly."

"Except . . ."

"There's always an 'except' with you," Miguel muttered.

Cady turned in her seat to face him. "I still think Sutton is going to return to the motel if he can. But he's probably not stupid enough to do it in broad daylight. They haven't managed to stay free this long by being careless."

"Unless he's desperate."

She nodded. That was true as well. The daily media coverage of this case had been continuous. After the murder this morning, it would be nonstop, making it increasingly difficult for either Sutton or Aldeen to easily secure another vehicle. As far as the men knew, the car at the motel was still anonymous.

Miguel was silent for a long time. Finally, he heaved a sigh. "You're like a bomb waiting to detonate. By the time we get there, the CMPD will have already tracked Neve down and we'll have wasted a trip."

Sensing her partner was wavering, Cady seized the advantage. "It wouldn't hurt to have a chat advising Andrew Neve on how best to keep the girls safe. He can't take them to the beach house. He needs to select a new location."

This time it was Miguel's turn to pick up his cell. "Fine. I'll call the command center and get a couple of replacements for us."

His words brought a surge of relief. Cady couldn't concentrate on anything else until she was certain Preston's daughters were hidden away in a place Sutton couldn't find them.

◆ ◆ ◆

Julie Neve arrived shortly after Cady and Miguel got to her home. A CMPD officer who'd been called to the house had already canvassed the neighborhood. None of the people they'd spoken to had seen Andrew Neve leave in the morning. While the officer joined Julie and Miguel on a walk-through of the house, Cady hung back. The woman had left her car in the driveway. Cady pulled latex gloves from one coat pocket and donned them before lowering herself to the ground cautiously. Some of her soreness had eased, but it was still a struggle to roll to her back and scoot her body under the vehicle.

It took a few minutes, but she finally saw exactly what she'd feared she'd find. Reaching up, she jerked the monitoring device free and began to wiggle out from under the car.

"If you're checking the oil, you're in the wrong place." Miguel's voice sounded somewhere above her.

"You're hilarious." It was a struggle, but she finally managed to shimmy free. She took his hand as he pulled her to her feet, biting back a groan as she rose. She wondered how long it would be before she could bend in any direction without pain.

In the next moment, she thought of Sheila Preston lying in the Charlotte hospital. Cady had gotten lucky. She'd be wise to remember it.

She held up the tracker to show him, flipping it over so he could see the magnetic back. "Damn." He looked in the direction of the house again, where the officer and Julie were coming out the door. "Looks like you figured it right."

"You must have thought there was a chance, or you wouldn't have agreed to head this way." It defied belief that anyone other than David Sutton had planted the tracker.

"I didn't notice any clothes or suitcases missing," Julie said as she approached them. "And Andrew's phone was still in its charger. He never forgets it. But it was a chaotic morning for all of us." She frowned as she came closer and saw the gadget in Cady's hand. "What's that?"

Cady held it out to show her. "It's a monitoring device. Whoever planted it would have been able to trace your car's movements."

An expression of bewilderment chased over Julie's face. "But . . . why?"

"The CMPD bomb squad found small remnants of a similar gadget on your sister's car," Cady explained. "The person who planted the bomb used it to keep track of where she was."

Her words elicited an instant flood of tears. Understandable, Cady figured, given the day the woman had had. The emotional storm passed quickly. With apparent effort, Julie wiped her eyes and drew in a deep breath. "Sorry. There was too much today. Sheila's stable, for now. And hearing how that animal found her . . . why would he want to keep track of me? Oh." Comprehension filtered across her expression. "Is it . . . he can't be . . ."

"We don't know he's near this area."

The woman raised a shaking finger to point at the street. "Oh, thank God. Andrew's home."

Cady and Miguel stepped aside to allow the car to swing into the driveway. She looked in the back seat of the vehicle they'd driven and found an evidence bag. Dropping the device in it, Cady labeled the bag and set it on the seat before turning back to her partner. "If we find another tracker on his car," Miguel said in a low tone, "you can bet there's one on Cindy Preston's vehicle too."

She nodded, watching Julie run to embrace her husband when he got out of the vehicle. Children spilled out of it. The Neves had two, she recalled. So did Sheila. "The entire family needs to lay low until he's in custody."

That suggestion, as it turned out, met with some resistance. Fifteen minutes later, the CMPD officer gone and the children dispatched to another part of the house, Cady and Miguel sat at the couple's kitchen table. "You stay with your sister," Andrew Neve was telling his wife. "I'll take all four of the kids to the beach house."

"How would you entertain them there at this time of year?" Julie tried a smile. "You had to spend all day at the mall and the movies today to keep the girls occupied until our kids got out of school. OBX is almost deserted when it turns cold."

OBX. Short for the Outer Banks. It took a moment for Cady to make the connection. "We found a second device on your car, Andrew. Sutton has been tracking your movements too. I'm afraid the beach house is out of the question. We know Sutton has its address. Stay away from anything familiar. Go to a place you've never been before."

"I'll bet the kids would love a hotel with an indoor water park," Miguel put in. "It's just for a few days." *Hopefully.* His unspoken word hung in the air between them.

"I'll look for a place online. We'll all go."

But Julie was shaking her head at her husband's assertion. "I'm not leaving Sheila. And neither will Mom. The hospital will accommodate us. There's space for us to sleep in her room. We'll be safe there with the guard right outside."

Miguel and Cady looked at each other. "It should be fine as long as neither of you leaves the hospital. Not even for a few minutes." It was hard to imagine Sutton would be capable of carrying out his plans for revenge while he was on the run. Cady had checked the latest task force update on the way to Charlotte. This morning's victim had been identified, as had his vehicle. Someone—somewhere—had to report a sighting eventually.

But there was a reason the men had remained in the state. And Cady couldn't forget the statement scrawled on the paper they'd found in Sutton's motel room.

They didn't leave until the Neves had finalized their plans. Julie supplied a description of her mother's car before they left. Cady swung by the hospital before leaving Charlotte. Miguel retrieved the GPS tracker they'd been certain would be on Cindy's car and placed it in yet another evidence bag. "We need to stop at the office to drop these off," he said as she left the lot.

Cady nodded. "What are your plans for tomorrow?"

He lifted a shoulder. "Depends on what the updates say. I figure I'll get some sleep, which was in short supply last night, check with the task force, and go where I'm needed. Good thing Gant authorized overtime on this investigation. We're racking up the hours. How about you?"

Cady was still trying to work it out. She'd missed spending last Saturday with her mom. She was reluctant to skip another. "I have something in the morning. I can join you later."

He nodded. They'd play it by ear. And hope like hell something broke on the case soon.

They were halfway back to Asheville when Cady's cell rang. The number was unfamiliar. But given the circumstances surrounding this investigation, she answered it anyway, her mind still filled with the Preston family.

"Deputy US Marshal Maddix."

"It's Eryn Pullman."

Miguel must have seen the shock on her expression. He mouthed, *Who?*

"Eryn. Hello."

"Would you be able to stop by today? I remembered something. At least, I think I did. I don't know what it means, really . . ."

"Yes, of course." Cady glanced at the clock on the dash. "It might take me a couple of hours." She could swing by the house before heading to her own.

"All right. I'll be waiting." The call ended.

"Eryn . . . Pullman?" Miguel guessed. "Any chance this is about Aldeen?"

"I have no idea." After the last time she'd talked to the girl—and her uncle—Cady had figured pursuing the Aurora Pullman angle was a dead end. But she was intrigued enough by the call to gladly make the trip to see the girl again.

It was nearly eight o'clock before Cady drove through the open Pullman Estate gates. When she got out of the car and walked up to the front door, it opened before she could knock.

"Come in." Eryn stepped aside for Cady to enter before shutting the door behind her. "I want to show you something."

Mystified, Cady followed the girl through the home. She glanced into the study she'd been shown to the last time she was here. Found it dark. There was no one in the large living area they walked through, either. "Where's the rest of the family?"

"My uncle and his wife took my cousin to a movie. Mary Jane is spending the weekend with her sister near Asheville. She's not a relative. She's . . ." Seeming unable to come up with a description, Eryn shrugged. "She's been with the family forever."

"So you're all by yourself in this big house?" Cady asked jokingly.

But the girl's voice was sober when she answered. "I don't mind. And I'm not really alone with the deputies outside. The family will be home soon." Eryn led her down a different hallway lined with doors. She opened one and flipped on the light. Cady could see it was a bedroom. "I'm sorry. I would have brought it out, but it's pretty heavy." Eryn gestured to an unframed picture leaning against the wall beneath a set of windows.

Cady knew nothing about art. In this case, she didn't need to. A sense of brutality leaped from the canvas, as much in the colors and bold strokes as the scene they depicted. Fascinated, she walked farther into the room to get a closer look. It would be difficult to remain unmoved by the pain portrayed in the work. The raw emotion. After studying it for a few more moments, she raised her gaze to meet Eryn's. "Did you paint this?"

"No. My mama did. I don't recall ever seeing it before. I found it earlier today when I was in the attic going through some of her pieces Uncle Bill had stored up there."

Remembering the explanation Eryn had given for her call earlier, Cady guessed, "Is that your mother in the scene?"

Eryn's attention returned to the canvas. "I think so," she whispered. "I think . . . I can almost remember seeing this before. But not in a picture. When it happened. The memory sort of melts away when I try to recall it more clearly."

The words struck uncomfortably close to home. Cady had experienced the exact sensation when she tried to force herself to recall that pivotal moment when she was four. She remembered sensations the most clearly. And only scraps of images. She was never sure how much of the memories were hers and how much had been implanted in her mind by others' retelling. And she knew she needed to be careful of not being guilty of the same: fixing an idea in Eryn's mind that sprouted a fabrication.

"When was this painted?"

"Before we moved here, I think." Eryn sank onto the mattress. "She signed all of the work she kept." A ghost of a smile flitted across her lips. "She was a ruthless self-critic. Maybe it comes with the creativity. She'd show me every piece she finished if she intended to keep it. And she didn't keep many. I remember the signature she used. It's a small *a* encompassed in a larger capital *P*. But this one"—she nodded at the canvas—"I'd never seen that signature before. It's on several upstairs."

Cady stepped close enough to see the identification in the lower right corner of the canvas. A lowercase *a* next to an uppercase *P*. A shrink would have a heyday figuring out the implicit meaning of the final initial dwarfing the first. "What do you think it signifies?"

"The paintings with the signatures I don't recognize must have been done when I was quite young," Eryn said simply. "My earliest real memory is sitting on Mama's lap while she put the final touches on a painting. It's the one to the left of the windows. I think I was about three."

Cady crossed to look at the picture. It was much smaller than the one on the floor. A busy beach scene covered the canvas. As Eryn had mentioned, the signature on this differed from the one on the other work.

"We moved here when I was three or four. And I only have snippets of memories before this house. Just a jumble of feelings more than anything. But then I saw the picture and felt . . . it's like I'm in it. I don't know why I'm certain of that, but I am. Someone hurt my mama when I was small. Badly." She shook her head. "It probably doesn't help you at all. I don't know who or why. But I am sure it happened before we came here. Does any of this help?"

Did it? Cady took a final look at the first painting. It raised more questions than it answered. "I'm not sure," she finally replied.

There was a distant sound of voices. The family had returned home.

Eryn walked quickly out of the bedroom. Cady trailed her. She could hear a child's voice above the others, waxing enthusiastic about whatever film they'd seen. As they returned to the living room, small footsteps pounded down the hallway toward them. "Eryn!" A boy's tones, his volume deafening. "Eryn, guess what?"

He skidded to a halt in the opening of the doorway when he saw Cady. "Who are you? Is that your Jeep outside? What's that star mean on your belt? Are you a detective?"

"Sort of."

He turned to holler down the hallway. "Mom! There's a detective with Eryn!" Two adults appeared quickly then. William Pullman and a woman Cady assumed was his wife.

"Eryn." The woman's voice was sharp as she laid a protective hand on the boy's shoulders. "Who is this woman?"

"It's fine, Rosalyn." But Cady could tell by William Pullman's expression that finding her here wasn't fine at all. "Get Jax ready for bed. I'll be in soon."

"But I want to tell Eryn about the movie!" the boy protested.

"You can tell her tomorrow." With a backward look in Cady's direction, Rosalyn guided the boy out of sight.

"Marshal, what brings you here this evening?"

Cady opened her mouth, but Eryn forestalled her response. "I called her."

"I see. Is there anything I can help with?"

288

She glanced at Eryn. The young woman gave a tiny nod.

"I have a few more questions, if you don't mind."

The man released a sigh but gestured for Cady to precede him out of the room. When she glanced back at Eryn, she saw her retreating in the direction of the bedroom they'd just exited.

Assuming they were headed for the study, Cady led the way toward it. Within moments they were settled in the same chairs they'd occupied before. She wondered now if Pullman kept the desk between them as a subtle way of exhibiting authority.

"I'm sorry Eryn bothered you." His words were abrupt. "I don't know how she got your number. Perhaps from the card I put in my desk."

"I wasn't bothered." Cady watched him carefully. He hadn't been especially pleased by her last visit, but today he seemed almost belligerent. "She had a memory she thought might help. Was your sister ever badly beaten or involved in a violent accident of some sort?"

"Of course not." His tone was dismissive. "Did Eryn claim otherwise?"

"There's some reason to believe it." Cady picked her way carefully. "Could something have happened to Aurora you didn't know about?"

"I can't claim she shared much about her life at college, but I am certain nothing like you mentioned occurred once she'd returned home to live."

"Maybe it did happen while she lived in Charlotte." Perhaps shortly before the move back to the Pullman home. The picture itself only gained significance with the snippets of memory they elicited in Eryn. And they were important to Cady if the violence captured on the canvas had stemmed from David Sutton. "Surely she would have told you about something so serious."

"She would have, yes. But she didn't. Which means it never happened." William stood. "I don't mean to be rude. But this is the second time you've kept me from my son's bedtime. Not to speak unkindly of my niece, but you're aware of her history. And the irony is, if it weren't for her, my sister would be here to put this nonsense to rest herself." Cady's interest sharpened. Apparently, the man was finished with diplomacy. "Please show yourself out."

She did so. Pullman might be right. It could be extremely unwise for Cady to give credence to an unsupported memory shared by a mentally ill young woman. It said something about the situation, she figured, that Eryn had been more convincing than her uncle.

◆ ◆ ◆

It was a measure of Cady's exhaustion that she was halfway home before the obvious occurred. She could easily discover whether Eryn Pullman was right. A police report would exist if assault charges had been filed. She could turn around and drive back to the office to check the database. But before she did she eased to the side of the road and called the office number. Marshals kept irregular hours. Maybe she'd get lucky.

She reached Allen Gant, who agreed to check the records for her, and then pulled back onto the road. Her cell buzzed almost as soon as she hung up. Cady saw Ryder Talbot's name on the caller ID and answered unceremoniously. "Do you have news?"

There was a pause. Then, "Deputy US Marshal Cady Maddix?"

She grinned at his falsely polite tone. "I'm surrounded by smart-asses."

"Always better to be smart than dumb."

Laughing out loud, she hugged the shoulder to allow a vehicle to roar past her. "Are you perhaps familiar with the driver of a red dually pickup whose customary speed is racetrack level?"

"Speaking of dumb-asses. Gilly Gilbert and I are going to have a come-to-Jesus moment as soon as Aldeen is behind bars."

The reminder of the investigation had her amusement dissipating. "Has anything worthwhile shown up on the tip line?"

"The only way we'll know is to continue to wade through each and every call. I thank God every day for the personnel to take care of things like the tip line. Even if I don't offer thanks for some of the personalities and red tape involved in supplying that manpower."

His wry tone had her smiling again. "So you just called to keep yourself awake on your drive home?" she asked.

"Plus I wanted to talk to you about the Pullmans."

She raised a brow and swerved to miss a roadkill carcass in her lane. "What a coincidence. I just left there." Cady filled him in on her recent experience, finishing with, "I got the distinct impression William was unhappy with my presence or my questions. Both, probably."

Ryder was silent for a moment. "I can guarantee he'll be far unhappier about the call I'm about to make. I got a nasty piece of news today. The source of those phone calls tipping off Frederick Bancroft, the crazy pastor causing trouble at their estate? They were made by none other than Rosalyn Pullman."

He'd managed to shock her. "Get. Out."

"We traced the number and got security footage of her making the contacts on a public phone at the times appearing on the pastor's cell."

Anger flared. It wasn't enough Eryn had to return to a family she barely knew. She also had to struggle with one of them working to sabotage her emotional stability. "What a bitch."

"My sentiments exactly. If William was in a temper before you left, it'll soon be worse."

"Worse for Eryn, maybe."

"It's bound to be unpleasant around the house for a while. But I'm betting the calls to the pastor will come to an end now. And I think I've got him wound so tight, Bancroft's church isn't going to be involved in any protests at the Pullman's anymore."

"At least there's that."

"Are you nearly home?"

"Just pulling up to my gates, why?" Hero was tearing across the property toward her. He wasn't barking. Cady wondered if he'd already learned to recognize her vehicle.

"Good. I wanted to make sure you were home before I hung up. I pulled into my garage a minute ago. After I call William Pullman, I'm gonna face-plant on the nearest flat surface and sleep for five hours. I figure you have to be in the same shape."

She got out of the car to deal with the gates. And the dog. "You really know how to spend a crazy Friday night."

"I used to."

His audible yawn summoned one of her own. "Okay." She cruised up the drive and under the carport. "Go ruin William Pullman's night."

Hero trotted along by her side as Cady walked to his doghouse and placed his food and water dishes into it before blocking off the entrance. After she unlocked the door he dashed through it ahead of her in what had to be a breach of doggy etiquette. When she sat down on a stool at the counter to eat the sandwich she made, he waited patiently at her side. Absently, she tore off a piece and fed it to him. She should be taking the opportunity to sleep too. Tomorrow she'd be up early to spend a few hours with her mom before heading back to work.

But Cady waited up to hear from Allen Gant. And when she did, sleep was the furthest thing from her mind. He'd pulled up both aggravated assault charges on Sutton's record. The first one had been seventeen years earlier.

And the victim had been Aurora Pullman.

Eryn: Then

Eryn was cold. The little room where the babysitter had put her made her shiver. The floor was hard, and so were the walls. Dark. Everywhere was dark. Maybe there were monsters. She'd screamed and screamed in her head. But there was a nasty cloth in her mouth. And he'd tied her hands and feet. *That's what happens to naughty girls. Naughty girls have to stay by themselves.*

She cried silently. Where was Mama? Why did she have to go out tonight? She'd danced Eryn around the kitchen before she'd gone. They'd laughed and laughed. When Mama was happy, Eryn was too.

But she hadn't been happy when the babysitter had come into her bedroom. Then she'd screamed and yelled. He'd slapped her. Hard. And then taken her to the nasty basement. Everything stunk down here. And there were scary dark rooms behind the washers and dryers. Rooms where no one would ever find her, he'd said.

Something crawled over her leg. She screamed in her head again, shaking her legs from side to side as hard as she could. It was scary! Eryn wanted out. She wanted Mama. She'd be good forever and ever if Mama would find her.

She didn't know how long it was before she heard the scratching at the door. Like a mouse. Or a monster. Pee dribbled down her leg. She tried to wiggle as far away as she could. But the cold wall was already at her back. The door creaked. Eryn hid her face against the cold, damp stone.

"Maybe you're ready for some company by now. It's chilly in here, isn't it? Are you feeling a bit friendlier?"

She shook her head, squeezing her eyes closed. If she didn't see him, it wasn't real. Just like a movie. A bad scary movie.

"There isn't room for both of us to sit." Eryn felt herself lifted. When he put her on his lap she started to shake. "There now. Why don't I warm you up?" His hands slipped into her pajamas. Touching her. Rubbing. Maybe there hadn't been monsters in here with her before.

But there was now.

Eryn: Now, the Next Evening

Eryn stiffened as her door eased open, but when she saw Jaxson framed in it, her tension vanished. Lowering the notebook she was writing in, she said, "Hey. What are you doing out of bed? It must be after midnight."

He approached her, his face troubled. "Can I sleep with you?"

"Jaxson." Concern chased through her. "What's wrong? Is it your ankle?"

He shook his head dolefully. "No, it's almost well. It's Mom and Dad. They're arguing again. Just like last night. Yelling, but in whispers. But sometimes they forget to whisper. I heard your name. Maybe they're arguing about you."

Her stomach clenched. A person would have had to be unconscious to miss the frostiness between Uncle Bill and Rosalyn today. Eryn had never seen her uncle so grim. And his wife swung between a state of near tears and a frigid demeanor. Eryn had played hours of video games with Jaxson just for an excuse to escape the simmering strain in the house. Neither of his parents had come to warn him he was spending too much time with electronics. That in itself was strange.

Maybe Rosalyn had done as she'd promised and told Uncle Bill about taking pain medication she hadn't been prescribed. If that was the cause of the arguments, her uncle must have been extremely angry about his wife's addiction.

The tension had only been exacerbated by Henry's presence at dinner tonight. Eryn had fled to her room as soon as possible to avoid the man.

Scooting over in bed, she patted the mattress beside her. "Hop in."

He scrambled up and settled himself against the pillows. "Are my parents getting a divorce?"

The question rocked her. Were they? Eryn had no way of knowing what the dynamics were between the couple. She'd seen her uncle frustrated and impatient, but she couldn't even imagine him yelling. "I don't know. But couples fight sometimes." At least, they did in the movies. That was as close to real-life experience she had in the matter.

"They were saying really mean things to each other." Jaxson looked small and forlorn against the pillows she'd mounded to prop herself up on when she was writing. "Bad things. I'd get in trouble for saying them."

"Sometimes adults have bad behavior. Just like kids." Eryn had no marriage experience to draw from. But she had plenty of experience with therapists to rely on. "They're working something out. Maybe it'll be better tomorrow."

"Maybe." The boy's voice sounded dubious. "Everything is weird. Henry is in the kitchen by himself."

Surprised, Eryn said, "He is? What's he doing?"

"He's pouring stuff from a bottle into his glass. He's sitting in a chair like this." He leaned against the pillows with his limbs splayed out. "He and Dad talked after dinner and when Dad left the kitchen, Henry looked real mad." The boy straightened on the bed, his expression a mask of worry. "Dad's making everyone mad lately."

It sounded like Henry had the misfortune of picking a particularly inopportune day to visit. Eryn wasn't going to waste sympathy on her older cousin. He'd spread his share of misery when he was younger. But as Eryn had been leaving the dining room tonight she'd heard Uncle Bill snap at his son about not smoking in the house. She hadn't thought anything of the man's temper at the time. If Mary Jane were here, she would have berated Henry too.

"It'll be better in the morning," she said and then wished she could recall the words. Eryn was in no position to make promises. Especially when she had no idea what was going on with Jaxson's parents. She searched for something to soothe him. "How about if you and me go to the mall in the morning?"

His eyes lit up. "For real? Because they have a visiting dinosaur display there, and it's super cool. I saw it once, but we could go again. And then we could get corn dogs. And ice cream!"

"Sounds like a great way to get a bellyache."

He made a face. "That's what Mom would say."

"We'll have to ask your parents. And we will. First thing in the morning. Get some sleep so you're not too tired to go."

"Okay." He pulled up the covers and snuggled into the pillows. "Thanks, Eryn. You're cool."

Something clutched in her chest. "You're pretty cool too."

She'd be wise to take her own advice. But Eryn already knew she wasn't going to fall asleep anytime soon. Her insomnia was worsening. She felt energized and revved all of the time, even though she was careful to take her medications. Anxiety gripped her. She'd have to share her symptoms with Dr. Ashland. Although she felt far better than she had in years, without the doped-up tired feelings, she knew the improvement could mean the medication wasn't working anymore. The tachyphylaxis had ruined her trial transitions in the past.

If she failed this time, as well, she'd be tempted to give up.

The boy's breathing was soft and even. Eryn closed her eyes. But she couldn't shake the hyperalert feeling. Every creak and groan of the old home seemed magnified. She wondered if Henry was still here, or whether he'd driven home even after it sounded like he'd been drinking.

She didn't know how long it was before a scream awakened her. The sound had Eryn sitting straight up, shaking off the drowsiness that had just crept across her consciousness. She listened, but the noise had ended as abruptly as it had begun. Eryn threw back the covers, stealing a look over her shoulder at Jaxson. He was still sleeping. Maybe Rosalyn had gone to check on him and gotten frightened when she found him gone.

Eryn opened her bedroom door and walked toward the living room. Bumps and scraping sounds could be heard. Her feet slowed, and a chill trickled down her spine. Taking refuge against a wall, she sidled along it until she could peek around the corner into the shadows shrouding the room.

It wasn't dark. Not completely. Two beams of light shone. Then one vanished. Moments later it reappeared. She could hear snippets of words. Eryn moved a bit closer.

". . . the others."

"Not yet. Help me get them tied up."

She blinked uncomprehendingly. For a moment, Eryn felt like she was having an out-of-body experience.

"He's coming around."

"Punch him again. No, let me." She winced at the sound of flesh cracking against flesh. "Fucker's had that coming for a long time."

Eryn didn't wait to hear more. She ran softly back to her bedroom and to the window. Unlocking it, she raised the sash and pushed on the interior hook keeping the old outer window secured. When she had it unlatched, she hurried back to the bed. She softly put her hand over Jaxson's mouth and shook him awake. His eyelids fluttered, then went wide when he saw her bending over him, a finger to her lips. Her lips close to his ear, she whispered, "We have burglars." But the nasty tangle of fear in Eryn's stomach put the lie to her words. Whoever was in the house was far more dangerous. "Listen to me. I'm going to lower you out the window. Understand?" He nodded, his expression frightened. "When you get outside, run to . . ." She stopped herself, comprehension dawning. The deputies should be parked on the road out front. How did the men break in if law enforcement was still outside? Making an instant readjustment, she said urgently, "Don't go to the boathouse. Don't run toward the road. Go past the gardens and hide behind the old gazebo." It was the opposite side of the property from the stable. She couldn't bring herself to suggest he hide himself in the structure that still haunted her memories. "Got it?" He nodded again. She lost no more time. Picking him up, she carried him to the window and, using her elbow to hold the outer one open, lowered him to the ground. The boy lost no time racing in the direction she'd indicated.

Eryn grabbed her phone and cracked her door open. Mary Jane's room was closest to the kitchen. The kitchen had weapons, and it was near the back coat closet. The image of the knife block flashed across her mind, followed by a bout of gut-wrenching nausea. But the closet had baseball bats.

She ran lightly down the hallway toward Mary Jane's room and hid in the closet there behind her clothes. Fear racked Eryn's frame as her fingers fumbled with her cell. She didn't dare make a call. But she looked up recent numbers dialed and found the marshal's. A text message would be safe. Her fingers were trembling as she typed.

intruders broke in home danger help

She silenced her cell so an answering text alert wouldn't give her away. Cautiously, she left her hiding place and went to the door. Pressed her ear against it.

"They're not there! The window's open in the girl's room. I'm going after them."

Guilt held Eryn rooted to the spot. She should have stayed with Jaxson. But how likely was it that someone unfamiliar with the property would find him in the dark? She needed to help Uncle Bill and Rosalyn. They had to be the ones the strangers tied up.

A small light winked on her cell, but she didn't have the time to check for an answering message. She raced down the hall toward the kitchen. If one man had gone out the window, there was at least another left. Unless there was a third she hadn't heard. Maybe keeping watch outside.

She heard an earsplitting shriek. Rosalyn. The sound resolved something inside Eryn. She stuck her head in the kitchen. Found it empty. For the first time in her life, she wished Henry were still here.

Eryn lingered a moment too long in front of the knife block. Her palms dampened as she reached toward it. When her fingers closed around the hilts of a couple of steak knives, something inside her wanted to weep. She tiptoed to the opposite doorway. To the left was the back entry. Across the hall was the closet, and to the right she could access the living room.

Voices drifted from the room beyond.

"William, William! Are you all right?" Another scream from Rosalyn, followed by a sharp crack.

Sick with fear, Eryn dashed across to the closet.

"Typical woman. He's half-unconscious and you're still yapping." There was the sound of fabric ripping. Rosalyn's muffled sobs. "He wouldn't help you if he could. He didn't have the guts to come after me himself when I put his little sister in the hospital."

Eryn's blood turned to ice. Uncle Bill's little sister. Mama. She clamped her jaw against the mournful wail that threatened. The painting. Violence. Blood. She still couldn't recall more than glimmers of perceptions. But now she knew the man in the other room had been part of the scene.

"He had to hire a small army to come after me. Right, tough guy?" Sickening thuds sounded. "Fuckers nearly killed me. Bet you thought you'd gotten away with it."

It took effort to move. To grab a coat and slip it on because she didn't have pockets in her pajamas. The knives were placed in one. Her cell in the other. Then she went to the equipment box in the closet. Grasped a bat and drew it out. She tiptoed back to the doorway, then remembered to check her cell. There was a return text from the marshal.

On my way. Get out now!

Eryn released a quick shuddering breath and stuffed the phone back in her pocket. That was excellent advice. Because someone needed to check on Jaxson.

But the man who'd hurt her mother all those years ago was only yards away. And Eryn knew she wasn't going anywhere. She crept out of the closet, her fingers clutching the bat.

"I'm gonna fuck your wife in front of you, Billy. The bastards you sent after me crushed one of my balls. Turns out, everything works just as well with one. Then when I'm done, I'm going to beat you to death before burning the whole damn place down with both of you in it. And then we'll be even. Somewhere out there Aurora is probably applauding this. I always figured you killed your sister to get the whole inheritance."

"No, that's not true!" Rosalyn's words were a hysterical mixture of screams and sobs. "He never would have! He loved Aurora."

Eryn inched closer down the hallway. Close enough to glimpse where her uncle and his wife were. To catch sight of a shadowy figure bending over Rosalyn. Then the woman was hauled out of her chair and thrown to the ground.

Eryn was at the wrong angle. She couldn't see the entire room. Turning, she ran back through the kitchen. Down the hall. She needed to come up behind the man. She'd only get one chance.

I can help, Mama. The thought drifted across her mind like a wisp of fog. *This time I can help.*

"You don't know a damn thing about it. Ouch! Bitch!" Eryn peered around the doorway into the living room. Rosalyn had knocked the man off her and had gotten to her feet. He snaked out a hand and caught her ankle, yanking her to the floor with a crash. "That's gonna cost you." He flipped her over, his hand gripping her hair. "What do you, say, Billy? I never took no shit from a woman. Maybe a candy ass like you is different."

"Leave her alone! You've got a problem with me. Let everyone else go." Bill's voice was weak.

"Best part of this?" The stranger ripped Rosalyn's nightgown away as she struggled. "Right now my buddy has killed your niece and is feasting on your kid."

The visceral howls of rage and fear from Bill and Rosalyn echoed inside Eryn. No. Her mind skittered away from believing it. How could this guy know that? Jaxson was safe. He was hiding. She had to believe it.

"What kind of man lets his woman and kid get raped while he just sits there, hm-m?" Eryn took a step into the room. And then another. The stranger was grappling with Rosalyn, who was fighting like a mad-woman. She swung wildly. Her fist just grazed the man's jaw. "The kind that lacks the guts to come after me on his own. Who's so damn cowardly he frames his own niece after he kills her mother for money. Piece of shit."

"No, he didn't! He never would! It was an accident! I . . . I just wanted to scare her! She would never have let us be together." Rosalyn's shrieked words were intermingled with ragged sobs.

"Rosalyn! No! Please don't say . . ." The horror in Uncle Bill's voice echoed in Eryn's brain. She stilled for a second, her brain grappling with the woman's meaning. Rosalyn? Wanted to scare . . . Mama? It was all too much to take in, and she could feel a part of her shutting down. *Don't think. Don't feel.* The inner litany battered her insides. There was something . . . urgent. She mentally shook herself. Jaxson. She had to help Uncle Bill and go to Jaxson.

She inched along to hug the wall opposite the side of the room where her uncle was tied up. He didn't seem to notice her. Maybe he'd escaped to a place deep inside. A place where the horror couldn't touch him. "I didn't mean to . . ." Rosalyn's face was turned toward her husband's. "Please, William, you must believe me . . ."

"And I'm the one who got locked up for ten years. Jesus, you people deserve everything that happens to you tonight." The man's back was to Eryn. She closed the gap, cocking the bat.

The stranger half rose above Rosalyn. Loosened his pants.

Time crawled, like a movie clip in slow motion. As if from a distance, Eryn saw herself swing the bat. The man crumpled on top of Rosalyn, who screamed. A long quavery screech that reverberated in Eryn's head and scraped ragged nerve endings. The stranger was unmoving. Like a sleepwalker, Eryn ran behind her uncle's chair and put one of the knives in his fingers.

And then, the bat still in her hand, she raced for the back door.

Jaxson. The jumbled emotions in her head were bumping and colliding too fast for comprehension. She held the thought of her cousin fast. She'd deal with the rest later. Eryn couldn't handle anything else right now.

She burst out the back door without a shred of caution, running toward the gazebo. The boy had to be there. He had to. Eryn raced through the gardens, not registering the icy chill beneath her bare feet or the stab of shorn stalks. She ran toward the toolshed just past the garden.

And then something grabbed her foot and pulled. The bat fell out of her hand as her body crashed to the ground.

"Eryn!" A slurred hiss. She felt herself being dragged, but she couldn't draw a breath. Couldn't breathe. Lights were flickering behind her eyes, bells clanging in her head. She was suffocating. Gasping for air.

It was a long minute before oxygen refilled her lungs. When it did—when she was able to haul in a breath—her mind began to clear. The shadow next to her took shape. Recognition filled her. "Henry." She struggled to her feet. "What are you doing out here?"

Then a sneaky sliver of suspicion struck, and she backed away. "Have you seen Jaxson?"

"He's got him." Henry was leaning heavily against the side of the shed. At first Eryn thought he was wounded. A moment later she realized he was drunk. Disgust surged.

"Where are they?" When he didn't answer, she reached out and shook him. She followed the direction he pointed with her gaze, and her heart dropped.

The stable.

Cold. Dark. Smelly. Clawing fear smashed into her at the thought of following Jaxson and the second man into the structure. She should wait. The marshal had said so.

But what would happen to the boy in the meantime?

"It's too late," Henry mumbled. "I saw 'em when I was outside having a cig. They sprinkled the perimeter of the house with gasoline before they went in. Didn't you smell it? Dropped my phone. Can't find my phone."

"C'mon!" She stood and pulled at him. "I hit the man inside. He might be dead. You have to help me find Jaxson."

He stumbled to his feet. Swayed. "The guy who took him could have a gun. What are we supposed to do then, huh? They musta killed the cops who were out front. If they can kill them, what chance do we stand? Wait."

"I need your help." Desperation had her yanking harder at his arm. "Two of us might be able to stop him from hurting Jaxson."

He lost his balance and went to one knee. "Think." Henry clutched a handful of her jacket. "There's nothing we can do. No one would expect . . ." His next words were almost too low to make out. "We'd be the heirs, you and me. Everyone else would be gone."

She wasted precious moments staring at her cousin in horror. Then she wrenched her jacket from his clutching fingers and fell to her knees, searching the grass until her fingers closed around the bat. She rose and began to sprint.

The distance to the other structure had always seemed vast, but now it was closing much too rapidly. Two invisible forces warred inside her. One, a terrible sense of urgency, impelled by fear for her younger cousin. The other, a sense of dread, hauling her back, constraining her with a terror rooted in her past.

When she stopped outside the structure, her lungs were heaving. One of the big double doors yawned open. Eryn stared at the funnel of darkness before her and took an unconscious step back. Evil lay within. Her certainty came from a visceral place deep inside her. The bat slipped in her damp grip. She wiped one palm on her pajamas and then another. Shudders racked her body. Eryn's brain ordered her limbs to move. They didn't obey.

Casting a wild glance over her shoulder, she searched the darkness for Henry. Had he followed her? But the tenuous hope was dashed. There was no approaching figure. Lights flickered outside the house. No, not lights. Flames.

Panicked, Eryn looked frantically from the house to the stable. Where was the marshal? How much longer before she arrived?

Nearby, screams sounded, each tearing through her like jagged shards of glass. One after another. Desperate and terrified. Jaxson. They released her from the paralyzing fear rooting her in place. With trembling fingers, she turned on the cell's flashlight app and plunged into the shadowy structure.

So dark. Cold. Her body quaked as she tiptoed through the building, following the sound of the shrieks. They didn't come from the stalls. Eryn already knew where they emanated from. Her veins turned to ice. A desperate shred of self-preservation careened through her mind. *No farther, no farther.* But her feet continued to move forward even as everything inside Eryn wanted to flee.

She crept toward the small room in the back corner of the building. Holding the bat behind her, she reached out a hand and pushed the door open. The thin beam of her cell landed on the two people inside the room. Jaxson was struggling, his cries sounding harsh and guttural. But it was the man holding him fast that drew her attention.

As if feeling her eyes on him, the intruder shifted his attention to her. He smiled a hideous smile. "Hello, Eryn. I hoped we'd meet again."

It was like stepping off a cliff. Arms wheeling, desperate to stop the fall. Eryn felt herself descending into the vortex of a nightmare. But her voice sounded calm to her ears when she spoke.

"Hello, Uncle Arlo."

Ryder

"We've got two teams dispatched to Tennessee. The tips came from here. Here. And here." Ryder tapped the red pushpins in the large map covering a bulletin board they'd erected in the command center. "There's another crew surveilling Sutton's Cherokee motel. Yet another staking out the area surrounding the cabin rental in Bryson City." He faced the team members working the third shift of the investigation. "You've read today's updates. Questions?"

"How reliable are those tips coming from out of state?" The voice came from the back of the room. Greg Jensen, Swain County Sheriff. "I hate thinking we're putting so much manpower in one place if it's a wild-goose chase."

"The callers claimed to have sighted either the truck or one of the men riding in it in three different locations within twenty miles. The timeline works. Law enforcement there have questioned the people who called in. They deemed them credible enough for us to check out. But our people have found no sign of Aldeen at any of the areas yet." Jensen's question touched a chord in Ryder. There had been robust discussion yesterday on how much personnel to dedicate to the tips. It left them shorthanded here, but leading by committee was a lesson in compromise.

"Any other questions?" He patiently answered the ones called out, then pointed at the whiteboard on the wall. "Your shift duties are listed on the board." His cell buzzed. Withdrawing it from his pocket, he glanced at the screen. Cady Maddix.

"Jerry." He jerked his head toward the team members milling around the duty list, and his chief deputy nodded. He'd facilitate if necessary. Ryder walked to the corner of the room. "Cady. What's up?" She'd taken a shift on the surveillance of Sutton's motel in Cherokee, he recalled. But someone should have relieved her by now.

"Break-in in progress at the Pullman place. Got a text from Eryn just as I was getting home. I'm not sure exactly what's going on. I'm on my way. I don't know what to expect when I get there, but send backup."

"I've got . . ." Comprehension slammed into him. He waved over Cal Patterson and told him, "Radio Fitzpatrick and Cahalan. Get an update." To Cady he said, "I've had pairs of deputies stationed in front of the estate round-the-clock since we discovered Aldeen had Eryn Pullman's audio files on his MP3 player." Their reports had been uneventful. A sense of foreboding lodged in his chest. "I'm on my way with a team."

"Oh, and Ryder?" The urgency in Cady's tone stopped him in the act of disconnecting. "Last night I discovered that one of Sutton's assault charges stemmed from an attack on Aurora Pullman seventeen years ago."

The news hit him with the force of a vicious left jab. "Got it." It all made a terrible sort of sense now. He hung up and strode over to FBI Special Agent Tolliver, briefly outlining the call.

With a sick feeling of inevitability, he left the agent to round up the task force while he ran out of the building toward his vehicle. There wasn't a doubt in his mind now that those "sightings" in Tennessee had been staged to direct attention away from the area.

They'd wondered what was keeping Sutton and Aldeen in the region. Ryder unlocked the SUV and climbed inside, backing it out of its space. And despite the precautions the task force had put in place, the two fugitives were currently enacting the plan they'd had all along.

Samuel

"I always wondered if you'd remember me. You were so young, of course. And one of the few of my guests I let go." That was before he'd known the true extent of his divinity, he recalled. Before he'd learned how to recognize the Takers and their mission to deplete him of organ, tissue, and blood to use his strength for themselves.

Before he knew what it took to regain what was stolen from him.

"You look so like her, you know." Samuel cocked his head as he studied the young woman in front of him. It was like seeing Aurora again, the way she'd appeared all those years ago. Eryn shifted slightly, attempting to hide whatever she held behind her back. Poor dear. She'd sealed her fate the moment she stepped inside the room. "I was always fond of your mother. I wasn't pleased at all when she called a few months after leaving Charlotte and told me what David had done to her. I abhor senseless violence."

"That's an interesting claim, coming from you."

Like a mighty fish on the end of a fishing line, the boy in his lap struggled in his grasp. Samuel had him scissored between his legs with an arm clamped around his chest, while holding the gun in his free hand. He tightened his grip to quiet the boy. Samuel's wasn't a catch-and-release program. He chuckled softly at the witticism. At least not anymore.

"Sassy. Like your mama. I'm so gratified that I made an indelible mark on you. That's ego, I suppose, but there you go. I had my friend Joe bring me some of your early progress notes that were converted to audio." He'd dreamed of obtaining a collection of recordings of a nine-year-old girl lisping a retelling of her murderous deeds, or a sobbing recount of the time they'd spent together.

He'd been doomed to disappointment. The recordings were merely the doctor's dictations about the sessions. But there had been some pleasure in learning he'd stayed with the child in some fashion. A man liked to believe he'd made a difference.

"Why did you come here? What do you want?"

She was surprisingly calm. Almost eerie in her lack of expression. Perhaps he'd had a hand in teaching her those qualities as well. There was no use wasting energy when the outcome was already predetermined.

"My assistance was required. But it's not all work for me, thanks to your young cousin, here." He caressed the boy's cheek with the weapon. "I'm afraid it's you who's not needed any longer." He swung the barrel of the gun toward her. "Goodbye, Eryn. Tell your mother hello for me."

Cady

She could see the flames a half mile from the house. Reaching for her cell again, Cady pressed redial as she continued to speed toward the Pullman Estate. "Send fire trucks. And ambulances, just in case."

"You got it. I'm five minutes out."

"I'm here."

"Keep me posted."

She slowed beside the sheriff's car parked down the road a ways. Throwing the Jeep in park, Cady grabbed her Maglite from beneath the seat while drawing her weapon with her free hand. Trepidation closed her throat as she approached the SUV, aiming a beam at the front seat. Empty. Her tension eased a fraction. She stepped close enough to see there were no slumped bodies in the front or back. She flicked the light about. No bloodstains or bullet holes inside the vehicle or near it.

That didn't explain where the men were now. She jogged back to her vehicle.

The gates were closed, she realized as she drew closer to the drive. Smoke plumed in the air beyond the tree line. Her stomach sank. The house was on fire.

Cady got out of her vehicle again and surveyed the wrought-iron spiked sections of fence framed between brick pillars. It was designed more for looks than security, she determined. Without another thought, she ran back to the Jeep. Backed up and stomped on the accelerator. It smashed through the gates without even triggering the airbags. She pulled off into the grass to allow room for the emergency vehicles to enter and then parked, grabbing her Maglite and drawing her weapon before leaping from the car. As she drew closer to the house, she saw a car parked in front of it. Flames prevented her from accessing the door. She rounded the house at a sprint, intending to try the back. Before she got there, the beam of her flashlight caught three figures in the grass.

Her heart stopped for one brief moment. "Hands in the air! US Marshal!" she shouted. Two figures were prone. Unmoving. She moved close enough to see the remaining man with both hands half raised. She didn't know him.

"Don't shoot, for God sakes." He coughed violently. "I'm Henry Pullman. I've got Rosalyn and my dad here. They need help. They were beaten pretty bad. The guy that did this is still inside. He might be dead."

She didn't lower her weapon. "You have ID?"

"Yeah." When he started to reach for it, Cady said, "Use two fingers. Toss it over here."

He did as she demanded. "You can point the gun somewhere else now." He coughed violently.

Ignoring him, she flipped open his wallet. Shone the light on his license. It matched the guy in front of her. But that didn't necessarily clear him. "Lay on your belly."

"What? Why?" But he obeyed.

"Hands behind your back." She set down the flashlight to swiftly cuff him.

"Some fucking thanks I get for risking my life to get my dad and his wife out of a burning house."

She noted the slurred speech. Ignored the bitter tone. "I'll apologize later." Until Cady knew for sure what was going on, she wasn't taking a stranger's word for anything. She moved on to William Pullman and crouched beside him. His face was a battered mess. Feebly, he struggled to sit, raising an arm to shield his eyes. "Jaxson," he croaked.

A loud wail emanated from the woman by his side, who was wrapped in a blanket. "My baby! Find my baby!"

"Where're the boy and Eryn?"

Henry Pullman nodded toward a looming structure in the distance. "The second guy took Jaxson in there. Eryn followed them."

Sick comprehension slammed into her. Samuel Aldeen had the boy. And Eryn. One armed lunatic with two hostages. Without another word, Cady began running.

She snapped her light off as she approached the open door of the stable. Strained to hear anything that would give away Eryn and Jaxson's location. She crept inside, sweeping the vicinity with her weapon as she stepped deeper into the building.

You afraid of the dark, girlie?

Cady swallowed. She wasn't. At least not anymore. Because she'd be damned if she'd let the old man keep a grip on her, even after his death.

The big drafty structure couldn't be further from the cramped space she'd been imprisoned in more than once. But there were still arrows of dread shooting through her veins. It shouldn't remind her of the shooting in Saint Louis. She was inside here, not out. She was alone. Not with another marshal. There was no one standing over her partner with a gun pointed at the man's temple.

But the situation had parallels. She had a man nearby with two captives. Which made the situation even more grim than the one that still haunted her.

There. She stopped. Listened. Heard a murmur of indistinct voices. Cady moved toward them, halting every few feet to listen again and make sure she was headed in the right direction. As she drew closer she could make out a second sound. Quiet sobbing.

She took shelter in a stall close to the front. It still smelled faintly of hay and horses. She was close enough to hear most of what was being said.

". . . let him go. You have me." Cady winced when she recognized Eryn as the speaker.

"A lovely offer. You're too old, I'm afraid. The younger my guests, the greater replenishment to my strength. You wouldn't understand. You've never had an army of Takers ready to ambush you at every turn."

The sound of Aldeen's voice had an icy finger of trepidation tracing down Cady's spine. They'd long known Eryn and Sheila's families had factored in this investigation. What they hadn't counted on was the men getting to the Pullmans even with armed deputies posted outside the home.

"After what you did to me, you owe me an explanation first."

Good girl, Cady thought silently as she slowly straightened. Stall him for as long as you can. She stared through the darkness until she spotted the half-open door. A room of some sort in the corner of the building. She could be sure that Aldeen and Eryn were in there.

But she didn't have a view inside it. Easing to a crouch, she went to the edge of the stall and looked for a better vantage point.

"A sense of entitlement is so unattractive. Now drop the bat, or I'll shoot your cousin. I'd be quite unhappy about the waste. You have no idea how needy one can get in a loony bin." His laugh sounded unhinged. "Or maybe you do."

Cady moved silently, tiptoeing to avoid having her boots sound on the cobblestone floor. There. She had a view into the partially opened door leading to a small room. Two small beams of light split the darkness inside. One came from Eryn's cell. The other from a low spot Cady couldn't see. A small flashlight on the floor, perhaps.

"I don't recognize you," Eryn was saying. Her voice was eerily matter-of-fact. "But I know your voice. I heard it whispering in my head when I was little."

"You have no idea how that pleases me."

And the sick fuck looks gratified, Cady thought, staring into the shadowed space. The walls and floor were stone. Aldeen was sitting with the boy draped carelessly across his lap, the child's legs confined by the fugitive's. One arm was wrapped around both of the kid's. Aldeen's free hand held the weapon. And it was trained on Eryn.

Trepidation dampened Cady's palms. Drawing the man out of the space would be the safest scenario. It was chancy to risk a shot while the three were inside. The boy was too close. Eryn was moving nearer Aldeen. Even a miss would be potentially dangerous. A ricochet off the stone could kill any of the three.

"Uncle Arlo was my mother's brother," Samuel said. "My, I certainly wasn't fond of the time I spent alone with that man. But I survived him, just as you did me. Until now. Drop the bat." He shifted his weapon from Eryn to the boy. There was a loud clang on the stone floor. Then a metal bat skittered out of the doorway, as if it'd been kicked. It landed a foot from where Cady crouched. "Much better. I'm afraid you're interrupting this young lad and me. Three is indeed a crowd." Aldeen raised the gun.

Mini snippets of the scene in Saint Louis flashed across her mind. Deputy US Marshal Gagnon on the ground, writhing in agony. The kid standing over him with a Glock aimed at his head. There'd only been one decision then. Only one now.

Adrenaline mingled with dread as Cady sighted her weapon at Aldeen's forehead, sending up a silent prayer.

In the next instant, there was a blur of movement. A scream sounded, turning Cady's blood to ice. "Bitch! Oh, you bitch!" She rushed into the compact space, shoving Eryn away from the man. One of his hands was raised to his face. He continued shrieking as blood poured down it. A knife was buried to the hilt into one of his eyes.

"Get out!" she shouted. Eryn bent and pulled the boy from Aldeen's loosened grip and half carried him from the room. Cady took position behind the half-open door and trained her weapon on the fugitive. His gun was still raised, but his free hand was clutching at the knife, a wild animal-like keening coming from his throat. "Drop the weapon! It's over, Aldeen. Put it down and we'll get you medical help." She saw the intent in his expression a split second before he fired. She dove out of the way. The sound of his shot echoed and reechoed in the cavernous structure as the bullet tore through the old splintered door and slammed into her chest.

Even with the ballistic vest she wore, the force of it knocked her backward, driving the breath from her lungs. Cady battled to breathe. Long moments ticked by. Laboriously, she got an elbow beneath her and aimed, her weapon more unsteady than she would have liked. The two shots she fired through the door sent fragments of wood flying like tiny missiles through the air. Aldeen screamed.

Cady used her heels against the damp cobblestone floor to leverage herself close to a stall. Used its support to struggle to her feet. When she could stand without swaying—much—she approached the ruined door. Swung around it, her weapon ready.

Aldeen was slumped motionless against the stone wall at his back. The knife still protruded from one eye. His gun was by his side. Cady took a gulp of oxygen to feed her burning lungs. He was bleeding from his eye, right leg, and side. But she knew better than to lower her guard.

The man's fingers twitched. Then slowly closed around the weapon's grip.

"Don't even think about it," she warned, inching nearer. "Your wounds might not kill you. But I will." She watched cautiously as he slowly withdrew his hand from the gun before she sidled farther inside, kicking it away from his body.

There was a sound at the entrance of the stable. She shifted so she could keep it and Aldeen in her sights.

A moment later, she recognized Ryder approaching. "We're back here."

"Is he alive?"

"He might live." A mingled tumult of emotion washed over her, shocking her with its intensity. She knew what it said about her that her words were tinged with regret. Cady just couldn't bring herself to care.

Eryn: Then

"It's so beautiful." Eryn stared, awestruck. Mama held her hand tightly. Eryn hadn't meant to get so close to the edge of the lookout point. There was a fence there, anyway. It wasn't like she would have fallen over it. But she couldn't help dancing from one foot to the other. This was her first time at Mount Mitchell, and the view below was the prettiest thing she'd ever seen. Autumn had painted the rolling hills of the Smokies with splashes of brilliant reds, oranges, and golds. Gray wisps of fog drifted over hills, winding between mountains. She tugged at Mama's arm. "I want to learn to paint fog!"

"If you're good, I'll teach you to do a wash," Mama promised. "It's a simple technique. You'll have fun experimenting with it."

"I don't think I'll ever be able to paint anything as pretty as this." Eryn never wanted to leave. When she got older, she'd buy a house right where they were standing. And she'd look at this scene every day forever and ever.

"That's why artists keep trying. C'mon now, Eryn. If we don't eat lunch soon you won't be hungry at dinner. And then Mary Jane will scold us."

But Eryn didn't care about Mary Jane. She wished she could get close to the fence again and look way down to the bottom. If she were a bird, she could get as near as she wanted to the treetops below. "I wish I could fly," she said wistfully.

"You will, baby." Mama let go of her hand and wrapped an arm around her waist. "Not like a bird, but by following your heart. Make every day a memory. That's what dreams are made of."

Eryn thought about Mama's words. If dreams were memories, this day would be her favorite.

Eryn: Now

"How are you dealing with Rosalyn's confession?"

Eryn looked out the window of the doctor's office. They were nearing the end of the session. She'd hoped to conclude it without the inevitable subject that seemed to rise at every appointment. *How,* she wondered, *am I supposed to feel?* She'd been locked up most of her life for a crime she didn't commit. And she had no doubt that if Sutton hadn't been about to rape Rosalyn, she'd have let Eryn go to her grave believing she'd killed her mother. How could anyone handle that kind of information? It was like surviving an earthquake, only to be rocked daily by the unceasing aftershocks.

"It doesn't seem real yet." She'd said the same the last time they'd met. But nothing had changed in the intervening time. She finally looked at Dr. Ashland. "I don't understand why she allowed me to take the blame. I was a child. She didn't even know me."

The other woman laid a reassuring hand on her arm. "No. She didn't. I doubt she planned any of it—killing your mother, or the aftermath of the murder. But she still allowed you to be scapegoated and held accountable for her actions. People who refuse to take responsibility can rationalize the most reprehensible behavior. But from what I understand, she's going to be held accountable now. She's being charged with manslaughter, I read."

Eryn nodded. She knew little more than what was in the news. Uncle Bill certainly didn't talk about it. He didn't talk about much of anything, unless she asked him a question. Once, Eryn had happened by the makeshift office in the rental house. He'd had his head down on his desk. His strangled weeping had been heartrending. She'd never felt so helpless. He was going through as much as she was right now. And she wasn't at all certain how to help him.

As if reading her thoughts, the doctor said, "How are things at home?"

Eryn hesitated. Even that simple question was fraught with complications. Did she have a home anymore? The rental in Waynesville certainly didn't feel like it.

But neither had the Pullman Estate. So maybe home depended on wherever family was.

What was left of it.

Finally, she answered, "Weird." In some ways, it seemed like months instead of just under two weeks since the fire. The house hadn't been a total loss. One wing was livable. But she didn't know if they'd ever move back.

The psychiatrist frowned a bit. "I still think we may need to talk about another placement for you, until things settle a bit more."

Raising her gaze to the woman, she asked, "When will that be?" When would Uncle Bill get over the knowledge of all his wife had done? When would Eryn, for that matter? When would Jaxson stop wandering around the strange home looking lost and afraid? It would be so easy for her to agree with the doctor and leave the stress of the last couple of weeks behind. It would also feel like running. "Real life is messy."

The woman nodded her dark head. "It can be, yes."

"But I have to learn to handle the messy parts too." She gave a slight smile. "With your help, of course." Eryn knew she didn't have all the necessary tools to grapple with the suffocating weight the truth had brought. It still brought her awake, her heart squeezing so tightly it was a struggle to breathe.

"Besides, Jaxson needs me. So does Uncle Bill." Mary Jane had moved with them to the new house. There wasn't as much for her to do, but Eryn was glad she was there. Right now, the woman seemed like the only "normal" in the entire situation. And all of them were desperately searching for normal.

The doctor was wearing pink today. A pretty pastel sweater that contrasted with the dreary November day showcased in the windows. Eryn liked her far better than she had Dr. Steigel. Someday she might like her as well as she had Dr. Glassman.

"With all that's happened, you have a lot to work through. What else do you want to discuss today?"

They'd talked frequently since Samuel Aldeen and David Sutton had tried to kill Eryn's family. Eryn was seeing Dr. Ashland nearly every day now. They'd started to process some subjects. There were others Eryn wasn't ready to broach.

Like dwelling on the specifics of how Mama had died. Dr. Glassman had always said that Eryn had suffered a psychotic break the night it happened, which explained why she'd never been able to remember a single detail. But now Dr. Ashland said the cause was more likely the trauma of what she'd seen. Eryn's mind skittered away from the thought. She knew she wasn't strong enough to deal with the topic yet. She wasn't sure she ever would be.

Realizing the doctor was waiting patiently for an answer, Eryn cast around for one of the subjects she *could* handle. "I told you I followed Jaxson into the stable. The first time the man who took him spoke, I recognized his voice." She still couldn't wrap her mind around that. How a man she didn't remember could have lived in her head while she was a child. How one of the voices in her mind back then sounded just like him.

"It's complicated. Your childhood auditory hallucinations were a symptom of your mental illness. Bipolar disorder is a brain disorder. It may have existed even without the traumatic events you endured, although the trauma and associated PTSD could have triggered it." The doctor's eyes were as kind as her tone. "Your file says the voices went away once you were properly diagnosed and treated. It's not unusual for a child not to remember events that occurred at ages two or three. But it doesn't mean the incidents didn't affect you psychologically. Your fear of small, dark spaces, for example."

"Dr. Glassman always said the voices were really my thoughts."

The woman nodded. "That's true. You said the voice with the name of your abuser was the one telling you to hurt yourself and others. Perhaps you subconsciously made a correlation to him forcing you to do things you weren't comfortable with."

"If Uncle Arlo was a real person, what about Mr. Timmons?" She hated discussing the very things that were symptomatic of her illness. Despised knowing that there was no cure for it.

But there was treatment. And understanding her symptoms gave her some control over them.

"An interesting question." And the doctor did look intrigued. "I've actually done some research on the issue myself. But I'm afraid there's no way to be certain. It's possible that you came in contact with someone by that name when you were very young and impressionable who was kind to you. Perhaps a policeman or medical worker. And then your mind equated that name with your more responsible thoughts."

The veiled reference to the violent scene between her mother and David Sutton had Eryn wincing a little. She'd had enough for the day. What she'd learned about her past was almost too unwieldy to handle. But they'd take small bites at it. Like the baby steps Eryn was taking toward independence. Neither would be easy. But in the last couple of weeks, she'd learned she was stronger than she'd ever realized.

Ryder

Deputy Cal Patterson scrambled to his feet when Ryder walked toward his station outside Samuel Aldeen's door in Asheville Memorial Hospital. "Ry. It was a quiet night."

There was an Asheville cop stationed on the other side of the door, who rose more laconically from his chair. "Sheriff."

Ryder inclined his head. "Officer. The other two inside the room?"

Cal nodded. "We've been trading off positions."

"Why don't the two of you go get some coffee. Your shift should change soon." Not waiting for a second invitation, the men bolted down the hallway. Ryder mused that he should have asked for some himself before mentally dismissing the idea. He could do better hitting a drive-through on the way back to Waynesville.

He pushed open the door, noting the immediate attention of Deputies Logan Middleton and Kara French. They exchanged greetings and looked toward the bed. Aldeen was unmoving, his good eye closed. The other was swathed with bandages. Ryder knew the gunshot wounds would bear similar treatment. Both wrists were manacled and chained to the bed rails.

He jerked his head, and the two deputies followed him outside. "Any change?"

Aldeen had lost his eye after Eryn's attack. Ryder took a moment to appreciate the irony. Rosalyn Pullman would stand trial for the murder of Aurora Pullman. Ryder didn't need the guilty verdict to be convinced Eryn hadn't been responsible for the knife attack that had killed her mother. But attacking her abuser with a similar weapon had a certain poetic justice.

"The doctors have already been by this morning. They say the surgery earlier this week for the gunshot wound in his leg went well. He'll likely be transferred to Fristol's infirmary within the week."

With far more security during his stay there than in the past. Ryder had already had that conversation with Dr. Isaacson. "Okay. I have a few more questions for him." He left the two deputies in the hall and reentered the room.

"Sheriff Talbot." Aldeen was awake, but his voice was slurred. The effects of the sedation, maybe. Or from the medication for his mental illness. "Have you come for another chat?"

"Just a few more questions." Ryder dragged a chair close to the man's bedside. "Who started the fire at Pullman's? We know you poured accelerant around it."

"David, I presume." Samuel looked amused. "He'd scouted the property beforehand and hidden the gas cans we'd use in the stable. After helping him with the owners, I was in too much of a hurry to get to the boy. And David was still inside at the time."

The man has no reason to lie, Ryder reflected. He was going to remain locked up for the rest of his life. On the other hand, given his mental instability, anything he said was suspect.

"Sutton never got out of the house."

"Which is a pity. A horrible death."

There was zero compassion in the man's voice. For his friend or the victims he'd meant to die in the fire.

"Your deputies have me to thank for their lives, by the way. David wanted to kill them. It was my idea to lie in wait until they made their hourly rounds and ambush them. I trust you found them bound and gagged in the trunk of their car?"

Anger flared. Five hundred acres was a large territory. They'd found the place where Sutton and Aldeen had entered it, driving the stolen pickup across the property until they abandoned it later to walk in behind the house, out of sight of the deputies.

"Tell me again about your plans after the escape."

"Aruba maybe for the winters. Europe in the summer. I do so love Paris. Have you ever been?"

Ryder shook his head. From what he'd learned of the man's finances, he could have afforded to live out his life exactly as he wished. "But you didn't head out of the state. Why did you stay to target Eryn Pullman?"

"Target," the man mumbled. "Takers are wily, but incredibly dense. How do you think I got the accomplices I needed for my escape?"

"Money and coercion," Ryder said bluntly.

"I prefer the term *persuasion*, but yes, of course." The chains on his wrists jangled as he shifted position in the bed. "And how would I persuade David to help me if he wasn't strongly motivated by money? God rest his soul, the man had his hand in all sorts of illicit enterprises."

"Revenge," Ryder guessed.

"Exactly. David never could ignore even the smallest slight. He might have been reluctant to get involved with my escape having so recently gotten out of prison." A small satisfied smile crossed his face. "So I appealed to the side of him he couldn't control. I was once quite fond of Aurora, you know. And when she started allowing me to baby-sit . . . well, I grew even fonder of her daughter."

A slow burn ignited inside Ryder. His fist clenched. *Fond.* An enraging rationalization for sexual abuse.

Aldeen was obviously tiring. His words were getting harder to make out. "We kept in contact for a while. She told me what David had done to her. And also what her brother had done to David. Hiring a trio of thugs to beat him within an inch of his life. I never told David that. Back then."

"But you used the information to elicit his cooperation," Ryder said grimly. It fit. It matched Eryn, Rosalyn, and William's accounting of that evening. Although he hadn't pinned William down on the accuracy of the accusation, it was clear now that it was all too true. And Aldeen had known exactly what the revelation would do to David Sutton.

"He helps me, I help him." Aldeen's voice was little more than a murmur now. "He . . . gets me out. Genius, really. To force Preston's . . . involvement. And plan to destroy her . . . afterwards."

"I guess I'd use a different term." *Murderous. Callous.* With complete disregard for anyone and anything that didn't serve Aldeen's purposes. Ryder rose. He'd require more information, but it needed to be in small doses, given the man's condition.

Ryder strode for the door. Limited amounts of time with Samuel Aldeen was probably best for both of them.

◆   ◆   ◆

The home William Pullman was renting was spacious, but it was a sliver of the size of the family estate. Of course, Ryder conceded as he rang the doorbell, almost anything would be.

He recognized the spare, unsmiling woman who opened the door from his interviews almost two weeks earlier. The housekeeper. Mary Jane.

"I'm here to see William."

She held open the door. "His office is downstairs." She surprised him by following him through the living room. "I should have said something the last time we spoke." He turned around at her words.

"About what?"

Mary Jane smoothed her palms down the front of her crisp black slacks. "It might be nothing. But I saw Rosalyn in Eryn's bathroom. Saw her nosing around in the medicine cabinet too. I asked what she was doing in there, but she said she was just checking that Eryn had everything she might need." The woman shrugged her bony shoulders. "Might have been just that. Or she might have been messing with the girl's medication."

Her observation fit neatly with Rosalyn's statement the night of the fire. The woman had admitted as much. Of course, from what Ryder had heard, the defense attorney was attempting to have her confession dismissed. But Mary Jane's words would be damning. Lab results had already verified that Eryn Pullman's medication had been switched. And he'd already scooped up Rosalyn's accomplice. "Thank you for telling me that." But he was speaking to Mary Jane's back. Her duty done, the woman was already walking toward the kitchen.

Ryder descended the stairs to the basement. He'd been surprised to get a phone call from William asking for him to stop by. After what he'd been through, the man could be forgiven for wanting some time for him and his family to heal. And Ryder would surely have given him that space, had the man not contacted him.

The area was finished but sparsely furnished. An unused wet bar occupied one end of the space. Ryder found William in one of the two bedrooms, which contained only a desk and a couple of chairs, with a filing cabinet in the corner.

"Sheriff." The man got up and grabbed a folding chair propped in the corner. Opened it in front of the desk and motioned Ryder to it. "Thank you for coming."

"How are you, William?"

The man's smile looked like a grimace. "Well, I have bad days and . . . bad days. My therapist says that's to be expected." He sat down at the desk again.

"I'm glad to hear you're talking to someone," Ryder said sincerely. He couldn't imagine the emotional burden the man was carrying right now.

"It helps to talk things through with an objective observer. That's why I called. There are gaps in my understanding of what happened."

The man raked through his hair, which didn't look as though it'd been trimmed recently. "You told me before it was Rosalyn making those calls. Inciting the wackos at Bancroft's church to protest. To upset Eryn, I suppose. Another way to sabotage her transition. But the girl told me about some lights she'd seen on the property. She caught Rosalyn in the boathouse with another man, she said. Did Eryn tell you all that?"

Ryder nodded. He was still impressed as hell at what the young woman had gone through. He knew plenty of people without her problems who wouldn't have exhibited a fraction of the bravery she had. "Rosalyn confessed she was meeting another pharmacy tech she used to work with when she was employed there years ago. He's admitted she was paying him cash to change Eryn's meds. They were the same prescriptions, but lower dosages."

An expression of grief crossed William's face. "She asked so many questions the times we met with the doctors at Rolling Acres Resort. I thought she was just concerned that Eryn would suffer another psychotic break when she came home. But she must have been planning a way to disrupt the girl's mental condition without bringing about a complete breakdown. Eryn's earlier transitions were unsuccessful. She has a condition . . . her system gets used to the meds and they have to be changed . . ." He swallowed hard.

"Why?" Ryder asked bluntly. Once Rosalyn had retained a defense attorney, Ryder's access to the woman was limited. "What would she get out of having Eryn returned to Rolling Acres?"

"That damn trust," the man muttered, one hand going up to rub his forehead. "She and Henry. Both of them were obsessed with it. But she was wrong if she thought having Eryn declared mentally incompetent meant the girl would no longer get her share. It's no secret that I'd like to sell the property. Move somewhere smaller. Less of a financial drain . . ." His gaze flicked around the room. It was obvious that this house wasn't what he'd had in mind. "I suppose, if Eryn was back at

Rolling Acres, I'd have guardianship over the entire trust. Which meant I could do whatever I wished with the property." His voice choked.

And selling it would have vastly added to the family fortune, even if he would be recipient to only half the sale. Carefully, Ryder asked, "Was anyone in your household a smoker?" The arson investigators had found the remains of cigarette butts outside the back of the house. And more deeper in the yard. There'd been no cigarettes found on Aldeen or Sutton.

William started to shake his head, then stopped. "My older son smokes. Henry. He was visiting that night. I thought he'd left until I saw him outside after I managed to get Rosalyn out of the house."

The man's words just underscored Ryder's interest in Henry Pullman. They'd caught him in several inconsistencies since the night of the fire. He'd told Cady that he'd rescued his father and stepmother. Their account disputed that fact.

His refusal to help Eryn rescue his half brother and his mention of them inheriting if the rest of the family perished were especially damning. Ryder's office would be looking hard at the man's possible involvement after the fact. "Rosalyn's accomplice is facing charges as well."

"How many times did she meet with him?" William asked.

Understanding dawned. "Have you talked to Rosalyn since the fire?" The man's lack of response was its own answer. Ryder couldn't blame him. The woman was accused of killing his sister, and she let his niece assume the blame for a horrendous crime. Although Rosalyn was now claiming that she'd merely concocted her admission to distract Sutton and keep him from hurting her husband, her initial story carried a lot of weight. Coupled with the actions she'd taken against Eryn, murdering Aurora fit a pattern of behavior. "Both she and her accessory say they met three times. He stole only a few pills a day, to avoid suspicion."

William was silent for a moment. "But Eryn says she saw lights outside several times that week."

"I think David Sutton was probably scouting the property even before we connected him to Aldeen." Aldeen had been honest about the accelerants. They'd found empty cans in the yard and a couple more full ones in the stable. Forensic testing had identified the bones of the body found inside the Pullman house as belonging to Sutton. By the time the fire department had arrived, it'd been too late to get inside that part of the home. Ryder couldn't find it in himself to regret that. Sheila Preston's family wouldn't have to live in fear anymore. And neither would the Pullmans.

"It's my fault." William's words were tinged with self-recrimination. "I lied to the marshal twice when she asked me about knowing David Sutton. I'd never met him, but I hated the bastard. He beat my sister half to death, and he got a few months in jail. I wanted him to pay. I wanted him hurt as badly as he'd hurt Aurora. I hired someone. He rounded up a few others."

He clasped his hands together on his desk so tightly his knuckles showed white. "I'm not proud of it. I've never done anything illegal in my life before. But I'm not sorry. At least I wasn't." His throat worked. "I'm responsible for everything that happened . . . Jaxson and Eryn in the grips of that madman . . . the fire . . . even Aurora's death. It was my fault Rosalyn was in the house earlier that night. We were seeing each other, but my sister didn't approve. That part of her story . . . it rang true. Aurora was making things . . . difficult for us. Rosalyn stayed with me in my room for a while and left after midnight. I never knew she'd come back. Never even considered . . ." He shook his head incredulously. "I didn't mention it to the investigators. Why would I? It seemed so clear. I'd woken early in the morning and got up. I thought I heard voices, but . . ." He swallowed hard. "It was just Eryn. In Aurora's room. *Humming*. And the blood . . ." He shuddered. "Eryn's prints were on the knife. Hers and Mary Jane's."

Ryder had pulled the old file on the murder investigation. His father had handled it. And there was nothing in the records to indicate Butch Talbot had seriously considered anyone other than Eryn Pullman.

"My niece needed help." William straightened. "I can't count the number of times I told my sister that. I walked in on that scene and the first thing I thought was 'I knew something like this would happen.'"

"The police report said that Eryn would frequently go to her mother's room at night." The man nodded miserably. "Her medical file noted she suffered a psychotic break that night. It might have been from witnessing her mother's murder . . . or finding her dead . . . rather than killing her mother herself." The bedclothes had been soaked in blood. Ryder could imagine all too easily how some of it could have transferred to the girl sitting next to the bed. "I wanted to tell you that I'm reopening the investigation into your sister's death."

William's head came up swiftly. "There's no statute of limitations on murder."

In North Carolina, there was no statute of limitations on any felony, which meant William could be charged for his part in the assault on David Sutton seventeen years ago. Ryder already knew he wouldn't be sharing the man's admission with the county attorney. William Pullman was already living with enough.

"This is my fault. All of it. I withheld the information about Rosalyn being there, which caused Eryn to spend most of her childhood in a psychiatric facility thinking she'd killed her mother. My actions brought Sutton to our home." The raw agony in the man's voice was difficult to hear.

"I don't claim to have all the answers, William. But my experience in the military and in police work has taught me one thing." Ryder leaned forward, his voice taking on a note of urgency. "David Sutton is responsible for hurting your sister. He's responsible for siccing Samuel Aldeen on your son and for the fire that destroyed your home. If Rosalyn killed Aurora, she alone is to blame for Eryn being locked up for years. Don't you take on any of their responsibility. Don't you absolve their culpability. Guilt can be a terrible thing. It'll eat you alive if you let it. You can't afford that. You have two sons and a niece who are counting on you."

William drew a shuddering breath. "You sound like my therapist."

Ryder sat back. "I don't know about that. But it sounds like she's giving you good advice."

Cady

"I'm glad you could join me," Eryn said shyly, when she and Cady had finished their dinner. Cady had been surprised by the young woman's invitation. But she hadn't hesitated to agree to meet her at the restaurant she'd named. "Your face looks better." Eryn immediately looked chagrined. "Sorry. That was probably rude."

Cady smiled easily. "It is better. I can even cover the last of the bruises with makeup now." More importantly, the stitches were out. The soreness had faded considerably. "How are you doing?"

They'd skirted topics related to the night Eryn had stabbed Aldeen. Eryn had talked about her driving lessons. Her uncle's promise she could get a car when she passed her test. Her family's temporary house. Cady had followed Eryn's lead. The last thing she wanted to do was to force the young woman to confront the recent trauma.

Eryn shrugged. "Okay, I think. I'm worried about my uncle. Today before I left the house we spoke about the estate. Both of us decided not to rebuild. We're going to sell the property. I didn't care so much, except for losing my mama's paintings. It wasn't really home to me. And I guess Uncle Bill doesn't ever want to go back to it. I wouldn't make him." She was silent for a moment. "Maybe . . . when I'm ready . . . I'll have my own place built. Something small. With a view of the mountains."

"That sounds like a great plan."

Neither of them spoke for a few minutes. But Cady waited. She had a feeling Eryn wasn't finished.

"If you hadn't come when I texted we'd all be dead now."

"You were very brave." Cady had a mental flash of Eryn moving in front of Aldeen with the knife while Cady was taking aim. She squelched a shudder at the thought of how things could have gone drastically wrong.

"I wasn't. Brave, I mean. I just . . . too much was coming at me. I couldn't process it all, so I focused on one thing. Getting Jaxson away from Aldeen."

"You saved him. That makes you a hero."

Eryn shook her head. "I'll never believe it. You don't know how hard it is to think of yourself one way for most of your life. To have your entire identity wrapped around one moment. One decision."

A boulder lodged in Cady's throat. She did know. She lived with the same. And unlike Eryn, there wasn't a possibility that the guilt she carried was unwarranted.

The young woman looked at her hands where they were clasped around her water glass. "Now I have to untangle that perception. It's hard to manage. It took years for me to come to terms with thinking I killed my mama. Now I have to unlearn it. It's harder than it sounds."

Cady waited for Eryn's gaze to meet hers again. "I know there's a tough road ahead. It'll take time. But it seems to me, there's one huge thing to focus on. Although Rosalyn is recanting her confession now, she's been charged with your mother's homicide. A terrible wrong was done to you, but the state believes you didn't kill your mother. You're innocent. Concentrate on accepting that first. It will make everything else to come easier to deal with."

Eryn gave a half smile. "Thanks. I'm going to try."

Cady remained in the booth long after the young woman had left. The parallels between Eryn Pullman's history and her own had disturbed her from the start of the case. And in the coming days, Eryn had to muster the same strength she'd used to tackle her past. *There are no completely happy endings,* she mused, raising her water glass to her lips. Only accepting what was and moving on.

She'd muted the cell before setting it on the table. A tiny light winked in it now. She picked it up and answered.

"What are you doing?"

Ryder Talbot. The quick clutch of pleasure at the sound of his voice surprised her. "I'm off duty. So I'm doing absolutely nothing."

"So am I. Do you want to do nothing together?"

Off guard, she hesitated. She'd missed their conversations more than she wanted to admit. That, coupled with a purely female appreciation for the way the man filled out a pair of Levi's, caused an inner alarm to sound. A deeply rooted streak of caution had her hedging, "That depends."

"Meet me in an hour at Legends for a beer. I'm through most of the paperwork for this case. I'm calling it a night."

Something inside her eased. *A beer is casual,* Cady mused. Casual was her forte. "I'll see you then." She strode out of the diner and across the lot, enjoying the slow rise of anticipation. She could allow herself to be defined by the dark moments in her past. Or she could concentrate on the future.

Her step quickened. It was really no choice at all.

ACKNOWLEDGMENTS

As usual, my imagination surpassed my actual knowledge. I'm always grateful to the experts who take time out of their busy days to help fill in the plot gaps with pesky little things like facts! A special thank-you goes to Deputy US Marshals Marc M. and Robert S. for all things USMS related. I appreciate your assistance as well as the job you do. Many thanks, Robert, for the tour and for answering my endless questions.

I owe a debt of gratitude to Dr. Gary Keller, who supplied in-depth answers on types of mental illness and associated behaviors. Your information was absolutely fascinating, and if I managed to capture even a smidge of your expertise, I'll call it a success.

I'm also grateful to Rick Hopper, North Carolina Deputy Sheriff (ret.), for your patience answering my process and procedure questions. You gave me some good ideas to add to the story!

And to Bill, correctional officer extraordinaire, many thanks for the explanation of security measures taken at correctional facilities. I have no doubt my bad guy would never have escaped with you at the helm. :)

Megathanks go to my intuitive editors, Jessica Tribble and Charlotte Herscher. I appreciate your patience and insightful guidance during the required surgery ☺.

As usual, any errors are the author's alone. Sometimes it's all about asking the right questions . . .

ABOUT THE AUTHOR

Kylie Brant is the author of forty novels and is a three-time RITA Award nominee, a four-time RT Award finalist, and a two-time Daphne du Maurier Award winner. Her books have been published in twenty-nine countries and have been translated into eighteen languages. Brant is a member of Romance Writers of America, including its Kiss of Death mystery and suspense chapter; Novelists, Inc.; and International Thriller Writers. Visit her online at www.kyliebrant.com.

Made in the USA
Middletown, DE
20 February 2023

25175412R00208